Wrinkle

A NEW MEDICAL THRILLER

SCOTT ALAN ROSS

Barringer Publishing, Naples, Florida
www.barringerpublishing.com
Cover, graphics, layout design by Lisa Camp

ISBN: 978-0-9851184-9-5

Library of Congress Cataloging-in-Publication Data
Wrinkle / Scott Alan Ross

Printed in U.S.A.

This is a work of fiction. All characters, organizations,
and events portrayed in this novel are either products of the
author's imagination or are used fictitiously.

CHAPTER 1

The overwhelming bolt of pain arrived forcefully and without warning while Shirley Herold was entering the exit ramp on I-75. Grabbing the steering wheel tightly, she tried to focus on bringing the car safely off the road and to a stop. An all-encompassing pain tore through her skull; leaving her nauseated with fear and pain. While traveling at 65 miles per hour, Shirley lost control of her vehicle. As she closed her eyes, Carrie Underwood's song, "Jesus Take the Wheel" fought through the pain into her awareness. The last thing Shirley felt was a crushing jolt as her body began turning upside down in unison with her Grand Cherokee.

Cars and trucks swerved to avoid the vehicle resting perpendicular to the north bound lane. A Good Samaritan pulled off the road to dial 911. Meanwhile, a Hispanic landscaper pulled his truck over next to the Good Samaritan. Both reached the driver's side simultaneously, the Hispanic man calling out first.

"Hey lady, are you okay?"

Raising his voice above the hissing of the punctured radiator the Good Samaritan shouted;

"I don't think she's breathing. Let's get her out!"

Both men tried in vain to extricate the trapped woman. The driver's door was crushed inward and the deployed air bag partially obscured her face. The position her vehicle had landed, along with the relatively small window, made removal of her body impossible.

"Hey man, my car insurance is expired. I'm gettin' out of here before the cops come. We can't help her anyways." With that, the landscaper hurried back to his vehicle, skirted the strewn parts on the road, and drove away.

The first screeches of an ambulance could be heard in the distance, followed by the deeper clang of a fire truck. The blue strobes of two police cars quickly joined the scene as darkness settled on the patch of highway. The "jaws of life" and brute strength of the firemen allowed Shirley's body to be removed. The task was completed in less than fifteen minutes.

"Go ahead," the static voice of dispatch rose above the noise.

"I've got a 51 year old female MVA. Pulse is absent. No respirations and both pupils are blown."

The paramedic calling in the information to the hospital looked young enough to be in high school but spoke with the authority of experience.

"You know the drill, continue CPR and we'll be waiting for you. Anyone else hurt?" inquired dispatch.

Motor vehicle accidents in Florida were all too common for the doctor taking the dispatch call. Between young kids driving at sixteen, and half-blind seniors driving at ninety, the roads in Florida could be more dangerous than walking the mean streets of an inner city at night.

"Negative dispatch. Sole driver wearing her seatbelt. Cause of accident is unknown. Our ETA is five minutes."

"Copy that. See you when you get here."

Dr. Sebastian Bradley performed an aggressive CPR, especially considering the moribund state of the patient. Her neck did not appear to be broken.

There were no apparent rib fractures and the only significant physical findings had been fixed, blown, pupils and a complete lack of response to resuscitation. There were some small puncture marks and faint yellow bruises apparent on her face. Bradley recognized these as the likely stigmata of plastic surgery. Scars appeared abundant in this patient who also had white lines beneath her breasts from apparent breast augmentation and visible incision marks behind both ears from a facelift. The puncture marks and recent bruising were probably from either one of the wrinkle filler agents such as collagen or Botox. In addition, she had facial burns from the airbag abrading her skin.

Shirley Herold was pronounced dead twelve minutes after her arrival.

"Debbie, any luck contacting next of kin?" the emergency room physician addressed his charge nurse.

"We called the number listed as home in her cell phone and only got her machine. She has several business cards in her wallet from a Dr. David Layton, a plastic surgeon here in Pelican Cove. She was wearing a nurse's uniform and she also has an American Nursing Association ID so she might work for him. His office is closed, but we have a call in to his service to see if they can reach him. There were no pictures of kids, just a cat and an older man, perhaps her husband. The police are sending a cruiser by her house to see if anyone is at home."

"Thanks Deb, I've got a call in to the medical examiner. I've ordered drug screens and other preliminary blood work. Dr. Jack Shea is taking most of the calls for the examiner's office and he can be finicky. I don't know if he'll want to do a post on this one or just attribute it to bad driving," finished Bradley.

"It's just such a shame. She looks so healthy and obviously took care of herself. One minute she's driving, and the next minute-BOOM-she's lying unconscious trapped in her car."

Debbie walked away from the desk and to an alcove behind the nurses' station and ate the last of the donut holes.

CHAPTER 2

"Nate, would I look sexier to you if I got rid of these wrinkles?" As she asked the question, Lisa placed each of her hands on the sides of her face, palms pushing upward as she stretched her skin absurdly towards her temples. She looked grotesque, vaguely oriental, and not like the attractive thirty-nine year old that he loved dearly.

"Honey, I adore you just the way you are, wrinkles and all," he replied.

"You're supposed to say I don't have any wrinkles!" she retorted half in jest.

Lisa had always prided herself in staying in shape and had looked younger than her years for as long as Nate could remember. Her beautiful green eyes offset honey-brown hair that she wore attractively to her shoulders. She could still turn heads but this past December the extra five pounds that she had gained had stayed on- maybe with a few more added since. This summer was the first in which she caved in and wore a one-piece bathing suit to hide her extra weight. He would never let her know that he preferred her to be thinner. He loved her too much to tell her the truth and still demonstrated his adoration for her in little ways that would endear him to her and make her feel good about herself. The problem was that he felt that he was failing.

These days, more often than not, she would just roll over and go to sleep, without as much as a kiss good night. He found her up late at night, sometimes watching TV, sometimes "surfing" the internet or reading a book and she always seemed tired. Although their love-making was still good, she never seemed to have the desire to initiate it and generally seemed less full of life than in the past.

"Should I get some of that collagen injected or maybe do some Botox? It's not as drastic as a face lift. Marie had it done and she looks ten years younger."

Lisa dropped her palms from her face and squinted as she raised her eyebrows slightly, furrowing the skin between her eyes and causing deep tracts between them.

"Lisa, you're just fine!" Nate's response was automatic but sincere.

This time he smiled at her. Was it all women of a certain age or only his wife? He felt himself caught between his feelings of unconditional love for his soul-mate and life partner and sadness at the harsh marks life's advance was leaving on her body. Nate felt wrong at allowing this consumption with outward appearance to have importance. He couldn't help but reach out to his wife; touching her shoulders, pulling her toward him, trying to chase away any of his unpleasant thoughts.

"I love you honey, just the way you are," Nate whispered softly.

"I love you too sweetheart," Her response seemed flat and ineffectual; more like a habit rather than any true sentiment.

Nate looked into her eyes and perceived sadness and despair. In a final attempt to push away her forlorn early-morning melancholia, Nate let his hands caress Lisa's breasts. No longer firm as they had been, the passage of two pregnancies and time had given gravity its certain victory. Still, he knew that if anything could change his wife's mood it would be his attention here.

Nate reached under her loose-fitting sleep-shirt, touching the soft edges of her breasts. Lisa shivered with anticipation and then excitement at his touch. At last he saw a true smile form at the corners of her mouth and saw the return of the woman he loved, the same woman he had married when he had finished law school.

Thanks for putting up with my silliness," she whispered, as her hands reached down to his groin, reciprocating attention on her husband where she knew he enjoyed it most.

"Let's go back to bed," Lisa whispered. "I'll go lock the door so the boys don't interrupt us."

"Now you're talking," Nate responded huskily, excited by the unexpected and of late, too infrequent rendezvous.

Lisa clicked the lock on the bedroom door. Nate had already crawled back under the thick covers. Hooking his fingers around his underwear, he pulled them down to his ankles and tossed them aside under the sheets, anticipating his wife's return. Before getting into bed, Lisa stopped in the adjoining bathroom and brushed her teeth, and he was about to get up and scrub his own, when she leaped into the bed beside him.

"Now, where were we honey? Show me how much you love me. Do you think sex helps fight wrinkles?"

"Stop with the wrinkles already," Nate responded smiling as he felt himself becoming aroused by the proximity of his wife's warm body at his side. The smell of her hair in his face, the faint whiff of her fresh scrubbed face and sweet-smelling shampoo made his heart skip a beat.

"Besides, I don't know if it fights wrinkles, but it has to keep away frowns!" Nate slid closer to Lisa, pulling her body even closer to his.

Lisa tossed aside her skimpy panties while Nate ran his hand over her small, soft breasts. He felt the nipples harden as he touched their tips gently with his fingers. She moaned softly and drew closer to him, pulling their bodies tightly together, their warmth radiating one to the other under the thick covers in the cool, air-conditioned room.

"Now, isn't this better," Nate cooed, his breath catching.

"Yes, honey, I want to show you how much I love you," Lisa responded warmly as she lowered her head between the sheets.

As her head fell between his thighs, he felt his body tensing with excitement and desire. Her soft hair was touching and teasing his skin.

"I love you honey," Nate moaned passionately.

Nate heard Lisa begin to say something but it was muffled by the covers over her head. Just as she began placing lingering, moist kisses on his upper thighs he heard another voice that fought for his immediate attention. At the door, he heard first one soft knock, then a second, louder knock followed by a rattling of the door handle.

"Mom, why is the door locked?" It was Josh, their younger son.

Nate never understood how, but their kids seemed to have radar that alerted them to come to their door on mornings like these. All Nate or Lisa had to do was try to get some quiet adult time alone and miraculously Shawn or Josh would show up at the most inopportune time.

Nate felt his manhood melt like a piece of chocolate left in the midday sun. Lisa's head jumped out from under the blankets followed so quickly by her body that Nate had to avoid her as her flying elbows almost connected with his jaw. It reminded him of a scuba diver surfacing from below the sea in a rapid ascent. He would have chuckled at the thought if he hadn't been so disappointed at the termination of another unsuccessful rendezvous.

"Coming Josh!" Lisa shouted, pulling her panties on and grabbing her robe off the bedside table as she leaped from the bed.

"Maybe we can resume later honey," Lisa said over her shoulder as she flew over to open the bedroom door.

"Is that a date?" Nate asked, knowing as he responded that the best chance of a liaison had just passed and that the odds of a second romantic encounter twice in the same day were low enough to make a bookie cringe at taking the bet. He felt guilty at his disappointment and the apparent ease with which Lisa left their bed.

"We'll see," drifted back to Nate.

Lisa bolted from the room like the concerned mother that she was, eager to reassure their eight-year-old that the closed door wasn't meant to keep him out. It wasn't the way he wanted the day to start out, but maybe; just maybe, this might be that rarest of days where they could get back together at night and renew their vows.

He walked over to the sink and ran the toothbrush half-heartedly across his teeth. Nate was on his way to another day at work.

Both Josh and Shawn were off on the bus to school. This was the time of day Lisa often enjoyed most. Her time to herself to sit and drink her coffee and let her thoughts drift away as she watched the morning television and flipped through the newspaper. Most of the time it was nice but today she felt uneasy; not that she knew why. Life was pretty darn good. She sensed that maybe it had something to do with turning forty in a few months. Maybe she just needed to go back to work; she had enjoyed bringing home a paycheck during the time she had worked before the boys were born. Maybe she should return to nursing. God knows, with her skills as an RN she could certainly find a job easily enough.

She sat down at the kitchen counter and gazed out the large bay windows that over-looked the eighth green of the Egret's Nest golf course. Lisa loved the view, not for the golfers that passed through from dawn to sundown, but for the greenery and birds which frequented the rough that bordered her property. The small hills reminded her of her childhood home in Ithaca, in northern New York State. Though the winters had been brutally cold in New York, and the spring brought buckets of rain, she still missed it. Especially during the hot monotonous summer weather in Southern Florida. She missed her childhood environs, and though she had spent the past ten years in Pelican Cove, on Florida's quiet West coast, she feared that she would always consider New York, and the North, her real home.

As she sipped her first cup of coffee, her mind wandered to the morning's events. She knew Nate loved her dearly and she smiled at the thought of her husband. Then, almost as quickly she felt sad. It seemed that each morning she would look in the mirror and notice another sign of advancing age, each time catching her like some nasty surprise--- "Gotcha! A new wrinkle. There you are! A new brown spot on your cheek and neck. Here you go! A spidery vein bulging like a Rorschach blotch on your thigh." All those infomercials for beauty creams seemed to be directed at her, calling her name – "Make age spots fade away, let Dr. What-cha-ma-call-him make you look years younger!" Her own mother had died when Lisa was only nineteen from aggressive breast cancer and Lisa felt her own mortality reflected in the mirror. She felt that she was looking much older than her forty year old husband. Lisa knew he loved her but wondered if it had merely become a matter of habit and dedication to his marriage vows, rather than true underlying love and physical attraction. The fact that he was always keeping such long hours at work also made her worry sometimes.

Switching on the TV, she saw a perfectly coiffed, attractive female newscaster read the story of the most recent lotto winner, a retiree from Pennsylvania who was going to buy a houseboat and travel the world with her new-found fortune. A lump gathered in her throat and she was glad that the boys were both off to school and couldn't see the tears welling in her eyes. Darn it! She should be happier. She missed her carefree youth, her childhood friends and her family up North and she resented the loneliness like an unwanted visitor who came too often. Wiping her tears away with her bathrobe sleeve, she gulped down the rest of her coffee.

"Okay Lisa, stop feeling sorry for yourself. There's grocery shopping to do," she muttered sarcastically speaking out loud to herself as she rose from the kitchen table, deposited her mug in the dishwasher and turned off the chatterbox TV.

CHAPTER 3

David Layton knew an opportunity when he spotted one. When he arrived as one of the younger plastic surgeons in affluent Pelican Cove, he decided to establish himself as a cosmetic specialist for the privileged who could afford his services. He knew that most new doctors in town joined an established physician group, thereby acquiring a ready patient base from the 'over-flow" of the other members of the group and their referral sources. Alternatively, he could "hang up his shingle" and advertise like crazy, schmooze all the established doctors and their nurses and hustle every opportunity he had to acquire new patients to make a name for himself. Now-a-days that often meant joining every crummy, low-paying HMO and taking lots of late night call at the emergency room just to get busy enough and have enough income to pay the bills. Unfortunately, with reimbursement schedules constantly being reduced, participation in these plans really did not guarantee a sound financial base for the practice. By providing cosmetic procedures he knew that his income might achieve much higher levels and not be affected by decreasing insurance reimbursement. The wealthier patients almost seemed happy to pay high fees established by a skillful plastic surgeon. It was as if by charging more he could establish that he was truly worth more; a better and more qualified physician.

The famous Dr. David Layton Sr. When it came time to set up his practice, David made the difficult decision of approaching his father for a personal loan. The senior Dr. Layton was from the "old school." He had attended Yale, finishing his training in family medicine. Dr. Layton had practiced in Melrose, Connecticut for over forty years, and at the age of sixty-eight was still working fifty hour weeks. He never spoke of retiring, though his work required late night call and a commitment that the younger Dr. Layton found unreasonable.

David had always found talking to his father difficult. His older brother seemed to be the genuine favorite, even though Philip hadn't followed his father into medicine. Philip had excelled in school, surpassing David in academics and sports. However, his calling was in business and he had been one of the fortunate souls who had gotten in early with a start-up dot-com. He had cashed out in time to avoid the crash in 2000 and now lived comfortably on his savings. He had the easy life David longed for along with a nice summer house in Connecticut and a winter home in San Diego. David was willing to do almost anything for a life like his older brother's.

The only arena where David had Philip beaten was in his charm and quick tongue. It wasn't that Philip didn't have his share of friends and popularity, but David always was the one to get the prettiest cheerleader and the one who always seemed to come up with just the right thing to say. He could always talk his way out of trouble, though usually he was smart enough to avoid difficulties. However, his charm and way with words failed him around his father. He always sensed that the senior Dr. Layton found him wanting in some way. David felt that his choice of plastic surgery had disappointed his father. He knew his dad had hoped his son would become a "real" doctor such as a family physician or general surgeon. But he knew that what had really infuriated Layton Sr. the most was his choice of specialization.

Unfortunately, setting up a private surgical practice required some extra money for necessary advertising, equipment and facilities – money he didn't have. Even with past help from his father he had significant debts from medical school. It was difficult, but he had finally found the nerve to ask his father for a loan of $120,000. It was granted, though David could almost feel the bitterness in the senior Layton's mouth as he vouched for the funds he had earned saving the lives of his patients.

"So I suppose it's too late for me to talk you into taking a position with the faculty at Yale teaching meaningful surgery and perhaps helping with some indigent medical care. You know you're quite gifted surgically, they could use you."

David swallowed back the bilious lump in his throat and wanted to explain to his father that having to fight the politics of the institution for relatively low pay wasn't his cup of tea.

"Dad, you know it's hard enough for me to have to ask you for money at the age of thirty-three. Please don't make me explain why I want to do cosmetic surgery," David pleaded.

"So that you can suck fat out of women and men who should diet or at least accept themselves as they are? Or get rid of a few wrinkles? I had hoped for far more from you David," the senior Layton commented disdainfully.

"Dad, just give me the check and let me go," David said; angry and hurt at the same time.

It always came down to this: I had hoped for more from you David. God, how he could hate his father. All he wanted at that moment was to leave his father's study with his check in hand and some measure of pride remaining.

And so it had passed. That had been seven years ago. Now, at forty, David had a thriving and (what he at least imagined) a well thought of cosmetic practice. He had no ties to the dreaded HMOs, saw no Medicare or Medicaid patients, hadn't killed anyone and had a very healthy bank account.

David had never married, though with his good looks, including bright blue eyes and a full head of light brown hair on his six foot-one inch frame, he never lacked for female companionship. Though he felt that perhaps he should settle down, he never entertained such thoughts for long. He always enjoyed meeting and getting to know new, attractive members of the opposite sex. With no big commitments and no one to answer to. He liked it that way. All-in-all, life was good for David Layton II.

The phone rang and interrupted his daydreams.

"Dr. Layton, this is your service. The emergency department at Pelican General has been trying to reach you regarding Shirley Herold. They want to know if she works for you."

"Did they say anything else?" He responded.

"No, they just asked that you call back."

"Okay, thanks."

David hoped there was nothing wrong with his nurse. She had been with him from his first days in Pelican Cove and was as much part of his family as any blood relatives. He hit the speed dial and connected through from the operator to the emergency department.

"Hi, this is Dr. Layton, I understand someone has been looking for me regarding my nurse Shirley Herold."

The receptionist of the ER department paused. She knew that the nurse had been pronounced dead, but passing on such information was not in her job description.

"Please hold for a second doctor, and I'll get Dr. Bradley on the line."

Layton had only enough time to switch his phone from his right ear to his left before the ER physician came on.

"Dr. Layton, I'm Sebastian Bradley, one of the ER docs. Do you know a Shirley Herold?"

"Yes, she's one of my nurses. Has she been hurt?"

Bradley hesitated for just a moment.

"I'm sorry to have to tell you this, but Ms. Herold died this evening from a motor vehicle accident. She was dead on arrival."

"Oh my God! How did it happen?" Dr. Layton cried.

"We really don't know. Apparently she lost control of her vehicle. Had she been ill?" The doctor queried.

"Not at all, she was the picture of good health."

"I'm so sorry, Dr. Layton. Does she have family in town?"

"No, her husband passed away a few years ago and she has no children," David responded.

"Do you have any idea what her wishes might have been for her body?"

"I sure don't," he replied. "We never discussed it. Her father is still alive and lives in Miami Beach. I can try to contact him for you. He would have a better idea of what should be done."

"Thanks, that would be helpful. In cases of unexplained accidental death the ME usually wants to decide regarding the necessity of an autopsy. Please have her father call us and we can follow-up with any arrangements after the medical examiner has made his decision and done whatever he has to do," the ER doctor finished.

"Okay, I just can't believe she's gone….."

Bradley could hear the pain in Layton's voice. No matter how many times he had to deliver such horrible news, it never diminished the feelings of sadness being the bearer of such tidings brought him.

"I'm so sorry for your loss, David."

"Thanks, I'll call her dad and help him make any arrangements. Goodnight."

David hung up the phone. The clatter of the receiver hitting the cradle echoed in his ear. Not only had he lost a loyal and valued employee, but also a cherished friend. He glanced at his watch. It was 8:30 in the evening. David knew that Shirley's father's name was John Kilkenny and was able to get his phone number from information.

He made the call. Having to tell the old man that his only daughter had died was horrible. The father was clearly in shock upon receiving the news but was managed to recall his daughter's prior expression of preference for cremation. She had said that when she died she wanted to have her ashes spread out at sea in the Gulf of Mexico at sunset, joining her husband who had been disposed of similarly several years earlier. Mr. Kilkenny said he would drive over to Pelican Cove in the morning to take care of the arrangements. David felt guilty at the relief he felt at not having to make all of the preparations himself and offered the grieving father his help.

CHAPTER 4

David Layton entered the back door to his richly decorated office in Pelican Cove's most prestigious shopping district, Palm Drive. He half expected to be met by his head nursing assistant, Shirley, who always greeted him with a smile and an offer for a hot cup of coffee. The office was unusually quiet, although it was almost noontime. Instead of Shirley, he was greeted by Barbara, one of his other nurses.

"Dr. Layton."

Barbara's thin face was tear-stained and her mascara was smudged by fresh droplets running down her face. David had notified the entire staff of Shirley's death by phone shortly after he had received the news.

"I can't believe Shirley is gone. I just can't." Barbara began to sob.

"Are you okay to work today? I can close the office if we have to," offered David.

"We were able to reschedule all of the early morning patients, as you asked, but honestly, I'd rather work than sit at home and think about Shirley every minute. I've already spoken with everyone else and we'd all rather work, at least for a few hours and you've still got your Botox seminar this afternoon. Will there be a funeral for Shirley?" Barbara questioned.

"Her father is coming over from the other coast and he may arrange a small ceremony. As far as I know she's going to be cremated. I'll let you know for sure after I speak to him."

"Okay, Dr. Layton, you've gotten two calls from Dr. Manzari at Youth Labs in the last hour. He wants you to call him right back."

Barbara had worked with David for the past three years. She was reliable and professional and was great with the patients. Barbara had silky chestnut-colored hair and a slim figure, enhanced by breasts which two years earlier had been enlarged and uplifted by Dr. Layton's skillful surgery. At forty-six years she had the appearance of a woman of thirty-five. Early on, David had initiated a policy of free cosmetic surgery for his staff as a Christmas bonus. Over the past years Barbara had received a full face-lift, liposuction of her hips and abdomen and the previously mentioned breast surgery.

More recently, Barbara had been the recipient of a new Botox. David had developed this in conjunction with his partner and collaborator at Youth Labs, Sal Manzari. In the past, David had found it necessary to give Barbara additional Botox shots every four months or so. However, the most recent injections had already lasted over seven months. This improved formulation was not yet available for general distribution. Dr. Manzari and Dr. Layton were equal partners and so far, they had resisted the financial temptation of turning over their new compound to a larger firm. Their hopes were pinned on attracting venture capital. By doing this, they would be able to pocket the windfall of money resulting from a closely held patent and small group of investors. David's goal of obtaining a life of extravagance would be fulfilled in this way.

"Barbara, please get me Dr. Manzari, I'll be in my office."

David sat down in his plush office office. The walls were decorated with several expensive old maps; cartography was a hobby he had acquired from his father, who also collected ancient maps. Perhaps it was the similarities between the impermanence of nations and their geography and how that compared with the impermanence of cosmetic surgery that appealed to David. In any case, he found the décor pleasing and always enjoyed the solitude of his cozy office. The red light on his phone lit up, indicating a successful connection with Manzari.

"Dr. Manzari on line one Dr. Layton."

David spoke into the speakerphone.

"Thank you Barb, I won't be long. Let me know when the first patients are here."

"Certainly doctor, would you like your coffee too?"

Having Barbara so quickly take on Shirley's former accustomed task of bringing him his coffee was jarring, but he fought off the sad emotion in appreciation of Barbara's gesture.

"Thanks, yes please."

He switched off the speakerphone and picked up the receiver in order to speak in private with Dr. Manzari.

"Good morning Dr. Layton. I read about Shirley in the paper this morning. I'm so sorry," Dr. Manzari began.

"Thanks, Sal. We're all in shock here."

"What happened to cause the accident?" He continued.

"They're still not sure and are considering doing an autopsy. No other cars were involved and she wasn't drinking or anything. We just don't know yet," David volunteered.

"Is there anything I can do, David?"

"Thanks for the offer, but I think we'll mull through okay here. How are things at the lab-is my order for more Botox ready yet? We're running low."

"Almost, David, I'm waiting on a delivery of one of the reagents by FedEx today. If it comes in I should have a new batch for you tomorrow. We're going to have enough for about forty more patients, depending upon how much you need for each treatment. All the little ladies still happy with their results?" Dr. Manzari inquired.

"Yes, Sal. I've even used some on my own wrinkles. I had Barbara treat several spots on my face and I'm looking great, even if I do say so myself. This afternoon I'm running another free question-and-answer seminar and expect to attract some new patients. I'll need you to call me tomorrow and let me know if the new batch is ready. How are the mice doing?"

"They're thriving. No side effects in eight months. Things couldn't be better!"

"Good, the last thing we need are problems. We're so close to the venture capital money I can almost taste it. Then we can retire and sip strawberry Daiquiris by the pool."

David had to chuckle at the thought of the three hundred pound Manzari lying in a bathing suit by the pool. Dr. Manzari was an extremely gifted doctorate biochemist whom David had met at a cosmetic surgery conference in Florida. As one of the largest users of Botox in South Florida, Manzari knew that Dr. Layton's practice was an excellent choice for testing of his new formulation. When he was approached by the corpulent researcher, Layton was initially hesitant to invest money in the new drug, aware of the expense and time involved in obtaining FDA approval. The vision of where he wanted to be in comparison to where he was now helped to persuade him. David had huge dreams for himself that required a large amount of funds-and he wasn't the most patient of men. Yes, his brother's success in business and a desire to do better than his sibling pushed him to take this chance. The biochemistry appeared extremely sound, with modification of the compound only consisting of one new carbon and hydroxyl unit, providing increased longevity of the chemical after injection.

Chester Jankel, at the FDA had advised that it would be at least eleven months before the results of Phase II trials could be reviewed and approved. Then, licensing of the drug could slowly progress, requiring perhaps one or two more years. He and Manzari had decided to move ahead on their own, with their own timeline. David trusted Sal as a genius chemist and an easy partner. If needed, Dr. Layton could manipulate Sal to his own advantage.

"So are we on track for our meeting with the BioVenture money guys?" Sal asked.

"Absolutely! The data we have should be sufficient to open their wallets right up. They're already talking about moving the operations to a new lab in Singapore where licensing and testing is easier. From there, we'll get the drug approved in Europe and then bring it back home to the good ol' U.S. Anything else I can do for you?" asked David.

"No doc, keep up the good work and you'll make us both wealthy. And again, I'm so sorry about Shirley."

"Thanks, Sal. Have a good one, and don't work too hard."

"You too, Dr. Layton," Dr. Manzari broke the connection.

Barbara tapped on the door softly.

"Come in," David called.

He picked up a plastic surgery journal and glanced at the cover, reviewing the newest lasers for less-invasive liposuction.

"Here's your coffee, Dr. Layton," Barbara said softly.

Her voice sounded shaky and David thought she might have been crying.

"Thanks, Barb. When's our first patient due?"

"You've got about forty-five minutes. We've been busy on the phones.

A lot of our patients have been calling expressing their condolences for Shirley. Everyone loved her," Barbara answered.

"She was a great woman. I'm going to catch up on my journals and mail. Buzz me when the first patient is ready."

"Okay."

Barbara closed the door and David's thoughts returned to Shirley as he tried to read his journal. The forty-five minutes passed quickly. A buzz on his speakerphone alerted him to the start of his work-day.

"We have a Botox consult for you, Dr. Layton."

"Thanks Barb, I'll be right out."

As David got up to leave the room, he momentarily forgot what he had intended to do. He had been having more and more of these episodes lately – he was just so darn busy. Several times he'd found himself standing up or wandering into a room for a reason that was lost to him. Remembering the two waiting patients, he opened the door onto the brightly lit corridor. Barbara's somber face greeted him; she had redone her makeup and placed a smile on her face.

"You okay Barb?" David asked.

"I'll be okay, Dr. Layton. Let's get to work. It'll help me put things out of my mind," Barb stated.

"Sure, and thanks for being here today Barb."

David entered Exam Room #1 and was greeted by Christy Moore; a new patient. David glimpsed down at the chart.

"Good morning Mrs. Moore, I'm Dr. Layton. I see from the chart that Ann Childs referred you to me."

"Yes Doctor, she spoke so highly of you. I know you must hear this all the time, but what you did for her really changed the way she felt after her divorce. She's so happy."

David remembered Ann Childs well. A recently divorced, now single mother who wanted breast implants. He had agreed that a change from her "A" cup to a "B" or maybe a small "C" with some firming might help, but had failed to convince her not to go all the way to a "D". It often seemed to be that the women wanted more than what he felt fit their body type.

"I'm so glad she was happy and referred you. So how can I help you Christy?" David looked her over quickly trying to determine which part of her body might displease her. She was an attractive thirty-year-old, with a well toned body and fair skin. Not tanned or very wrinkled, unlike most of his patients here in Florida.

"I would like to get rid of these wrinkles." Christy replied. I know they're not real serious, and you're probably going to laugh, but they bother me, especially when I'm out in the sun and squint."

She squinted in demonstration, revealing exaggerated furrowing between her eyebrows.

David smiled.

"No, Christy, I understand. And it's very easy to correct the problem. I've had great success in treating just that spot. Would you like me to treat you today?"

"Wow, I didn't know you could do it now, I thought today was just a consultation. Sure. Will it hurt much?"

"No, not too much Christy. I use a fine needle and only insert tiny amounts of the medication. Are you familiar with Botox?" Dr. Layton questioned.

"Just from what I've read in the supermarket magazines and from Oprah. How long does it last?"

"The literature usually suggests three to six months. My patients have generally been very satisfied. I've consistently been able to get the effects to last six months or more. Let me have Barbara review the treatment with you and get your signed consent and I'll be back in a few minutes, okay?" Dr. Layton walked to the phone.

"Thanks Dr. Layton, that sounds great."

David buzzed for Barbara. "Barb please get me a vial of Botox and a new patient info package. I'll be injecting four units to the left side and right sides and another eight centrally."

David exited the door, as Barbara returned with a folder which included information on Botox, before and after pictures, a standard informed consent and a list of charges. There was also a form advising the patient that all charges were not likely to be covered by insurance and payment would be required at the time of service.

"Do I have to read all of this?" asked Christy.

"Dr. Layton would really prefer that you understand everything before we start so that there are no problems later. Spend a few minutes, and don't rush. I'll be back soon and answer any questions before Dr. Layton comes in.

"Okay," Christy responded, a little nervous at the expected discomfort of the shots but excited to get rid or her wrinkles.

The next patient for Dr. Layton was a post-op. It was the cousin of one of his former employees. These days, he rarely did anything involving any insurance company claims, but when one of his former employees almost begged him to remove a small skin cancer from her uncle's nose he reluctantly agreed. The 'small' cancer ended up being larger than anyone had expected and he had spent over two hours removing it and another hour repairing the hole it left behind. He had been forced to use a skin graft to recreate the shape of the man's nose.

"I see Barbara has removed your stitches. How are you Mr. Germaine?"

"I'm great Doc, you patched me up good. Look you can hardly see where you put the skin on. It won't even hurt my movie career!" Mr. Germaine quipped.

Pleased with the result, David laughed at the joke. He felt remorse only in the fact that for his three hours of work he was not going to be paid well. The man had a high deductible with his insurance, had limited income and was the family of his former employee – all factors which united to limit what he felt comfortable charging.

"Well, it does look like you're doing very well. I think if you're having no problems, I won't need to see you again, and can discharge you back to the care of your dermatologist."

"So soon? Don't you want to see your handiwork again?"

"Only if you have a problem," responded David. Time to cut my losses, was the thought running through the surgeon's head.

David sensed disappointment from Mr. Germaine at the brevity of the meeting. However, he was very eager at the thought of getting back to his Botox client. After shaking hands with the patient he exited the room. On the way out, when he was just outside the door, Layton couldn't help but hear the older man say,

"Isn't he a great doctor!"

David checked his schedule. At one p.m. he had the second of his in-office Botox luncheons. Although it was somewhat frowned upon to trivialize the treatment by having "Botox parties," he found free lunch conferences an excellent way to increase the number of patients in his practice. It had been crucial in expanding his base for the new Botox - he needed as much data as he could get. The more trials and data offered to investors the more money to be had. Besides, everyone loves a 'free' lunch.

Barbara joined him with Christy Moore. By now Christy had read through the papers, signed her consent, and she was waiting nervously on the examination table.

"Any questions Christy?" David asked.

"None, Dr. Layton, I'm ready."

"Great, now just try to relax. I'm going to have you lean back a little on the table."

After cleaning her skin with an alcohol solution, David skillfully injected minute amounts of the Botulinum toxin to paralyze the fibers of the frontalis muscles. The musculature here was actually quite complex, including muscles known as the corrugators, depressor supercilli and also part of the orbicularis oculi and procerus. David knew them all well, completing the treatment in less than a minute.

"Is everything okay Christy?" asked the doctor.

"Fine, Dr. Layton," she responded sincerely, "it wasn't anywhere near as uncomfortable as I thought it might be."

Now you may have some temporary swelling or even a sensation of heaviness around your eyes." If you have any questions or problems please call. Otherwise, I'll have Barbara finish up with you and you're free to go."

"Thank you so much doctor, you're great!" Christy beamed.

Barbara was already gently blotting the small puncture wounds with dry gauze and preparing Christy for home. Dr. Layton's abbreviated late morning schedule included a mixture of brief post-op visits, a new evaluation of a potential face-lift patient, and a guy who wanted liposuction of his 'love-handles'. Before he knew it, it was time for his office seminar.

CHAPTER 5

Lisa opened the door to her Volvo. Nate had insisted on the car after reading about how safe they were. She promised herself a minivan next time. Let the Arabs get rich on all the gas money she'd spend on fuel, she didn't care. Getting all the groceries in and out and carrying the boys all around town in the Volvo was a pain. Her hands engulfed a heavy bag of Coke bottles and Home Style Tropicana just as her cell phone rang. An abbreviated version of a Matchbox Twenty song cried out from her purse.

"Hi Lisa, are you just about ready? I'm leaving my house now to pick you up."

It was her closest friend Janetta. Like Lisa, Janetta was a displaced Northerner. Unlike Lisa, Janetta was all alone. She had moved to Pelican Cove on a job transfer, only to lose the job in a corporate takeover of her company. Now she was a very successful real estate agent. Her success was probably helped by the fact that she was gorgeous as well as very hard-working. At age thirty-five, Janetta already had her own home, a new Beamer, and a nice stock portfolio. Even with the recent drop in the market she was secure. Unfortunately, she just hadn't met Mr. Right. In fact, she had just ended a two year relationship with an asshole who she found out had been cheating on her for most of the past year.

"Oh my God, I totally forgot about our get together today for that lunch seminar. I'm just leaving the supermarket, let me rush home. I'll be there in ten minutes," blurted Lisa.

"Okay, I'll meet you at the house. I don't think Dr. Wrinkle will wait for us so hurry up!" Janetta finished with "see you in a few."

"Okay, Janetta".

Lisa tucked the phone back in her purse and finished packing her groceries in the car. She had mixed emotions about the lunch meeting and wondered if maybe she had intentionally forgotten the seminar. She was embarrassed at being seen at the plastic surgeon's office and didn't want anyone to think she was vain and unhappy with her appearance. Then again, maybe it would be interesting or even fun. Knowing Janetta, her single friend probably wanted to check out the eligible bachelor. She drove home lost in thought and was at her house and unpacking before her friend arrived.

"I've always wondered what they do with the edges when they cut them off these little sandwiches." Lisa Martin took a nibble from a tiny corner of a smoked salmon and caper hors d'oeuvre.

"I don't know, but for what Dr. Layton gets paid for doing his work, you'd think he could afford the entire sandwich!" Janetta joked.

Lisa gazed around the opulently decorated room in the offices of the renowned plastic surgeon. The ceilings boasted rich, dark-toned crown moldings and the walls were covered in prints of European Masters' paintings. Included were some Reuben's classics, which Lisa thought were somehow out of place---after all, Dr. Layton spent so much of his time helping women reject the idea of the robust, full-figured woman depicted in the classic works of art; it seemed a contradiction.

Lisa looked toward the door that connected the meeting room to the rest of the office. She had never been to a plastic surgeon's office before, and was a little embarrassed to be at one now. She hadn't told her husband she was going and didn't really want to tell him. Lisa wondered how much he noticed the wrinkles that used to be around her eyes only when she smiled but now were there all the time. And then there were the little brown spots-like water stains on a dirty glass-appearing on her forehead and hands.

David Layton entered the meeting room carrying himself with dignity; his head held high. Today's turnout was excellent, with seventeen women in attendance.

Janetta caught herself staring at the doctor. She had heard that he was handsome, but found herself unprepared for his movie star quality good looks. It was his brilliant blue eyes that especially struck her as they glanced around the room and rested on hers momentarily before moving on. She noticed that she wasn't the only one captivated by the doctor.

"He looks like a Greek god," Janetta whispered into Lisa's ear.

"Yes and quite single, though I hear from the grapevine that he's never lacking for companionship," Lisa responded.

"Another one of those I don't need," barked Janetta, almost loud enough to be heard.

The meeting was rather brief. Dr. Layton presented slides representative of his work, including before and after Botox photos. Barbara discussed her own satisfaction with Botox, advising everyone of how pleased she had been with her recent results.

"I don't think her boobs are real," Janetta intoned into Lisa's ear.

"No, and her face looks a bit tight, I think he's done a little face-lift on her too," Lisa responded quietly.

Despite their catty comments, both women were impressed by the final outcome, especially when Barbara advised the crowd that she was forty-six.

"Not bad," whispered Janetta.

Dr. Layton then pitched his final remarks:

"I realize that many of you may be concerned and have unrealistic fears that the press has produced regarding Botox. I can assure you that it is completely safe in practiced hands. Any potential side-effects are reversible and short-lived and the benefits are truly remarkable. If you wish, on the way out you may schedule your first session at half the usual fee as my way of saying thank-you for coming to hear me speak today."

With that, Dr. Layton thanked everyone for attending and exited the room to the applause of the group.

"What do you think, Lisa, should we do it?"

"I don't know Janetta, Nate really isn't in favor of plastic surgery stuff".

As an attorney, her husband was quite aware of the potential for complications in any surgical procedure and generally wasn't a big fan of doctors.

"Why don't we just do one session? It is half price. Then if we don't like it, we'll never come back-- no one has to know." Janetta spoke as if her mind was already decided.

"Okay, just once. I really don't mind the idea of losing some of my wrinkles, even if it's only for a few months," Lisa sighed.

On the way out the door, women were given appointments – Lisa was worked in for the next day, and Janetta was scheduled for the following week.

David sat at his desk—four p.m. and no more patients. This part of the day was his favorite. Removing his shoes, he rubbed his feet on the soft carpet and then lifted them up on his desk. Taking a deep breath, he relaxed, appreciating the peace and solitude of his empty office.

Generally a technophobe, he did enjoy some of the technological advancements of recent years. He tolerated the computer only in a limited way, realizing its importance in billing and scheduling, but he still enjoyed his paper records. The new plasma TV was cool but he dreaded having to program it. He was about the only person he knew who still had a VCR. It was only a matter of time before he might have to automate his office further and place all of his charts in the care of his computer, but for now he still utilized records he could hold in his hands. The best invention he did enjoy was his new iPod. Becky had helped him program it and it was a minor luxury for him to be able to lean back at the end of the day, read his mail, and listen to the little iPod while sitting at his desk. He pressed some invisible buttons on the miniature wonder and called up an old Sam Cooke song, "Chain Gang". Somehow it seemed to fit the end of the day. From there, he jumped to Willie Nelson, and "On the Road Again". Finally, he listened to two from a Norah Jones CD—"Cold, Cold Heart" and "Come Away With Me". His relaxation was interrupted by Barbara's voice as she entered the room.

"I'm going to be heading out Dr. Layton. Is there anything you need before I go?"

"No Barbara, thanks. Any big plans tonight?"

"Only if you consider curling up in my recliner and watching a DVD from Blockbuster big plans! You know me Dr. Layton, no going out on a school night, and hardly any going out on the other nights." She sighed.

David smiled at Barbara who really was rather alone in the world. She had married a younger man that David had genuinely liked. The guy had seemed normal enough. Then one day he takes Barbara aside and tells her he's been having an affair—with another man. She was devastated and almost left town when the gossip became too much. Now two years later, she was still bitter. Barbara was the only child of older parents, both of whom were deceased. Dr. Layton was employer, family and confidant to her.

"Well, I hope you enjoy your movie, I'll see you bright and early. We've got a busy day tomorrow."

"I'll be here, have a good night, Dr. Layton."

"I'm following you right out the door Barbara, goodnight."

She exited the office, followed closely behind by her boss.

CHAPTER 6

It was Thursday evening and dinnertime in the Martin household. At seven p.m. Nate came in the door with a bouquet of flowers and an apology on his lips.

"Sorry I'm late honey. We're swamped with Jointrex cases and it's just so hard to get home. We signed on another nine cases today."

Jointrex was Wagner Pharmaceuticals promising drug for rejuvenating damaged joints. One or two injections seemed to delay the need for knee surgery for several years. Unfortunately, the company had concealed information from the FDA indicating a higher than reported incidence of abscess formation in the areas of injection. When the product became widely used, new reports of joint infection and total joint destruction surfaced. Records were subpoenaed and it was like minting money for the attorneys who were fortunate enough to represent patients with damages. Nate's firm had been aggressive in creating a web site to acquire new cases and had developed a television ad campaign. Projections were for 10-15 million dollars in revenues for the partners.

"I understand Nate but I already fed the boys. It's past seven o'clock and they came home from school starving. I did pick up some apple pie we can share with them after dinner. So does all this extra work mean partnership this year?"

"I think so honey. And a nice Christmas bonus too. Maybe we can all go on a Caribbean vacation over winter break."

"That would work for me—we could certainly use it." Lisa served Nate chicken breasts and fresh green beans.

"What's the matter honey, there's no skin on my chicken. Are you trying to keep me alive forever?"

"What I'm trying to do is serve you healthy food instead of that fried crap you grab when you're too busy to take the time to eat healthy," Lisa responded smiling.

Walking over to his wife, Nate wrapped his arms around her and buried his head in the side of her neck.

"Thank you honey, I do appreciate everything you do." He exhaled into her ear. Lisa shivered and smiled.

"Nate, you smell like chicken, go finish your dinner. I want to give the boys their dessert and get them off to bed-then maybe we can have our fun later."

"Okay, okay, I know when I'm not wanted," Nate teased. He sat back down and finished his meal.

"Josh, Shawn, come on downstairs for dessert," Lisa called up to the boys.

They raced each other down the stairs, elbows flying in an attempt to achieve advantage on the way to the kitchen.

"I won," gasped Shawn, slightly out of breath

"Sure, 'cause you cheated," snapped Josh. "You always cheat."

"Come on boys, stop bickering. I've got apple pie and whip cream for you."

"Real whip cream, Mom?" asked Josh.

"Real whip cream only if you behave. Now sit down and Dad will cut the pie for you."

"How was school today, boys?" asked Nate.

"I hate school, Dad," blurted Josh. "I just wish I could fish all day. It's not like I have to know that much to be a fisherman."

"Josh, unless you go to school, you won't be able to get a good job and buy a nice boat so you can fish in style. Besides, you always do well in school," Nate answered smiling.

"I know, I just get bored."

"Give it some time, Josh," Lisa interjected. "It's only the third week of school; I bet things will get better."

"Probably just harder," Shawn pushed the words out around a huge bite of cream-covered pie.

Shawn had already wolfed down his entire dessert; seemingly able to eat anything and everything without gaining weight. He was a great student, already reading two grade levels above his fourth grade classmates.

"Am I excused? I've got some reading to do."

"Me too," chimed in Josh.

"Sure, but make sure you're reading and not spending all night messaging your friends on the computer," admonished Lisa. "And I want you both in bed by nine."

"But Mom, I'm older," Shawn argued.

"Yes, but I don't want you falling asleep in class. Okay, nine-thirty-but that's the latest. And nine for you, Josh," Lisa finished.

Josh looked like he was about to ask for another half hour for himself, then decided to race his brother up the stairs instead, beating him to the computer. In no time at all, he was messaging his friends.

CHAPTER 7

David drove his Mercedes to the hospital early the next morning. Shirley was scheduled for an autopsy that morning and the pathologist, Dr. Jack Shea had asked to meet with Dr. Layton. The medical examiner hoped Shirley's employer could assist with any background information. David made his way into the lower level of the administration area of the hospital. It always seemed that the pathology section of the hospital was kept as far away from 'live' patient care as possible. Layton was greeted by a receptionist who directed him to Dr. Shea.

Dr. Jack Shea was the most experienced pathologist in the Medical Examiner's office, and also had a reputation as the most meticulous. Besides being meticulous Dr. Shea was also fast and efficient. He made the standard "Y" incision from the breastbone to the umbilicus as he dictated into his recorder, anchored behind his ear.

"Shirley Herold, Caucasian, 51, medium build. Victim in MVA. No foreign bodies in mouth, teeth intact. Small bite marks one side of tongue. Slight ecchymoses on temples and at glabella,-yellow. Estimated three to five days old. Small puncture marks with scabs at glabella and lateral canthi of eyes. Sclera clear." He paused as he continued his incision.

"Heart grossly normal. 292 grams. No clots noted. Valves appear normal. No evidence of Atherosclerosis. "Liver grossly normal, weight 1350 grams. Capsule intact, no hematoma. Intestines normal. Kidneys grossly normal, right 9.2 cm, left 9.4 cm by 4.1 and 4.3 cm respectively. Weight right kidney, 145 grams, left kidney, 154 grams. Capsules intact."

David arrived at the medical examiner's on time. When the door opened Dr. Shea saw a distraught and disheveled Dr. David Layton.

"Hello Dr. Layton. I'm so sorry about your nurse. I understand she worked for you for a quite a long time."

"Call me David, and yes, for as long as I've been in Pelican Cove."

Jack Shea noted the grief on Layton's face. It was a look he saw all too often.

"Anything abnormal on the autopsy, Dr. Shea?" asked David.

"Please, call me Jack. Not yet. Everything looks pretty much normal. It looks like you've had your hooks into her though-had you been giving her collagen shots?"

David hesitated before he answered.

"No, just a little Botox lately. Actually, I gave her some three days ago."

"Well that would explain her old bruises and small puncture marks on her face. I doubt we're going to find anything, but I plan to complete the autopsy with an examination of her brain. If it ends up normal, we'll sign this out as due to 'natural causes'; likely an arrhythmia or seizure. I understand her husband is dead and she has no kids."

"Yes, she lived alone."

Dr. Shea felt sorry for his colleague. He never really felt much camaraderie with the medical staff, least of all the plastic surgeons, but he could tell that David Layton was truly beside himself over the loss of his employee and friend.

"If I find anything, I'll let you know. I'll be able to release the body this afternoon. My office will contact the next of kin and we'll let the funeral home know when we'll have the body ready for them."

"Thanks Jack." With that, David was more than happy to leave the surroundings of the morgue. He opened the door, left the hospital and was confronted by a wall of sticky warm muggy air and another bright, steamy Florida day.

Traffic was light and on the way back to the office David's thoughts wandered. With Shirley gone, he had lost his most experienced and dependable employee, as well as a friend. His receptionist, Becky, only handled clerical duties. His nurses, Paula and Barbara were good, but much less experienced than Shirley. Barbara was able to assist with surgeries but Paula was newer to his staff, having replaced Kandi, who was on maternity leave. Neither wanted the full-time hours Shirley had worked and David was feeling lost without her.

Upon reaching the office, Barbara greeted Dr. Layton, but she was unusually reticent. She reeked of too much Bath and Body Works vanilla lotion and was chewing gum. She stopped in mid-chew, looking like a sad cow chewing its cud. David prohibited chewing gum inside the office- today he decided to let the gum chewing violation go.

"Hi Dr. L, we've got a full day today. Did the medical examiner have any information regarding Shirley's cause of death?"

"He thinks she probably died of an arrhythmia or seizure. So far, they really haven't found anything."

"Shirley was such a great person." Barbara's big brown eyes were tear-filled.

David walked over and hugged her. As he relaxed his grasp he looked into her eyes with sympathy.

"Are you going to be okay?"

"You know me, Dr. Layton, I can handle it. I guess we're going to have to hire someone to replace Shirley."

"We will. I hated to have to think about it so soon, but I placed an ad in the paper already. Hopefully we'll start getting some resumes soon."

"I'll work extra hours if you need me to, Dr. Layton."

"Thanks, Barbara. You don't know how much I appreciate it. I'm going to make some calls. I'll be in my office. Let me know when the first patient arrives. Do you know how long I have?"

"Your first patient is a post-op lipo at 9:30."

"Okay, so I have about 45 minutes. Just buzz me when she arrives."

Mrs. Kay Chase was the perfect patient. Not too demanding, pleasant, always on time and polite to the staff. Her surgery had gone perfectly. She had liposuction of her hips and abdomen and had recovered without complications and with only minimal bruising. David was happy to see her.

"Good morning Kay, how are you?"

Kay was a beautiful woman. She worked as a newscaster for the local NBC affiliate in Pelican Cove. The liposuction had been her first treatment by a plastic surgeon and she preferred to keep her visit confidential. Thus, her early morning appointment.

"Dr. Layton, you are amazing! I'm having no problems at all and I was able to work after just one day off. I'm so grateful. I'm already fitting into a size 4–I haven't been able to do that for years!"

"Have all of your wounds healed?"

"See for yourself." Kay lowered her jeans and raised her blouse. Her liposuction treatment sites were pink, but healing well.

"Looks good to me. I think you're all set. Is there anything else I can do for you?"

"No, Dr. Layton, but there is something I'd like to do for you. Would you be interested in some free publicity? I'd like to do a piece on plastic surgery for the station and can highlight your office. The TV execs have already given me the green light."

"Wow, Kay. That would be great! I'd especially like to showcase the great results I've been having with Botox."

"I'm going to let you take it wherever you want. You'll look great on TV. I'll have my production crew get in touch with you to set up a date and make all the arrangements."

"Thanks, Kay." They shook hands and David escorted Kay from the office.

After seeing several follow up patients Paula buzzed him.

"You have a new Botox patient, a Lisa Martin."

"Thanks, Paula. Have her brought to the consultation room and I'll be right there."

Lisa was escorted by Paula to Dr. Layton's consultation suite. The exam room was small, but tastefully decorated. She sat in a soft leather chair and admired a framed oil painting of a young couple sitting on a swing under a tree, gazing into each other's eyes. They seemed to have no cares in the world, sharing the boundless glories of youthful love. Dr. Layton quietly entered the room.

"That painting is my favorite. It speaks of the unlimited potential of love and youth."

Lisa found the handsome doctor's presence somewhat unsettling. He had caught her off-guard when he entered. She felt her heart flutter like a wild bird caught in a cage.   It occurred to her that she was weak, having allowed herself to get excited by the surgeon's presence. To cover, she smiled at the doctor in what she hoped was a friendly, but not too friendly, manner.

Dr. Layton looked briefly at the questions in the chart that Lisa had completed moments earlier.

"I see this is your first elective procedure, and we're to inject around your eyes and between your eyebrows. Do you have any questions Mrs. Martin?"

Lisa assumed by "elective" procedure Dr. Layton meant cosmetic. She again felt guilty over her vanity.

"No, I attended your seminar and feel very knowledgeable and any other questions I had Barbara answered for me."

"Great, well let's get started then." David buzzed for assistance and the nurse promptly appeared at the door with a small tray. It contained a very small syringe, some gauze and a vial of what Lisa assumed was the Botox.

"This will hurt a little bit as I inject the medication, but only briefly," Dr. Layton said in his practiced, reassuring manner.

He had Lisa sit on the examination table at a sixty degree angle, and steadied his hand on the side of her face as he injected minute amounts of the medication into the small wrinkles at the corners of her eyes. Next, he injected the deeper furrows at the area between her eyebrows; her "frown lines." It was uncomfortable, but certainly tolerable. The proximity of Dr. Layton to her face as he administered the treatment gave Lisa the opportunity to once again notice how handsome he was. Smelling his cologne, Lisa felt embarrassed at how drawn she was to stare at him. She felt a strange urge to reach out and touch the doctor. Except for her husband, it was rare for any man to touch her skin, other than Robert at the hairdresser's, who had no affinity for women and was more like a woman than a man. Her heart again fluttered involuntarily. He seemed so confident, so skillful and in control. Appearing to sense her thoughts he smiled at her.

"Well, that's it Lisa. You may notice some swelling and bruising for a few days. The results vary, though some of my patients have had corrections lasting longer than six months.

Lisa was surprised.

"What's your secret Dr. Layton, I thought Botox usually lasted only three or four months. Do you use a higher concentration or lower dilution of medication?"

Dr. Layton was surprised by her choice of words – dilution sounded unusually 'medical' to him.

"Have you been around medicine much Lisa? I don't think anyone has ever asked me that question quite that way before."

"Well, yes, before I became a mother, I worked at Pelican General Hospital and before that I worked in Connecticut as a charge nurse on a surgical ward."

"That explains it. No, I don't use a lower dilution; that wouldn't work. I use only fresh Botox and I don't want to brag, but my results have been very good—and I do have a lot of experience. Have you ever thought of going back to work?"

"Actually I have, but my boys are still young, only seven and nine, and it would probably be hard to find a job to fit with their school schedules. I have been thinking of doing visiting nurses' service though."

"Lisa, I don't know if Barbara mentioned this, but one of my nurses died in a car accident just two days ago. We've been working short-handed and had just placed an ad in the paper for help. I know this is really kind of out of left field, but if you'd like to return to nursing and work for me, at least part time, I could give you hours that could work around your boy's school schedule. You could call the 'shots' as far as your schedule – sorry, pun intended. It could be beneficial to both of us."

Lisa didn't know what to say. She had heard of the horrible auto accident. On a certain level she believed in fate – maybe this job was just the thing she needed at this point in her life.

"Thank you so much Dr. Layton. I just don't know what to say. You know I've been out of the work place for several years……

"Don't worry, Lisa, we can help you catch up. It's really not that hard a job and the staff are all great to work with."

Lisa sighed. This was just the type of opportunity she had secretly been hoping for as the boys had finally reached the age where they were both back at school and becoming more independent. She didn't want to let it pass her by. She found herself responding, "I may not be able to be as much help as you need, but I'm willing to give it a try."

"Fantastic! I'll do everything I can to make sure that you don't regret your decision. I'll have you speak with Barbara. She'll arrange for an orientation, paperwork, background checks, etc. and then we'll get together regarding your schedule. Are you sure this will be okay with everything at home and with your husband?"

Lisa frowned. She hadn't considered David's reaction to her rather rash decision, and appreciated Dr. Layton's concern. Anyway, she was happy to hear that he had placed an ad – at least she could tell Nate that she responded to the ad, and not that she had been at the office to receive Botox.

"I will have to discuss it with him, but I'm sure he'll support my decision."

She hoped that things would go as easily when she broke the news to her husband.

"Well, I'll count on it then. We'll plan on having you start next week."

"Thanks Dr. Layton, I'm looking forward to it."

"Me too, Lisa. Have a great weekend and either Barbara or I will be in touch with you over the weekend to set up your work schedule."

David finished two other examinations and was finishing up a consultation for a face lift when Becky came to the door.

"Sorry to interrupt, Dr. Layton, but I put that call through for you to

Dr. Manzari. He's on line two."

"Thanks, Becky, I'm just finishing up here. I'll be right out"

"Mrs. Conroy, if you have any questions, please don't hesitate to call. If you decide to have the surgery, Barbara can go through all the necessary paperwork and scheduling."

Mrs. Conroy, a sixty-year old 'trophy wife' for an eighty-year old Pelican Cove Toyota dealership owner smiled at Dr. Layton and thanked him for his time. David left the room.

※ဒ

"Hi Dr. Layton, what's up?" Dr. Manzari sounded tired.

"Were you able to make the new lot of Botox ?"

"Yes, I received the FedEx shipment of reagent and was able to make the new batch. I can have one of the techs bring it over to you later today."

"Thanks Sal, that would be great."

"Have you heard anything else about your nurse?"

"Actually, yes, I met with the medical examiner this morning. He did an autopsy and wanted me to help with some questions he had."

"That's gruesome. Why anyone would ever want to go to medical school to take apart dead bodies is beyond me."

David didn't know that as they were speaking, Manzari was folding a computer-generated hand of Texas Hold-Em—a five of diamonds and eight of clubs. The Giant Poker website Sal was playing on was for high rollers only, with minimum opening blinds of $20. As much as he tried to stay away, Sal Manzari couldn't stop gambling. His credit card account at Giant Poker was becoming worrisome. He knew his luck was bound to change, it had to. In the last three weeks he had lost over $30,000 and knew that he would barely be able to cover the minimum charges on his credit card balance which stood at over $21,000. His busy job helped to keep him out of the casinos, as did his lack of money, but computer gambling was just too accessible. And there were more chumps online to beat. He muttered a soft, "shit" under his breath as the flop came with both a five and eight, giving him what would have been a great hand if he hadn't folded.

"Say something Sal?" asked David.

"No, just spilled some coffee on my shirt." Manzari exited the game and gave the phone his full attention. "So what did the coroner say?"

"He didn't really find much. He said she probably had an arrhythmia or seizure and will have the final results in a few days."

"Anything else I can do for you, David?"

"Other than provide me with nursing help, not much." Shirley was my right hand in the office. I was able to find some part-time help so things could certainly be worse. Everything okay at the lab?"

"No problems here Dr. Layton. When can we wrap up the trial in your office and present the data to the Venture Capital guy?"

"I'd like a few more weeks so that we can have enough data to reassure the money-men that the drug is safe. It wouldn't hurt either to have more cases to show them. I've got plenty of before and after pictures so it should be a slam-dunk." David was getting excited as he filled in Manzari.

"Well, rest assured that the production end is running smoothly. I have to admit, I envy you out there in the real world with all those pretty wrinkled women to treat while I'm stuck here in the lab with my rodents."

David laughed.

"You keep up the hard work, and very soon, we'll both be able to spend our days lounging around the pool in our Speed-Os, sipping our Pina Coladas and ogling all of the beautiful women we want, without worrying about working ever again."

"Sounds like a plan to me David, have a great day. I'll send out the batch of Botox today."

"Thanks, Sal, stay well."

"You too. So sorry again about Shirley."

David reflected on the conversation. He didn't think Sal would ever be able to do much more than ogle the beautiful women he might admire. Though a more than capable biochemist with a brilliant mind, and a pleasant enough guy, the appearance of the scientist at pool-side would not be a pretty sight. Sal Manzari was a bachelor at forty-eight, had never married, and had a very inactive social life. David knew that at one time he had frequented the casinos of Vegas and the Seminole Indian tribe of Florida, but had recently stopped venturing out for gambling. David felt sorry for his business partner and wondered what it was that had led Sal to let his appearance and social life deteriorate so completely.

Before he knew it, it was time for David to see his afternoon patients. The distraction improved his mood, though he found it very tiresome to discuss Shirley with every patient; all of whom knew of her death. Those that were returning had only nice things to say of his cherished nurse. Each inquiry left him saddened and his sense of loss was reopened, like the pulling off of a fresh scab from a wound. Several times he found himself distracted and had to re-focus on the task at hand. The one bright note was provided by knowing that at least he had found a partial replacement for Shirley. He looked forward to spending time getting to know Lisa Martin and smiled as he reflected on their office conversation.

CHAPTER 8

It was almost eight o'clock when Nate stepped through the door. He had called at six and advised Lisa not to hold dinner for him. She absently wondered whether he was really at work all these long hours or could he be having an affair? She shook her head, trying to push the negative thoughts from her mind.

"Hi honey, sorry I'm late, but I wanted to get some of the new cases finished up before the weekend. If I don't tie them up some other firm might. It's just hard to get away these days." Nate had been saying the same thing for some time.

"I know Nate, but the boys miss sharing their day's events with you and I miss you too. Besides that, I have something we need to discuss."

Nate looked at Lisa and noticed that she seemed trimmer and seemed a little more radiant lately.

"Have you been working out?" he asked.

"Nice of you to finally notice!" she chided. "Yes, I have been." She was about to tell him about the Botox, but decided against it.

"Well you look great honey, not that you didn't look great before."

Lisa didn't know if he was being honest or not, but enjoyed the compliment none the less.

"So what did you want to tell me?" asked Nate.

"You know that I miss working. Well there was an ad for a part time nurse's position with a plastic surgeon and I went to his office and he offered me the job."

She was careful not to lie, wanting there to be truth in her words. An ad had certainly been placed and the job had been offered. She still didn't want to 'fess up' to the Botox injections.

"Honey, the boys count on you so much. With the house chores, their school work and all, do you really have the time?"

Lisa felt herself becoming uncharacteristically angry; she felt a fight coming.

"I know you're used to being the breadwinner in the family, but it's just not working for me anymore. I want to pull a paycheck and spend more time around adult people, not just the kids. I miss nursing and using my mind. You know, you could help out a little more too."

Almost as the words left her mouth Lisa regretted saying them. She really didn't want this to get ugly but the conversation was not progressing in the direction she had hoped.

Nate felt bile rising in his throat. It had been a long day and this wasn't what he wanted when he came home tired. He resented Lisa thinking that he needed to help more around the house.

"I'm tired of feeling that no matter what I do, it's not enough. If you want to take the job, go ahead. But right now I'm working as hard as I can for this family. You'll have to work out the arrangements with getting the kids in the afternoons. If I can, I may be able to help get them to the bus stop in the mornings, but sometimes I've got to be out of here before they're even awake."

Lisa sensed the futility at arguing further and wanted the conversation to end. With a sigh, she responded,

"I'm going to take the job Nate-and with or without your help I'm going to make it work."

Lisa felt empowered by her decision, despite what she felt was a lack of understanding on the part of her husband. She perished the thought of telling him about the Botox, and after placing his dinner out on the table, busied herself in tidying the kitchen.

CHAPTER 9

Saturday morning David Layton was awakened by a ringing that he thought was part of a dream. It was 8:30-he had slept later than usual. Grabbing for the phone, the source of the ringing, he knocked the cradle to the floor but managed to hold onto the portable device.

"Hi David, Jack Shea. I hope I'm not calling too early, but I wanted to catch you before you head out to the golf course."

He didn't know that David despised golfing. If David was going to spend four hours 'exercising' he wanted to break a sweat and burn some calories.

"No problem". David tried to sound sincere.

Actually, he hated being woken by phone calls, though it didn't happen often.

The reason I'm calling is that we've had some interesting findings on the post of your nurse. Everything checked out normal, including the blood tests, until we got to the brain. Even that was okay for the most part, but when we sectioned the brain stem we found several small vascular occlusions, clots, that most likely caused a cerebral-vascular accident. That stroke may have killed her. In addition, there appeared to be small plaques present, similar to those seen in Alzheimer's disease, scattered in her brainstem in the area of the fornix. Had she been complaining of feeling ill or acting unusual lately?"

David reached inside his memory to probe his long forgotten neurological anatomy.

"Jack, what is the fornix?"

"Sorry, David, I forgot it's been awhile for you. It's a portion of the brainstem that regulates simple emotions- rage and anger in some. I've also read where it may be the seat of our response to sexual stimuli."

"Shirley seemed fine. I would never have guessed anything was wrong at all."

"Any family history of Alzheimer's?" asked the pathologist.

"None that I know of, at least Shirley never spoke of it. I really don't know much about her medical history, except she was rarely sick and seemed in excellent health."

"Well, this is a very unusual case. I'm going to search the literature and see if there are any similar reports. Again, I'm sorry for calling so early on the weekend, but I knew you'd want to know what I'd found and was hoping you might be able to shed some light on her prior medical history before I do my medical search."

"Don't be silly, I appreciate your call. Have a great weekend. Maybe you should be golfing!" David teased the hard-working pathologist as he ended their call.

David pulled himself out of bed and reflected on the conversation with the pathologist. Poor Shirley. Well at least she didn't suffer the ravages that Alzheimer's might have brought. A brainstem stroke. How odd. In the seat of anger and sexual drives. She had certainly seemed normal. He ambled to the bathroom and looked out the window.

"I think I'll go for a run," he thought to himself, as he patted his firm stomach in self-admiration.

CHAPTER 10

David usually tried to get to the office early on Mondays. He arrived at 8:30. It was still jarring to not see Shirley's face in the office. Barbara and Becky were already there.

"Good morning ladies. Did you have a good weekend?"

"Nothing special for me, Dr. Layton."

"Me neither," responded Becky.

"So Lisa Martin is starting today, right Barb?"

"Yes, Dr. Layton, she should be here now."

"Well, go easy on her. I think you'll like her, she seems very nice."

"I think it's you who should go easy on her!" Barbara teased him back.

Ten minutes later Lisa arrived. She had her shoulder-length silky hair tied back with an elastic band and wore a new, fashionably-cut nurses white coat and pants that showed off her figure nicely. Her green eyes were offset by a tastefully applied small amount of makeup.

"Good morning, Lisa, you don't know how glad we are that you're here! You've met Becky and Barbara. Barb is going to help train you. And don't worry; you'll have lots of help from everyone."

"Thanks Dr. Layton." Lisa tried to hide her nervousness.

Between the new job and her quarrel with Nate, she had hardly slept the entire weekend. Change always stressed her out and she had been up since 5:30 in the morning- before her alarm. Lisa had just enough time to wash her hair and dry it before waking the boys for school. She wished Nate could have driven them, but he had to be at the office by eight, the same time their school began. What had she gotten herself into? Bringing her attention back to Dr. Layton, Lisa tried to force a smile.

"I don't think you've met Sam, who is really Samantha. She's our office manager and girl Friday. She'll need you to fill out the forms for Uncle Sam and new-employee paperwork. Also, you'll have to read over the new employee folder and sign it. We have some OSHA training that Barbara will take care of. Have you had your hepatitis vaccinations?"

"Yes, when the kids got theirs for school I did too." At least that was taken care of she thought.

"Okay, I'll leave you in Barbara's hands this morning. We're not scheduled too heavily this week and I won't add anybody until we're back up to speed. You can just shadow Barbara and we'll all help you." He smiled at his new employee.

Lisa had begun to feel that she might master her emotions around the doctor. Wrong. Her heart fluttered and she turned away from his eyes.

"Thanks Doctor," she forced herself to respond calmly.

Her heart retreated back into her chest as she began concentrating on the job. Lisa was amazed at how easily she dove into it. Most of the office care she had to provide was 'common sense' and not stressful at all. The staff was great, though clearly suffering through the sadness of Shirley's passing. There was much she had to learn regarding the various plastic surgical procedures offered by Dr. Layton, but Barbara did most of the talking and as Barbara answered questions posed by the patients Lisa listened intently, attempting to soak up all the new knowledge like a sponge.

There was a break in the schedule at 10:30 and Lisa finished her paperwork and reviewed some of Dr. Layton's patient information and consent forms.

"Barbara, does Dr. Layton do any surgery at the hospital?"

"No Lisa, he does it all in our surgical suite here in the office. We have everything he needs right here."

"Do you assist him?"

"Shirley did most of the assisting, though I've assisted too, and Paula is learning. Have you had much hands-on surgical experience?"

"Not really, most of my experience was in the post-op area. I only assisted in surgery back when I was in training." Lisa felt her stomach tightening into a ball. "How did you learn, Barb? Were you trained in school?"

"No, about the same as you. Dr. Layton and Shirley trained me. Don't worry; he's a great teacher and very patient. You'll be fine."

Lisa wasn't so sure, but forced a smile.

"I hope so," she managed to say.

CHAPTER 11

Work was physically more tiring than she imagined it would be. Perhaps even more difficult had been the mental strain of learning new things and feeling inadequate and stupid at times. Dr. Layton had been more than patient and the nurses were most pleasant, but by the end of the day, all Lisa wanted to do was go home and put her feet up and watch the news. Fat chance that might happen. She left work promptly at 3:00 to pick up the boys. Both were waiting for her at the school and excited to see her.

"What's for dinner, Mom. I'm starving," declared Shawn.

"I'm starvinger," chimed in Josh.

"Hungrier honey," Lisa corrected. She hadn't given dinner much thought.

"Can we have McDonald's?" It was Josh again.

"No, we're going to have real food and eat as a family. I've already called your father and he promised me he'll be home for dinner at six."

"I can't wait that long."

"Me neither, I'm starrrrrrrrrrrrvvvvvvvvving." Josh dragged out the word for emphasis.

"Okay, how about I get you each a burger at McDonald's to tide you over till dinnertime?"

"Can we have shakes too?"

"Don't push your luck, Shaw," Lisa warned.

"Okay, okay, Mom. Don't be so grumpy! We liked you better when you weren't working." Shawn pretended to sulk.

Maybe working wasn't such a great idea after all. It wasn't the first time that day that the thought had crossed her mind. Lisa took in a deep breath, sighed and thought to herself, "I am going to make this work."

At 5:30, Nate called to say he'd be late for dinner. He asked Lisa not to make the boys wait and promised to make it up to her. Holding her disappointment in check, she apologized to the boys for her husband. She was saddened by how little it mattered to them. They were becoming too used to his absences.

Her own mother had always tried to keep their family together and had used dinnertimes as an anchor for the family. Her father had been a loser who drank too much. Finally, when she was eight, he left the family, taking up with a much younger woman. He never kept in touch, and died in a driving accident after a long night out drinking three years after he had left the family. Lisa had promised herself that nothing like that would ever happen in her own household. She wanted them to eat together. Lisa felt tears forming at the corners of her eyes, swallowed hard and fought back the painful emotions.

For her first meal as a working mom, she had managed small steaks on the grill and French fries. She added some green beans to help make the meal healthier. After dinner, they had some Ben and Jerry's Chunky Monkey ice cream, the boy's favorite. She felt guilty as she dipped the spoon into the quart container and served herself a small portion.

"How am I going to find the time to stay in shape on my new

schedule?" she muttered aloud, mostly to herself.

"You look great Mom, and we're proud of you for working," declared Josh.

Lisa beamed.

"When did you get so smart, little man? That's the nicest thing anyone has said to me all day." She heard Nate's car pull up.

"I'm truly sorry. Time got away from me and I was interviewing a client."

As disappointed as she was at his tardiness, Lisa better understood the pressures of work on home life after having returned to the workforce. She kissed him softly on the cheek.

"How was your first day at work honey?" he asked.

"Not too bad, but I've got a lot to learn and I'm exhausted."

"You don't have to do this," Nate responded.

Lisa felt resentment rising in her. Nate was too quick at advising her she "didn't need to do it". She wanted his support, and didn't feel as if she really had it.

"Would you rather I just quit?" she retorted.

Now Nate felt taken aback.

"Whoa, honey, I didn't mean anything bad by that, just that I work hard enough for both of us and don't like to see you stressed out."

Lisa felt too tired to carry on this conversation, a repeat of the one they had had earlier, and looked her husband in the eyes full on.

"Nate, I am going to make this work. It will be easier with your help, but I need to do this for me and I am not going to give up."

"Okay, okay, I didn't mean to offend you. I'm sure it'll be alright. I was only thinking about you."

Nate walked over to Lisa and wrapped an arm around her. She allowed herself to be hugged, but wondered why she felt like crying. She forced her emotions back inside and allowed herself to be comforted by her husband. His touch soothed her but she felt herself pushing him away.

"Duty calls, I've got to get your dinner heated up."

Nate felt his arms drop to their sides, decided that he was best off keeping his mouth shut, and so just sighed heavily and took his place at the table.

CHAPTER 12

The Pelican Cove police had been summoned by the dead woman's neighbor, Mike Starns. The victim and Starns had been living in adjacent apartments for many years and had gotten to know each other's schedules. He golfed with his retired friends three times a week, she played bridge on Wednesdays. Both were widowed, she was the younger, at sixty years. When Starns didn't see her for several days, and when she didn't answer her doorbell, he notified the police. The stench that greeted them when they forced open the door to the apartment announced that they were too late. The victim's name was identified as Mrs. Roberta Cook.

"Does she have any family in town Mr. Starns?" asked the patrolman, a huge bear of a man who had identified himself as Sergeant Joe Walker.

"She has a brother in Tampa, Peter Camisa. I remember because she told me that when she was younger, people always teased her about her last name, and called her Roberta T-shirt, since camisa means shirt in Spanish."

Sergeant Walker phoned in the death to dispatch, which routed the call through as a non-emergency ambulance summons. There was no evidence of violence but the medical examiners office would need to be notified. Examination of the apartment medicine cabinet revealed only Tylenol and cold remedies. Most likely it was heart-related, though even in death, she appeared younger than her age and physically fit.

Her brother's name and number were in the Tampa directory. He picked up on the second ring.

"Mr. Camisa?" the officer asked.

"Yes, can I help you?"

"My name is Joe Walker. I'm a sergeant with the Pelican Cove police department. I'm sorry to have to inform you that your sister has passed away, at home, apparently from natural causes."

The sergeant heard Camisa gasp. "When did it happen?"

"We found her body when her neighbor said she hadn't been seen for several days. Do you know if she had been feeling ill?"

"No she was always in excellent health. She did her treadmill, yoga and all that. Not like me, I like to eat. Actually, I think she did tell me she was having a headache last week, but I didn't think it was any big deal. It wasn't like she was going to the doctor for it or anything. She hardly ever went to the doctor. The only time she ever went to one was to get her boobs done and I think she also had one of those face peel things. Except for plastic surgery, that's about it for her and medical care."

"Do you know if she had a family doctor?"

"I really don't, but I do know that she had the plastic surgery from a guy in Pelican Cove. Maybe he can help you. I know sometimes they require physicals before some of their work. I guess I'll come down and make the arrangements tomorrow. I'm just so shocked, she was so healthy. Is there anything else I can do?"

"Well, I know this is awkward, but the medical examiner may want to do an autopsy. Is that okay with you?" The officer always felt awkward asking that.

"Absolutely, I'd like to know what happened to her if possible." Anyway, I'll be down tomorrow. Where will the body be?"

"Either at the medical examiners office or the county morgue. You'll have to determine which funeral company you'd like to use."

"I remember the guy whose funeral parlor she used for her husband; it was run by some guy Pietro. He did a good job, even though she said it cost her more than two thousand bucks. I guess they've got you when someone dies. Now there was a guy who looked like he might not be long for this earth; the guy that ran the funeral place."

The officer knew of whom he spoke immediately. Bob Pietro was an obese chain-smoker. He was also rumored to handle some betting action on the side. But he was still alive and kicking. Only the good die young.

"I know the place Mr. Camisa. It's the Astin Funeral Home. Please contact them. If the medical examiner finishes before you arrive we'll have them send the body over there. Sorry again for your loss."

Camisa's voice sounded strained as he responded tiredly, "Thank you officer," and broke the connection.

CHAPTER 13

Jack Shea figured this must just be his lucky week. His job as medical examiner usually involved obese, elderly or abused specimens of humanity. But in the last two weeks he had had the more 'pleasant' experience of having to study two relatively healthy younger women. He was still intrigued with the findings of the brain tissue of the plastic surgeon's nurse. He had been unable to find similar cases described in his computer literature search. Though busy, he was considering writing the case up to publish in one of his medical journals. The new autopsy seemed less interesting. She was slightly older, and the heart had revealed some atherosclerosis, probably indicating an arrhythmia or heart blockage as the cause of her death. The vessels were slightly calcified though grossly, the heart appeared fairly normal. He continued his work in relative solitude. It was a quiet day and hers was the only case posted. Dr. Shea submitted all tissues for histology slide preparation, submitting specimens in formalin for the lab.

The next day he was surprised by the results. There was mild atherosclerosis, but not enough to close any coronary vessels, and not likely the cause of death. It was her brain sections that had been most peculiar. The specimens from the brainstem revealed findings of early Alzheimer's disease and there were plaques in the fornix. He wondered if these slides had been mixed with those of the prior week, but on checking the names, realized that this was indeed a new case, Roberta Cook. Extremely unusual. The pathologist placed a call to Dr. Layton for the second time in two weeks.

"There's a Dr. Shea for you on line two," Becky paged Dr. Layton through the office phone system.

David wondered if the pathologist had discovered anything new on Shirley's case.

"Hello, Dr. Shea?"

"Good morning, David. At least I'm not calling as early as last time! I've got some puzzling findings here. I'm finishing up another case and the brain findings are amazingly similar to those of your ex-nurse. The plaques in the fornix are there and I've found no other significant cause of death. There were also small emboli in the brain. She may have had a stroke or a seizure."

"Had she been ill?" asked Layton.

"She lived alone. Her brother had been in touch with her and described no illnesses. She has had some plastic surgery done locally. I know it's a shot in the dark, but I was wondering if you might recognize her name, Roberta Cook."

The surgeon shivered involuntarily-he did indeed remember Roberta Cook. She had already had breast implant surgery completed by another surgeon when they met several months ago. He remembered her as being most pleasant and she had come to the office twice, both times for Botox. In fact, her last office visit had been just two weeks earlier. Layton was not in the habit of concealing information from another doctor, but sensed a possible pattern which concerned him.

"Sorry, Jack, the name doesn't ring a bell, but you know, I see a lot of patients. I can check my records if you want."

"Please do. Any information might be helpful. If something is going on here of an epidemiologic nature it would behoove us to find out the cause and at least see if the CDC has other cases. Please give me a call if you find anything in your files."

"No problem. Will do. Anything else on Shirley?" David tried to steer the conversation away from the new case.

"No, I've sent the slides to the Armed Forces Institute of Pathology for review. They're the experts in pathology, and if anyone has had similar cases, they may know about it. It may be weeks before I hear back from them."

"Well thanks for keeping me in the loop, Jack. I'll be sure to call you later if I have anything. Have a great day."

"Thank you, David. Bye." Jack Shea sensed tenseness in the plastic surgeon's voice. He presumed it had something to do with the recent death of the doctor's long-time nurse. Probably Layton was just getting tired of receiving gruesome news from the medical examiner. If so, he wasn't the first. Many found his chosen profession on the macabre side.

David placed his head between his hands and rubbed his temples. It was an old habit, brought on when he was under stress. These deaths couldn't be linked to his treatment, could they? The Cook woman had received hardly any Botox at all and had noticed no problems with the treatments. And Shirley had been fine too. David walked to the area of his files and pulled two charts, the one for Roberta Cook, and the file for Shirley Herold. Placing them under other papers he was carrying, he quietly walked back to his office. He certainly didn't need these two cases to conflict with all the successful data in his study. Any problems now and he could kiss his venture capital money goodbye. Most importantly, he wouldn't realize his dreams of phenomenal wealth and the easy life it would bring.

Dr. Layton sat down at his desk, opened a side drawer, and removed a small key. Attached to the underside of his modern teak desk was a locked file containing personal documents. Dr. Layton utilized one section for the data pertaining to the in-office Botox testing. Copies of the records of all eighty-nine patients he had treated with the experimental Botox were inside. He actually had two sets of records on each of these patients–the official one, in which he identified the treatment and results, including the type and quantity of commercially available Botox and the private record, containing data of the enhanced drug dosage used and the response. These records were kept private, and he made the entries into the study charts at the end of each day. No one in the office knew of these records and no one had access to these charts. He placed Shirley and Roberta's office records next to the 'unofficial' documents. Next, David logged onto his computer and accessed the record for Roberta Cook. He went into the scheduling prompt and found her two appointments, from August and May. She had paid for both visits with cash and no other evidence of the woman existed in his office.

David took a deep breath and sighed. He could almost feel his father's presence as a weight on his shoulder, judging his next planned action. Then his connection to his father was broken and an image of his successful brother flashed through his thoughts. He found a wry smile press his lips,

"Here's to you Daddy." He pressed the 'delete' key for the payments page. Next, under patient record, he clicked on another delete prompt. Roberta Cook ceased to exist as a patient in the practice.

CHAPTER 14

The computer dealt him a pair of Kings—a great hand and a chance to win some money. Sal Manzari typed in a $100 bet on his screen. Two players stayed in and their money joined his in the center of the pot. He could feel his heartbeat speed up and the metallic taste of adrenaline in his mouth. All his senses were sharpened as he focused on the game. The 'flop' of three cards were a two of diamonds, three of clubs and nine of hearts. Crappy cards. Sal was glad there were no real live players in the offices of Youth Labs to see how excited he was getting. He wanted to bet enough to keep the other computer players in the game and not enough to scare them away. Sal bet $50 and both players stayed in. The next card, the 'turn', lit up as a Jack of spades. His hand was looking strong, time to cash in. He bet another $100 and one player dropped out. With $650 in the pot, the final card, the 'river' popped onto the computer screen, a two of clubs. Now there was a pair of twos on the table for both players. Sal became more excited. No one would have stayed in this far with a two in their hand and only three twos looked strong enough to beat him. He bet $200. The response from the other player was slow, then he saw that he was raised $300. Shit. What could this sucker have? Two pair? His Kings looked strong. There would be no going out now. He clicked in his own $300 to 'call' the bet. There was now $1650 on the computer table.

Both players' cards were simultaneously turned up by the computer. Sal felt his stomach drop into his groin and he felt like vomiting. His opponent had another two in his hand, giving him three twos and giving Sal the losing hand. Shit, Shit, Shit, Shit, Shit. In less than a minute he had lost $750 even though he had played everything right and had good cards. Manzari exited the game, knowing that his credit card balance had just ballooned further. The eggs and sausage he had had for breakfast rose in his throat giving him a bitter acid taste. As he searched in the desk draw for his Tums, he heard the automatic buzzer indicating someone had entered the lab. It was five-thirty and all his techs had gone home for the day. Visitors to the lab were rare.

Two men entered. Sal knew who they were immediately. Sam Prano, who was better known by his nickname, "Knuckles" and Vic Chifolo. Vic had no nickname and never spoke much, though at about six foot-four and two hundred and forty or so of muscle and bone, no one challenged him. He came along with Knuckles to reinforce the message Sal knew was coming.

"So what's the good word Sallie? We aint been seein' ya much. Hard at work or have ya found some other suckers to take yer action?"

Manzari cringed. He owed Prano's boss, Bobby Volpe, over $60,000 from two year's worth of gambling debts on horses, baseball and football games. He actually had a good run for a while on the computer last year and had paid some off. The last six months had been an entirely different story and he was having trouble finding the money to pay the exorbitant interest and balance on his debt to the organized crime family. But today they weren't there for money.

"Hi Knuckles. Vic. What can I do for you? I thought I had an understanding with Bobby about my debt."

"And so ya do, so ya do my friend. We're here to make sure you's hard at work on 'is investment. How are those little animals doin'? Ya curin' all their diseases? Bobby wants to know if ya could give 'im some of your results to look over. It seems that you's doing some hot-shit work and he wants ta make sure it's all as good as ya say."

Sal thought he felt crappy after losing the poker hand but now he felt ten times more lousy. The last thing he wanted was outsiders reviewing his data. He recalled his conversations with Dr. Layton and past agreements of secrecy regarding their research. He wondered how good these goons were at keeping things quiet.

"I'll have something for him over the next few days. I'll get it together and organize it so it makes sense without him having to be a scientist."

"Ya do that Sallie, ya do that. Jus' remember, he's bein' very generous with ya. Don't push it."

Sam laced his fat hands together and cracked his knuckles with a loud orchestral popping – reminding Sal how he had gotten his nickname. Or maybe it was the brass knuckles he was rumored to use. Walking over to Sal, Sam gently pulled on his ear.

"Ya know better than to let the boss down. Ya got two days to have somethin' for us to show 'im. He aint the most patient of men, and when he aint happy, we aint happy and ya' know what that means?"

"I guess it means I better make you all happy." Sal answered sheepishly.

"See Vic, I told ya he's smarter than he looks. We'll let ya get back to work Sal. And have a nice day!" The men left Sal alone in the laboratory.

֍

Whenever Sal found himself feeling stressed, losing himself in his work served to calm his nerves. He walked over to the cages in which the mice were contained. The lab housed nine dozen mice. They had received

Botox injections over the past eight months. They were of several species, specially bred for laboratory work. The mice he liked best were the hairless wrinkled variety; they reminded him of those Char Pei dogs with all the wrinkles. He always carefully documented the dosage of Botox and the responses, both with photographs and microscopic histology date. Rarely, one of the mice would be sacrificed to be certain that no effects of the drug had caused organ damage. They had outsourced their slide preparation to a lab in Minnesota and outsourced their slide interpretation further; to a pathologist in Delhi, India who did their pathology work for less than twenty percent of what it would have cost them in the States. Most of their funding came directly from Dr. Layton. Manzari knew that the plastic surgeon was stretching his resources to run the lab privately and badly needed the funding from the BioVenture group.

Sal walked over to the second of the multiple rows of cages and peered inside. The water bottles were full and the mice were sleeping. Advancing to the next row, he found the four mice in the cage also sleeping; however one of the mice was uncharacteristically lying in the middle of the cage. They usually preferred to sleep in the corners. The biochemist slid the cage out and opened the latched door finding the mouse cold and clammy. It was the first unexpected death the lab had experienced since the trials had begun. Sal quickly examined the remainder of the cages and found no other surprises. The dead mouse had received its last injection of Botox two weeks earlier, from the newest batch he had prepared. Manzari placed the rodent on a small board and began the task of dissection, separating the various organs and tissues for placement in formalin. The specimens would be mailed to Minnesota and then on to India for analysis. The entire process would take no longer than a week. Manzari finished his work efficiently and without interruption. He imagined that maybe his luck was finally changing – for the better.

CHAPTER 15

Peter Camisa arrived in Pelican Cove to arrange the affairs of his deceased sister Roberta. Rummaging through her apartment was very depressing—he felt like an intruder. He planned to donate most of the clothing and possessions to the Women's Shelter. It was only the personal mementoes and a few pieces of furniture he considered taking back to Tampa with him. He had a large garbage can he had brought into the apartment and was disposing of many things while organizing the objects for either donation or destruction. His cell phone rang. He checked the ID on the screen and didn't recognize the number.

"Hello," he answered curiously.

"Hello, Mr. Camisa?"

"Yes, who is this?"

"Hi, my name is Dr. Jack Shea, and I'm the medical examiner who completed the autopsy on your sister. Sergeant Joe Walker gave me your number. I'm sorry for your loss. I'm calling because I've discovered something curious in your sister's autopsy. Mostly, everything was normal and for a woman of her age she was in unusually good health. But her brain had some abnormalities that were surprising. I found swelling and enlargement in one area of the brainstem and evidence suggestive of Alzheimer's disease. Has anyone in your family ever had a neurological disorder?"

"Thanks for calling sir. Actually, both our father and our uncle died with Alzheimer's disease. So far, I've been fortunate and seem to have been spared-I had thought Roberta was too. I guess she wasn't so lucky, but she never seemed ill. Do you think that's what killed her?" Peter questioned.

"I'm not sure. There was some swelling, but she may have suffered from a cerebral-vascular accident. Swelling, or what we call edema, in the brainstem can be quite serious in that it can alter important functions such as breathing. We may never know for sure. I've sent her slides to specialists in brain pathology for review. Do you know if autopsies were done on your father or uncle?'

"I doubt it though I'm really not sure, since it was over twenty years ago. I think both of them died in Providence, Rhode Island-where we're from. My dad was in a nursing home, I'm not sure if my uncle died at home or somewhere else, I was away at college when he passed away."

"I may try to find out, but it sounds like it may be difficult to unearth those records even if an autopsy was performed. Thanks for your time Mr. Camisa, I'll let you know if I find anything else out."

"Thanks for calling Dr. Shea, I appreciate your inquiries.

As Peter resumed cleaning the apartment his morbid feelings returned. He felt the presence of his departed sister around him and the apartment had the faint odor of his her perfume. He half expected her to walk in the door and ask him what he was doing. Peter felt tired and wondered if he would be the next family victim of Alzheimer's disease. Instead of giving into his despair he opened a small kitchen drawer which looked like a catch-all space for miscellaneous small objects. It contained paper clips, pencils, receipts and an assortment of reminder pads and papers. A business card from a handy-man, a paper menu from a Chinese restaurant and an insurance company calendar all went into the trash. Beneath these, he found a parchment-like business card with an appointment date written on it in hand. On the card in bold script was the name Dr. David Layton II, Plastic Surgeon. He wondered whether Dr. Shea would be interested in obtaining his sister's medical records from the local physician. Couldn't hurt. He decided to do another hour or so of cleaning, then call the medical examiner when he felt ready to take another break from his task.

CHAPTER 16

Lisa enjoyed work even more than she had anticipated. She thrived on caring for the patients and the camaraderie of her co-workers. Being around the younger staff made her feel more full of life. Her home schedule was working well too at least for now. The boys were both playing soccer after school and she had no trouble getting off work in time to pick them both up. Although Nate wasn't really helping her any more than he had before her employment, she was surprised at how she managed to 'do it all'. She patted herself on the back. Even if no one else noticed how hard she worked, she was proud of herself. Dr. Layton treated her with respect and rewarded her labors well; she earned $25 per hour and would have worked for less happy just to be back in the work environment. Though she loved being a mother and wife, Lisa was more content than she had been for years.

These were her thoughts as Lisa turned the key to her Volvo and was greeted with the dull, slow grinding of a battery gasping its' last breaths. She turned the key again to one final groan and then nothing. Thinking about how to get the boys from school Lisa saw Dr. Layton in her rear view mirror. She got out of her car to seek his assistance.

"Dr. Layton, I can't get my car started, I think it's the battery. Do you have jumper cables?"

"Yes, I do. Let me bring my car over." He responded quickly.

In no time at all, Dr. Layton had both hoods opened and the cables attached. Lisa got back into her vehicle and turned the key.

Nothing happened.

"It looks like either your battery is really dead or it's the starter or something else. Do you want to call a towing service?" he offered.

"I'm not sure, I have to get the boys picked up or have my husband leave work early to get them," Lisa responded distractedly.

"I'd be happy to help you pick them up, or you can drop me off and use my car," he countered.

For days, she had been able to respond coolly and professionally with her boss. Now, anticipating being in the car with him had her nervous. She really couldn't deny her attraction to this man she found physically appealing, intelligent and generous. In any case, she needed his help.

"I don't want to put you out—I'm sure you have other things to do. But if you could take me home I'd be most grateful. One of my neighbors can help me get the boys."

"Well, the offer stands, Lisa. If you can't get a neighbor to help and your husband isn't available please call me and I'll pick them up for you. I really don't mind." His offer was very sincere.

"I'm sure my neighbor or best friend will be able to help me from there, thank you." Lisa was just as sincere.

"Okay, hop in."

David walked over to the passenger side and opened the door for his employee as all gentlemen do. As Lisa came next to him and approached his Mercedes convertible she came close to his arm and brushed past the doctor's body. Their eyes met for a moment that felt like minutes. Her heart froze and she felt paralyzed with the attraction his gaze aroused in her.   Part of her wanted him to take her in his arms just like a young thing in one of those romance novels she occasionally read. Thankfully, she loved her husband and was able to push these thoughts from her mind.

David smiled. He was drawn to her and found her strength, sincerity, intelligence and beauty most attractive. The fact that she was married as well as his employee presented obstacles to his following-through on his interest. For now he was happy just to have her working for him. David closed the door for Lisa and got in the other side. He revved the engine loudly as he pulled away from the parking lot.

CHAPTER 17

S al was greeted by Ed Neouri, his tech in charge of recording vital signs on the laboratory animals, as well as Sal's main treatment assistant. Being the opposite of his boss, Ed was thin and groomed to a "T". He also sported a thin mustache - having the sparse facial hair common to those of Japanese heritage. Ed called himself a 'mutt', as his mother was of Irish descent while his father was Japanese-American. Sal knew that his assistant was gay, and also knew that Neouri's parents were unaware of his tech's proclivities. It was Ed that administered the Botox injections to the lab animals.

"Dr. Manzari, I'm afraid we've got a problem. I found another mouse dead this morning. Until today she had been healthy."

"When had the mouse received its last treatment?" Manzari asked.

"Two weeks ago, and before that, six weeks ago," Ed responded.

"Which a Botox lot was she treated from?"

Neouri checked his clipboard. "She was treated from the most recent batches you and Dave synthesized; lot numbers B11 and B13. Was the mouse that died yesterday treated with the same batches?"

Manzari seemed less tense as he responded to his researcher.

"Yes, both mice received treatment from the newer lots."

"Maybe the deaths are due to the esterifcation of the Botox molecule. It might have allowed entry of the drug across the blood-barrier. I'll do the autopsy if you'd like."

"That's okay Ed. You finish up what you're doing and I'll take care of getting the tissues sent out for processing."

"Do you want me to stop administering the esterified Botox? I've still got some of the previous hydroxyl/carbon formula on hand. It had been working without any problems."

Ed knew that Manzari was a brilliant chemist, and rarely questioned him, but failed to see any benefit to testing the newest Botox molecule when the original formula had seemed to be working just fine..

Manzari considered his next words carefully.

"Administer both Botox formulations for now. It would be a shame if the esterified formulation was found to have unanticipated side effects. Just keep super- accurate records on the lots used."

Ed thought his boss was making a mistake, but was also aware of the importance of having as much data available as possible for the planned presentation to the Bio Venture group next month. Why the two versions though? He hoped Manzari knew what he was doing. Ed was counting on a big raise and stock options once the money started coming in to the company.

"I hope so, boss. I'm counting on it!" Ed got back to his work.

Sal absorbed the morning's news. He knew he would soon have to call Dr. Layton and advise him of the demise of the animals. However, right now he had more urgent business-Volpe. Sal went through the office and collected data sheets containing informcation on many of the animals, specifically the oldest data from the first few months of trials. He tried to do this as inconspicuously as possible and when the sheets had been collected went into his office to photocopy the information. Manzari attached photos of his subjects with pretreatment and post-treatment pictures clipped together for several of the files. Tomorrow was the day he knew Knuckles and Vic would be returning to pay a visit. They would need some good data and he would be ready.

CHAPTER 18

Janetta was excited. She had just received a signed contract from a cash buyer for a two million dollar condo on the beach. Her share of the commission was going to come to over $30,000. She thought of calling Lisa to share the good news, then reconsidered, thinking that her friend might still be at work. She logged in online and instead of checking her mail decided to see if anything good was happening in the chat room of SingleFun.com. She had only been a subscriber to the service for two weeks and had posted her picture five days earlier. These last weeks, she had found her desire to meet someone had resumed. Truth be told, she was rather horny and considered going out to look for a guy in one of the few clubs in town. Unfortunately, Pelican Cove was rather small and she really didn't want to run into people she knew cruising the bar scene-and she was rather picky. Perhaps it would be more efficient to find someone who fit her 'profile' through some internet dating service. The chat rooms were just more of a distraction and she really didn't take them seriously. Janetta had heard all the stories of bald fat married and unemployed guys pretending to be suave single good-looking businessmen. She clicked in her user id and password and entered the website.

"Anyone looking for some action tonight?" It was a posted message from SlimJim77. Janetta ignored it.

"What kind of action you offering Slim?" The response from Dahlia8 flashed on the screen.

"Wherever you want it and whenever you want it," popped up quickly. These guys were good typists, Janetta thought to herself.

"Want to go to a private room?" offered Dahlia.

"K" was all Jim needed to type, and the meeting had been arranged.

"Boy that was fast!" Janetta muttered to herself. She saw both names leave the list of those in the chat room. Janetta imagined they were already furiously hitting their keyboards like some "Sleepless in Seattle" characters run amuck.

"Any Southern gurrls out there?" A message from WinerTom joined the chat list.

Janetta thought to herself, "Lisa would be so ashamed of me for wasting my time here chatting with morons." At the same time, Janetta had to admit that for some reason, on some level, it was fun.

"Florida sunshine here," Jan responded. Janetta wondered who Janetta one through eight were; all eight were taken when she had joined as a member and applied for a screen name.

"Tom from Atlanta here Jan. Nice to meet you." As she read the message, Janetta clicked on his name and was able to call up his profile and picture. "Not bad looking." She said softly. Light brown hair, athletic build, profile listed him as six foot and 180 pounds and thirty-three. Although Janetta was thirty-five in the real world, online she had placed her own age at thirty-one. After all, who would ever know? Under interests he had written, hiking, travel, all kinds of music (except rap). He loved sunsets and drinks on the beach. His profile was very similar to hers.

"Janetta in Florida. Nice profile Tom."

He must have been reading hers at the same time. He responded, "Yours too, we have a lot in common. What do you do when you're not chatting to strange men online?"

Janetta chuckled. "I'm a realtor, and I like to travel. And I love sports. Actually, I'm a big Atlanta Braves fan. We get all the games here on cable."

"I think everyone here in Atlanta loves the Braves, though this year hasn't been a good one for them. Ever been to Atlanta?"

"Yes, a couple of times, but not recently. You ever been to Southern Florida? That's where I am, on the west coast."

"I've been to Miami lots of times, I'm a wine wholesaler and a lot of the buyer's meetings are held there. I've only been to the west coast once, to Naples."

"I'm very close to there. The town is called Pelican Cove."

"I've heard of it. So how's real estate there?"

"Well, not as good as it used to be, but I'm managing to pay the bills. So, no Mrs. Tom in your life?"

"No, I've actually never married. It just hasn't happened for me. I was engaged once though. I came home from a wine-buying trip to New York early one day and caught my fiancé in bed with some guy who had come to the house to do trim carpentry work. Wood wasn't the only thing he was 'trimming.'"

Janetta thought of typing in 'lol,' the computer abbreviation for laughing out loud. She imagined that anyone typing what Tom had just submitted to a stranger must be over his loss. She gave in to the urge and 'lol' appeared next to her name on the chat list.

"Go ahead, laugh," Tom responded. "It is the fastest way to get a woman excited they tell me. Do you cyber?"

Janetta was new at this, but had learned that most of the time, when someone online asked that question, they wanted to have a sexually oriented conversation on the internet. Usually, she found the thought unappealing, but didn't want to scare Tom away; he seemed interesting. What the heck. Janetta typed, "Not really, but if you promise to keep me laughing we can chat in private if you like."

"I'll go save us a spot. Follow me to the private room section. Janetta and Tom left the general chat site and entered a room called "Closer Encounters."

"Thanks for joining me, Janetta. How about a glass of wine?"

Janetta didn't know what he meant.

Tom typed, "I'm going to get a glass of white from the fridge. Can I get you something?"

Janetta chuckled. "Actually, I'm more of a red drinker myself—I have an open bottle from last night. I'll go get a glass. brb." Janetta felt smart knowing the abbreviation for 'be right back'.

"Ok" responded Tom.

Janetta felt nervous. She filled a glass of wine, looked at it and thought, "I could use some courage right now." She slugged down the glass of wine and filled another. Almost immediately she could feel the alcohol create a slightly light-headed sensation in her head. Janetta returned to the computer screen.

"Tom?" she typed.

"b" the abbreviation for 'back' appeared.

"What are you wearing Janetta?"

Janetta looked down at her silk blouse and black pants. She fingered the buttons on her blouse as she responded,

"I'm wearing a white blouse and tight, black pants. But I'm feeling a bit warm. Would you like me to take something off?"

Somewhere in her mind she also was thinking, "What the hell am I doing?" but she was becoming aroused by her conversation and thoughts.

And the wine didn't hurt.

"That would be very nice." Tom replied. "I should probably take something off myself; my pants are getting a bit tight in front here. I may have to move away from the computer screen."

Janetta opened the buttons on her blouse and let it slide off her shoulders. She then removed her bra. After finishing the second big glass of wine she touched her fingers lightly to her breasts. She began to feel flushed.

"I've taken off my blouse," Janetta typed online. "And bra. I'm getting excited Tom."

"I had to take my pants off Janetta. I'm sitting here in my boxers. It's warm, so I'm taking my shirt off too. Can I touch you, Janetta?"

Janetta was surprised at how excited she was becoming. She lowered her hands to her groin and began to touch herself. She was more excited than she could remember being for months.

"Oh Tom, go for it."

"I'm touching your breasts now, Janetta. Is that okay?"

"Yes, don't stop."

"Now I'm taking my hand and bringing it."

His typing had stopped in mid-sentence. Janetta stared at the screen—hanging on to his words and waiting impatiently for him to continue. She watched as his name dropped from the list of those in the room.

"Shit," she muttered. Either he had lost his internet connection or maybe his wife or girlfriend had caught him misbehaving online. Janetta stared stupidly at the screen and after a couple of minutes of computer silence rose from her chair and made her way to the bathroom to replace her torrid online romance with a cold shower.

Despite its premature termination, the online tryst had been very exciting-even if it wasn't real. Janetta couldn't remember the last time she had felt so horny. What had come over her? She stepped into the shower and allowed the cool water to bring an end to her torrid thoughts.

CHAPTER 19

Usually at mid-morning, about 10:30 or so, David would take a short break. It gave his nurses a 'breather' and allowed him to catch up on his morning phone messages. He scanned the small pile of little stick-on notes. One was from Jack Shea.

"Becky, get me Dr. Jack Shea please. When he's on the line, just beep me. I'll be in my office."

"Okay, doctor."

The ME answered his own phone, "Medical examiner's office."

"Good morning, Dr. Shea? This is David Layton, I'm returning your call."

"Yes, hi David. The reason I'm calling is related to the case I spoke to you about the other day, Roberta Cook. Her brother was cleaning out her house and getting her possessions in order and came across a card with your name on it. It had an appointment listed for August 16th. Did you have a chance to check your office for her records after we spoke?"

"Shit." David thought, this was getting more and more complicated. The line, "Oh what a tangled web we weave when we first endeavor to deceive" popped into David's head. He tried to sound smooth as he responded,

"I believe she came to one of my Botox introductory seminars and went ahead and made an appointment. She failed to come in for her scheduled return visit in August, and probably she forgot all about it when her card got misplaced. We don't open formal records on anyone at the seminars and that would explain why no record of her was found in my office." David took a deep breath.

The explanation sounded good enough to him. He listened intently for the response from Dr. Shea.

"I was afraid it would be something like that. I had hoped to have some records to review that might provide some added insight into her case. I'm coming up empty. We may have to wait to see what the pathology experts have to say regarding my two cases. Anyway, I'll let you know when we get the report on your nurse, Shirley Herold."

"Thanks Jack. Sorry I couldn't be more help." David swallowed hard and felt like he had just dodged a huge bullet.

"Don't work too hard. You know they say nobody ever died wishing they had another day to work." David joked.

"Actually, David, nobody ever says anything after they die. That's what makes my job so hard! Have a good one. Bye."

CHAPTER 20

Youth Labs wasn't in the best part of town, but even the 'low rent district' in Pelican Cove wasn't too shabby. The offices were in an industrial park and they filled the 2500 square foot unit completely. Sal Manzari heard the front door open as he was finishing up the autopsies on two additional mice that had died. The soft echo of raindrops on the walkway and street beyond entered the lab and the faint odor of the rain as it hit the warm tarmac outside the door mingled with the chemical odors of Youth Labs. A bell chimed as the door opened, letting those inside know someone had entered.

It was someones, not someone.

Knuckles and Vic had returned. Knuckles had only one color suit – black. Vic was a fashion statement, wearing a too small shiny blue suit and a yellow shirt and red tie. Rainbow colors were supposed to be a gay thing, right? Sal knew better than to ask Vic if he was gay. The gray weather outside matched Manzari's mood. He wished he could somehow make these guys just go away. Having them show up in the lab was going to raise questions with other employees and what if Dr. Layton happened to be here?

"Top o' the morning' to ya, Sal. I think ya got somthin' for us."

"In my office please Knuckles, let's get some privacy." Ed Neouri recognized the men from a prior visit to the office and had suspected that the swarthy hulks had something to do with his bosses gambling habit. Neouri kept his head down and pretended not to notice their entrance. The other two lab techs working that morning took their cues from Ed and lost themselves in their work.

"It don't look like nobody even knows we're here. Look how they're all workin'. Ya oughta teach your help some better manners Sal." Knuckles followed Sal into his office and Manzari closed the door behind them.

Sal slid open a file cabinet attached to his desk and extracted two manila envelopes.

"I'm sure Mr. Volpe will be happy with the information Sam." Manzari handed off the files.

"You know betta than to call me Sam."

The thug reached around behind the desk and softly punched Sal in the side of the arm. A 'love tap' that Manzari knew would leave a bruise. Such assholes.

"From what the boss tells me, Sallie, he's got big plans for ya and your little mice. Maybe if ya play your cards right, he can help ya find some digs in the good part of town. The place is a shithole. Let's go Vic, if we stay too long we're gonna to start smellin' like somethin' the cats should be chasin.'"

Vic turned and followed Knuckles out of the office, through the lab and out into the street. It had stopped raining outside and the sun was once again cooking the tar of the parking lot hot enough for steam to rise from the baking asphalt.

Large rings of sweat had gathered beneath Manzari's armpits, though the lab was kept at a relatively chilly seventy degrees. "I guess that could have been worse," he thought. However, there was still more nastiness to take care of. He still had to call Dr. Layton. Sal closed the door to his office and dialed David's cell phone. Manzari knew that he was honored to be one of only a few that could get through to the doctor during working hours.

From the caller ID, David knew it was his biochemist partner.

"Hi Sal, what's up?"

"I'm afraid I've got some bad news. Everything had been going fine, but we've had four mice die in the last two days. We haven't been able to determine any immediate cause of death. They hadn't been febrile and none of the usual signs of illness appeared. All the other mice seem okay. I'm really at a loss to tell you what happened."

"The obvious question is, do you think the deaths were treatment related?"

Sal paused. He had to answer this carefully.

"Well, I think we have to consider the treatment as a possible cause. I think we're going to have to wait several days until the pathology slides can be reviewed. I've already sent some specimens out and will have the rest done by the end of the day. In view of their deaths, you may want to hold off on treating with the new Botox."

"Sure, Sal. Please be sure to keep the files from the deceased mice separate for me to review. I'd like you to lock them up in your office. I don't want anyone in the lab to get too nosey until we know exactly what's going on. I also don't want there to be any way any of the venture capital boys could find anything negative out unless we tell them." David was rubbing his head again.

"We can't really keep this information from them can we Dr. Layton?"

Now it was Layton's turn to choose his words carefully.

"If our alternative data continues as good as it is, I think we may need to 'adjust' our laboratory data to better fit our clinical trials. After all, it really matters how it works in humans and not in mice, right?" David held his breath for the response.

Sal was surprised and more than a little shocked. He had expected that any problems with the laboratory results might discourage his partner. He had not considered that Dr. Layton would so easily disregard the deaths of the laboratory animals.

"David, surely we couldn't reasonably try to get the drug released for use in people if it's unsafe in mice. The FDA would never approve it."

"You let me worry about that, Sal. You just keep those mice alive. For now I will take a break from using our Botox in my patients, until we get the path results back. You're okay with that, aren't you?"

"Sure Dr. Layton." He tried to sound sincere but Sal had rarely been less okay.

CHAPTER 21

The boys had gotten off to school on time. The day was a bit unusual in that Lisa and the boys had been joined by Nate for breakfast. She had returned home after dropping the boys off at the bus stop and was disappointed to find her husband no longer at the breakfast table. She went into his study imagining he'd be there working on some Jointrex cases but the room was empty. Lisa called his name, the words echoing through the house.

Finally Nate replied, "I'm up here honey. Come up, I have something to show you."

"Can't you come down here? I've got to take you to work so I can use your car. I really don't want to drive a loaner from the dealer."

"Please, Lisa. You won't be sorry........."

"Okay, okay." Lisa slowly padded up the stairs.

Nate was lying in bed with the covers pulled up to his chin. He had a goofy grin on his face and winked at Lisa.

"Come back to bed honey."

Now that she was a working woman, Lisa found she had very little time to call her own. She had planned on working out at the YMCA gym that morning; hoping that she wouldn't be called in the middle of her workout to pick up her vehicle which had been towed to the dealership. Grinning at her husband, she thought, "One workout is as good as another I guess."

"Only if you promise to make it worth my while." she played.

"I promise to make it worth both our whiles and then some."

Nate pulled the covers down to his waist and reached out to Lisa as she brought herself over to the bed. He loved the way she smelled in the morning and the feel of her hair in his face. As he wrapped his arms around her, he nuzzled his face in the crook of her neck and nibbled on her ear lobe. Lisa reciprocated by wrapping her arms around his neck and kissing him on the shoulder. After a half hour of being lost in giving and receiving pleasure, their climax came powerfully as they came together in a great union of passion.

Lisa sighed dreamily trying to remember the last time she had been this aroused. Before she had started working, she had been rather depressed and her love life with Nate had suffered. She hadn't discussed it with her husband, or even Janetta, but in the last two weeks she had found herself distracted with thoughts of sex at all times of the day. Maybe it was the satisfaction she found in her new job, or working side by side with the handsome plastic surgeon- whichever, she was happy to have her sex drive return.

"I love you Nate Martin."

"I love you too honey." He emerged from the sheets and ambled over to the bathroom as he made his way to the shower. Lisa followed close behind him.

"I may never get to work if you join me in here Lisa." Nate grinned.

Lisa grabbed a pink shower cap, knowing that if she got her hair wet she would lose another half hour or so drying and combing it. She needed that time to get her errands done.

"You look like a pink mushroom." Nate chuckled.

Lisa let the comment pass because she did look silly in the pink shower cap. And because she was still at peace with the world after her morning session with Nate. Lisa kissed him on the shoulder, climbed into the shower and let the warm water run over her body. Nate turned toward her and she was surprised to see that his excitement had only apparently only partially subsided.

"It looks like you've been working out too honey." Lisa quipped.

"I took a Viagra at breakfast."

Lisa didn't know if Nate was kidding or telling the truth, but she felt herself getting aroused. Her heart fluttered and she wanted him inside her again. It had been so long since they had given each other an encore performance-especially in the morning.

Lisa wanted him again. Nate joined Lisa in the shower and began rubbing her shoulders. Pouring conditioner onto his hands, he then began caressing her breasts. His palms slipped and slid over her nipples while she struggled to remain standing despite the passion shaking her legs and the slippery floor. Nate lifted her legs and supported her in his arms as he filled her completely. One wave of orgasmic pleasure filled her, then another. Shaking spasmodically against Nate, she wasn't sure she was done with him when she felt his excitement fade. Her legs fell back to the shower floor as Nate released her.

"Wow honey that was awesome -what's gotten into you?"

"You know what's gotten into me. You. Twice."

Lisa couldn't remember when she had last been so happy.

CHAPTER 22

Another two weeks passed. No additional mice had died in the lab and the practice was running as smoothly as ever and David was impressed with his new nurse, Lisa Martin.

She's got it all, he thought to himself. Brains, looks and confidence, a loving family and now a job too. Lisa had easily assumed many of Shirley's duties and was great with the patients. David felt lucky to have her on his staff. He imagined she was probably great in bed too. Sadly, he expected he would never have the opportunity to find out.

David had begun to look forward to Monday's, one of the two days Mrs. Martin worked with him. He spent a few more minutes getting dressed and chose the dark pants, shirt and tie which he felt complemented his features best. He looked into the mirror a few moments longer, and plucked some wayward hairs from his eyebrows and ears. Why the hell these hairs started growing where they didn't belong he'd never know.

He often came to work a little earlier on Mondays to catch up on weekend messages that might be waiting for him and to check the weekend mail. Since no one else was in the office yet David would usually answer the phone. This morning was no exception.

"Hello, Dr. Layton's office." David tried to sound like the answering service so that if it was a patient calling he might be able to 'relay the message' and not have to seem unprofessional answering his own phones.

"Hi, David, glad I caught you." Layton recognized the voice as that of his brother, Philip.

"How are ya, Phil, I didn't know you retired people got up this early. Are you in San Diego or Connecticut?"

"Neither, I'm actually in Boston, visiting some friends and taking in some Red Sox games. I was hanging around the airport on my way out yesterday and decided to call Dad. I hadn't spoken to him for a few weeks and was just checking in to see how he was doing. Anyway, he seemed alright but he told me that he had been having some problems with his memory. He went to his friend, Dr. Chuttani at Yale and had some tests done. It's not for sure, but the neurologist thinks he has mild Parkinson's disease and also early Alzheimer's. He's also having a little trouble walking – I'm no doctor, but he said his 'gait' had changed."

David was aware of the shuffling steps, the gait change that Phil was referring to. "That's sucks Phil. Did he start him on any medication?"

"I think he did, but Dad really didn't want to talk to me about it much. I just thought you should know. To tell you the truth, he asked me not to tell you. I think he wants to tell you himself and is somehow embarrassed about it. Probably worried that we'll want to put him in a nursing home or something. He's even turning his practice over to his associates, and you know how important his work has always been to him."

David was at a loss for words. He thought his dad was immortal. Their mother had developed multiple sclerosis when he and Philip were teenagers. When her care at home became too difficult she was moved to a skilled nursing facility. The senior Dr. Layton had suffered through three years of her deteriorating health and watched as his wife's dignity diminished with her ability to care for herself gone. The disease left Mrs. Layton blind, and unable to bathe or clean herself. Eventually, she had to be fed and remained in diapers and in bed much of the day. David's father had made the boys promise that he would never have to spend his last months in a similar facility. He even formulated a living will stating as much.

"I appreciate the heads up Phil. I'll wait a few days and give Dad a call. Maybe he'll broach the subject himself. I promise I won't bring it up until he does. So when are you going to visit sunny Florida?"

"About when you visit sunny San Diego!" It was always the same between the brothers. Both rarely got together, though they made it a point of visiting their Dad in Connecticut every Christmas. David had visited his brother twice in San Diego, both times when he was attending a medical conference there. Philip had never come to Pelican Cove.

"Well anyway, I'll see you up at Dad's for Christmas. Maybe I'll send him a ticket and see if he'll come down to Florida for Thanksgiving. Want to join us Phil?"

"That might work; let me get back to you in a month or two. I was planning on a possible trip to Australia in November with Jacqueline."

"Still with the stewardess?"

Philip had gone through a messy divorce three years earlier and had dated several women since, but this was the first time they time had spoken since the divorce that David recognized the same woman's name from one phone call to the next. Usually by the time he spoke to Phil, he had moved on to a new object of affection.

"They're called flight attendants now. And yes, I'm still with the same one. I may even bring her home at Christmas."

"Now you've got me really worried! Well good for you. At least one of us should be settled down. I'll call you soon and let you know about Thanksgiving, and thanks for the head's up."

"Ciao Dave, you take care."

❧

Almost simultaneously, Lisa and Paula entered the office, followed by Becky.

"Ready for another day ladies?" David called out.

They all smiled at the doctor. He felt fortunate to have such great employees. Becky was the only single employee among them, and she was seriously involved with a fireman from Pelican Cove. All three represented the practice well. David would never admit so in a court of law, but he hired his employees partially based on their appearance. He didn't feel it would do to have a plastic surgeon with unattractive employees. He tried to choose women who seemed similar to his patients so that they might perceive potential outcomes similar to the visages of the nurses around them. Not model pretty perhaps, but certainly attractive. Mrs. Martin fit the bill to a "T". As he greeted the staff, David couldn't help but linger a few seconds longer as he admired her beautiful 'Ivory Girl' looks. She smiled easily and he smiled back at her.

"Back for more Lisa? I guess I haven't scared you away yet." He couldn't help but speak to her individually.

She blushed. If the doctor noticed, he was kind enough not to say anything.

"Good morning Dr. Layton. Yep, back for more. I'm enjoying it." Lisa thought, "I sound so stupid. I hope he doesn't notice my blushing."

The doctor's smile widened. He wondered if Lisa realized how sexy she looked. He had noticed her flushing several times and found it somewhat exciting. Knowing he had to keep his hands off his staff (especially his married staff), didn't stop him from fantasizing about a rendezvous with Mrs. Martin.

"That's great. Well, we're all glad you're here. Keep up the great work. Today looks pretty busy, we've got a lot of Botox cases and a full face lift in the afternoon. Becky, can you please get some coffee going?"

"Of course, Dr. Layton, and look what I've got!" Becky produced a bag she had been hiding behind her back. It was white with pink lettering. His favorite— Dunkin Donuts.

"Thanks Becky, I'm in love." Becky blushed, but she knew the doctor was only kidding. Well, probably kidding. She smiled back and walked to the kitchen to start the coffee brewing.

CHAPTER 23

"So what do you think, Fred? Deal or no deal?"

Bobby Volpe couldn't believe that Howie Mandel had a successful TV show with suitcases being held by models on stage and morons guessing where the big payouts might be. How lame. Well, no one ever got poor overestimating the stupidity of the American public. Someone had said that.

"I think it's a winner, Bobby. I mean, you've got the cash to invest from your legitimate business holdings, and you can move some of the production overseas and fund that with your 'off the books' endeavors. Botox is hot and its safety is already established. Unless something bad shows up in the trials on real people, the new Botox should be a big winner and get everyone rich."

Bobby Volpe was meeting with his counselor and attorney, Fred Mancouso, while eating lunch at "Jasper's," Volpe's favorite restaurant in Pelican Cove. They were at the mobster's usual table; in the corner furthest from the door. Vic was standing out front by his boss's shiny new silver Cadillac, always vigilant.

Fred stuffed his face with another mouthful of greasy calamari dipped in marinara sauce.

"This is great, Bobby, maybe you should just franchise this restaurant."

"Don't think I haven't thought about it," Bobby replied.

Volpe neatly folded a white napkin over the lap of his tailored dark blue trousers. A trim and well groomed man, he took pride in his appearance. At sixty, he looked fifty and still had a thick crop of fashionably trimmed hair. Alert, dark brown eyes with unusually long eyelashes never missed a thing.

"But let's get back to the Botox business. Do ya think we can show enough funds ta run this thing? I mean I expect making the drug, gettin' all that FDA shit together and creatin' a company will cost millions."

"You're right of course, Bobby. What we need to do is just get the ball rolling. Incorporate the business and maybe grease the wheels a little at the FDA. A little money in the right place will go a long way toward easing approval when the drug is reviewed. It probably wouldn't need our help anyway. Then we shop the drug around to some of the bigger drug companies. Maybe not the giants, who might ask too many questions about who their partner is. But we ought to be able to retain control over the rights to the drug, and have a company with established lines of marketing and advertising sell it. Eventually, if we play our cards right, one of the big companies will buy us all out for more money than we've ever imagined. It is important that we keep control of the company and have patent rights to the drug. Is that taken care of?"

"Ya know me better than that Fred, of course it is. The sad guy who's done all the work on the drug is just about bankrupt from gamblin' debts. I've arranged to have him make me his partner in exchange for forgivin' what he owes us. He seems to know what he's doin'. As long as he plays by our rules, I plan on keepin' him along. But if he gets outta line, we know how to handle that too. He gave us his lab records ta review and I'm no Einstein, but it all looked Kosher ta me."

"It looked good to me too, Bobby. But if you want some expert opinion, I know a couple of physicians who would be glad to make their expertise available in exchange for being kept abreast of any developments. Before this drug goes public, a lot of people with inside information will become millionaires by owning stock early. God Bless America."

"Amen, counselor." Bobby smiled, and wiped the marinara from the corner of his mouth. "Amen."

CHAPTER 24

Janetta was again seated in front of her computer terminal. She logged on to the Single Fun website.

Janetta entered the chat room for "casual, just looking". A few seconds passed, before BigJim10 messaged "hey Jan9, nice profile, want to go to a private room with me?"

Janetta clicked on his profile. How gross. He was about 250 pounds, with a fat round face and an apron of fat falling across where his thighs would normally be. He was naked. What a pig. No way was she going any where near a private room with him. Still, trying to be polite, Janetta responded,

"Looking for someone who isn't here right now, sorry Big Jim."

"I can make you very happy Jan," he messaged back.

Janetta signed off the computer. She wanted to be held by a real man. It was Monday night, not a great night for going out, but she figured it might be worth a try. Janetta went back into the bathroom and touched up her makeup. She was pleased at the results of her recent Botox treatment – wrinkles that made her look like she was frowning were gone. Janetta slipped into a tight top that showed off her cleavage. Between the top and her snug jeans she thought she could pass for a five or maybe even ten years younger than her age. She hopped into her Beamer and headed to Pizazz, a new restaurant that doubled at night as a dance club.

It had been open only six months, but was already established as the 'hottest' place to go in Pelican Cove. There was no cover charge, and usually no band, but a DJ played good dance music and the floor was always packed with a crowd of twenty to fifty year olds gyrating to the deep bass of the music. The drinks were expensive, but free for the ladies until 11PM on Mondays and Tuesdays. The ceiling was painted black., making it dark inside. As was the trend, the ventilation system was exposed and the lighting and speakers hung on wires and pipes from the ceiling. The walls were decorated with posters of rock stars from the disco era – KC and the Sunshine Band had a spot next to the entrance, right next to Donna Summer. Coincidentally, the hit "Shake Your Bootie" was playing as she entered—a classic hit from KC and their band.

It was nine o'clock and the floor and bar were already packed. Janetta walked over to the bar and ordered a glass of cabernet. It was too sweet. She made a face, and the handsome guy next to her said, "What's the matter, don't like the drink?"

"Too sweet," she replied, "But I guess you can't complain much when it's free." She looked down and saw the wedding ring on his finger. No use wasting her time with that one, she thought.

"Wanna dance?" married guy asked.

"No thanks, I'm waiting for someone." Janetta walked away from the bar and ventured into the crowd.

It seemed that everyone was talking to someone they knew, and Janetta felt alone. She was often reserved in crowds, and thought that it had probably been a mistake to come here alone. Careful to avoid the man she had already spoken to, Janetta returned to the bar. When her glass emptied, she ordered another and pretended to be interested in a basketball game on the bar television as she looked around the room for any attractive single men.

It was almost ten o'clock and Janetta was ordering her third glass of wine. She was about to give up on Monday nights in Pelican Cove when two very handsome guys walked in together. One was maybe thirty or thirty-five years old, six foot with short sandy hair, an athletic build, broad shoulders and a big smile. Even from the bar, Janetta could see the twinkle in his eyes. "He looks like trouble," she thought. His friend was perhaps a little younger, maybe twenty-eight or so, five-ten with longer blond hair. He looked like a surfer dude. "Wouldn't kick either one out of bed," Janetta mused.

As they entered Pizazz, they scoped out the room. Janetta laughed to herself—it was like watching one of those periscopes from a submarine surface and scan around to see what was out there. Her seat at the bar was a bit out of their line of sight and she doubted they saw her, but as they entered they approached near where she was sitting and ordered drinks from the bartender.

Two frosty Budweisers appeared on the bar and blond boy paid the tab. "Probably gay," Janetta imagined. She noticed that neither man had a wedding ring. Sandy hair looked down the bar and his gaze met Janetta's. He had bright blue-green eyes. But rather than try to shout over the music and the two people sitting at the bar between them, mouthed a silent "hi". It was accompanied by the sexiest smile she thought she had ever seen.

He touched his friend on the shoulder and they walked over to Janetta. Fortified by the two glasses of wine in her system, she had no trouble smiling back at them. The pair looked like a couple of models out of an Abercrombie and Fitch catalog. They were easily the two best-looking men in the club. Probably gay......

Surfer dude spoke first.

"Hi, I'm Dave."

Twinkling eyes was next,

"And I'm Jonathan."

"I'm Janetta, pleased to meet you." She extended her hand. Jonathan took it in his and held it gently.

"Pleased to meet you Janetta." Jonathan smiled and stared into her eyes as if he could read her thoughts. "What a hot-looking guy," she thought again.

"Are you from here?" she asked. Pelican Cove was a resort town much of the year, with many 'Snow Birds' coming south in the winter to get away from the northern winter weather. Now, at the end of summer, it was mostly 'locals' in town and in the bars.

"Actually we're here for business. Dave and I are models and we're doing a 'shoot' for Gentlemen's Week. We get to put on all kinds of nice clothes and bake in the sun while they take pretty pictures of us."

Janetta complemented herself for guessing their careers.

"And no, we're not gay," added Dave.

Janetta laughed so hard she almost sprayed red wine on her new friends. "Thank God, it would have been such a waste," she thought smiling at the handsome men.

"Are you from here?" asked Dave.

"For quite a while now. I'm from Pennsylvania and work in real estate."

"I guess you keep pretty busy here. Seems like everyone in the U.S. retires to Florida," noted Dave.

"Where are you two from?"

"Dave is originally from Colorado and I'm from Toronto. We both live in New York City now. Hey, would you like to dance?"

"Sure," Janetta responded casually.

Jonathan led Janetta to the dance area, which was already packed. The DJ was playing a song by Blondie, "Heart of Glass".

The music was too loud to allow reasonable conversation. Jonathan moved like a dancer, not herky-jerky like most guys, but with fluid movements—almost ballet-like. Every now and then he gently touched her on the shoulder or back and smiled seductively. What a hunk. After two dances she was sweaty and ready for another drink.

They returned to the bar. Janetta ordered another glass of wine, then left it on the bar as she excused herself to go to the bathroom.

"It's lady's night and we're feeling right, yes it's lady's night. Ohhhh, what a night," blared across the sound system.

When Janetta was out of sight, David extracted a small vial from his pocket. Inside were two pills. He crushed one in his hand and dropped the powder in the glass of red wine on the bar.

"Don't be a jerk, David. You saw how she looks at you. She wants it bad."

David had to admit, he was excited by the attractive Floridian. He didn't think he would have any trouble 'hooking up' with her tonight, and hoped things would work out.

"If she passes out, you're the one who can pay for the cab to get her home. And remember, I had no part in it."

"Sure, Jonathan. I just thought this might make it more fun, that's all."

Janetta returned from the restroom and joined the men back at the bar.

"All better?" Jonathan teased.

"Yes, all better. Where are you two staying in Pelican Cove?" she asked.

"Now don't go trying to sell us real estate," Dave joked. "We're staying at the Ritz. Fortunately we're not paying for it. That place costs like $500 a night."

"Yeah, it's not the cheapest in Pelican Cove, but it's one of the nicest.

You guys are lucky to be staying there." She took a swig of her glass of wine.

"Cheers, Janetta, here's to new friends." Jonathan raised his glass to meet hers and Dave joined in. Janetta smiled at the men and had another sip of her wine.

The Rolling Stones hit "Satisfaction" blasted from the speaker from across the bar.

"Hey, Janetta, my turn for a dance."

"Sure Dave." Janetta quickly finished off the glass of wine and walked to the dance floor with the blond model.

Jonathan was the more handsome of the two, but Dave was more seductive. He winked and smiled at Janetta the entire time they danced, and even stuck his tongue out at her once. Normally, she would have found the demonstration rude, but he made such a silly face as he did it that she couldn't help but laugh. His body was also great and she found herself imagining what it might be like to sleep with him. She made a mental note that she probably should not drink any more wine if she wanted to stand a chance of driving home.

The DJ's next tune was "Everybody Have Fun Tonight", by Wang Chung. They continued dancing. Dave had gotten closer to her and had his arms loosely holding her by the waist. Janetta was attracted to him and felt herself becoming slightly aroused at his touch on her skin. She didn't notice it as Jonathan came up behind her and lightly touched his thighs to the back of hers and 'sandwiched' her between he and Dave. They continued dancing as a threesome. Janetta noticed that the space between her and the two men had diminished and as she danced to the beat her body invariably touched either Jon or Dave. She imagined that at least a couple of times she could feel what might have been a bulge in Jonathan's pants nudge her from behind, and Dave's grasp on her waist had become more persistent. Excitement was overwhelming her.

However, she was becoming embarrassed at the attention their performance was generating- people were staring. Thankfully, the song was over and the men gave her room as she made her way back to the bar.

"You're a great dancer Janetta."

Jonathan was looking at her with his beautiful eyes. She wanted to go home with him and wondered what had come over her. The last time she had gone home with a man she met in a bar she had been in college.

"I'd say," Dave echoed. "Listen Janetta, it's silly for us to stay here all night. We can hardly hear each other talk. They've got a jazz club at the Ritz, we can dance there and the wine is better."

Janetta didn't know what to do. She wasn't sure which of the men were more interested in her. But then again, she didn't really care-she would take either one.

"I probably shouldn't drive. I wouldn't mind going, as long as you don't mind bringing me back here at the end of the night when I'm sober so I can drive home."

"No problem, Janetta, Dave and I would be happy to be your drivers."

Their car was parked in the lot just behind the club. It was a rental Chrysler Sebring convertible. Dave drove with Janetta up front. Jonathan insisted on sitting in the back. Janetta was glad to feel the fresh air on her face as Dave lowered the top. The Ritz was only a five minutes away and before she knew it, they were there. Dave handed the keys to the parking attendant and the three entered the lobby.

The Ritz was opulent. It had a large marbled entranceway with fantastically high ceilings. To the right of the entrance was a tuxedoed white-haired man playing gentle tunes on the piano accompanied by a harpist. Their destination was near one of the restaurants at the end of the reception area. The jazz club was called "Andy's Way" after the cove by the same name adjacent to the Ritz property.

Immediately upon entering the club they realized that leaving Pizazz had been a mistake. There was one grey-haired senior citizen at the bar, a couple of blue-haired older women at a table, and a tired looking trio playing sleepily on stage. That was it. Dave and Jonathan looked at Janetta.

"Looks like this wasn't such a great idea. Sorry to take you away from lady's night, Janetta. Can we get you a drink upstairs? We're on the executive floor so we have our own bar staff and club room upstairs. It's really quite nice."

Janetta hesitated. She was feeling the effects of the alcohol and felt a little sleepy.

" Sure, but just one last drink for me. Then I think I better get back."

They exited the club and made their way to the elevator and the eleventh floor.

The club floor included larger executive rooms and a separate meeting room. The meeting room had a sign hanging on the door, "Please excuse our mess. The room is being cleaned and will reopen in the morning." The trio could hear the melodious chatter of Creole and the muted roar of vacuum cleaners as the cleaning crew went about their work.

"Looks like we're striking out all over. How about a quick drink in our suite, then we'll take you back to your car," Jonathan offered.

Janetta felt light-headed. She was alone with two gorgeous hunks who both seemed interested in her. Her mind was buzzing like an overcharged electrical grid. This was her libidinous fantasies come true. How could she say "no" to one and "yes" to the other? Or would it be "yes" to both? Well, another drink might make her decision easier.

"Okay, just one more drink. I've had too good a time to go home now."

Jonathan slid the key card in the door. Their room was small, but tastefully decorated.

Dave walked over to the mini-bar.

"Let's see, we've got red and white wine with a screw cap, gin, Jack

Daniels and a couple of Amstel Lights, and there's a Heineken. What would you like?" asked Dave.

"I'll live dangerously.   Pop the 'cork' on the red and I'll have that."

Dave removed the six ounce bottle and poured it into a glass. Simultaneously, he removed a Roofie from his pocket. With his back turned to Janetta, he crushed the pill and dropped the powder into the glass. It dissolved, as he swirled the mixture gently.

"Here you go Janetta. It looks like a fine vintage, probably April last year." Dave handed her the glass.

Janetta laughed. Alone in a hotel room with two men. What had gotten over her?   And she was so turned on by them.

"And what are you two going to drink?" she asked.

"Amstel for me."

"Me too," added Jonathan. Jonathan was walking over to the television. Dave lightly tossed him a beer.

Janetta admired the room. They were high up and could see the lights of the town stretching eastward. The hotel was on the beach and contained a balcony from which to admire sunsets and listen to the surf.

"What a beautiful view." Although the words came out clear, Janetta felt a little difficulty with her speech. And her mouth felt dry.

"I'll say," answered Dave, admiring Janetta from behind as she walked through the room.

Janetta opened the sliding windows on the balcony and stepped through to the humid warm air. She enjoyed the taste of the sweet wine and drank half the glass in two swallows. Dave was right behind her on the balcony.

She had thought that the fresh air might wake her up. Instead, she found herself excited by Dave's presence, but sleepy at the same time. His blond hair blew lightly in the Gulf breeze. He smiled at her as they both leaned on the railing of the balcony. Before she had a chance to consider what was happening, he leaned over and pulled her toward him. Dave kissed her on the lips.

"I couldn't let you leave here without kissing you Janetta," Dave blurted.

He wondered if she was some kind of Superwoman or something. She had had several glasses of wine and been given two Roofies and seemed totally with the program. Even her speech was clear.

Dave didn't know the effect his kiss had on Janetta. Feeling it all the way down to her toes, Janetta was frightened by how much she wanted to continue the passion with the relative stranger. Surely he must be able to see it in her eyes.

Janetta impulsively pulled Dave back to her mouth, aggressively kissing him back and sliding her tongue into his mouth. He responded by pulling her closer to him and letting his arms drop down around her waist and chest. They kissed, forgetting completely about Jonathan, who was still in the room and had been checking to see what was on the TV.

Janetta felt Dave's hands move up her blouse and across her sheer bra. Warmth rose within her as she felt a flush of desire. They continued kissing as Dave slid his hands under her bra and across her left breast. She shuddered with excitement.

No words were exchanged. Dave lifted Janetta in his arms as her legs wrapped around his waist. He carried her to the bed, removing his shirt as he dropped her slowly and lowered her onto her back. Janetta removed her blouse and bra in one tangled heap. She was naked to the waist as Dave lowered his mouth to her breasts. Janetta wanted him, but even through the haze of the wine knew one thing she had to do before letting this continue.

Breathlessly she gasped, "Do you have a condom?"

"We both do," Jonathan answered.

Janetta had forgotten that there were three of them in the room. Jonathan was standing there naked and had been watching his friend and Janetta on the bed. His manhood clearly indicated that he wanted to participate and he had already slipped a sheer condom on. He looked like a Greek god. Janetta felt her heart racing with anticipation.

Jonathan walked over to the bed and handed a condom to Dave, who slid away from Janetta. Jonathan then lowered his body onto her and kissed Janetta gently on the lips. He lowered his head to chest and began to kiss her body softly. Janetta felt as if she was going to explode. Her head was throbbing and she was unable to think coherently.

Lifting his head, Jonathan smiled as Janetta moaned. He pulled his body away and then approached her again. She spread her thighs wide, in eager anticipation.

Jonathan joined Janetta as she arched her back and met his thrusts with contractions of her thigh muscles; squeezing him as he moved inside her. The first waves of an orgasm began within her, joined by a dense foggy feeling in her brain. The sounds in the room were becoming muffled. Through thick air, she heard herself moaning as an orgasm coarsed through her body. She thought she heard herself scream out as Jonathan came within her, but the fuzziness in her brain confused her – she couldn't tell whether she was imagining what she had heard or actually had screamed out loud. The orgasm passed and she regained some awareness of her surroundings. Janetta felt very short of breath. She just couldn't get enough air. Jonathan suddenly felt very heavy and she pushed against him to free herself of his weight. Fatigue washed over her. Sensing a change in his partner, Jonathan lifted himself away from her.

"Are you okay, Janetta?"

"I can't breathe, and I can't think. My head feels tho woozy. I'm tho tired."

Dave had been planning to have a turn with Janetta next and had been sitting next to the bed. He looked nervous.

Janetta's eyes fluttered, then closed. Although her chest moved slightly, her breathing was very shallow and rapid. She let out a single deeper gasp before her breathing stopped entirely.

Both men were terrified. Jonathan knew CPR and checked her airway. He saw no obstruction to her breathing. Her chest had stopped moving, though her heart was still beating.

"Call 911!" Jonathan shouted to Dave.

Dave peeled the condom from his now flaccid penis and pulled on his pants. He tried to dial 911 from the hotel phone.

"Shit, it won't let me dial a nine."

He grabbed his cell phone and got through to the 911 operator. An ambulance was on the way.

Jonathan began CPR, breathing intermittently for Janetta. Between breaths he began to gather her clothes back around her and had been able to get her panties back on. He wondered if he had somehow killed her.

"I think I fucked up Jon. Maybe I gave her too much Roofie."

"No one ever stopped breathing from one Roofie." Maybe she's sick or something.

"No, I gave her two Roofies."

"When the fuck did you do that?"

"When the first didn't seem to do anything, I gave her another when we got here. It sure looked like everything was okay. I mean she seemed fine. Maybe she had some rare reaction to your condom or something. I read where if you're allergic to latex you can die during sex."

Jonathan gave Janetta some more breaths.

"If she was allergic she would have stopped me before we started. Shit, it better not be the Roofies or we're screwed. Man, Dave, you're such an asshole sometimes. Let's get her all dressed before the ambulance gets here. I think you better get some clothes on too."

"Should we tell them you had sex with her?" Dave asked.

Jonathan considered their options as he puffed two more breaths into Janetta's silent body.

"I don't think we should lie. I saw an episode of CSI where even though the woman wasn't raped; they knew she had sex with someone just from traces of the powder and spermicidal agent left behind from the condom. We can't just go away, and anyway, this room is registered to us. I think all we can do is tell the truth."

"I think we should deny the Roofies, Jon."

"I think we never should have given one, let alone two, to her in the first place. But we're screwed now. At least if we stick around and try to help and tell the truth they'll probably go easier on us. And remember, the Roofies were all your idea; you have to admit to them, they'll find out about them from her blood anyway. First we've got to make sure she's okay. I hear sirens."

The ambulance had arrived on the street below. Within moments, the paramedics were in their room. As one asked them about what happened, another attached Janetta to a monitor and administered oxygen. The screen indicated normal heart activity, but she was not breathing. There was no evidence of obstruction and the paramedic noted that her lungs sounded clear.

"What happened?" one of the three paramedics asked.

Jonathan and Dave began to explain the events of the evening. Shortly thereafter, the police were called to the scene.

CHAPTER 25

"Janetta Fannestack, 11 Whispering Pine Way, Pelican Cove. Not bad for a DMV picture," the doctor commented.

Janetta's personal affects had accompanied her to the emergency room where a chart was being created. Her driver's license and effects were being examined for pertinent information. She was stable. A tube had been placed in her trachea to facilitate her breathing. A ventilator was being prepared and admission to the intensive care unit was arranged.

Dr. Gary LaStella joined Janetta in cubicle seven. Gary was actually Giovanni, an Italian born and trained physician. He was the most capable of an excellent staff, and the fifty-year-old father of five girls.

"What crap!" LaStella vented. "These guys think its okay to slip pills into this woman? And what the hell is she doing in their room anyway. They said they just met her. For their sake, she better come around."

LaStella, was known in the emergency department for his blunt honesty and conservative values. His ranting was directed at no one in particular. He was examining Janetta and ignoring the IV team, who were busy placing a large bore access line into her left forearm because the line placed by the paramedics had become dislodged.

Blood tests had been drawn and her alcohol level was reported at 1.4. Enough to diminish her capacities, but not enough to explain her respiratory failure. A drug screen, including a blood level for rohypnol, had been ordered but would not be available until the next day. Charcoal had been administered via a nasogastric tube into her stomach. Routine blood chemistries had revealed no abnormalities. Her chest x-ray revealed normal appearing lungs. Only her neurological exam was abnormal. Janetta had diminished response to pain and there was mild papilledema, swelling of her optic nerve, noted on her eye examination. Her neurological examination was not 'focal' meaning there was no evidence of a stroke on either side of her brain, but in view of her altered mental status, a CAT scan had been ordered. The preliminary reading had shown no abnormalities. An MRI was planned for the morning.

LaStella had learned from the police that the two men who were with her admitted to an act of consensual sex and heavy drinking. One of the men admitted to slipping the "Roofie" into her drink. No additional pills were available for examination, which could have helped in determining if the drugs had been adulterated, though the blond jerk who had given the medication to the victim admitted to taking one himself and had not experienced any unexpected side-effects. Both men were being held in the jail, pending determination of bond by the judge.

"Is she married?" inquired LaStella of his unit clerk.

"The police were able to contact her mother in Pennsylvania when they checked the numbers on her cell. Apparently she's single and lives alone. Her parents are going to book a flight in tomorrow. They gave us the name of her best friend, a Lisa Martin, in Pelican Cove. Do you want us to call her?"

"Wait. Did her mother know of any medical problems? Did her daughter use drugs or anything that mom knew about?"

"No, Dr. LaStella., her mother said she had no history of any illness or diseases and other than an occasional social drink, didn't take any mind-altering substances."

Dr. LaStella's question had been answered by the nurse in charge of Janetta's care in the ER, Gloria Bilch. Gloria was old enough to be Janetta's mother and had worked in the emergency department for twenty-three years. She related to every patient as part of her own family. Janetta reminded the nurse of her own daughter, who had tragically died at the age of twenty-four, the victim of a drunken driver when she was only a graduate student in college.

"Her mind is certainly altered now," replied the doctor. "Let's wait until later in the morning. Before I go off shift at eight, I'll call Ms. Martin myself and see if she knows anything useful. I don't see any point in calling her now at two in the morning. In a few hours, the drug screen information will be available, we can get the MRI done and maybe we'll have some answers. The ICU will be taking over her care. I've given her some Medrol and the steroid should help with any swelling in her brain. We're hyperventilating her a little to help reduce the intracranial pressure and she's stable, so hopefully, if it's a drug, it'll work its way out of her system," LaStella finished.

"I hope so, Dr. LaStella."

CHAPTER 26

Lisa was awakened by her alarm which was set for seven. She heard Nate in the bathroom already getting ready. She rolled over and pulled the covers over her head for a few moments of sleep. The bed felt so nice. Lisa knew that Nate would be sure to get her up before he left. Without looking at the clock she tried to guess the time. Of course, she knew it was seven when the alarm went off, so if he came in soon, she had a good chance of guessing. Some days, she fell back to sleep and had little idea if five minutes or fifteen had passed.

Lisa felt Nate's hand on her shoulder.

"Wake up sweety, time for work."

"Nate, it's Tuesday, I don't have to work today! But I've got to go get the boys up."

She kissed Nate on the corner of his mouth as she awkwardly lifted her head from the bed. At the same time she made a mental guess, 7:08, and looked at her digital clock on the bedside table. The light green numbers read, 7:07, but as she watched, turned to 7:08.

"Close enough!" exclaimed Lisa. Nate knew of her game and smiled knowing that his wife's day had started with a small victory.

"Nate, can you please go out and get the newspaper so I can read it with my breakfast."

"Sure honey. Sorry I can't eat with you, but I've got a ton of stuff to do at the office." He kissed her on the cheek and exited the room.

After showering, Lisa woke both boys and made sure they pulled themselves out of bed. Sometimes, if she wasn't vigilant, Shawn would go back to bed. Today though, both boys came down the stairs hungry for breakfast.

"Can I have a Toaster Strudel?" asked Josh.

"You can have one if you eat your oatmeal first."

"Come on Mom, I won't be hungry after I eat the oatmeal. How about if I eat half the oatmeal, and then eat half a Toaster Strudel."

Lisa laughed at her younger son.

"Okay, you win. Some day you'll make a fine lawyer!"

Lisa prepared breakfast for the boys. As they ate, she removed the newspaper from its plastic bag and scanned the large print of the headlines. The big story involved a land developer who had destroyed the burrows of several gopher tortoises, protected animals in Florida. Pelican Cove wasn't known for having the wildest news events.

The next caption she read made her gasp. There in the lower right corner, probably added to the paper as a 'late-breaking story' and in bold print she read, "Local Woman Hospitalized After Alleged Date Rape." Then the opening line, "Two male models are being held in the county jail after allegedly providing alcohol and the date-rape drug Rohypnol to local realtor Janetta Fannestack, who has been hospitalized and is in serious condition."

"Oh my God!"

"What's the matter Mom?" asked Shawn.

"Janetta is in trouble honey. She's in the hospital."

"What happened?"

"I'm not sure Shawn, but it sounds like she may have been given something bad to eat by some bad men. Finish up so I can get you to school."

"What would Janetta be doing with two men on a Monday night?" she wondered. Janetta rarely went out. Lisa automatically began cleaning the kitchen and put away the milk and juice. Cleaning was something she always did for some reason when things were bothering her. Even Nate had noticed and commented on it in the past. She was jarred from her thoughts by the ringing of her phone.

"Hello, may I speak to Ms. Martin?"

"Yes, this is she."

"Hi, my name is Dr. Gary LaStella. I work in the emergency department at Pelican Cove Hospital. I'm calling because a friend of yours, Janetta Fannestack, has been admitted to the hospital with an apparent drug overdose."

"I know, Dr. LaStella, I read it in the paper this morning. How bad is it?"

"She's still in a coma and not breathing on her own. We can't identify any injuries. Blackouts in people who combine rohypnol with alcohol can be very serious and can often last over twenty-four hours. We are concerned that there may be some brain damage, either from the drug or lack of oxygen before she got to the hospital."

"Will I be able to come see her?"

"Absolutely. I was hoping that you might be able to shed some light on her behavior. Has she ever experimented with drugs before? Does she take any medication?"

"No, if anything, Janetta is a bit of a health nut. We drink together sometimes, but Janetta's limit is usually two glasses of wine. I've never known her to take any drugs and as far as I know, she takes no medication."

"Well, it appears, she may have taken theses drugs unknowingly. Two guys apparently seduced her and one of them slipped the drug into her wine."

"They admitted to it?"

"Yes," replied the doctor. "Apparently, they feel that she consented to whatever they did, but felt remorseful when she ended up in a coma. I hope for their sake and hers that she wakes up soon."

"What are her chances doctor?"

"Well, she's young and otherwise seems healthy, so I am optimistic. The next twenty-four hours will be important. Do you know if she has any allergies, Mrs. Martin?"

"As far as I know, only to shellfish. She ate some lobster mixed in a sauce at a Chinese restaurant once and swelled up like a balloon. Other than that, nothing else that I know of."

"I'm coming off shift and going home Mrs. Martin, but if you think of anything else that might be helpful, please let me know. Just leave word in the ICU with one of the nurses. The ICU doc who will be in charge of her is great, Dr. Sanchez, so you can be sure she'll be in good hands. Sorry about Janetta. Hopefully, next time we speak she'll be making her plans to go home."

"Thank you, Dr. LaStella."

Lisa said a silent prayer for her friend. Deep in thought, she finished her kitchen chores and got the boys packed up for school. Josh and Shawn sensed tension in their mother and were unusually quiet in the car on the way to the bus stop.

"Is Janetta going to be okay, Mom?" asked Josh.

"I hope so Josh, I hope so. I'm going to visit her as soon as I drop you guys off."

She deposited both children at the corner, just three blocks from their house. She remembered the days when a mother could just let her seven and nine-year-old kids wait at a street corner without supervision. Not anymore. She waited for the bus and pondered the loss of innocence that surrounded her.

CHAPTER 27

Despite his cavalier attitude with Sal, David Layton was concerned. The meeting with BioVenture was only a few weeks away and things were not running smoothly. Four mice had died. No causes could be determined for the first two mice; the third appeared to have a congenital heart defect. The fourth was the one that concerned the doctor—the reading from their pathologist described inclusions in the brainstem and cerebral edema. The findings were similar to those identified in Shirley and Roberta, whose cases were both being reviewed by the experts at the Armed Forces Institute of Pathology. The dead mouse and Roberta had received only small amounts of the experimental Botox, and both had received the medication relatively recently. Perhaps one vial had been contaminated in the lab.

Any inability to enter additional patients into the study would weaken his data. He and Sal needed to open the wallets of the BioVenture guys. Of course they would be swayed by the animal findings, but the human data would be more convincing. Millions of dollars were at stake. David's mind continued to reel. He thought of his father with Alzheimer's disease and a life of hard work brought to an end by disease. Then he thought of his brother, rolling in dough and enjoying the good life. He hoped his own future might be more like his brother's than his father's.

Reaching for the telephone, he dialed the number for Manzari at Youth Labs.

"Hello, Gemini Construction," someone answered.

"I'm sorry, I must have dialed the wrong number," answered Layton. He disconnected and began to re-dial Manzari but realized he had once again forgotten the number.

"Just too many damn things to remember these days," David muttered.

He pulled the number from his cell phone directory and connected to the lab.

"Hey Sal, David here."

"Good afternoon, Doc. What's the good word?"

"How are your pets doing Sal?"

"All the mice are doing fine. How are your patients faring?"

"No problems there, but that's why I'm calling. I've reviewed how we're doing here, and wonder whether perhaps an impurity got into one of the Botox vials. Everything else is going so smoothly and all the data appears so perfect; I'm tempted to just ignore the death of the mice as a fluke."

Sal asked quickly, "And your nurse?"

Layton had not revealed the death of Roberta Cook to Manzari. They had discussed Shirley's demise. The similarities in the brain pathology between Shirley and the dead mouse could not be dismissed easily---Sal was aware that there was a connection.

"I am concerned, but I think as long as we're very careful in preparation of the Botox and limit patients to only one injection of the new formulation I think we'll be okay. Has anything changed in the preparation of the Botox that could have caused the problems?"

Manzari swallowed hard. He had counted on Layton to respond

ethically and follow the Hippocratic Oath in protecting his patients. Sal knew that Shirley's death had shaken the doctor and thought human trials of the Botox would be shelved. The chemist expected the doctor to call and advise that they would be 'cutting their losses' and perhaps close the lab.

"No, nothing has changed in the formulation of the Botox. You know how careful I am. I'm as perplexed as you are over the problems. Maybe we can just present our animal data to the FDA, end the human trials and let the chips fall where they may."

Manzari knew that this was an unacceptable alternative to the doctor, who needed funding from BioVenture quickly in order to advance the drug's development, keep the lab afloat, and hopefully cash out. He also knew that getting funding with the limited data would be impossible.

"Sorry, Sal. I can't keep the trials going that long. I've already sapped most of the money out of my home equity line to make payments on the lab debts we're incurring. If it weren't for the cash from the practice and selling off some of my stocks, we'd be dead in the water right now. We've got to get this together for presentation next month. I'll need about ten or twelve new vials to treat the additional patients I plan to enlist in the trials. Can you have them ready this week?"

Sal sighed, careful not to allow any anxiety to be heard in his voice.

"Sure Dr. Layton, no problem. I hope what we're doing is the right thing. David, if anyone gets word of these trials and Shirley's death it could create big problems. And I don't want to be held responsible for hurting anyone."

"Don't be such a worrier Sal; I've got things under control over here. Nothing has happened but a small bump in the road. We'll be fine."

Sal wasn't surprised at the 'bump in the road' at all. It was the rest of the trip that was worrying him.

CHAPTER 28

Lisa came to work on Wednesday happy to be kept busy by the responsibilities around her. The previous day had been very difficult as Janetta's condition had deteriorated. The MRI had shown diffuse edema, suggestive of a lack of oxygen, and brain damage. In addition, the swelling did not seem to be responding adequately to treatment. The intensive care physician had been guarded in offering a prognosis for her friend.

"Good morning, Lisa. How's everything?"

"I'm okay Barbara, but I had a terrible day yesterday. My best friend is in the hospital and she's not doing well at all. She went out and some guys laced her drink with Roofies. It looks like she's overdosed; she's unconscious and may have brain damage."

"Wow, that is terrible. I'm so sorry. Can they give her medication to get it out of her system or something?"

"They're doing all they can. They're giving her respiratory support and hoping she comes out of it. They're concerned with swelling in her brain. I wish there was something I could do, but there isn't. In a way, I'm glad

I have work to distract me."

"Well, if there's anything I can do, just let me know," Barbara volunteered.

Dr. Layton joined the ladies in conversation. Looking dapper as always, David was wearing a canary yellow Brooks Brothers Oxford shirt with a black and gold-striped tie and crisp black slacks. His white 'doctor's' coat hung sharply over his broad shoulders. Lisa never tired of noting how much he resembled a movie star; maybe Richard Gere. These days, her heart didn't jump as it did on her first days on the job, but a part of her still felt an intense attraction to the man.

David noticed how serious and subdued his employee appeared.

"Why so glum?" he asked.

"Lisa's friend is in a coma in the hospital," Barb volunteered.

"What happened?"

"Some guys laced her drinks with Roofies and she may have brain damage. You actually met her Dr. Layton. It's Janetta, my friend who came to your office with me when I came here for your Botox seminar."

David hesitated. "Yes, I remember her. I think she came back afterward for treatment. I hope she recovers."

Dr. Layton wondered whether her eventual outcome would require further modification of his Botox clinical data. Surely her accident should not alter the statistics. He pushed these thoughts from his mind and hoped the young woman would fully recover.

"Let me know if you need some time off Lisa. I understand if you need to spend time at the hospital. Does she have family here in Pelican Cove?"

"No, unfortunately not; I'm the closest thing to family she has here. But her folks flew in from Pennsylvania yesterday afternoon. They're in shock, but seem to be holding up. I appreciate your offer, but I should have no problem working my hours. As I was telling Barbara, work is good for taking my mind off Janetta and there's really nothing I can do for her anyway."

"Alright then, if you change your mind let me know. Barb, I'm ready to start whenever you two are. We've got a liposuction consult first, then I think we have three Botox cases in a row. I'm going to get some coffee while you get the patients in the rooms. See you in a few minutes."

Dr. Layton went back to his office and the nurses went about their duties.

CHAPTER 29

"Paging Dr. Blue. Paging Dr. Blue, intensive care unit." The message came over the hospital intercom system. Dr. Blue was the semi-secret message utilized by many hospitals, including Pelican General, to alert all staff physicians that there was a hospital emergency requiring their presence. In this case, it was in the ICU. Normally, Dr. Sanchez, the intensivist on duty, would have been on the scene, but he had stepped out for a bite. The emergency was answered by both an internist and a cardiologist.

Dr. Odom, the cardiologist, was the first on the scene. He appeared winded and his comb-over hair was askew, falling across the side of his face. Self-consciously, he placed the hair-spray-coated hair back over his balding pate. The patient's nurse pretended not to see the action and tersely briefed the cardiologist on the patient.

"She had been stable, after a drug overdose. Cerebral edema had caused respiratory problems and she's been on a ventilator. About two minutes ago heart rate slowed suddenly and she became rigid—as if she were having a seizure."

Dr. Lugo, the internist, reviewed the most recent lab chemistries and vitals attached to the bedside clipboard.

"Everything looks okay here Dr. Odom."

"Give her fifty of lidocaine and we'll need to add atropine for the heart rate. Also an amp of bicarb. Have the tech draw a set of blood gases too. Get her attending on the phone."

Dr. Odom placed his stethoscope over the patient's chest.

"Her heart and lungs sound normal." Next he examined her pupils. They did not respond to the light he trained across them.

"I think she's herniating her brainstem. Has she had cerebral edema?"

"Yes, she's been on Medrol and we've been trying to lower her intracranial pressure."

Despite the medication, her heart rate was now down to thirty.

Dr. Odom removed the ophthalmoscope from the wall and endeavored to examine her optic disc.

"She has massive edema at her optic nerve. That probably explains her problems. First she lost her ability to stimulate breathing, and now it's affecting her heart."

"Start CPR, we need to try to get some blood to her brain. I'll try to insert a temporary pacemaker. Do we have permission for invasive measures?" the cardiologist inquired.

"The parents wished to be notified of any changes in status, but until now we have had Carte Blanche," replied the nurse. "There are also other legal issues here."

"Oh, this is that young woman with the date-rape thing, isn't she?" asked Dr. Lugo.

"Yes, it's such a shame. Would you like to talk to the parents?"

"Yes, but also call the intensive care physician. He will want to remain in the loop. I don't want to step on anyone's toes. And give her another amp of atropine and 250mg of mannitol for the cerebral edema."

Dr. Sanchez, the intensive care physician, immediately returned to the hospital, and contacted the patient's parents by phone.

"Mr. Fannestack, I'm sorry to have to inform you that your daughter has taken a significant turn for the worse. She is no longer responsive to any stimuli and her heart is not beating fast enough to get oxygen to her brain. The cardiologist is preparing her for a temporary pacemaker to stimulate her heart, but with the degree of swelling and damage to her brainstem, we are no longer optimistic of a recovery."

"Please do whatever you can for her." Dr. Sanchez could hear Mrs. Fannestack crying in the background. "We'll be right over. Please save our Janetta."

"We'll do all we can, Mr. Fannestack. I'll be here when you arrive."

Janetta Fannestack was pronounced dead on Thursday morning, September 29th at 6:27AM. Her parents were at her bedside. The body was transferred to the morgue and came to the urgent attention of the senior medical examiner, Dr. Jack Shea.

CHAPTER 30

Jack usually enjoyed the generally slow pace of medical examiner work. He had previously been in a group practice with other pathologists but found the politics and stress of being a partner intolerable. Now, his salary was paid for by the hospital and nicely subsidized by his work for the county on cases requiring a police investigation. His most recent case fell into this category. Still, it was one he would rather not have had to tackle. As head of the department, any cases with potentially serious political or legal consequences were often delegated as his responsibility. The death of Janetta Fannestack was one such case. Her death was allegedly due to drugs administered to her by two unscrupulous 'pretty boys'. They were already being called the "Abercrombie Date-Rape Murderers" in the press and there was significant heat from the police for him to have the case 'wrapped up' as soon as possible. It was an election year, and the sheriff of the city and the mayor of Pelican Cove had no intention of looking soft on crime.

Jack proceeded with his autopsy. Each finding was meticulously placed into his dictation as if a defense or prosecuting attorney were peering over his shoulder. Every clinical feature was carefully described, photographed and each organ weighed before separation for histological preparation. Dr. Shea was careful to document changes to the body that were the response to the attempted resuscitation, avoiding any subjective description that might be challenged by an overeager attorney. His work was impartial; though if some scum had caused this tragic death his opinion was that a life in jail would be too good for them.

There were no surprises during the autopsy. Some respiratory trauma was evident from the placement of the endotracheal tube, and bruising from the intravenous lines, but otherwise, the autopsy was unremarkable. The only gross abnormality was edema of the cerebellum and brainstem. The changes were subtle, and he might have not even noticed them if not for the notations from the chart and medical records prior to death. In addition, two recent abnormal brainstem cases had sensitized Jack to check for abnormalities in this generally uneventful area. Jack finished up his work and submitted his gross specimens for histological slide preparation. It would be the next day before the slides would be ready for review. In the meantime, he knew he would be fending off the police and reporters as they awaited his findings prior to bringing formal charges against the two young men. The pathologist looked forward to putting this case to rest. He was locking up the office and getting ready to go home for the day, just as two athletic-looking men exited the elevator and entered the morgue.

"Dr. Shea?"

It was the taller of the two men, a thin, heavily freckled six footer in a dark blue suit. A bulge at his hip tipped Jack off that these were police officers.

"Only if you're not here because I owe you any money or to tell me that my ex-wife wants me back."

Both officers smiled at the humor, though their demeanor quickly became serious.

"We're here about the Fannestack case. I'm Kevin Collins and my partner is Dan Levine."

Both men extended their outstretched hands in greeting to Dr. Shea who reciprocated.

Levine spoke.

"Have you found any evidence that will support the cause of death as due to drugs she may have been given?"

The shorter man was the more muscular of the pair, obviously no stranger to the weight room. He wore a black suit that was a little too small around his beefy shoulders and his neck stretched his shirt collar broadly apart. A thick black mat of curly hair poked from the top of his shirt. His thick, large, nose appeared as if it had been broken in the past. and his speech suggested an upbringing in New York or New Jersey.

"It's a bit early to tell, but I expect her autopsy to do nothing to counter the impression that an overdose of drugs and booze caused her death. We will know more tomorrow when I have had the chance to review the microscopic findings of her tissues."

"Thanks Dr. Shea. Hopefully, your work will satisfy the District Attorney that there was nothing else wrong with the woman that could have contributed to her death. The DA will then likely want to avoid the circus of a trial and allow the guy who admitted to giving her the drugs to plead to involuntary manslaughter. He'll be back on the street in seven years."

"Personally, I find that disturbing Detective Collins- I'd like to see him hang. Anyway, I'll be sure to call you when I've finished my work— probably tomorrow."

"Thanks, we'll be heading out then." Both detectives handed Dr. Shea their business cards. "Sorry to interrupt your work Dr. Shea."

"No problem at all, I was just leaving anyway. I'll call you tomorrow afternoon. Nice meeting you both."

Jack shut the off the lights. He left within a few minutes of the detective's departure.

CHAPTER 31

Thursday morning was bright and sunny. Lisa found herself wide-awake before her alarm and pressed the button, inactivating the buzzer. Nate sensed her movements and his eyes fluttered open.

"Morning, honey. Do you have work today?" Nate asked.

"Nope, I'm off. How about you? Busy day?"

"No rest for the weary. I've got to take a deposition for one of the Jointrex cases and have to review a bunch of new cases with the paralegal to see if they're worth pursuing. But with any luck I shouldn't be home too late."

"It would be nice if we could all eat together, on time, for a change. I've got some great steaks I picked up yesterday. If you call me when you're about to leave the office I can get them on the grill and we could have a nice dinner."

"I'll call – I promise. Should be about five, or five-thirty at the latest."

Nate's response was interrupted by ringing of Lisa's cell phone.

Lisa felt a foreboding – with Janetta in the hospital, a call first thing in the morning had her concerned.

"Hello."

"Hi Lisa. It's Vicky Fannestack, Janetta's mom. I'm sorry to call you so early in the morning, but I wanted to catch you before you went out. Janetta passed away. She died early this morning." Mrs. Fannestack's voice trailed off and Lisa thought she heard the older woman sob.

Lisa was shocked.

"Mrs. Fannestack, I'm so sorry. Do they know what happened?"

"Her heart failed and she wasn't breathing. They've ordered an autopsy but other than that we really don't have any more information.

"Is their anything I can do?"

"The medical examiner has her body, and I suppose I'll have to get to her apartment and take care of her things. I just can't even begin to think about it all right now. We'll be bringing her back to Pennsylvania for burial when they've finished with her. I'll call you as soon as we have any arrangements set, but please don't feel obligated to go to the funeral– I know you've got young boys and a job and don't want to put you out. You might be able to help me go through Janetta's things if that's not too much to ask."

"Vicky, there's no way I won't be going to the funeral. Janetta was my best friend – I can't believe I have to say was. Whatever I can do for you—just call me as soon as you know what's up as far as helping with Janetta's things or making any arrangements here in Pelican Cove.

"Thanks, Lisa. I'm having trouble talking right now, so I'm going to let you go. Thanks for being Janetta's friend, and I'm sorry I called so early."

Lisa's voice caught in her throat. "I'm sorry you had to call. It's just not fair. Please call me later so that I can help."

"I will Lisa. I'll call you this afternoon. Bye."

Lisa gazed at her phone through misty eyes, magically wishing that by staring at the silent phone long enough it could bring her friend back to life. She placed the phone on her nightstand and collapsed in Nates's arms, tears streaming down her face.

CHAPTER 32

There was quite a bit of pressure on Jack to finish the Fannestack case. The newspapers were having a field day. Yesterday's headline in the Pelican Daily News read, "Prosecution to Pursue Murder Charges in Date-Rape Case." In the Pelican Cove Gazette the headline was "Will Models Get Chance To Be Model Prisoners?"

The national news services had also joined the bandwagon. Jack found himself hiding from the circus in the relative solitude of the pathology department physician's cubicles, reviewing the slides from yesterday's autopsy.

"Good morning Dr. Shea."

It was Courtney, one of the histotechs. The hospital kept the technicians working on eight hour shifts 24-7 and Courtney worked the weekends to supplement her income.

"Morning Courtney. Have you finished the Fannestack case yet?"

"I finished it an hour ago. The slides are on the table by the dual-headed scope."

Courtney was the most skillful of the technicians. He was glad that she had been involved in this sensitive case.

Jack carried the large stack of trays, containing twenty slides each, over to the microscope. When the slides were from a younger, relatively healthy person like Janetta, it was simple work to read them as there was usually little deviation from normal. When the technicians marveled from time to time at how fast Jack could read the slides, he drew the analogy to that of a normal person looking out across a parking lot for a yellow school bus. The 'skilled observer' would quickly be able to identify a bus in the lot and ignore all the other information surrounding the bus: the cars, buildings and pavement. The body and its tissues were similar for the skilled pathologist; his eye was trained to spot the stray 'bus' and ignore all the relatively unimportant and normal surrounding data.

One by one, the trays were transferred from a stack on his right side to the growing pile at his left elbow. Jack had progressed through samples of Janetta's heart, lungs, kidneys, liver, intestinal tract, stomach and skin. The pathologist knew that there had been cerebral edema and wanted to work his way up to the more significant pathology he expected he might encounter in the brain tissues. Sections had been taken from multiple areas of the brain with special attention given to the more edematous areas of the brainstem, cerebellum and cortex.

Jack was immediately impressed by the degree of edema noted on the specimens. The slightly increased size of the brainstem noted clinically was also appreciable under the microscope. Nerve cells were separated by paler areas of edema. However, not only was there edema, but increased thickness of the tissues was detectable and in the area of the fornix, which Jack had specifically sectioned in view of his recent cases, hypertrophy was evident. Could the enlargement here translate to abnormal function? Loss of impulse control might have led the young woman to uncharacteristic behavior and poor judgment. The pathologist could only imagine the ways that the defense attorneys might use his pathology findings toward their own benefit. And what was causing these unusual findings? They could not be explained away as the result of insult to the brain from hypoxia.

Jack had taken the initiative to order silver stains for several areas of the brain, in an attempt to detect any degenerative fibers or foreign substances that might be better visualized with the special staining. The effort was rewarded with subtle evidence of small tangles of fibers, possibly degenerative nerve tissue or nonspecific substances gathered in the cortex. These were also present in the specimens from the brainstem. The findings were almost identical to those of Dr. Layton's nurse Shirley and Roberta Cook, the Pelican Cove woman found dead in the apartment by her neighbor. The cases were remarkably similar in that all three involved women who had seemed healthy but had demonstrated abnormal brain tissue findings. Of course, this case was complicated by the presence of drugs and alcohol, but Jack was unaware of Roofies causing cranial hypertrophy in the fornix. Roofies were known to lower inhibitions and alter behavior, but those changes were short-term and did not result in cerebral hypertrophy or the deposits detected in Janetta's brain tissues. What could be causing these changes?

The pathologist carefully completed dictating the reports on the specimens. Only the brain tissue required customized dictation; all of the other reports, which were entirely normal, merely involved keying the menu item listing 'normal' in the pathology department's computer software, a speedy process. Jack was perplexed and intrigued by his findings and wondered what to do next. He would contact the pathology experts evaluating the other two cases regarding his findings so that they too could do special staining. He would then call the police to let them know that their case might be a little more complicated than they had anticipated.

CHAPTER 33

The Martin family spent a quiet weekend at home. Lisa was depressed and shocked over the passing of her friend. Initially, when the alarm awoke her she thought it was Sunday instead of Monday, and wondered why she had set the alarm to wake her on her day of leisure. Nate's absence in the spot next to her in the bed reminded her that it was Monday. The clock read 7:01, time to get up. Lisa pulled her tired body off the bed, trying to cheer herself before seeking out the boys for breakfast. She could hear the sounds of Nate preparing breakfast in the kitchen. Lisa smelled the beautiful smoky aroma of bacon. She found Josh and Shawn sound asleep, looking like two 'road kill' angels, flat in their beds.

"Wake up boys, time for school."

Josh rubbed his eyes and looked up at his mom. He appeared disoriented for a moment, then smiled, and dropped his head back onto the pillow pulling the covers over his head.

"Josh Martin! WAKE UP. I don't have time to hang around here. Shawn, you too."

Shawn arose from his bed, staking first claim to the bathroom. Slowly, Josh rose from the bed, seemed ready to plop down once again, and might have, if Lisa hadn't pulled him up by the shoulders.

Lisa was depressed. She wished that she could join the boys, go back to bed and reverse the events of the last few days. By the time she arrived downstairs her mood had lightened a bit. Nate had set the table for four. Scrambled eggs, toast and bacon were laid out on the table. She couldn't remember the last time they had sat together for an unhurried breakfast. Not that breakfast on a school morning could ever be totally unhurried. Lisa smiled at Nate.

"Honey this is so thoughtful of you. Mmmmm, the bacon smells great."

Nate looked across the room at his wife and wished he had stayed in bed with her longer, instead of getting up early to cook. Even in her pajamas she looked sexy.

"I thought you could use a break today. With everything that's happened, it was the least I could do to cheer you up."

Lisa walked over to Nate and hugged him. She kissed him softly on the cheek.

"Nate, I've got to get some clothes on and get ready for work, I'll be back down in a minute. Please be sure the boys start eating. I promise I'll be quick. Eat slow!"

Nate had almost forgotten that Lisa had to go to work that morning, he was still used to her dropping the kids off and coming home. He had considered getting in to work late, and maybe waiting at home for her to return from dropping them off at school for some morning fun in the bedroom. Her having to go to work changed all of that.

"Sure Lisa." I'll put your plate near the stove to keep it warm."

By the time Lisa came downstairs, all dressed in her nurse's uniform and ready for work, the boys had finished their breakfast and Nate was putting their dishes in the dishwasher. Lisa looked at her husband, walked over and kissed him for the second time that morning.

"Thanks, honey. Maybe I can pay you back later."

Nate smiled. "I think I've heard that at least once before!" He returned her kiss, then went up the stairs to put on his tie and jacket.

When Lisa arrived at the office for work she was surprised to find that the only one there was Becky.

"Lisa, I think we forgot to tell you when you were here last week. Dr. Layton is giving a presentation on cleft palate repairs at the hospital this morning and won't be in until ten o'clock."

"Well, it looks like I've got a couple of hours to kill then. I suppose I can help you with the charts and we can call tomorrow's patients to remind them of their appointments."

"That would be great, Lisa. I can show you a thing or two about how the front desk runs. Dr. Layton likes us all to be able to fill in for each other in case of an emergency."

At a little before nine, Dr. Jack Shea entered the office.

"Hi, I'm Dr. Shea, from the pathology department. I was driving past the office on my way to work and thought I'd stop by to talk to Dr. Layton for a minute before he started seeing patients. Is he available?"

"Sorry," answered Becky. He's actually at the hospital giving a talk. He'll be here in an hour. Can we help you?"

"I just came by to let him know that I've found another case similar to Shirley's and wanted to see if he had found out anything more from her past medical history that might shed light on her cause of death. I didn't want to play 'phone tag' and just thought I'd stop by and share coffee with him."

"I wish I could help you. You might do better just to call him around lunch time or I can have him call you. He won't be back until about ten," Becky offered.

Lisa caught the tail end of the conversation and introduced herself to the doctor.

"Hi, I'm Lisa Martin. I replaced Dr. Layton's nurse Shirley. Are you the medical examiner who worked on her case?"

"Yes, I am Mrs. Martin."

"Do you know anything about the Fannestack case?"

Jack assumed Lisa was another news watcher with curiosity regarding the death.

"Actually, I finished the autopsy on Saturday. Her case is also my responsibility."

Lisa looked sad.

"Janetta Fannestack was my best friend. We often went out together. Have you found anything out regarding her death yet?"

Jack found it unusual that all three of his cases somehow seemed to share something in common with Dr. Layton's office

"Lisa, did you work with Shirley?"

"No, she had her unfortunate accident before I arrived."

"I'm sorry, Lisa, patient confidentiality won't allow me to discuss Janetta's findings with you. I can only tell you that as soon as the case can be released to the public I will let you know about anything I've found. It's a little touchy with the police charges involved and all. I know it's a bit one-sided, but perhaps you can help me. Did she ever go to the doctor for medical problems of any type, or complain of feeling ill?"

Lisa understood the ethical dilemma facing Dr. Shea, and understood why he couldn't tell her certain things, but nevertheless felt some resentment at the one-way nature of their conversation.

"Janetta was the one of the healthiest people I knew. She took care of herself. As far as I know, she had no medical problems, though I imagine she went to her gynecologist every year. You might want to check with Dr. Brenda Pennington, we both go to her. Actually we both also saw Dr. Layton for Botox but that doesn't count I imagine."

Jack felt a switch go off in his head.

"You both got Botox?"

"Yes, at different times. At least I think she did. We went to an orientation together and I think she went back afterwards for treatment."

"Does she have a record here that we can check?"

"If she was seen here, she would. Let me check our files."

Lisa walked over and examined the file section labeled "FA" on the charts, for Fannestack. There were no charts with Janetta's name.

"Looks like she wasn't here. Let me check in the computer to see for sure."

Becky assisted Lisa in doing a computer search for Janetta Fannestack and found nothing. There was no record of Janetta having been seen in the office.

"I guess she never made it back here Dr. Shea, unless her office record was already deleted after her death. I thought for sure she told me she had been back to the office. I even remember noticing that her wrinkles looked better."

"Hmmmm. Well please let me know if her records turn up. In the meantime, I guess I'll try Dr. Pennington. Maybe she has some more information. If you think of anything else, please let me know Mrs. Martin. I'll be in touch with Dr. Layton later today."

Upon Dr. Shea leaving the office, Becky continued orienting Lisa to the front desk operations.

"Dr. Layton really isn't much of a computer guy. He still likes to have all his appointments recorded in this schedule book we leave at the desk. It's easy for him to glance at it quickly so he can see who's coming in, without being tied to the computer. We also keep a copy online, but he rarely goes in there."

Lisa looked at the dog-eared appointment book on the desk. It seemed simple enough. The computer scheduling was actually a little more inconvenient, in that multiple blocks of time had to be set aside, depending upon the planned length of Dr. Layton's various procedures. She imagined mastering both methods would not be too difficult at all.

Lisa picked up the book. She searched for her own appointment from a few weeks earlier. She flipped the pages and wished that she could as easily turn back time and bring back her friend. An entry on Tuesday, September 13th caught her attention. The ten a.m. appointment space read Janetta Fannestack.

CHAPTER 34

Detective Kevin Collins had been told more than once that he could double for David Caruso of CSI Miami. Of course living in Florida where the show was based made the comparisons more common. Kevin wasn't really vain, but felt that in the comparison he was getting the raw end of the deal. He thought Caruso was kind of scrawny and a little wimpy and not really all that handsome. But anyway, after fifteen years of marriage and four kids, he didn't give his own appearance too much thought. He was more concerned with paying the bills, catching the bad guys and finding time to spend with his family.

The only thing wrong in his world on this hot Monday Florida morning was the same thing that was usually wrong on Tuesdays, Wednesdays, Thursdays, and Fridays—all of the paperwork he had to complete. Between that, and the press hounding him about the Fannestack case, he had no time to do any real police work.

"Detective Collins, you've got a call."

"Thanks Connie." Kevin picked up the receiver. "Is it another reporter?"

"No, it's a Dr. Shea."

Kevin had been waiting for the call from the Medical Examiner's office. It came none too soon. The brass was breathing down his neck for the forensic results he hoped were completed.

"Good morning, Kevin Collins."

"Good morning Detective, I'm Dr. Jack Shea. We've finished with the autopsy on the Fannestack case. Not much to tell you about the overdose. There were no clinical or histologic findings to suggest physical trauma to the body or forced sexual activity of any kind. You already know about the drug and alcohol levels we found. The only red herring was abnormalities in her brain. It appears that she may have had early Alzheimer's disease and she had a lot of swelling of the brain with some hypertrophy of her brainstem."

"Talk English to me Doc, what does it all mean?"

Jack laughed. It wasn't the first time he had been admonished for speaking "Medicalese".

"It means that she was probably sick before she overdosed. Her brainstem hypertrophy may have caused some changes in her behavior or judgment, though you may want to find a neurologist to better advise you on that. In any case, we're finished on our end. The cause of death will be listed as cerebral edema causing respiratory and cardiac arrest. Complicating factors will be drug overdose, likely causing the acute respiratory event and possibly causing the coma. There was one more thing."

"What's that?" asked the detective.

"There have been a few cases with similar findings lately. Actually, we've had two other cases with almost identical abnormalities. The location of the findings in the brainstem of three otherwise healthy women is very unusual. I spoke with the chief of neuropathology at the Armed Forces Institute of Pathology and he verified our findings. He is unaware of any recent reports of similar cases. All three of the deceased had early Alzheimer's findings in the brain tissue with enlargement of the brainstem in an area called the fornix. The other thing is, they all had some type of connection to Dr. David Layton."

"The plastic surgeon?"

Kevin knew of the popular doctor from charity work. David had been a generous supporter of the Police Athletic League programs for kids. More recently, Kevin had heard the doctor's name in connection with inquiries his wife had made regarding possible breast augmentation. Mrs. Collins had considered breast surgery in an attempt to bring back youthful firmness to her breasts, lost after her four pregnancies. The eight thousand dollar price tag that the surgeon had attached to the surgery made Victoria Secret bras seem the much better bargain and so he told her he loved her just the way she was.

"What's the connection?" Kevin asked.

"One of his nurses died in a car crash, probably after suffering a stroke. A second woman died alone in her apartment and Dr. Layton's name turned up on an appointment card found in her apartment. He denied ever seeing her in the office. And the Fannestack woman had attended a seminar on Botox the doc gave to drum up business, but it seems she may never have made it for the appointment either. Their relatively excellent health and his name seem to be about all the three cases have in common. I dropped by Layton's office this morning to speak with him, but he was out giving a lecture. I was thinking of going back around lunchtime, but maybe it would be better if you did; I really don't have much to add at this point and I've got tons of other work to do at my office."

"Probably the similarities between the three cases are more interesting to you, as a pathologist, than to me as a detective, but I guess with the serious consequences of the charges in the Fannestack case I ought to at least make a call on the doctor. I'll drop by and let him know we spoke. I really appreciate your finishing up on this case and calling— I'm that much closer to getting the press and politicians off my back."

"Sure thing, Detective. Have a good rest of the day." Shea hung up.

Detective Collins was disappointed at the autopsy results. He had hoped to put the yuppy guys behind bars for a long time, at least the one who had admitted to slipping the woman the Roofies. Now it appeared that the asshole would get off lightly. In view of the freely-given admission of guilt, the apparent underlying previous disease, and now, the possible alteration of the victim's behavior due to pre-existing changes in her brain, a good defense attorney could make manslaughter impossible to prove. Three to five years of prison is all the perp would probably get, and his friend would get off with maybe a year or only probation—if his claim of no knowledge of Fannestack having been given any drugs held up.

"Well, at least now I have an excuse to leave this paperwork behind and get out of the office," he thought to himself. Kevin paged his partner, Detective Levine, and grabbed the Pelican Cove phone book to find the address for the office of Dr. David Layton.

CHAPTER 35

"Hi Dr. Layton, sorry to call you during office hours but this is important," Sal began.

David had just returned from his hospital talk. He thought it had gone well, helping to maintain his reputation as a "serious" plastic surgeon.

"What's up Sal?"

"I'm sorry to have to tell you this, David, but another of the mice died. I waited until we had our preliminary pathology reports back. They found brain tissue thickening and Alzheimer disease-like plaques in the brainstem. It appears that we may be dealing with drug-induced side effects from the Botox." Sal took a deep breath.

He had laid it all out as clearly as he could for the doctor. The Botox was causing the side effects and caused the death in the mice as well as in Dr. Layton's nurse.

David felt like the rug had been pulled out from under him. There had been some problems, but Layton still felt that the drug was safe enough to bring to market. He knew that there were risks involved in burying the data from Shirley and Roberta. He doubted that the Fannestack death involved anything more than side effects from her drug overdose. To be safe though, he had managed to make her chart records 'disappear' so that they would not need to be included in his series of office-based Botox patients. The newspaper reported an overdose of drugs and booze as her cause of death and he hoped to avoid any involvement in the case. After all, he wasn't responsible; those two young men were. Records were lost all the time and so much was at stake for David and his future plans. Who could fault him? And why was everything going so wrong all of a sudden?

"Has something changed at the lab, Sal? Everything was fine for months, now all of a sudden it's like the shit has hit the fan. Could there be any problem with our drug preparation?"

Sal paused before answering. He had prepared his answer.

"I've triple-checked everything. I even ran mass spec tests to be certain that the drugs are pure. No problems anywhere that I can tell."

Surely Layton would finally be convinced to abandon the drug, cut his losses and terminate the study. Sal waited for the doctor's response.

"Sal, I've got hundreds of thousands of dollars invested. I don't want to have to admit it, but something is wrong. I'm going to send some of the remaining Botox to Quantum Chemical Labs in Miami. Before we had our own equipment they helped us out and were reliable. I want to check the most recent vials you've sent me. Hold off treatment of any of the animals and just monitor them for now. But don't worry, we'll be able to get up and running soon. I should have an answer for you in two or three days."

"SHIT!" roared inside Sal's head. Why the fuck did things never work out for him. He expected his Italian 'partners' would be at his doorstep any day and didn't think they would appreciate Dr. Layton participating in their business. The doctor was not part of the package he had offered them when they promised to release him from his gambling debts. Sal knew that his leverage at bargaining with these dangerous men was very non-existent. Apparently he had fooled himself into thinking he could rid himself of Dr. Layton easily. The plastic surgeon's relative lack of concern regarding the side effects of the drug and tenacity in bringing the drug to market had not been anticipated by Sal. What could he do now? He had to think of something, but for the moment he had no option other than to agree with the surgeon.

"Okay, Dr. Layton. But no matter what the lab finds, I think the negative findings in our data are going to be a real problem in getting any FDA approval for Phase III human trials. I don't even know if BioVenture will be convinced by our animal data. I wouldn't want to do anything that could harm people. I mean who cares about mice but even overseas they won't tolerate the possibility of neurological side effects in a drug used for cosmetic purposes."

"Don't be so negative, Sal." David wanted to be optimistic, but realized the logic in Sal's words.

He was surprised that Sal didn't seem more disappointed. He knew that the biochemist needed this drug to succeed in order to get his finances in order. Accidents happen. Maybe something simple would turn up that would explain their recent problems with the injected medication. David wasn't ready to quit; to let go of an idea that would shut his father up and give him greater success than even his brother had achieved.

"Sal, we've got so much riding on this. Just keep the troops at the lab going for now, and try to keep those animals alive! I'll be in touch with you in two or three days."

"Okay, Dr. Layton," Sal sighed.

Time for 'Plan B', thought Sal. It definitely wasn't going to be as easy as he had hoped.

CHAPTER 36

"Looks like we missed the boat Kev," Dan winked at his partner as they entered the plastic surgeon's office.

In the waiting area of Layton's plush office, sat two very attractive women. It was obvious that both had received the attention of a plastic surgeon, with breasts disproportionately large for their relatively smaller frames. And both wore especially tight-fitting tops.

"We should have been plastic surgeons."

"You couldn't have handled all the temptation," retorted Collins. "You're much safer around a freckled hunk like me!" Kevin smiled at his partner, then turned his attention to Dr. Layton's receptionist.

"I'm Detective Collins, and this is Detective Levine. We were wondering if we may have a moment of Dr. Layton's time."

What an unusual morning, thought Becky. First the medical examiner, now the police- both unannounced.

"I'm sorry, but Dr. Layton is in surgery right now, and he's running late. If you take a seat, I'll have the nurse tell him you're here and see how long he's going to be. Are you here about Shirley?"

Collins hesitated to reveal the reasons for the visit. It was probably a 'wild goose chase' anyway.

"Not exactly; we're investigating the death of another patient of yours, Janetta Fannestack."

"I think I remember her. I know she was a close friend of one of our nurses, Lisa Martin."

"No kidding. Maybe she would know if Ms. Fannestack has received treatment here. We'll wait. Just let us know about how long it'll be. My partner here gets mean if he misses his lunch and it's getting past his feeding time!"

Becky smiled at the handsome detective, then noticed his wedding band. All the good ones were always taken. Lisa was assisting in surgery, and Paula was getting the rooms ready for other patients. When she was finished, Paula came to the window and asked the officers if she could get them a cup of coffee.

"Sure, that would be great," they replied.

"Why don't you come back here; I'm sure Dr. Layton would rather have you wait for him in his office and not scare away our patients!" Paula opened the door for the men.

Collins and Levine exited the waiting area and followed Paula down the hallway.

"Nice offices," declared Kevin. I'm Detective Collins, and this is Detective Levine."

"Thank you," responded Paula. "I'm Paula Ritter."

"Have you worked here long?"

"About three years."

"It must be very interesting."

"It is. We all enjoy it."

"Paula, maybe you can help us. We understand that Dr. Layton may have treated a woman who died after allegedly being given the date-rape drug."

"You mean the one in the paper?"

"Yes, the one and the same."

"I know she was good friends with Lisa who works here, but I don't recall ever seeing her. You know, we don't spend much time with some of the patients. If she received Botox, she may have only been here for a few minutes. One of the other nurses might have spoken with her. You may want to check with Barbara, but she's off today."

"How about Roberta Cook? Does that name ring a bell?"

"Sure, I do remember her; maybe late fifties or early sixties, in good shape. I remember because I was there when Dr. Layton gave her Botox and we talked about country music. We both love Kenny Chesney."

The detectives tried to keep their best poker faces.

"How many times was she here?"

"She didn't do anything wrong did she?" asked Paula. "As I recall, she was here maybe one other time. I think I remember seeing her name on the schedule one day, but I wasn't around to see her when she came back."

Dan responded, "Actually Paula, the only thing she did wrong was pass away. She died alone in her apartment, and Dr. Layton's name was on an appointment card that was found in her place. We just thought he might know something about her health."

"Well Dr. Layton is very good at remembering all of his patients, so if anyone can help you, he can. I'll go find her record for you."

When she was out of sight, Kevin whispered to his partner.

"What do you think Dan? Dr. Shea definitely told me that Layton said he didn't remember treating the Cook woman."

"It does sound a little fishy, but he must see lots of women with the same stories."

Paula returned empty-handed.

"I'm at a loss, I couldn't find the chart and I searched in the computer to see if I could find any information in there and she wasn't even registered as a patient. I also checked on Dr. Layton, and his case is going to take at least another half hour. After that we have two more patients in the waiting room so I doubt we will be free until about three o'clock. He wanted to know if it was possible for you to come back then."

Kevin looked at Dan. This was more interesting than he had planned. A return appointment would give the detectives a good excuse to ignore their paperwork, enjoy a long lunch and probably get to see more beautiful women in the doctor's waiting room when they came back.

"No problem, we'll be back at three." Kevin handed Paula his business card.

"One last question before we go. Do you delete the records of deceased patients?"

"Sometimes we do—that's probably what happened. Usually though, for legal purposes, we keep the hard copies in storage for seven years. The Cook record should be somewhere. We'll figure it out when Dr. Layton comes out of surgery."

CHAPTER 37

Manzari went into his office at Youth Labs and closed the door. He was having trouble keeping his thoughts focused as his dreams of success were fading. Layton's persistence in finding an explanation for the laboratory deaths was a disaster. He knew that there was a way he could eliminate Layton from the Botox trials. Bobby Volpe would be very angry that Layton was still part of the picture. Volpe was rumored to be very successful at terminating unwanted relationships. Shit. Sal wanted a cigarette, but hadn't smoked in two years and anyway, there were none around. He did what he too often did when stressed— he turned on his computer.

Sal entered Legion of Poker.com and waited for the site to show on his screen. This was his 'low stakes' site. Here he could play for as little as five dollars a bet. "I'll only play with forty bucks," he said to himself. "If I double I'll quit." Sal took an open 'seat' at a virtual table and waited for the round to begin. After two minutes, the ten positions at the table were filled and the play began.

His first cards were a three of hearts and a nine of diamonds. He folded without paying the 'blind' or ante into the pot. "Nothing lost yet," he thought. The flop came up with an eight, a nine and a five. He would have had a strong hand, the high pair. "My lousy luck, I should have stayed in." Three players stayed in and next came the 'turn' card, another nine.

"I give up; when I should win I lose and when I should lose, I still lose," Sal grumbled.

The pot grew as all three players bet against each other. The river card came as a six. Sal watched with minimal interest. Two players bet against each other as the third dropped out. "I wonder if somebody's got the seven." A seven in the pocket cards would give someone a strong hand. Sal smiled as the cards were turned up. One player had the seven, giving him a straight, but the other had a seven and a ten, an even higher straight. "For once I wasn't the one who got screwed." Sal knew that if he had stayed in, he would have had a hard time not betting big with what would have been three nines, and would have lost to either of the other two players who finished with straights.

The next round began. Sal's cards were an Ace of hearts and a six of hearts. "Not bad," he thought to himself. He paid his ante to stay in the action. Six players of the original ten stayed in. The flop was a Queen of hearts, a King of spades and a seven of hearts. Sal was one card away from a flush, a powerful hand, especially with the Ace in his hand. He decided to play possum and 'checked'. The player next to him at the virtual table bet $10, double the blind. Sal stayed in. There were now five players left.

The next card was an Ace of diamonds. Not bad, but not great. Sal imagined that there was a good chance that one of the remaining players might have an Ace with a higher 'kicker' or second pocket card. His six wasn't all that high, joined up with his own Ace. As if to confirm his suspicions, the player two spots over made another $10 bet. Everyone folded and it was Sal's turn to match the bet, raise it, or fold.

"One card to a flush, probably gonna lose to the asshole who just bet," he sighed.

He couldn't pass up the opportunity of getting the 'nuts' or winning flush hand. He pressed the key indicating he was still in and his account was depleted of another $10. The last card, the 'river' came. He had been the victim of finding himself going 'down the river' many times, getting screwed on the last card in the hand. On the screen, a King of hearts flashed. Sal's heart almost jumped out of his chest. "About time," he thought. Sal tried to stay calm. His partner at the table, the only other player remaining, bet the pot, the most allowed under the parameters of the particular game. The bet was for $130. Sal remembered his plan not to bet more than $30, but saw no way he could lose. His opponent would have to have a full house or four Kings to beat him, both unlikely. He matched the bet and raised it by the most allowed, another $130. The pot was now at $390. He waited. Sal could feel adrenaline course through his body and sweat began to form in circles under his armpits. His opponent re-raised another $130. The pot was now $650. Sal stayed in. No further raises were permitted.

After a two or three second delay, Sal watched as the pile of chips was moved by the computer 'dealer' from the middle of the cyber table to his seat. His smile stretched from ear to ear. He had WON!

"Nice hand" his opponent instant messaged, using the shorthand 'nh'. "I had three Kings."

"Tx" Sal messaged back—shorthand for thanks.

The next hand was dealt to the ten players. Almost simultaneously, Sal's cell phone rang.

It was Bobby Volpe.

"Hi Sal. How are ya?"

"Fine, Mr. Volpe." A four and a nine were his pocket cards. Sal folded.

"I hope so, I'm counting on ya. Listen, I've had a chance to present your drug data to my adviser. He tells me that this is a good thing. We are ready to commit some real money and are gonna want ya to continue with tests on your animals. We also think we'll be able to speed up gettin' your FDA approval. They might not be the easiest people to deal with, but I think we can speak a language they understand."

Sal imagined he was referring to bribing the FDA.

"That would be good," Sal answered lamely.

"I've got some papers I'm gonna need ya to sign to make it all legit. This is gonna be all above-board and legal. Can ya meet me at my office at the Structure Furniture Showroom Wednesday night?"

Volpe had business interests all over Pelican Cove, along with several in surrounding Florida towns. Some, like Structure Furniture, were for the most part legitimate. Sal knew he had gambling and extortion operations and probably also dealt in drugs and prostitution.

"Sure Mr. Volpe, what time?"

"Nine-thirty, after the store is closed—and call me Bobby. We're gonna be partners!"

CHAPTER 38

David hated running behind schedule at the office. Between giving his talk, the disturbing phone call from Sal, and the distraction of the police officers' visit, he was running forty minutes behind. He wondered what, exactly, the two officers could possibly want with him. Their interest in him left him feeling anxious.

The detectives were again seated in Dr. Layton's office.

"Look at the old maps, Kev. I bet they set the Doc back a pretty penny."

The officers had eaten at their favorite Mexican restaurant and Dan had managed to get refried beans on his pants. There was a wet stain on his thigh where he had tried to wash it off with water. In addition, there were traces of grease at the corner of his mouth that his napkin had missed. Collins looked at his partner and considered mentioning the greasy face, but just then Dr. Layton entered.

Both officers stood to greet the doctor.

"Good afternoon, I'm David Layton."

"Good afternoon, Doctor," responded Kevin. "I'm Detective Kevin Collins and this is my partner, Detective Dan Levine."

David shook both their hands and noticed a wet stain on the shorter detective's thigh. He didn't say anything and waited for the men to present the purpose of their visit.

"You're probably wondering why we're here Dr. Layton. We spoke to Dr. Jack Shea this morning and he's come across three unusual cases that have required his attention as medical examiner. None of his cases are related in any way, except for having very similar and unusual changes in their brain tissues. And all three women had some kind of link to your office."

Color drained from David's face as his anxiety mounted. He became light-headed; the lack of food in his stomach certainly didn't help.

"Doc, are you okay? You look pale." Detective Collins stared at the doctor.

"I'm fine," Layton tried to compose himself.

"I missed my lunch today and thinking about Shirley still upsets me."

David hoped that his quick response would appease the officers.

"I think you know about your nurse's autopsy already. Dr. Shea advised us that a second woman died with similar neurological findings." Dan looked at his notes and continued—"a Roberta Cook. The third case you might have read about in the papers. And we'll have to hold you to professional confidentiality here, but the woman involved in the Roofie date-rape death also had the same findings. Your nurse, Paula, informed us that the Cook woman had been treated here a few weeks ago....." Dan let the words trail off as a question, hoping to encourage a response from the doctor.

"I may have treated her, but we haven't been able to find her chart. I should probably have a better protocol for the disposal of the records of patients who pass away. If they have had any surgery in our office, we normally keep them for seven years. Sometimes, if they only come for a cosmetic surgery consultation or non-invasive treatment with Botox or a filler treatment we just shred the record. If Paula said she remembers her, I'm sure I did treat her."

"Has Janetta Fannestack ever been treated here?" Now it was Detective Collins directing the questioning.

Dr. Layton felt the lies piling up. He had placed Janetta's file with the others, in his desk under lock and key. Unfortunately, he knew his staff might recall Ms. Fannestack coming to the office for the Botox. Barbara had been the nurse in the room with him at the time. Fortunately, she was not present to answer the officer's questions. Surely they wouldn't be coming back to talk to the nurse about a case that involved a confession and an involuntary drug overdose. He decided to plead forgetfulness once again.

"I remember Ms. Fannestack because her best friend Lisa became my nurse. I may have treated her before Lisa came to work for me, but I'm afraid I'm not the best at remembering patients that don't spend much time in my office. Her record may have come to the same end as the others. I just don't remember."

Kevin thought to himself, "for a smart doctor, he sure has a crummy memory. Then again, maybe all he cares about is taking their money." He had an idea.

"If they came to the office, wouldn't there be a record of the payments they made for their visits. Like a credit card receipt or check entry?"

David recalled canceling the transaction in the computer for the Cook woman. The paper records were stored off-site and were not easily available. From watching TV cop shows, he new that he did not have to reveal his records to the officers without a warrant. Still, he didn't want to seem to be hiding anything. He also recalled deleting the Fannestack record from the computer, but her visit had been more recent. The receipts from her visit should be in storage by now but David was still uneasy. He decided to act as if he had nothing to hide.

"We can check the computer for their transaction records if you'd like."

"I think that would be a waste of time, Paula checked for Roberta Cook's record this morning and didn't find anything in the computer. I guess you can look for the Fannestack record, but it's really the medical history that would be more interesting. I don't imagine your Botox caused any damage to either woman," the detective commented.

Dan seemed to be losing his interest in the case. It was getting close to quitting time for the detectives.

"You didn't buy any of that cheap Botox from Canada on the internet did you?" asked Detective Collins half in jest.

There had been several cases of doctors buying budget-priced Botox that was impure. It had been implicated in illness in a few well known cases in Florida.

"Of course not Detective! I can show you our invoices if you'd like."

Detective Collins was highly trained in picking up on attempts at deception. He perceived a slight rise in the tone of the surgeon's voice during his last response. Voluntarily offering copies of his invoices, when not actually asked to produce them, was also suspicious. He had no doubt that if any contaminated Botox had been administered, any invoices or evidence of its purchase would be long gone. But only a fool would risk losing his license and harming his patients just to save a few bucks by buying cheap, adulterated medication. From the appearance of the office, Dr. Layton wasn't hurting for a few bucks. He might be hiding something, but probably not the use of Canadian Botox.

"No, that's quite alright, Dr. Layton, that won't be necessary. But could you please check for Ms. Fannestack in your computer?"

David buzzed over to his receptionist from his desk phone. "Becky, can you check the computer and see if we have a Janetta Fannestack."

Becky's reply was heard by everyone – the phone was set on 'speakerphone.' "I don't have to check Dr. Layton; I tried to find it this morning and came up with nothing. Dr. Shea asked me to search when he came looking for you earlier."

David was getting tired of all of the attention being directed at his patients and his office. Becky hadn't advised him that Shea had asked to search his computer records. He would have to speak to her about not allowing anyone into the records in the future. At least without first checking with him. Regardless, it was clear that the record wasn't available.

"I guess that's about as much as I can do for you detectives. I can try to see if we have any receipts in the archives we've stored offsite if you'd like."

Dan yawned while Collins answered.

"I don't think we'll need that, Dr. Layton. Thank you for your time. And sorry about the death of your nurse."

The doctor shook hands with each of the detectives, who then departed through the employee entrance. Doctor Layton had two patients waiting for him in the reception area and didn't want the sight of the detectives, in plainclothes but carrying holstered guns, to frighten his upscale patients.

Dan stepped outside and began walking to their unmarked police cruiser.

"He sure doesn't seem to keep his records around for very long," Dan remarked.

"Dr. Layton is hiding something Dan, I'm sure of it."

"I don't see how it has any relevance to our perps though. He couldn't have anything to do with the Fannestack death that I can see."

"Me neither Dan, unless it has something to do with the Botox, but that wouldn't make any sense. If it was unsafe, lots of people would be sick. I just can't shake this feeling that he's hiding something."

Detective Collins was a legend at the precinct for his ability to pick up on deception. Dan rubbed his chin.

"We've got a shit-load of paperwork already Kev. This case looks pretty straightforward to me. The roofie dudes plead guilty and we rap this thing up. Can't we just have an easy one for a change?"

Kevin got a far-away look in his eyes and got into the cruiser.

"I just know he's hiding something Dan."

The detectives drove away. They didn't notice Dr. Layton peering at them from behind the blinds of his office window.

CHAPTER 39

S al pulled his old Buick up to the Structure Furniture Showroom at 9:15 on Wednesday evening. He knew better than to keep Mr. Volpe waiting.

The store closed at nine and the employees had already gone home. Volpe had his own office in the back of the building. Vic Chifolo was standing at the plate glass entrance maintaining a silent guard. He looked like an enormous black vulture.

"Nice to see you again, Vic." Sal mocked friendliness at the stoic Sicilian.

Vic grunted what passed for hello.

"Mr. Volpe is waitin' for ya, come with me."

Vic let him into the store and locked the entrance behind Sal. The chemist felt trapped alone with the hoodlum. They weren't going to try to kill him, were they?

The store was a typical square showroom filled with furniture destined for condominiums in Florida. It contained low-end pieces, competing with the larger Rooms To Go type of stores. Some of the prices were cheaper here than in the larger stores. Sometimes, the furniture had been stolen from freight arriving from Indonesia and China which had been 'lost'. As long as the shippers got their insurance money, no one ever complained much.

In the back was the billing office and quiet meeting room where Bobby Volpe was waiting. He was busy watching the Yankees play the Twins in one of the final regular season games of the year.

"Hey Sal. Thanks for comin' early. I like that. Whadya think of this A-Rod the Yanks got? It's not enough the guy can run and catch the ball, but he whacks it harder than Bonds does. Ya think he does steroids too?"

"You know me Bobby, I'm trying to stay away from the sports. Too much temptation to bet for me."

Bobby laughed.

"Good to see ya can learn from your mistakes Sallie. You should stay away from that stuff if ya want to keep your shit in order. I was going to mention that to ya. Anyway, enough chit-chat. Let's talk business. Have a seat. I've got some papers here for ya to sign."

Sal sat down across from Bobby at a heavy mahogany desk. There were pictures of Bobby's family in little frames at either corner. He had two married daughters and three grandchildren. There was a bucolic picture of the proud grandfather with a little boy on his knee, and spaghetti sauce pressed on the mobster's nose. Just like the Sopranos, Sal thought to himself.

Bobby reached into his desk and pulled out a manila folder containing legal-size papers. He reached across and passed the papers and a pen to Sal.

"Go ahead and read them if ya want, Sal. I have to say, it's a good deal. We're going to give ya ten percent of all the profits in the business. On top of that, I'm going to give ya two G's a week salary. Not bad since we've got to swallow the $60,000 gamblin' debt ya were already into us for. Ya won't see that part in the contract; we'll just call it our little understandin'."

Sal wasn't in a position to bargain. He supposed he could live with ten percent and knew it really didn't matter; it wasn't negotiable. The deal he had arranged with Dr. Layton had included maintaining a 50% joint stake in the business, with the remaining 50% to be owned by the BioVenture group. Of course, they weren't going to pay off his gambling debts and they didn't have any [powerful connections at the FDA.

Sal signed the papers and handed them back to Bobby, along with the mobster's gold-trimmed Monte Blanc pen. He could smell Volpe's strong musk cologne on the pen as it passed from his hands.

"You're very quiet, Sal. What's the matter, ya don't think the contract is fair?"

Sal had anticipated this conversation, took a deep breath and steadied himself for what might happen next.

"The contract is very fair Mr. Volpe. It's more than fair. But I have a little problem."

"What type of little problem, Sal?" Bobby knew that when someone said they had a 'little problem' it sometimes meant they had a big problem.

"I have an arrangement with a doctor who has been paying the bills at the lab and we're kind of partners."

Bobby looked at Sal before he spoke.

"Sal, I don't know what shit ya got yourself into with any doctor, but the only partnership is between us and only us? Whatever other arrangement ya made, get out of it. If it's a matter of some money maybe we'll give ya another loan, but you're going to have to pay for it out of your ten percent. Don't make me regret being easy with ya on your debt. Ya won't get any second chances if ya screw up."

"It may not be that easy, Bobby. He's spent a lot of his own money and we have an agreement. I've been trying to discourage him the last few weeks—to get him to want out of our deal, but it hasn't worked."

"Look Sal, maybe we're not speakin' the same language here. I promise ya, whatever trouble he gives ya about breaking his partnership with ya is nothing' compared to the trouble we'd have if our deal isn't honored. He doesn't know about us does he?"

"Of course not, Mr. Volpe."

Perspiration was making his shirt stick to the skin of his armpits and he felt the back of the chair adhering to his sweaty spine-not to mention he had to pee.

"I've been trying to get the data from the lab to look less positive so he might just want to walk away from the whole thing. He should have already, especially after I arranged to have some of the lab animals die."

Volpe thought carefully before he spoke. He stretched his arms out in front of him and raised his voice.

"Sal, I can be a very persuasive man when I have to be. My 'persuasion methods' are a little bit different than yours-and they cost a lot. I think ya better keep working at convincing the doctor that he should give up on this drug. Get it all signed and legal so he can't come back after you and try to say ya stole his idea. But if ya absolutely can't, and ya need me to take over the persuadin', come back to me in a week and we'll talk again."

Bobby got up and walked across the desk to Sal's seat—towering over the balding biochemist.

"Don't mistake my generosity for weakness Sal. I am very angry at your not telling me sooner about this side agreement ya had with the doctor. Very angry. I'm a grandfather now; I want things to go easy. This was supposed to go easy. Don't fuck with me. Make the doctor think it's smart for him to give up his wonder drug. And do it soon."

He pulled Sal up by his shoulders and the heavy man's shirt tails pulled out from his pants.

"And lose some weight Sal, jeez you're sweatin' like a fuckin' pig."

Sal rose from his seat, the vinyl of the chair stuck to the sweaty seat of his pants, making an embarrassing sucking sound as he rose. He was happy to be leaving the meeting without bodily injury and worked at shaking off the verbal abuse and threats from Volpe. He had expected worse.

"Thanks, Bobby. I won't let you down. I know I should have let you in on things sooner. It won't happen again."

"Sallie that is one thing ya better be right about." Vic escorted Sal out of the Structure building and into the muggy sulfurous evening air.

"Goodnight Vic."

The thug looked at Sal with hooded eyes, stepped back into the store and grunted as he locked the door behind him.

CHAPTER 40

Lisa felt the bed move as her husband awakened to his alarm. Nate yawned like a bear rising from hibernation. It was still early, only 6:15 on Thursday. "All I have to do is get the boys to the bus stop and then I can go back to bed for a couple of hours," Lisa thought. Then, with a start, she remembered she had to go to work today to make up for taking time off in order to attend Janetta's funeral. Attending had been depressing. She dreaded having to discuss her friend's passing with anyone at work and wished she could just go back to sleep. Reluctantly, she forced herself to crawl out of bed and went to rouse the boys.

The children still shared a room, though she and Nate had discussed converting the study into a bedroom for Shawn. They got along well, but were growing older and had expressed a desire for rooms of their own. Josh wanted to decorate his space with pictures of fishing, while Shawn currently preferred pictures of stars of the Miami Heat and had photos of skyscraper-tall basketball players plastered on the wall on his side of the room. She cherished her two little angels lying motionless in their beds. Lisa walked over to Josh first, and wiped a stray wisp of hair from his eyes. Her sadness lifted, as it always did around her sons. Seeing them lying there, full of life's promise, made Lisa miss her deceased friend. She wondered what she would do if one of her boys ever became seriously ill or, God forbid, passed away. Pushing the thoughts out of her mind, Lisa kissed Josh on the forehead. He stirred, then slowly opened his eyes and smiled. "What a precious child," she thought.

"Good morning, honey."

"Good morning, Mom. Love you."

Josh was still young enough to be uninhibited at expressing his love for his mom. Lisa has noticed that lately, Shawn had been a little less openly affectionate. Her 'babies' were growing up.

"Love you more, Josh. Time to get up. I'm going to make you one of your favorites, blueberry pancakes."

"Mmmmmmmm, "Josh smiled and jumped out of bed.

Next, Lisa went over to Shawn's bed where he was still sound asleep, not disturbed at all by the conversation at the adjacent bed and the overhead light illuminating the room. Shawn's breathing sounded a little louder than usual; he was suffering through a slight cold and had been coughing the day before. Nate sent him to school Wednesday and he had made it through the day without the school nurse calling home to have him picked up. Lisa placed her hand on his head, and immediately noticed that he felt warm. Shawn was oblivious to her touch. Feeling panic, Lisa shook her son gently until the boy's eyelashes fluttered as he focused on his mom.

"I don't feel good Mom. My head hurts."

It was unlike her kids to get sick, especially Shawn. He was proud of his perfect school attendance, attested to by a certificate hanging over the desk in his room.

"Let's check your temperature." Lisa went back into her own bathroom and returned with a thermometer, popping it into his mouth.

"Leave it in for a couple of minutes, Shawn. I'll be back in a minute. Don't take it out till I get back."

"Mummmmpphh," Shawn mumbled around the thermometer, exaggerating his inability to speak with the thermometer in his mouth.

Lisa got Josh his school clothes and started some coffee brewing, then returned to check on Shawn. His face looked flushed.

The thermometer read just over 101 degrees.

"Looks like no school for you today big guy. Let me get you some Tylenol."

"I think I can go Mom."

"Sorry Shawn; I want you to take it easy at home today. If you're better, you can go back to school on Friday."

"What about my attendance record?"

"Even Lou Gehrig couldn't play every day honey. You need to stay home today. No arguments."

Then Lisa remembered that she had to go to work.

"Shoot, I've got to work until noon today."

"I can stay home alone Mom."

"No you can't Shawn. Maybe Dad can stay home with you in the morning until I get back. Let me go get you some Tylenol, you stay in bed."

Lisa went back into her bedroom where Nate had finished showering and was getting dressed.

"Nate, we've got a problem. Shawn is too sick to go to school and I have to go to work. Could you stay home with him this morning? I know that Paula has a doctor's appointment today and can't come to work. I'm still in my probationary period and don't want to leave Dr. Layton short-handed. I'll be home by around 12:30."

"Lisa, I'm swamped at work and if I'm not there it'll send the wrong message to the partners. I don't want them to think that I'm not committed 100% to the firm. If they think that I can be tied up babysitting, they may put me on the slow tract and I may never make partner."

"What about me, Nate; I'm already your partner and I need your help."

"Look honey, I appreciate your desire to work. But now it's interfering with your caring for the kids. I'm still the breadwinner and we need my salary and job to support us. You can miss work a lot easier than I can and it matters less."

Anger boiled inside of her. She had always done whatever he needed to promote his job and profession. For Christ's sake she had even stopped working. Sometimes there were weeks when she practically raised the boys single-handedly. All of the years of missed dinners, changed plans, disappointments she had put up with because of his job! She felt like she had asked for very little and worked very hard and put up with it very well- thanklessly.

"It may matter less to you, but it matters VERY MUCH TO ME. Fine, I'll take care of things at home, you go try to make partner. It must be nice to be so damn important!."

"Please don't be like that Lisa," Nate responded.

"I don't like you very much right now Nate. Just go to work and leave me alone."

Lisa began to cry out of frustration. Nate came over to try to console her but Lisa turned her back to him and moved away. She picked the Tylenol bottle out of the medicine cabinet. She walked out of the bedroom, leaving her husband staring at her back.

"What's the matter, Mom?" Josh was sitting at the breakfast table, enjoying his pancakes.

Nate was also seated, quietly filling his mouth with gulps of coffee and forkfuls of yellow pancakes soaked in syrup.

"I'm just concerned about Shawn, Josh. Finish up so I can take you to school."

Lisa averted Nate's gaze and directed her attention to tidying the kitchen. If Josh noticed their lack of communication, he chose not to mention it.

"I'll take Josh to the bus stop if you'd like, then you don't have to leave the house," offered Nate.

Yeah, right, keep me in the house, barefoot and pregnant, thought Lisa to herself. It was obvious that Nate was trying to make amends for his lack of consideration previously. Although she wanted nothing to do with it, she didn't want to make a scene in front of her younger son, and wanted to appear courteous.

"Okay, that would be fine," she managed to reply trying not to sound too angry.

Lisa felt herself beginning to cry again, but didn't want to break down in front Josh. She stood up and started out of the kitchen.

"I'm going to try to go back to bed with Shawn. Make sure Josh takes his lunch from the refrigerator." Lisa walked over to her son, kissed his cheek and managed a smile.

"I'll see you this afternoon, honey."

Lisa walked over and placed a dry kiss goodbye on her husband's cheek. There was little love for her husband in the demonstration of affection. She felt lonely and isolated and wondered what she would say to Dr. Layton about missing work. One thing was for sure, she wasn't going to give up her job without a fight.

Returning upstairs, Lisa handed Shawn two Tylenol and a glass of water and watched him swallow them. She knew she had to bite the bullet and call Dr. Layton. He had given her his home number so she thought she should try that first since no one would be at the office yet.

"I'll be back in a few minutes, Shawn." Lisa got out of bed and left the room, closing the door softly behind her.

David answered the phone on the first ring.

"Dr. Layton, it's Lisa Martin."

"Hi Lisa. Are you back in Florida?"

"Yes, Dr. Layton, and thanks for letting me have the time off."

"Of course—no problem. What's up?"

"One of my sons is sick with a cold and I don't have anyone to watch him this morning. I'm afraid I won't be able to come to work."

"Wow, that's tough. Paula has an appointment with her gynecologist this morning and Barbara called me yesterday evening. She went out for dinner and has been on the pot every hour since. She was going to call me this morning if she felt better, but left a message on my voice-mail this morning telling me that she was still sick. How bad is your son?"

"He just has a cold but his temperature was 101 this morning and he can't go to school. I've given him some Tylenol and he's resting in bed."

"I don't want to be pushy Lisa, but I have a pull-out bed in my private office. What if you brought your son here and came to work? I have a TV and DVD player that he can use. You're only supposed to work for half a day anyway. We've got a busy Thursday morning scheduled and we sure could use your help. If he feels crappy after he's here, you can always take him home."

Lisa considered his offer. "That sounds okay, Dr. Layton, as long as you know I may not be able to stay if he's feeling too sick. He's usually as strong as a horse. I may be a little late, but I can be there by a little past nine."

"Thank you so much Lisa, you're the best. I'll have the pull-out couch ready for him when you get here."

"Thanks Dr. Layton; I'll see you soon."

Lisa wished her husband had been half as understanding as her boss. Her mood lifted some as she showered and dressed for the day.

CHAPTER 41

The nicest thing about Thursday was that it was the day before Friday. Detective Collins was eager to leave work on Friday and head to the Florida Keys for a weekend of fishing with his college buddies. It had become more difficult to get away lately, but the group still managed to get together at least a couple of times a year. Kevin entered the building that housed the 13th Precinct offices and the jail for the city of Pelican Cove. He was assaulted by the sweet-sick odor of a passing alcoholic who had been released moments earlier. The building was quiet.

Kevin spied the open door of his department chief, Captain Fred Pincer. Pincer was not your typical police officer, having been in the department twenty-five years and had risen in the ranks after graduating from the police academy. Pincer was popular, but rarely mingled with the other men. He cared for his sister, who had Down's syndrome and lived with him. She worked full-time at the supermarket as a 'bagger' and helper, but needed supervision. Captain Pincer had never married, and now, at forty-nine, seemed destined never to do so. The Captain stayed fit, went to the gym daily and had a black belt in one of the martial arts, but his appearance betrayed none of this. He looked a lot like the guy who had starred as Mr. Rogers, in "Mr. Roger's Neighborhood."

"Good morning, Captain."

"Good morning, Kevin. What's up?"

"Glad to say, not much. Dan and I followed up on the Fannestack case. There may be a little problem there for the DA since it seems the victim may have had some complicating factors in her death. There were some abnormalities in her brain that may have caused her coma even without the drug overdose. The interesting thing is that there have been two other deaths with similar brain findings."

"Anything suspicious about those deaths?"

"That's the wrinkle, Captain. There may be. All three victims were women with some kind of tie to a plastic surgeon in town, Dr. Layton. One worked for him, and two had seen him for some cosmetic surgery."

"And?"

Kevin sensed his boss getting impatient, so he spoke faster.

"Dan and I went over to meet the doctor and he's legit and all, but I couldn't keep from feeling that he's covering something up. One of his staff remembered at least one of the vics having been there, but the doctor denied remembering her and the records are gone."

Pincer smiled. "Kev, you know I love you and your intuition, but this one sounds a little remote. I think it would be best if we just let the DA decide what to do with the Fannestack case now that the autopsy results are completed. Between that and the confession, John Q Public has been served and we can move on."

"Any chance of getting a warrant to check on the doctor's records? Something might turn up."

"Absolutely not. I'm not going to smear a doctor's reputation based on your hunch and I doubt the judge would give you a warrant just to 'go fishing' at the doc's office."

"Could Dan and I go back once more just to see if maybe our first visit jogged his memory?"

Pincer sighed. Things were pretty quiet at the department.

"Okay, just one more visit, tomorrow, after all of your paperwork is completed. I want all of your reports completed and on my desk today. I see you've put in for a day off Monday. Up to no good in the Keys again?"

"Yup, I'm gonna go fishing with the buddies."

"Well, make sure I don't read about anything you do down there in the papers." Pincer grinned at his detective.

"Don't worry Captain, what happens in the Keys, stays in the Keys." Kevin smiled as he walked out of the office and ambled over to his messy desk.

"Damn, I hate paperwork," he muttered.

CHAPTER 42

The drive to work was difficult for Lisa. Shawn had fallen asleep in the back seat, covered in a blanket. Lisa had dressed him in sweat pants and a sweat shirt, but he still said he felt cold. She imagined he would feel better once the Tylenol had taken effect. As much as she tried to fight the lingering feelings of anger, resentment at her husband boiled inside her and refused to go away.

Arriving a little late for work she recognized the cars of her co-workers parked in the lot. She found a spot next to David's Mercedes, parked her car and shook Shawn gently. He felt a little less warm.

"Whuuuut," he muttered.

Lisa realized that he didn't know where he was, after having fallen asleep in the car.

"We're at the office, Shawn. You have to get out."

Shawn looked around and regained his bearings. Lisa grabbed a bag she had packed with his MP3 player, some books and the bagged lunch she had previously prepared for him to have at school. They entered the building through the back entrance and walked straight to Dr. Layton's office.

The office door was half ajar. Lisa knocked once and entered. Dr. Layton was seated at his desk peering into a manila file. Lisa got the distinct sense that she had surprised him, and that whatever the doctor was reading was not intended for her eyes. The doctor seemed startled, quickly closed the file and placed it in his desk drawer. Only then did he look up and smile at Lisa and Shawn.

"Good morning! Your son looks just like you Lisa. He's a handsome guy. Sorry you're not feeling too hot this morning young man."

"Dr. Layton, this is Shawn. Say good morning Shawn."

"Good morning." Shawn looked longingly at the sleeper sofa which the doctor had opened and prepared for him. There were fresh sheets and an oversized pillow.

David reached in his pocket and removed a small key. He then locked his desk drawer, utilizing the lock integrated into the side of the cabinet. He shook Shawn's hand. "Pleased to meet you, Shawn. Would you like some breakfast? I picked up some Egg McMuffins for you and your mom on the way here this morning."

Shawn felt his stomach grumble.

"Can I Mom?"

Lisa was encouraged by her son's appetite, imagining that it meant he couldn't be too sick.

"Sure. That was so nice of you Dr. Layton."

Lisa looked at the doctor as she spoke and their eyes met. She had thought that she was over her attraction to the man, but her poise disappeared as she melted into his twinkling blue eyes. Her heart caught in her chest and she felt her face flush. Lisa turned away in order to regain her composure. The moment was not lost on David.

Layton was touched by the love and caring of Lisa for her son. He longed for the close relationship she shared with her offspring. And what a looker she was. If only he could find a woman who had her act all together like Lisa, he might finally settle down.

"Let's go get some food into you two, then you can crash in my office Shawn." David led the Martins to the kitchen where fresh coffee and the bag of McMuffins were waiting. There was also a stack of four small red paper boxes labeled "Apple Pie".

Shawn reached for the dessert. Lisa grabbed his arm.

"Eat the McMuffin first, Shawn, dessert after."

"Please Mom…"

David smiled. Living alone, he missed these common interactions. Lisa smiled at Shawn.

"I'm sure you'll have no trouble eating both, but hit the McMuffin first please young man."

"Okay, Mom."

"Lisa, I'll leave you two alone. We already have several patients waiting. As soon as you're done, settle Shawn in my office and find me."

"Okay, Dr. Layton."

David left the office, but as he walked out, and before he was too far down the hallway, he could overhear Shawn's comment to his mother.

"He's really nice, Mom."

CHAPTER 43

"Morning Ed."

"Morning, boss."

"You got here early. Is everything okay?" Sal questioned.

"Everything is alright at the lab. Problems at home, but I really don't want to talk about it," responded the lab tech.

Manzari knew that Ed had been living with someone for the past several months. He had never met Ed's 'friend', but thought that there had been problems of late. There had been several long cell phone calls which Ed had taken outside the lab for privacy, and Sal had a feeling they had been from Ed's partner. The thought of two guys together repulsed Manzari, though he was open-minded enough to appreciate his assistant's abilities and value him as an employee. Ed was irreplaceable in his dependability, knowledge and capabilities.

"All the animals look okay?"

"Yes, we haven't had any illness—at least none that I can see. Do you want me to administer any more medication this morning?"

"Not yet; I'm going to make some more Botox today. I'd prefer to use the fresh medication. We can inject it later today or tomorrow."

"No problem. I've got lots of paperwork to do anyway. It'll give me a chance to catch up," Ed stated with a relieved sigh.

Sal really wasn't sure what to do. He didn't want to harm all of his laboratory animals with the esterified medication, so he had to go back to the old formulation, which had been safe and successful. If he used the old formula, Dr. Layton would never be persuaded to stop the study – the results would be too good. To complicate matters further, the doctor was going to have the Botox analyzed and would know soon enough that the drug had been tampered with. He would have to go back to running the lab on the up and up and find some other way to get Dr. Layton to want to terminate the study.

Sal's mind tried to focus. How could he get rid of Dr. Layton? He knew he couldn't buy him out of the partnership. And the doctor had no inclination to voluntarily end the study. What could he do? Manzari went into his office to think, but no long-term alternatives came to mind. He absentmindedly watched Ed pouring over paperwork at the lab table as he thought to himself, "I need to at least buy myself some more time." His relationship with the doctor would certainly become more complicated if Layton discovered that intentional tampering with the Botox formula had occurred. A plan began to take shape in Manzari's turbulent mind. If it worked, it might buy him enough time to end his problems with at least one of his two partners.

CHAPTER 44

Lisa took the liberty of remaining with Shawn for a few minutes after they had finished their McDonald's breakfast.

"How are you feeling honey?"

"Better, Mom. I'm kind of tired. Do you think I could go to sleep on the couch?"

"That's what it's there for—just for you!" Lisa walked Shawn over to the prepared bed and tucked him in. She touched the back of her hand to his head.

"You don't feel anywhere near as warm, Shawn."

"I know. I don't feel cold anymore either. I think it was the apple pie that made me feel better." He smiled at his mother, and his eyes began to flutter closed.

"Don't worry about me Mom, you can go to work. I'll be okay."

Lisa gave Shawn a hug and kissed his forehead. He was growing up so fast. She adjusted the covers on the bed and quietly shut the door to Dr. Layton's office.

Fortunately, there was no surgery planned. The doctor had several consultations, including one for blepharoplasty, to repair droopy eyelids, and another for a complete face lift. He also had several follow-up visits for Botox and collagen injections.

David smiled warmly at Lisa as she joined him for the blepharoplasty consultation.

"I'm glad you're here, Lisa."

"I'm glad to be here, Dr. Layton. I can't even begin to tell you how much I appreciate your understanding and how you got everything ready for Shawn."

In the back of her mind she was thinking about how less considerate her own husband had been and how angry she still felt at his inadequate response to her needs.

David's smile was destroying her composure. She broke her eyes away from his gaze. At about the same time, David looked away.

"Let's get to work," he exclaimed.

Prior to entering the room, Layton reviewed the patient's chart. Mrs. Tonya Williams had been a patient for over four years. She had been to the office on multiple occasions for injections of collagen and Botox. Neither treatment had helped to improve her droopy eyes. She was here to discuss removal of excess skin from both her upper and lower eyelids.

"Good morning, Tonya. How are you?"

"Great, Dr. Layton. You don't seem to ever get any older. How do you do it?"

David smiled at Mrs. Williams. The sun hadn't been kind to her fair skin and at fifty-five years of age, she looked more like a woman in her sixties.

"Thanks, I hope I can look as good as you when I'm your age."

They both knew he was lying, but all the same, Tonya was beaming at the compliment.

"So what can we do for you today?"

"Well, I've already been to the ophthalmologist and they checked my peripheral vision. My droopy upper lids are blocking my vision enough so that my insurance will pay to have the upper lids done, but I want you to do the lower lids and get it all finished at the same time."

"You know we don't take insurance, Tonya."

"Oh, I know, Dr. Layton. I'll file my own claim. Whatever it costs, I know you're worth it. Everyone knows you're the best."

Now it was her turn to flatter him, and he had to admit that he didn't mind it at all.

"Thanks, Tonya. That's very nice of you to say. If you'd like we can schedule the surgery next week. This is my nurse, Lisa Martin. She can get you an information packet on blepharoplasty for you to read at home. You'll need to stop your aspirin and any blood thinners pre-op."

"I don't take anything, Dr. Layton. I'm as healthy as a horse."

"Great. How's your Botox holding up?"

"I'm very pleased Doctor. The crow's feet and wrinkles at my forehead are staying away. It's been over three months since the first injection, and four weeks since the 'touch up' and the results have been fabulous."

"I'm glad you're happy. I'll have Lisa help you make the arrangements for an appointment for your eyelid surgery. Is there anything else I can do for you?"

"No, Dr. Layton, I think I'm all set. If I have any questions after I read the information I'll call."

"Perfect, Tonya. Thanks for your vote of confidence and I look forward to seeing you soon." David shook her hand and exited the room.

After Dr. Layton was safely out of hearing range, Tonya exclaimed,

"I don't know how you can work with such a good-looking guy all day." Mrs. Williams looked down at Lisa's wedding ring.

"I guess it helps that you're married."

Lisa just smiled politely.

"I've only been here a few weeks, Mrs. Williams, but I can tell you, he's as good a doctor as he is good looking."

"I know, Lisa. But he's so handsome he could be a model. I almost opened my mouth and told him that I had a dream about him."

"A dream?"

"Yes, two days ago. My husband passed away last year and I've been all alone since. I really don't think about men all that much, but the other night I had a very exciting dream about your doctor. I'm too embarrassed to repeat it, but I had a hard time getting back to sleep, and in the dream, he wasn't wearing any clothes!" Mrs. Williams giggled self-consciously.

Lisa didn't want to share any of her own fantasies with the patient, and decided that it was time to end the conversation.

"Well, don't worry Tonya, your dreams are safe with me." She winked at Mrs. Williams and led her down the corridor to the front desk.

The blepharoplasty was scheduled for the third week of October.

CHAPTER 45

"Quantum Labs, can I help you?"

"Harold Linchitz please."

"Who may I say is calling?"

"Sal Manzari."

"Will he know what this is about?" the operator continued.

Sal was impatient with the perfunctory questions from the receptionist. He thought he could hear her chewing gum or something as she spoke.

"Please tell him it's personal."

"One moment please."

Sal was placed on hold and his ears were accosted by the loud staccato of salsa music from a station in Miami. His time on hold was mercifully brief.

"This is Harold Linchitz."

"Hi, Hal, it's Sal Manzari. How have you been?"

"Sal, great to hear from you. How are things in Pelican Cove?"

"Fine. How's your family?"

"Growing up, buddy. My oldest starts college next year and the youngest is fourteen. We're getting older."

"Tell me about it. The only hair I have left is white hair, and even that is falling out." They both laughed.

"So what's up?"

"I need a favor. You know, I'm working with Dr. David Layton on the Botox molecule."

"Sure, he called to tell me he was going to Fed-Ex over a couple of samples to test. I think we have them already. He's worried about impurities in the mixture."

"We both are. But since I'm doing all the biochemistry in the lab, I'd prefer to present the data to him myself when you're finished with the samples. I'll show him your findings, but would prefer to be able to 'soften the blow' if anything in the results is attributable to problems arising from the work in my lab. If the results are perfect, which I expect, it'll be simple. However, if I have to do any explaining, I'd rather be able to prepare myself to present the data to the doctor."

"No problem, old buddy. You know I'd do anything for you. I think I still owe you fifty bucks from the last time we played Texas Hold-Em at that chemistry conference in Boca Raton."

"Hal, consider us even. Just please help me out with this and I'll let you beat me next time."

Linchitz laughed.

"Sal, the day you let anyone beat you at Hold-Em will be the day it snows in Miami in June. Consider it done. I'll probably be able to fax you the results in a couple of days."

"No rush at all. Just slip it in the mail and that'll be fine. If Dr. Layton asks, just tell him you're still working on the material and don't even tell him I called. I'll take care of reviewing it all with him. It may end up saving my job, and right now I really need my work at the lab."

"Mums the word, Sal. He's lucky to have you; you're one of the most talented biochemists I know. I wish I could have you with me here. Are you going to the annual meeting in Orlando?"

"I was planning on it. Are you?"

"Absolutely."

"Well, you pick the place and dinner's on me. And thanks for the vote of confidence, Hal. You know how much I admire your work. If the night life in Miami ever gets too hectic for you, let me know; I wouldn't mind collaborating with you over here. We could be a couple of 'wild and crazy biochemists' here on the west coast."

"No doubt Sal, no doubt. I'll try to drop the results in the mail tomorrow and you should have them by Monday. If you want, I can send you a copy via your email. We can keep it confidential."

"That would be great. My email is 'SalHoldsEmAA88@aol.com."

"Aces and eights, dead man's hand right?"

"Yup, what Wild Bill Hicock was holding at the poker table when he was shot in the back in Deadwood by a deranged drunk. Anyway, thanks again, buddy. I'll let you get back to work."

"Great hearing from you, Sal. As soon as I know my hotel plans for Orlando, I'll mail them to you, so maybe we can stay at the same place. Take care."

"You too. My regards to your wife."

Sal hung up. He knew it would be difficult, but with just a little bit of luck, things might still work out for him at the lab. Luck, and a few carefully placed changes in Hal's report.

CHAPTER 46

Lisa enjoyed her abbreviated day of work. She was worried that Dr. Layton might be short-handed when she had to leave to pick up Josh. Fortunately, Barbara's stomach troubles cleared up and she came to the office in the afternoon. Lisa left shortly after Barbara arrived. Shawn slept until ten o'clock, then played video games and read in Dr. Layton's office until it was time for them to leave. She was relieved that Shawn felt much better and hoped he would be able to go to school in the morning.

"So how about some lunch, big boy. Are you hungry?"

Shawn looked at his mother and smiled.

"I'm starving, Mom. How about Arby's?"

"Why don't we go someplace a little nicer? There's a new Fonzi's Diner downtown. It's not too fancy, but the food is better than Arby's."

"Can I get a milkshake?"

Lisa looked at her trim son. Where does he put it all!

"Sure Shawn. Let's go say goodbye to Dr. Layton. Make sure to thank him for all he's done: for letting you use his office, videos, and the breakfast."

Moments later they were driving toward the diner. It was only six or seven blocks from the office. Parking downtown at lunchtime was a bit difficult, and Lisa was having trouble finding a spot. As she rounded a corner two blocks from the restaurant, she was surprised to see a familiar car – it was Nate's gray Lexus sedan. She scanned the neighborhood for her husband. He's probably at lunch with his coworkers, she mused. Lisa congratulated herself on finding a spot to park, vacated by a monstrous taxi-cab yellow Hummer.

Lisa and Shawn began walking to Fonzi's and they passed Nate's gray Lexus.

"Hey Mom, that looks just like Dad's car."

Lisa spotted one of Josh's hats in the back seat, confirming ownership of the vehicle.

"That's because it is Dad's car."

Lisa looked around, hoping to find Nate at one of the restaurants occupying the busy downtown district. She recognized a familiar shock of light brown hair and the silhouette of her husband at a distant table at one of the nicer restaurants, Chez Golton. He was seated in the outdoor dining area, with his back to Lisa and Shawn and busy in conversation with two other men and a younger woman, all smartly dressed.

"There's Dad," Lisa exclaimed to Shawn.

She imagined that Nate was lunching with attorneys from his firm.

"Come on Shawn, let's go say hello."

They crossed the street, and as they did so, the group at the table began to leave. One of the men handed a small tray with the check to the waiter who thanked him graciously. Nate got up and walked behind the young lady at the table and eased back her chair as she rose from her seat. Lisa watched aghast as the thin attractive woman got out of her chair, smiled at her husband then kissed her index and middle fingers and touched them to Nate's cheek.

Lisa didn't know what to do. She no longer wanted to chat with her husband. She felt pangs of jealousy over what she had seen. It appeared to her that whatever was going on transcended a normal business relationship. Not continuing over to say hello might seem weird to Shawn, so Lisa felt that she had no choice but to let her feet continue on in their relentless path toward her husband. They had entered the outside dining area of Chez Golton and Shawn shouted a raucous greeting to his father.

Shawn ran over to Nate and hugged his father's legs. Nate was surprised at seeing his son, who had been lying in bed ill just a few hours earlier.

"Hey little man. I guess you're feeling better!" Nate looked up and smiled at his wife.

Just to Nate's right, stood a thirty-ish statuesque brunette with big brown eyes and not an ounce of fat on her. Lisa hated her immediately.

"What are you guys doing down here?" Nate asked.

Lisa tried to swallow the bile rising in her throat.

"We both spent the morning at work. Dr. Layton let Shawn rest in his office all morning while I worked. He felt much better, so we decided to go to Fonzi's for lunch. We saw your car, and came looking for you."

Nate smiled.

"What a nice surprise seeing you. Lisa, you remember Jeff Lobdell. The scary-looking guy next to him is Wayde Seligman. I know you've met Jeff, but you may not have met Wayde, since he's in our tax department. They're both partners in the firm. This is Sandy Parker, she's working on the Jointrex cases with me."

Lisa smiled at the group and shook hands with Sandy and Wayde who were standing closest to her husband. She didn't like how close to Nate the female attorney was lurking. A part of her also resented that Nate had been able to find the time to have lunch with his co-workers, including this hot-looking female attorney, but couldn't find the time to help her earlier in the morning when she needed his assistance.

"Nice seeing you all. We've really got to be going. At 2:30 I've got to be at school to pick up my other son, Josh, and we're going to go catch lunch at Fonzi's so we're a little pressed for time. Nice meeting you Wayde, and you too Sandy. Nate, will you be home for dinner?" Lisa's words hung in the air like wet laundry on a clothes line.

"I'll try to be home by 6:30 Lisa, but Sandy and I have a lot of work to prepare on our Jointrex cases and we wanted to have them all tied up before the weekend."

Lisa wanted to give Nate a piece of her mind. She wanted to tell him that she had seen Sandy's act of affection and wanted to tell him that she thought he was a selfish prick. She wondered if Nate had more than a professional relationship going on with the shapely attorney. But this wasn't the time or the place for such a discussion. Lisa mustered the best fake smile she could.

"Well, I'll have dinner ready for you when you get home. We'll wait until 6:30. Please try to make it; Josh will be disappointed if he can't tell you all about his day all by himself on the school bus without his older brother along for the ride. It's the first time he's ever been on the bus alone."

Lisa hoped that she was subtly reminding her husband of his family and his fatherly responsibilities. She wanted to say something to Sandy, but stopped herself— maybe the 'kiss' had merely been an innocent gesture, nothing more.

Nate was oblivious.

"I'll try Lisa. I'll call you later. Love you." Nate leaned over and gave Lisa a peck on the cheek. The similarity of the kiss to the one that Lisa witnessed moments earlier wasn't lost on Mrs. Martin. Lisa turned her face so that she could return the gesture to Nate's cheek, but he was already too far away to be approached without Lisa having to cross awkwardly over the several feet that separated them. Instead, she just smiled and felt eager to just get away from her husband and the group of attorneys.

"Bye Nate, see you later," she responded flatly.

"Bye Dad." Shawn ran over and got one last kiss and hug from his father and then they were gone, back on their way to Fonzi's.

CHAPTER 47

Dr. Layton's Thursday at work was lighter than usual. It was a slow time of year for most of the physicians of Pelican Cove, including David. The snow-birds hadn't returned from up North and the year-round residents were busy getting back to work and school after their summer breaks. Barbara's stomach had again acted up after a couple of hours at work, and David had called the last few patients and rescheduled them to the following Thursday. Now the only other person in the office was Samantha, who was answering the phones and checking through the day's mail.

David sat at his desk and opened the file containing his Botox study data. The files held the key to his pursuit of easy street. If only things could run smoothly, as they had before. That morning, he had sent off two Botox vials to Quantum Labs for evaluation. He had been promised that the results would be ready the following week. Everything that he and Sal had studied and evaluated in the literature, and their preliminary results in the lab, indicated that their drug could not cross the barrier from the blood to the brain. Damage to the brain from their test molecule just shouldn't happen.

"What I need is a good run to clear my head," he thought to himself.

Dr. Layton closed his file draw, gathered up his briefcase along with a professional journal he planned to read that evening, and prepared to leave his office for the day. David called out a "goodbye" to Samantha as he departed. Although he remembered to shut the lights, he forgotten to put away a small brown key which remained on the blotter of his desk.

"Don't stay too late," Dr. Layton shouted to Sam, as he exited from the back door of the office.

CHAPTER 48

Lisa chopped carrots into small pieces, preparing a salad for dinner. Shawn and Josh were busy playing "Grand Theft Auto" in the next room. Shawn 'paused' the game and entered the kitchen.

"Geeze, Mom are you angry at something? You're attacking those carrots!"

Lisa hadn't realized how hard she was chopping the vegetables. Shawn was perceptive. She had been thinking about Nate's lunch companions, mostly the slender one who had assaulted her husband's cheek. She turned to her son, smiled, and tried to cover her true feelings.

"I guess I was cutting them a little hard, honey. I missed my workout today, so I was using the chopping to take their place. Wait till you see what I do with the chicken breasts! I'm going to pound them silly. How are you feeling?"

"I'm fine, Mom. I don't think I need any more Tylenol and I don't feel like I have a temperature anymore."

"You mean a fever, honey; you always have a temperature, though hopefully not an abnormal one," Lisa corrected.

"Sure Mom, whatever you say. I feel okay though. How long 'til dinner?" asked Shawn.

It was almost five o'clock. Lisa hadn't heard from Nate, but was still hoping that he would be home in time for dinner.

"We're going to eat at 6:30. Can you last until then?"

Shawn smiled at his mother.

"Maybe if you give me a couple of cookies to hold me over I can."

Lisa was amazed at how quickly her son had seemingly returned to normal. Shawn sure did like to eat. She reached into the cupboard and pulled out a bag of Oreos and placed half a dozen cookies on the plate. Next, she poured two glasses of milk and handed the plate and glasses to Shawn.

"Here, take the milk and cookies in to Josh and share them with him. That's it until dinner."

"Okay, Mom. Is Dad going to be home for dinner?" Shawn asked.

"I think so, honey."

"I hope so; he told me he'd play "Grand Theft Auto" with Josh and me tonight."

"Josh and I".

"I know, that's what I said." Shawn took his cookies and milk and went back to his video game.

At 6:15, Nate called to say that he would be ten or fifteen minutes late. When 6:45 came, and the boys whined about how hungry they were, Lisa gave up on her husband and quietly placed dinner on the table.

"What's the matter, Mom?" asked Josh.

Lisa fought back the tears. She was disappointed that she couldn't hide her feelings from her boys, and was depressed at her husband's lack of consideration. She worried if he was being honest with her about what he was doing in his long hours away.

"Nothing honey, I just had an eyelash in my eye," feigned Lisa.

She wiped back the start of a tear from the corner of her right eye.

Dinner was subdued. Try as she might, Lisa just couldn't pretend to be light-hearted in her present mood.

"So how was riding the bus without Shawn?" Lisa asked Josh.

"It was kind of strange. I wanted to talk to him and he wasn't there. Then Billy Jewell sat next to me. He's kinda weird. One of the other kids told me he saw him pick his nose and eat his boogers once!"

Lisa had to struggle not to laugh at the antics of elementary school.

"Now, now, Josh—be nice. I'm sure it was better to have someone next to you to talk to on the ride to school than sitting all alone on the bus."

"Not really, Mom," Shawn interjected.

"He's gross. He never brushes his teeth. He's got like mold growing on them."

"Never mind you two. Eat up and if you finish everything, you can have dessert. I've got some Cherry Garcia for you."

"Yummmmm," exclaimed Josh.

Just then, Nate walked in the door.

"I'm home," Nate bellowed.

"About time," thought Lisa to herself. It was past seven o'clock.

Nate entered the dining room and realized that the family had eaten without him. He glanced at his watch, and was surprised to see how late it was.

"I'm truly sorry, time just got away from me again. Well, at least it looks like I got here in time for dessert," Nate chirped.

Lisa held her tongue and said nothing.

Nate walked over and bent down to give her a kiss hello. He planted a dry peck on the corner of her lips.

"Let me get up and fix you a plate." Lisa began to rise.

"You sit; I'll do it," Nate replied.

"I've been a bad boy, I know. I'm sorry for being late. I'll make up for it; we can all go out for dinner tomorrow, okay?"

"That would be nice," Lisa answered without much enthusiasm. "I don't mind cooking, but I would appreciate it if you would try harder to be on time."

"Believe me; I tried to get out. These cases are just keeping me so busy. But it's going to pay off; it looks like Jointrex is going to settle out of court for a big chunk of change. It's going to impress the partners when we sit down to talk partnership. I think I'm going to make it."

"That's nice, Nate, but family life should come first."

Nate felt anger rising within him, but fought to keep it inside so that the boys wouldn't see it.

"Sure, Lisa," he mustered.

Here he was, working hard, almost ready to catch the big prize, and all she could do was scold him. Damn it, she should just be proud of him and cut him some slack. Silently, he gathered a plate of shredded pork and baked beans.

"Were you working late with Mrs. Parker?"

Lisa didn't know why, but she regretted asking him almost as soon as the words left her mouth. The question would have been better saved for when the boys weren't around. The sharpness of the inquiry wasn't lost on Nate. He didn't like the tone Lisa was taking with him; especially not in front of the boys.

"Actually, Mrs. Parker, is a Ms. Yes, we're working up the cases together. If it wasn't for her help, I probably would still be at the office. She's not up for partner and has less to benefit from for her efforts than I do. You're not jealous, are you?"

Lisa looked at her husband. There were lots of things she wanted to say. She was sick to her stomach at knowing that the attractive woman working late with her husband was single. How dense could he be? Did he really expect her to say that she wasn't jealous? She lied through her teeth.

"Of course I'm not jealous, Nate. I just wish I could have had her help me get Josh to school this morning."

Her sarcasm was setting the stage for a fight. The boys were silent as they tried to understand what was happening between their parents. Shawn broke the tension in the air.

"Mom, can I have my ice cream now? I finished my dinner."

His plate was clean. Lisa forgot about Nate for a moment and focused her attention on Shawn.

"Sure, honey."

"Me too, Mom." Lisa noticed that Josh's plate was almost empty, but that there was a suspicious bulge in the napkin, half hidden under his plate.

"What's in the napkin, Josh?"

"Just bones and stuff."

Lisa frowned at her son.

"There were no bones, Josh. I wasn't born yesterday. If you open your napkin and eat the pork you can have dessert."

Josh began to protest, then thought better of it and quietly opened the napkin and popped a wad of pork into his mouth.

"Dhere, I ay it dall," he tried to speak around the ball of meat in his mouth.

Lisa couldn't help but smile at her son's antics. She appreciated the break from arguing with her husband and prepared two bowls of ice cream.

CHAPTER 49

David ran his hands through Lisa's hair. It was soft and silky and smelled faintly of jasmine. He kissed her full on the lips and let his mouth open to meet hers. Lisa wrapped her arms around him as their bodies intertwined. He felt his excitement rising and gazed into her beautiful green eyes. The doctor opened the buttons on her white nurse's top and pulled it over her head. Next, he helped her wriggle out of her white pants. He peeled her socks from her feet and pulled her lacey panties down. David reached behind and unhooked her brassiere. Her breasts were two glowing white mounds and as he stared down at them, she smiled with a look of desire in her eyes.

"Your turn Dr. Layton," she exclaimed.

Lisa unknotted David's tie and threw it to the floor. She ripped his blue Oxford Brooks Brothers shirt from his body, the buttons exploding off his chest like popcorn popping in a microwave. She ran her hands across his chest, leaned over and planted little kisses across each of his pecs, then onto his toned abdomen.

"Your pants look a little bit tight, Dr. Layton. I think there's something down there yearning to be free."

David was on fire with desire.

"I think I need your help, Lisa."

She smiled. Lisa opened his narrow belt and tossed it in the general direction of his tie and shirt. Next, she opened the button on his pants and slowly lowered the zipper. Lisa playfully touched the bulge which confronted her as David wiggled out of his clothes. In an exaggerated impression of a stripper, she took his pants and swung them over her head, letting them fly after a few rotations.

His nurse lowered her head to his groin. Lisa used her teeth to pull down on the elastic band of his boxers. Her hair brushed up against his manhood as the pulled his underwear down to his ankles. David helped her bring them past his feet and threw them to the floor. He pulled her face to his and looked into her eyes. The pair exchanged a passionate kiss and Lisa allowed her body to gently fall onto David's as she felt his excitement against her thighs. The sensation of her warm, soft thighs against him was more than he could take.

"I want you Lisa. I want you now."

"Oh, Dr. Layton, I want you too, take me. Take me."

David began to enter Lisa, with excitement incomparable to any he could ever remember. It was heaven. He was preparing to thrust inside her, when something distracted him. A sound that at first seemed far away became louder and louder, distracting him. The sound called out to him, making continuation of their coupling impossible.

David started and opened his eyes looking around. He was alone in his bed. His alarm clock was beeping, beeping seven A.M. He was going to be late for work. David remembered the erotic adventure with Lisa as if it were real; as well as the disappointment at finding himself alone and aroused. It was Friday morning; time for a cold shower and work.

206

CHAPTER 50

Nate and Lisa tried as best they could to ignore the events of the prior evening. Both awoke early Friday morning; Nate's six-thirty alarm getting them both out of bed.

"Nate, do you think you can drop the boys off at the bus stop this morning? I'd like to get to the office early today to make up for working such a short day yesterday."

"Sure, Lisa. How about dinner at Luigi's tonight?"

Luigi's was a good choice. It had pizza and pasta for the boys and more elaborate dishes for the adults. The boys loved the pizza.

"That would be nice. Can you make it for six?"

"I promise, Lisa." Nate placed his arms around his wife and gave her a hug, followed by a soft kiss on her lips.

"I'll count on it, honey. Let's have a nice dinner together tonight." She hoped Nate wouldn't disappoint her yet again.

"Absolutely." He ran to bathe in the shower and Lisa walked off to the kitchen in order to prepare the boy's lunch. She considered joining Nate in the shower, but was still feeling some anger and jealousy left over from the day before.

When she heard the water stop running, she entered the bathroom to take her turn at bathing. She avoided Nate and quietly entered the shower. Lisa dressed for work, then woke the boys who joined her for breakfast.

"How come Dad is taking us to the bus today?" asked Josh.

"I'm going in to the office early since I missed all of Wednesday and only worked a few hours yesterday. Dad wanted to be with you boys. And guess what?"

"What?" asked Shawn.

"We're going to Luigi's for dinner."

"Really?" asked Josh.

"Cool."

"Can I get the veal parmigana?" It was Shawn.

Her older son was rapidly becoming a sophisticated eater. The days of spaghetti and meatball kid's meals was disappearing way too quickly.

"Sure Shawn, whatever you want. Are you feeling okay for school today?"

"Yah Mom, I feel perfect. Ready to start my next run of days in school without being sick."

Lisa felt fortunate at having two such normal, healthy children. She knew she should probably be more grateful for all she had and not be so hard on Nate.

"You're a good boy, Shawn. You too, Josh. I love you both so much." Lisa walked over and kissed each of her boys on the head. She placed their bag lunches at their elbows.

"Here are your lunches. I'm heading out. Have a great day and I'll see you at school at three-fifteen."

"Love you Mom," It was Shawn.

"Love you more," chimed in Josh.

Lisa left the house with her spirits buoyed by the love of her sons, who almost always managed to cheer her up. Her thoughts shifted to her job and Dr. Layton. He had been so considerate the previous day. "I should do something for him," she thought.

As Lisa entered one of the busier streets of Pelican Cove she passed a CVS 24-hour drug store. "They probably have something I can get him in there," Lisa thought as she made a U-turn and entered the empty store.

After a few minutes of searching, she found a suitable gift. It was a "Zen Garden"—a little tray, with small wooden tools for 'tending' the garden, including a small rake and hoe. There was beach sand to be moved around and the total effect was intended to soothe the owner. Anyway, she mused, it's the thought that counts and the doctor would certainly appreciate the idea of trying to ease his tension. She made the purchase, accompanied by a small "Thank You" card. Despite the stop, it was only a little after seven-thirty in the morning and she would still be early for work.

It was the first time Lisa had arrived early enough to be the first one in the office. She entered through the front door. Her arms were full, bearing the gift for the doctor and her purse. Lisa switched on the lights and walked to the doctor's office to deposit her present. It felt eerily quiet in the empty office. She felt like an intruder. Lisa pulled the card from the bag and sat at David's desk while she tried to think of something to write in the note.

She immediately noticed a small key on his blotter, and also was able to see that the normally locked file at David's desk was slightly ajar. Lisa recalled the file he had in his hand when she entered the office the day before. Was there something in there that she shouldn't see? Curiosity got the better of her and she slid open the drawer.

There were almost one hundred alphabetized files. Most of them had a small white label with a handwritten name. There were three other charts which were similar to those used in the office and contained larger colored letters on the outside representing the first letters of the patient's last name. Lisa was shocked to see the names on the three office records – Roberta Cook, Janetta Fannestack and Shirley Herold. Lisa pulled Janetta's chart from between the others and was about to open the folder to review its contents when she heard a key in the lock to the back door.

"Shit," she muttered. Her hands trembled as she returned the chart to the two others and closed the drawer. She rose from the chair and went around the desk to the other side so as not to appear as if she had been snooping in the office. With a shaky hand, she began to write in the card, "Dear Dr. Layton, Thank you so much….." Just then David walked into the room.

"Hi, Lisa. I wasn't sure if you were coming to the office alone or with Shawn. Just in case, I brought him something to eat." Lisa noticed a box of Dunkin Donuts tucked under his arm.

Lisa felt like a burglar caught red-handed, and tried her hardest not to appear flustered.

"Dr. Layton, you're so thoughtful. Shawn was fine this morning and his father took him to the bus stop, so I was able to get here early. I got you a little something."

Lisa reached onto the desk and handed David the Zen Garden.

"I haven't finished the card yet, but I just wanted you to know how much Shawn and I appreciated how thoughtful and understanding you were yesterday."

As she spoke the words, Lisa looked into David's eyes and lost herself in their shimmering blue pools. Their eyes locked and she felt herself drawn to the doctor as his face moved nearer to hers. Her heart soared and excitement built inside her. She knew he was about to kiss her and at the last moment, just before their lips could touch, she remembered who she was and where she was and moved her head away from the doctor. She looked at David, and he looked back at her—both seemed to be embarrassed by what had happened.

David spoke first.

"I'm sorry, Lisa. I'm so sorry. I don't know what came over me…….." His voice trailed off as he seemed unable to come up with the right words to explain his feelings.

Lisa was too embarrassed to speak. In all the years that she been married to Nate she had never experienced anything like what had happened in that brief moment. Lisa knew that she felt an attraction to the doctor and the 'almost kiss' had not been all Dr. Layton's doing – the attraction had definitely been mutual. Even though she hadn't kissed him she felt guilty, knowing how thoroughly she had wanted to.

"Dr. Layton, I like you very much, and you're a great boss, but we can't let anything happen between us like that."

Lisa didn't enjoy saying the words and felt confused, but knew that she had to say them; it was the right thing to do. A part of her regretted what she had said, even as the words left her mouth. A part of her wanted him.

For David, it was a continuation of the dream from earlier in the morning. He felt as if he were still partially continuing his imagined passion. What was coming over him? He had never had any trouble controlling his feelings for a woman before. Lisa was very special, but he did not want to do anything that would endanger his practice. She was his employee, with kids and married – to a lawyer no less. He certainly didn't want to be sued for sexual harassment!

"Of course, Lisa. I understand. I apologize. Let's forget it ever happened. But I do want you to know that you are very special and I appreciate how you've stepped in and worked so hard in the office." His own words sounded awkward in his moment of embarrassment.

A sound at the back door halted their conversation as Becky entered.

"Good morning Dr. Layton. Hi, Lisa." Becky got the distinct feeling that she was interrupting something. Then she spotted the box of Dunkin Donuts.

"I should make some coffee to go with those!"

"Yes, Becky. Could you please get some going."

"Sure thing, but if there's a chocolate one, save it for me!"

CHAPTER 51

"I don't think Dr. Layton will appreciate us coming to his office unannounced."

"I don't think he'll appreciate us coming to his office unannounced or announced, Dan. But we may learn more if we surprise him," answered Kevin.

The officers had finished their work for the week and were now free to pursue their curiosity regarding the deaths of three women, all of whom had some kind of tie to Dr. Layton.

"This is like that Kevin Bacon thing. You know—how someone said that everyone in the world can trace themselves to Kevin Bacon in six steps or less."

"Stop being ridiculous, Dan. Let's just give this one more try before we close the files. I can't help feel that there's something more than meets the eye here."

"Yeah, your woman's intuition," Kevin teased.

Dan was driving, but Kevin pretended to have no concern for their safety as he playfully punched Dan in the thick part of his arm.

"You're lucky I'm driving, partner, or you'd be begging for mercy right now."

Kevin smiled at Dan. Levine was a good man and Kevin appreciated his good fortune in having such an easy-going and hard-working partner. It was almost eleven-thirty when they arrived at the doctor's office.

"I feel my stomach starting to grumble, Kev. How about you promise me we're out of here by noon so we can grab some grub, okay?"

"Okay, I'm eager to be finish up too. The Keys and fishing are calling."

To the chagrin of the officers, the waiting area was devoid of attractive patients. The room was empty.

"Guess no pretty ladies waiting here today, Kev," Dan whispered to his partner.

"They're probably getting ready for lunch." Collins walked up to the receptionist's window and greeted Becky.

"Hello, Becky, right?" Kevin asked the receptionist. If he wanted confirmation, all he had to do was glance at her name tag.

"Yes, Detective Collins and..." Becky couldn't remember the other detective's name—only that he had been the hungry one.

"Levine," Dan interjected. "Detective Dan Levine." He reached out and shook the attractive young receptionist's hand.

"We were wondering if we might have a few moments of Dr. Layton's time—if he isn't too busy," asked Detective Collins.

"He just went in the room with his last patient of the morning. We're only working half a day today. I'll see if he'll be able to meet with you when he's finished. Can I get you a cup of coffee?"

"None for me, but maybe my partner would like some. Dan?"

"No, I'm all coffeed out. But I sure could use some cold water."

"One ice water coming right up. Just wait out here, and as soon as the doctor is available I'll come and get you."

"Becky, are any of the nurses available to speak with us?"

"Only Lisa Martin is here today, Detective Collins, and she's with the doctor right now. Do you want me to see if I can get her?"

Kevin had hoped for some time alone to converse with the nurses, but now it looked like that might not happen.

"Maybe when we've finished speaking with the doctor. We don't want to impose on anyone's time while you're still seeing patients."

"I'll be sure to let her know. Let me get that water."

The wait was brief. Within ten minutes, the detectives found themselves seated back in David's office.

"Detectives Collins and Levine. What can I do for you?" David had none of Becky's difficulty at remembering the names of the two detectives.

"We're probably wasting our time and yours doctor, but we wanted to be certain to leave no stones unturned in the Fannestack case. Since three deaths in a short time all seemed to have loose ties to your office, we felt obligated to investigate a little further; even when those ties seem rather insignificant. Were you able to find any treatment records for the Fannestack woman or Roberta Cook?"

David felt uneasy. Why were they questioning him again? Did they know something already? He really had no choice. He had to continue with his denial. Surely they would give up and go away.

"No Detectives, I haven't been able to find any evidence of treatment for either of the two ladies. Actually, I haven't been able to find their records at all."

The door to David's office was ajar. Lisa had finished cleaning the exam room of their final patient and was waiting outside Dr. Layton's office at Becky's instruction, ready to answer any questions they might have. She was able to hear parts of the conversation taking place inside the room and had overheard Dr. Layton's denial of knowledge of the whereabouts of the records of the dead women. What was he hiding? As much as she hated to, Lisa moved away from the doorway and forced herself to walk down the corridor so that she would not appear to be eavesdropping.

David remembered something his father had told him when he used to play tennis in high school—the best defense is sometimes a good offense. David decided it was time to go on the offensive with the inquisitive detectives.

"Look, I feel very badly about the dead women. But I'd like to get out of here and I've already searched for whatever records we may have had in the office and couldn't find anything. In any case, whatever cosmetic work my nurse Shirley had done certainly didn't cause her neurological problems or car accident. I don't really recall Roberta Cook, though she may have been here once, and the Fannestack woman died from a drug overdose and had the misfortune of also having unrelated neurological difficulties. I understand your desire to tie their medical problems together in a nice tidy package, but I think you're barking up the wrong tree. Nothing that caused the misfortune of these women had anything to do with my practice or my office."

Both officers remained silent. Years of experience told Collins it was a waste of his time to continue. He also sensed that Layton was hiding something.

"Dr. Layton, we're very sorry if we've bothered you. We're just trying to do our jobs. We'll be on our way. Please get back in touch if you think of anything else about the three women, or come across any information in your office pertaining to their care. Would you mind if we spoke with your nurse for a few moments before we leave?"

David felt eager to have the detectives out of the office, but didn't want to arouse their suspicions by refusing to allow them to speak to Lisa.

"Of course, Detectives. Take as long as you'd like. But it is Friday, and we're finished for the day, so if you don't mind, I'll be leaving."

"Thank you Doctor. Have a nice weekend. We won't be long."

David picked up the phone and paged the front desk.

"Becky, can you send Lisa in please?"

"Right away, Dr. Layton."

Lisa entered the office. All three men turned their attention to the nurse as she passed through the doorway. David wondered whether his newest nurse sensed the way the detectives were looking at her, undressing her with their eyes, before addressing her.

"Lisa, the detectives wanted to ask you some questions about a few of our patients. Would you mind speaking to them for a few minutes?"

"Of course not, Dr. Layton. We're finished with patients for the day, aren't we?"

"Yes, I'm heading out; I've got errands to run. You and Becky can lock up and call it a day when you're done."

"Have a good weekend, Dr. Layton. I'll see you on Monday."

"You too, Lisa. Good-by, Detectives."

The officers turned their attention to the nurse.

"Mrs. Martin, I'm Detective Kevin Collins and my partner is Detective Dan Levine. We promise not to keep you long. We were just wondering if you could answer some questions for us."

"Certainly, officers, but you'd probably learn more from Barbara or Paula. I'm the newest one here. I only started a few weeks ago."

"That's okay. We know that Janetta Fannestack was your friend and were wondering if she ever mentioned anything about her treatment here. Did she ever come back to the office for care?"

Lisa was distraught. David had denied knowledge of Janetta's visit to the office, but her record in his desk suggested otherwise. After all Dr. Layton had done for Lisa, the last thing she wanted to do was cause any problems for her boss. Then again, Janetta had been a great friend and Lisa wanted to do the right thing and tell the officers whatever she knew that might help them in their investigation.

"Officers, I really hadn't been able to speak to Janetta much since working here. I've been very busy. She might have been here; I know she planned to come and have some Botox injections. I'm just not sure if she ever got around to doing it. She certainly didn't have it done on a day when I was working or I would have known."

"Do you assist Dr. Layton in administering the Botox injections?" Dan asked.

"Not really. I bring him the vials of medication, and sometimes measure out the amount he wants, but he does all the actual treatments himself."

"So you don't dilute the medication with anything?"

"No, it all comes directly from the manufacturer in ready-to-use sealed vials."

The detectives were running out of questions. It appeared that their boss had been correct and that this visit was a waste of their Friday afternoon.

"Mrs. Martin, thank you for your time. Here's my card. If you think of anything else, even if you think it's unimportant, please feel free to call me. You can leave a message at the precinct if I'm out." Dan held out the card.

"My pleasure, Detective." Lisa took the card and shook both officers' hands.

"We'll let ourselves out, Lisa. We know the way."

Detectives Collins and Levine stood and walked from Dr. Layton's office to the back entrance of the suite and departed.

Kevin looked at Dan.

"She seemed nervous, Dan. Did you notice?"

"She was probably nervous at the way you were staring at her chest while you were talking to her Kev."

Collins made a pretend slap at Levine's face.

"No, be serious."

"I am being serious," Dan teased.

"Actually, she did seem a bit tense. And did you see the way she diverted her eyes for a moment when you asked her if she knew anything. She's hiding something."

"Maybe you're right, Dan. All I know is I'm ready for the Keys."

The men got back into their car and drove away. Lisa Martin remained in Dr. Layton's office.

Lisa's hands were shaking as she walked across the office, back to Dr. Layton's desk. She had lied to the officers and now she felt obliged to find out the truth for herself. She placed her hand on the drawer containing the files she had seen previously. It was locked. Lisa could hear Becky on the phone confirming Monday's appointments. Any opportunity to have another look at Janetta's file was rapidly disappearing. Lisa frantically gave the drawer another tug but nothing happened. There were three smaller drawers on the other side of the desk. Trying the first, she found it was unlocked. Her heart racing, she eagerly searched for the key to the section containing the files.

The drawer contained Dr. Layton's extra cassette tapes for his portable dictating equipment. Lisa found a few coins, several old Post-It notes and a box of David's personal stationary, but no key. "What the hell am I doing?" Lisa thought. "I'm prying through my doctor's personal things." Remembering her dead friend though, Lisa continued her search. She opened the second drawer.

Pencils, pens and erasers were arranged in a plastic organizer. In one of the little spaces were two keys. They looked to be about the right size for the file drawer. Lisa quickly grabbed them both. Her hands were sweating and her ears were attuned to any sounds in the hallway. If Becky walked in she would have a hard time explaining what she was doing.

Lisa dropped the keys. They fell under the big leather desk chair. She bent down and found them both. Lisa tried to calm herself. She inserted one of the small brown keys into the lock. It entered but wouldn't turn. "Damn," Lisa muttered. She removed the key and quickly inserted the second. It turned and Lisa felt the lock release. The drawer slid backward slightly. She pulled it open and viewed the collection of files hidden within.

Lisa wasted no time. She withdrew Janetta's file and scanned the pages. There was an intake sheet containing Janetta's medical history, another page with a signed informed consent and a page of office dictation. It was dated September 13th and coincided with the entry in the appointment book that Lisa had seen previously. Botox had been administered to Janetta at the 'crow's feet' areas of her eyes and at her forehead. She had also received several units at the corners of her mouth. The dictation had been signed by Dr. Layton.

Lisa placed the chart on the desk and looked back into the drawer. She quickly removed Roberta Cook's file and confirmed what she already suspected. The woman had been in the office for Botox on two separate occasions. How could Dr. Layton have forgotten?

Lisa continued her inspection of the contents of the drawer. The white-labeled charts were also alphabetized. She searched for Janetta's name. Sharon Davidson, Gerri Ehrlich, Joyce English, Janetta Fannestack. Lisa removed the file from its place in the alphabetized group.

This was not the same as other office charts Lisa had seen. In addition to space allotted to "Patient Name, Date of Birth, and Sex, were spaces for Date of Service, Amount of Botox Administered, Location of Treatment, Number of Units, Response and Side Effects. The 'Date of Service' was entered in black pen as September 13, 2008. Janetta had been listed as Subject Number 66. Another space, under 'Batch Number' contained the entry B6. Lisa recognized the handwriting as that of Dr. Layton.

Lisa was seated at the desk and noticed that the red light, indicating Becky's usage of the phone at the reception desk, had gone off. Her co-worker was no longer on the phone. Lisa listened carefully for any sound in the office. Lisa quickly closed the file and placed it back in the drawer directly in front of the chart for Joyce English. She heard footfalls in the hallway. Focusing her concentration, Lisa carefully returned Roberta Cook's and Janetta's office records to their original locations. She closed the drawer and locked it as quickly as she could. Her hands were shaking. Lisa smoothly slid both keys back into their place in the desk drawer, then quietly slid it closed.

Mrs. Martin rose from the chair and was almost away from the desk and about to leave the office. Her exit from the room was halted by Dr. Layton entering his office.

CHAPTER 52

Sal couldn't resist. The lab was quiet—the assistants having gone for the day. Ed was the last to leave, as per usual lately, and had said his good-bye's moments earlier. Manzari was alone with the occasional squeak of the mice to keep him company.

Sal's computer screen glowed light blue as the chemist typed in the link for Giant Poker.com. "Just a few rounds to clear my head," Sal thought to himself. He was about to register to play some Texas Hold-Em when he heard the alert from their fax machine indicating an incoming message. Sal got up to see what was printing out.

A three-paged faxed report from Hal Linchitz at Quantum Labs appeared. His friend had kept his promise and forwarded a copy of the mass spec report on the Botox specimens. It was apparent to Sal that David had sent more than one bottle from more than one lot. The chemists at the lab had correctly identified the ester bond in one of the specimens, causing a visible spike on the mass spec printout. The second result coincided with the non-adulterated Botox study chemical which had been effective in their early laboratory and office-based cases. No unusual peaks were present on the data from the second specimen. The third sheet of paper was the cover page with a brief handwritten note scribbled across the front,

"Sal, hope this helps you out. There appears to be two different chemical substances here, both similar to Botox. I guess I know where I can go to get rid of my wrinkles! Mailed the original hard copies to you today by snail mail. Talk to you soon, Hal"

The results from the lab were about what he had expected. The words of one of his professors came to mind; "All data can be manipulated to lead you to the desired conclusion." Manipulation time was at hand.

CHAPTER 53

Hi Lisa, what's up?"

Lisa felt like a criminal. In addition to feeling distraught by what she had seen in Dr. Layton's files, he had caught her by surprise—she had expected to see Becky. Lisa didn't know what to say.

"I thought you had gone home for the weekend Dr. Layton."

"So did I." David smiled at Lisa and momentarily put her at ease. "Did the officers just leave?"

Lisa was a bad liar. She could pretend that she had been with the detectives for the last few minutes while she had actually been snooping in his files, or make up a different story to cover what she had actually been doing. If he checked with Becky and asked how long the officers had been gone, her boss would quickly know if she lied. Maybe a half-truth would work.

"They left a couple of minutes ago. They asked questions about Janetta. They wanted to know if she had been treated in the office. The same questions they had asked before. But they didn't seem to believe me when

I told them I didn't know. Talking about Janetta shook me up and I've just been sitting here trying to get myself back together."

Lisa couldn't tell if the doctor doubted any part of her explanation. He walked over to her side and joined her at the edge of his desk.

"This must be very hard for you, Lisa. I'm sorry I've had you working so hard so soon after losing Janetta. I appreciate all you've done since Shirley's been gone." David placed his left arm around Lisa's back and pulled her slightly toward him in an embrace.   The nurse didn't want to rebuke Layton's apparent attempt at demonstrating concern, but she was worried where this might be going.   She felt her heart skip a beat and it began to race as her body was drawn against his chest. His right arm came across her back and joined his left as he pulled her toward him. There was no longer any distance between their bodies and Lisa felt herself become light-headed in his embrace. She could smell his cologne and the stiff, pressed cotton of his shirt collar touched her cheek.

Lisa had promised herself that she would not allow any more events to occur between her and her boss that might interfere with their professional relationship. But despite the unsettling revelations she had seen in David's files, she couldn't keep herself from fantasizing and wondering what the feel of his lips on hers would be like.

Lisa wasn't sure, but as he pulled her body against hers she perceived his arousal as a pressure against her thigh. It startled her, and helped break the trance. Lisa took a deep breath and extricated herself from the doctor's hold. David had been lowering his head to hers for a kiss that was not to be. Their eyes met, as David's arms fell from her shoulders. In place of the bright sparkle in his eyes that she had seen on prior occasions, Lisa sensed only sadness.

"I'm sorry, Lisa. I really only wanted to comfort you. I hope you don't take this wrong, but sometimes I wish I had someone as special as you in my life. Please don't be offended by my actions. I won't let it happen again."

Lisa felt grateful for the space between them and took another half step back, away from temptation.

"Dr. Layton, I don't know what to say. I love working here with you." Lisa hesitated, not knowing what to say next. "You're a great man— smart, handsome, successful,............ but I am married, and love my husband very much. I appreciate your concern, but we can't allow anything to happen between us."

Layton looked at Lisa. Were Mrs. Martin's words the entire truth? He was fairly certain that he could feel her desire for him. Or was he totally off-base since she had clearly expressed her desire to be true to her husband and her marriage.

David allowed the moment to pass.

"I understand, Lisa. I promise to behave. Go home. I'm sure you have better things to do on a nice Friday afternoon than to stay here."

He didn't mean to sound cold, but Layton was eager to be alone. He felt depressed; feelings which were made worse by her tempting presence in his office. Though he had promised to act professionally, the embrace lingered in his mind, and acted like a breeze on hot embers, ready to be stoked at the slightest provocation.

"I do. I've got to pick up the boys from school. We have dinner plans. Have a nice weekend." Lisa quietly left the office.

David sat down at his desk. He had returned because he had forgotten whether he had locked it. He knew that it was unlikely that anyone would be in his office over the weekend or have access to his files. But never the less, with the officers snooping around he had become concerned about the need for maintaining the security of the materials relating to the Botox study.

Layton gave a gentle tug on his file drawer and was comforted to find it locked. He opened the smaller compartment containing the key and found it just where he had left it.

"I'll have to keep this safer," he thought to himself as he opened the drawer. Layton placed the key in the lock and accessed his files. Everything seemed fine—at first anyway. David wrinkled his brow slightly as he noticed something unusual among the charts. Several of the files sat slightly askew in the drawer and were minimally higher than those in front and behind them. Any other person might not have noticed, but Layton was meticulous in everything he did. He did not recall leaving the records in disarray. David pulled out the cluster of charts that were protruding slightly. Davidson, Ehrlich, Fannestack and English.

The surgeon felt uneasy. His training encouraged precision and accuracy in everything he did. These charts had been placed in the file drawer incorrectly alphabetized, with Fannestack before English, instead of after. Furthermore, they appeared to have been placed back among the others with disregard for the neatness David prided himself in maintaining. He considered the frightening possibility that someone else had been looking at the records. One of the charts that was askew had been that of the Fannestack woman, and it had been the file that was incorrectly alphabetized. Both the detectives and Lisa had been alone in his office. David shuddered. He opened the files and found the contents intact. Nothing seemed altered.

I have been forgetful lately; maybe I just made a small mistake myself when I filed these. The thought helped to comfort the plastic surgeon. He placed the charts back in their proper places and locked the cabinet. This time, he pocketed the key.

I'll have to keep this key with me for now on. Maybe the files would be safer at the house? David decided that would definitely be a wise move, and planned a return visit to the office during the weekend, when Becky would be gone and no one else around. He would remove the files then.

CHAPTER 54

It was Sal's weekend to check on the lab. Rick, one of the part-time lab techs, worked two weekends each month, taking a few hours on Saturday and Sunday for the extra pay. Sal went in at least one weekend a month and Ed Neouri worked the final slot.

The mice were tattooed for identification. Each mouse had between one to four green dots tattooed on the inner top portion of the right ear. They were then placed according to sex, four to a cage, and each mouse in the cage bore a different number of dots. Otherwise, they all appeared quite similar. One hundred and four mice remained in the study.

On the weekends, unless there was an unusual event such as an illness to record, laboratory duties were fairly simple. Sal was amused at the unusual activity that greeted him today at cage number twelve. One of the male mice was attempting to 'mount' another. This happened from time to time, but these two were staying together longer than usual. Sal tapped on the cage and the distraction was enough to cause the mice to uncouple. Manzari recorded the activity on the chart clipped to the cage. He continued past the remaining cages and noticed that Ed had documented similar activity the day before in cages fifteen, nineteen and twenty-one.

"I guess all the mice are getting a little bored," he mused to himself. "I'll have to see how much of this is going on; we may have to separate the mice if they get too frisky with each other." Sal continued with his chores.

Manzari was preparing to close the lab. He spotted the familiar boxy silhouette of the USPS mail trunk leaving the area. He wondered whether the copy of the lab report from Quantum Labs might have arrived. "Probably won't get here til next week." He went back to the lab and grabbed the key to the post office delivery area provided for the lab. Sal opened the door of the office and was confronted by the ninety degree heat of early fall, October the 8th.

"This global warming is gonna kill me," he muttered.

Sal wiped a few wisps of hair out of his eyes and pushed the sweaty strands back over the top of his balding head. He made his way over to the postal boxes, and opened the Youth Labs box, number 59.

Bills and credit card offers. A couple of trade journals. A supply catalog from Southwestern Chemical Marketing. On the bottom of the small pile was an elongated envelope with the return address of Quantum Labs in Miami.

Sal placed the letter on top of the pile and returned to the lab. The cool air that greeted him when he opened the office door was refreshing, and after more than twenty years of working in and around laboratories, the chemical and medicinal odors of the lab were as comforting as home.

Manzari placed some drops of water on the back flap of the Quantum Labs envelope. Next, he placed the letter in the kitchen microwave and started it on low power for ten seconds. When he opened the door, the flap of the envelope had partially peeled open. A few more drops of water and eight more seconds in the microwave produced the desired effect;

the envelope was opened without being torn.

Inside, Sal found two sheets of paper, bearing the same info he had received the day before. The mass spectrometry data identified the two compounds. A hand-written note from Hal Linchitz, read, "Hope this helps, buddy. Hope to see you soon, Hal."

Manzari looked at the envelope. It had a clear cellophane window, and had been stamped with the return address in Miami. Sal examined the mass spec page containing the first specimen. It demonstrated the peaks for the added hydroxyl and carbon bonds, the features which made their drug different that the original Botox. This was their study compound. At the bottom of the page, an addendum read: This result matches the data from a prior sample submitted on February, 12, 2008." He walked over to his desk and removed a bottle of 'White Out'. Sal carefully covered over the words of his name and address. Next, Manzari used a label-maker and printed out three labels; one for Dr. David Layton, a second for 101 Palm Drive, Suite B103, and the third read, Pelican Cove, FL 34610. Sal placed them neatly over the White-Out covered address on the sheet of laboratory data and printed a copy of the report.

"Not good enough," he grumbled.

Thin black lines were visible between the entries of the address where the labels had been placed. Sal adjusted the brightness on the machine and ran another copy. This time the result was perfect. He now had a laboratory report containing mass spec findings identical to the original data which they had obtained at the start of the study. Sal made two copies; representing the two lab specimens submitted. He carefully folded the sheets and was about to place them in the envelope, when he realized that they both listed the specimen number as B15. Sal checked the other sheet of data from Quantum. It listed the specimen as B20.

"Wow, that was close," thought the chemist. "All I needed was for Dr. Layton to see that both sheets were from the same vial." Sal again utilized the White-Out and label maker, this time creating a new label for each sheet, creating matching typesets of numbers to cover the B15 typed on the first page, and one with B20, for the second specimen. New photocopies were made. Sal now had two laboratory reports, for two different specimens, each reporting the same data—two identical chemicals matching their original study drug. Manzari folded the sheets of paper and placed them in the envelope. He utilized a glue stick to seal the flap and taped the envelope shut. The tricky part was still ahead.

Sal closed the lab and drove to Dr. Layton's office on Palm Drive. He scanned the parking lot, searching for David's Mercedes sedan. The doctor's private parking spot was unoccupied. Sal parked the car and walked over to the postal box area for Dr. Layton's complex. Before leaving his office, he had attached a 'sticky' note to the front of the Quantum Labs envelope and scribbled on it, "Not our mail, incorrectly delivered". Sal placed the envelope in the outgoing mail slot provided by the USPS. Tenants of the complex utilized it to leave their outgoing correspondence for the postal carrier to bring back to the post office for sorting and delivery. Manzari knew from experience that letters were sometimes misdirected and hoped that this letter would automatically be redirected to Dr. Layton when the mail was sorted by the postal carrier on Monday. With any luck, the note would be removed and the envelope and its laboratory data placed in the doctor's box. Sal hastily departed from the complex. Mission accomplished.

CHAPTER 55

D avid enjoyed a peaceful morning at home. The condominium
penthouse he had purchased when he first came to Pelican Cove
had been a steal. When Henry Johnson, a former CEO of a large
Midwestern department store chain died, his widow decided to move
into a retirement facility where she could be around other people. David
was able to obtain partial financing from the widow, while he became
established in his practice. The condo, which had cost him $600,000,
was now worth over five million dollars. It was the cornerstone of his
retirement nest egg. A home equity line on the property had helped fund
Youth Labs. The apartment afforded the doctor with a beautiful view of
the Gulf of Mexico and the surrounding community. David had
converted one room into an exercise compound, including free weights,
a treadmill and a rowing machine.

His study had a window view of the Gulf and included plenty of room
for his ancient maps, files and library. The décor in the study was more
traditional than the rest of the home. It contained a small complement
of antiques, including a massive Shaker style desk he had purchased at an

auction and an early seventeenth century wall unit made of solid oak. It contained mementoes of his life, including awards and souvenirs from his travels. Part of his cartography collection occupied one of the walls. The ancient maps were enclosed in glass. A wall safe was hidden behind one of the old maps, and held his important papers, some jewelry, and cash.

David yawned—his sleep had been interrupted by dreams, though he really couldn't remember any of them. He thought that there might have been a beautiful young woman in one of them, and imagined that the subject of the dream may have been Mrs. Martin. Thoughts of Mrs. Martin and work rekindled David's concerns regarding his Botox study. Could someone have been reading his private files? Layton reminded himself to head over to the office and remove the study data to his home for safe-keeping. It would be inconvenient in that any additional Botox treatment data would have to be recorded at the office and he would then have to bring the information back to his home to enter it into the study files. However, the peace of mind of knowing that the data was out of the reach of prying eyes would be well worth the added efforts. With this matter settled in his mind, David's thoughts wandered to preparing for his evening plans.

David liked to spoil his dates. Tonight's plans included dinner at Cote d'Escargot, a country French restaurant with one of the best chefs in town. David was a regular at the small exclusive restaurant. This time of year, tables were easy to get, but when the seasonal residents returned in the winter there would be a two month wait for a table on a weekend night. This was to be his second time out with Kerri Colle. She was his pharmaceutical rep from Realagen, the manufacturer of the collagen agent he used in his practice for treating wrinkles. Kerri, was a statuesque brunette with all-American-girl good looks. Her comely appearance certainly assisted her in obtaining appointments with the physicians she called on, but was not her only attribute. Although only twenty-five-years-old she was astute, and knew her product line thoroughly. David respected her knowledge and professional attitude and always enjoyed her visits to his office.

Just after seven-thirty David left his apartment in order to pick up Kerri. Layton pulled up to her townhouse and Kerri made her way over to the sedan. She was frowning.

"David, I've been waiting for you. It's almost eight o'clock."

"I know, but our reservations are for eight, and the restaurant is right around the corner."

"You told me seven-thirty."

"I don't think so. I remember eight." As they spoke, David pulled out his cell phone, pulled up the number for Cote d'Escargot and dialed it through.

"Cote d'Escargot, may I help you?"

"Yes, this is Dr. Layton. I believe I have a reservation for eight o'clock."

"Good evening, Dr. Layton. So nice to hear from you. But we had you down for seven-thirty."

"Gosh, I'm sorry; I could have sworn it was for eight. Do you still have a table available?"

"Certainly, Doctor, we've saved it for you. You will be coming for dinner then?"

"Yes, and please uncork a bottle of my favorite 1996 Canyon Vineyards Cabernet. By the time it's had a chance to breathe we should be there. My apologies."

"No worries, Dr. Layton. We'll look forward to seeing you."

Kerri leaned over to David and gave him a light kiss on the cheek. She looked stunning with just the right amount of make-up to highlight her beautiful big brown eyes. She had on a light blue form-fitting blouse from Abercrombie over a cream-colored camisole. Her long legs were covered in tight black pants finished off in Dolce and Gabbana stiletto heels.

"Do you forgive me?"

Kerri smiled coyly.

"Maybe, you'll have to make it up to me."

"And how can I do that?" David smiled back with a big grin.

"I'm sure we can figure something out before the night is over." Kerri flashed a perfect smile at the surgeon and seductively flicked the tip of her tongue over her glossy lips.

This had all the markings of a great evening.

David ordered lobster bisque which was the richest, most savory concoction he had ever tasted. Kerri started with a simple salad of baby greens. It was expertly prepared with the addition of small orange slices and candied walnuts. For his main course, David ordered the Coq au Vin, the chef's specialty. Kerri's entrée was a delicately prepared red snapper with a dusting of macadamia nuts. The sauce was a buttery delight that melted in the young woman's mouth. Jacques, the chef, was known for his way with vegetables and both dishes were complemented by perfectly sautéed French green beans almandine and baby carrots with pine nuts.

"Do we have any room for dessert?" asked their waiter, Peter.

"I'm afraid I'm stuffed, Peter."

"And the lady?"

"Ditto for me. But everything was delicious."

The waiter smiled.

"Perhaps an after dinner drink...... some cognac? I also have some very special late-harvest dessert wines."

David appreciated the waiter's excellent service and desire to increase their tab, which already had climbed to almost three hundred dollars.

"No thanks, I think we're ready for the check. Next time I think we'll have to skip lunch so that we have room for one of your excellent soufflés."

The waiter smiled. "I'll have the check for you right away, sir."

The waiter returned with a small ceramic tray containing their check and two small squares of Ghiradelli chocolate wrapped in bright gold foil.

David unwrapped his sweet and reached across the table. He placed it in front of Kerri's delicate lips.

She winked coyly at the doctor and opened her mouth invitingly. David gently dropped the chocolate onto her lower lip, which she then helped guide into her open mouth with the side of her tongue.

"I think we should go now," Kerri softly exclaimed with some huskiness in her voice.

David paid the check, which included a generous tip, and the handsome couple exited the restaurant.

CHAPTER 56

6:58. Lisa had heard Nate flush the toilet and had remained in bed several minutes. She was playing her game and guessing the time again. Sleepy eyes focused on the digital clock. It read 7:06. Not that good she thought. "I hope the rest of the day goes better." She considered it a bad omen when she couldn't do better with her time-guessing game. Lisa hopped out of bed.

To her surprise, Shawn was already out of bed. Lisa could hear the unmistakable sound of the boy emptying his bladder into the toilet. The door was ajar.

"Wake up Josh." Lisa shook her seven-year-old gently. His eyes fluttered open and he smiled lethargically.

"Good morning, Mom. I love you."

"What a nice thing to say first thing in the morning, Josh. I love you even more." She pulled her son close to her and held him tightly against her chest.

"This is one of those things that American Express would show in one of their commercials as priceless," Lisa said half to herself and half to her precious child.

"We have to get going, Josh. Up and at 'em." She released her hold on her son. Shawn came back into the bedroom.

"Good morning, Shawn. Three things; first – close the door when you're going to the bathroom; second – flush the toilet when you're finished; and third – wash your hands before you leave the bathroom. Now go back in there and wash up please."

Shawn frowned.

"Come on Mom, I just woke up!" Shawn walked back into the bathroom and gave his hands a perfunctory rinsing.

"I'll be downstairs. Waffles for breakfast. Your clothes are on the chair, Shawn and yours are on the edge of the bed, Josh." Lisa made her way to the kitchen.

Lisa removed the package of frozen Aunt Jemima waffles. In an hour or so she would be at work. Should she say something to Dr. Layton regarding her questions from the detectives? Now that she knew that Janetta had been treated at the office, and now that she knew that Dr. Layton appeared to be hiding something, what should she do? Her thoughts were interrupted by Nate's appearance in the kitchen.

"Good morning. Did you have a good night's sleep?" Nate was dressed for work.

"Morning, honey. I guess I slept okay. Do you think you could get the boys to the bus stop this morning? I still have to wash and dry my hair and it's going to be hard for me to get it all done and still be on time for work."

Nate sighed.

"If you really need me to, I guess I can, but I got up early so that I could get a jump on the day. I've got so much work piled up at the office. Is there any chance you could get your boss to agree to let you start work later so you won't have trouble getting the boys off to school and still be able to get to work on time?"

Lisa hated those 'sighs'. Nate's response left her feeling angry. She didn't want him to agree to do something after a heavy sigh and a long explanation of how much trouble it would be to do it. More than that, she hated it when he made her feel guilty over having to ask for something.

She let out her own sigh.

"Don't worry, I can do it all. I'll just let my hair dry on the way to work." Now it was her turn to lay on the guilt.

"Next time, just let me know in advance, and I can get up early enough to help." Maybe Nate was trying to make her feel better, but the damage had been done. Her mood had been soured. She knew it wasn't going to be a good day as soon as she hadn't guessed the time on her alarm clock more accurately.

"Sure, Nate," Lisa responded with a total lack of emotion in her voice. She continued preparing breakfast for the boys, and turned her back on Nate.

"Please don't be mad at me, honey. I'm under a lot of pressure at work."

In her mind, Lisa wanted to respond, "You always are." Instead, she muttered, "I appreciate how hard you work, Nate. I work hard too."

"I know you do, and I appreciate it."

If only he would show it with his actions. Lisa tried not to sulk.

"Come on down boys, breakfast is ready."

CHAPTER 57

The mundane routine of work was a welcome change from her tension-filled breakfast with Nate. It had been a busy Monday morning. One of the patients had returned to the office with an unexpected hematoma, a collection of blood, beneath her face-lift incision. It had taken Dr. Layton an extra half hour to correct and the doctor was now forty-five minutes behind schedule. Their tardiness forced them to work a little harder and eliminated some of the usual banter of chit-chat in the office. Not having the time to make conversation made it easier for Lisa to camouflage some of her discomfort around Dr. Layton.

Lisa found herself alone with their next patient, Carolyn Toscano. Clearly, the woman was addicted to sun bathing. She had a very dark tan and bleached blond shoulder length hair. Lisa examined the chart and noted that the patient was only thirty-eight, but appeared to have the skin of a woman ten years older. She was heavily freckled and had more wrinkles than most fifty-year-olds. It was also apparent that she had previously had breast enhancement surgery. This was her third visit to the office; she had received Reallagen last year, and Botox injections three months earlier.

"Good morning, Mrs. Toscano. I'm Lisa. I understand you're here for some more Reallagen."

"Maybe. Actually, I was really pleased with the results from the Botox at the last visit and was hoping that the doctor might be able to give me some more. It costs less than the Reallagen and seems to last quite long."

"You'll have to discuss that with Dr. Layton. Sometimes, the Botox can't help the deeper wrinkles, and sometimes the best results happen when the two are used together. He'll be here in a just a minute. He'll know."

Dr. Layton knocked on the door; then entered.

"Good morning Mrs. Toscano. How have you been?"

"Great, Dr. Layton. But I still have some wrinkles I'd like to get rid of—especially these deep ones by my mouth, and a few of the smaller ones by my eyes and between my eyebrows."

David furrowed his brow and frowned.

"Carolyn, as much as I love having you in the office, I'd much rather see you come in without that nasty tan. It's ruining your skin and giving you all your wrinkles."

"I know, I know—you sound just like my mother. But I feel so unhealthy without a tan. I promise, if you help me with my wrinkles I'll try to get less sun. I'll even use sunscreen."

David doubted the sincerity of her reply, but appreciated that she had at least promised to try to improve her ways. He brought his face closer to hers in order to better examine her prematurely aged skin.

"I think we can give you significant improvement with Botox for the smaller wrinkles of your upper face, but for the deeper wrinkles around your mouth we'll need to use the Reallagen."

"I had a feeling you were going to say that. How much will it cost me?"

"The Botox would be the same as last time, $450. The Reallagen is a more expensive material; it costs $950 per vial. You may need more than one vial to treat the area around your mouth."

"I think all I'll have you do today is the Botox, if that's okay. Let me save up for the Reallagen."

"That's fine, Carolyn. I wish I could charge you less, but that Reallagen is costly material. The price of beauty."

"Tell me about it Dr. Layton."

An hour later, Lisa found herself escorting another young woman, Alex Lankin, to an exam room.

"Good morning, Alexa, I'm Lisa, Dr. Layton's nurse."

Lisa glanced at the chart while the patient took a seat. Ms. Lankin was apparently divorced, as the 'Mrs.' had been crossed out in the chart and her last name had been changed. New letters had been placed over the old ones on the outside of her record in order to correctly alphabetize her chart with her new/old name. Alexa was tall, about five foot-ten, and in great shape for a woman of fifty-five. A review of her chart revealed that Alexa appeared to be what Dr. Layton had referred to as a 'Botox junkie.' Ms. Lankin had been in the office eleven times in just over two years. Her last visit had been only four weeks earlier.

"What can we do for you today?"

"The usual. I just need a little touch up of this little wrinkle by my left eye and one by the glabella."

It was always a 'red flag' when the patients knew their anatomical areas by their scientific names. It indicated that they had been in the office many times or on the internet researching their treatment.

"Has anything changed in your medical history?"

"I'm taking glucosamine now for my joints, and a multivitamin. Otherwise, no, nothing has changed. Oh, I do take Ambien every now and then."

"Do you have a lot of trouble sleeping Alexa?"

"Yes and no. Most nights I sleep okay, but for the last few weeks, about twice a week I've been having dreams that interfere with my sleep. If you want to know the truth, the dreams haven't been all that bad. They're all very erotic and sexual. Sometimes, I even wake up remembering parts of them. But they do interfere with my sleep."

Lisa remembered Tonya Williams from the prior week who had also had erotic dreams.

"Well, I guess if you're going to dream, those are the kind of dreams worth having! I'll let Dr. Layton know we're ready. I'll be back in a minute."

"Thanks, I'll be right here."

Lisa placed the chart outside the door, a signal to Dr. Layton that there was a patient awaiting his care. It also gave the doctor an opportunity to review the chart before entering the room. David had just finished with another of his patients and Barbara was giving the woman her instructions and escorting her to the front desk. The doctor quickly removed Alexa's chart from the slot at the door where he was joined by Mrs. Martin.

"I see Ms. Lankin is here for a tune-up. Same old thing Lisa?"

"Seems so, Dr. Layton. She seems happy with her treatment, she just wants some more."

"Let me show you a little office secret, Lisa. See these little letters on the bottom of the inside of the chart?"

Lisa looked below Dr. Layton's thumb on the corner of the chart and saw 'BJ' in small black letters. The nurse turned red, wondering what the letters BJ might mean and having only one possibility come to mind.

"It stands for 'Botox junkie'. We've got another one, 'CJ' for cosmetic junkie. When we have a chart like this, we know right away that it's someone who is demanding—either wanting a lot of appointments, a lot of attention, or both."

"I probably should let you know, Dr. Layton. She's been having weird dreams."

"What kind of dreams?"

"Erotic ones, for the past several weeks. She's been losing some sleep and has been taking Ambien sometimes because of it. She's not taking any other medications, and otherwise is doing well. It's funny. I didn't think to tell this to you earlier, because I didn't want to embarrass the patient and I didn't think it had anything to do with her treatment, but Tonya Williams, who we saw last week, also mentioned having the same sort of thing."

David recalled his own dreams involving his nurse and became somewhat self-conscious. He also wondered if there might be any connection between the dreams and the Botox treatments. Could it be related to the Botox? David recalled the changes in the fornix, the area possibly involved in sexual arousal, noted in the string of recent deaths in Pelican Cove.

"Thanks for the information, Lisa. I don't think it's related to our treatment, but I'll go online later and research it. In all the years I've been administering Botox I've never heard of this before so it's probably just a coincidence."

David hoped that he sounded convincing. He certainly had his own concerns and a growing apprehension regarding the chances for success of his research drug.

Alexa's treatment was over in a few minutes. The nice thing about a frequent 'customer' was that very little explanation was necessary. The appointment was more like a touch-up at the manicurist than a doctor's visit. It was all still new to Lisa, and she found every patient interesting. She imagined that after a while it must get boring for the doctor. Of course, he was paid quite well for his time.

At two-thirty Lisa prepared to leave. She had been busy all day and had not had much time to think about the files in Dr. Layton's office. She walked past the room, in search of the doctor. The hallway was empty as was the doctor's office. Lisa entered the room. A small scrap of paper was visible on the doctor's desk, containing the names of Tonya Williams and Alexa Lankin. Lisa was able to read, "check Botox lot" in Dr. Layton's handwriting. Were they somehow linked to the group of files in the doctor's desk? Lisa took a deep breath and gave a tug on the file drawer which housed the records she had briefly examined on Friday. She was a little bit surprised when the compartment opened easily. The reason was immediately clear – not only was the drawer now unlocked, but it was also empty.

CHAPTER 58

David had a lot on his mind. First, there were the pathologist Jack Shea's findings of possible neurological damage in several of his patients. Shea had mentioned thickening and hypertrophy of the fornix. The lab animals had died with similar findings. And now his patients were experiencing sexually-tinged dreams. As a matter of fact, even he had had a pretty erotic dream. "Now that's probably not so bad a side-effect if we could fine tune it," he mused. That thought was rapidly replaced by his concern regarding the possible intrusion into his records and the questioning by the detectives. As a distraction, he decided to read his mail. The first envelope grabbed David's attention. It was from Quantum Labs.

David tore open the back of the envelope and pulled out the contents. He reviewed both sheets of paper. The mass spec findings were identical. Layton noted that both samples had been evaluated and that each sheet identified a unique test vial.

David picked up the phone and dialed Sal Manzari.

The phone was answered on the fifth ring.

"Youth Labs, can I help you?"

David recognized the clear, somewhat effeminate voice of Sal's assistant, Ed. "Hi, Ed, this is Dr. Layton. Is your boss there?"

"Sure, Dr. Layton, let me get him for you."

Sal picked up the line.

"Hi, David?"

Layton could hear slight breathlessness in Sal's voice from the relatively minor exertion of walking quickly to the phone.

"Hi, Sal. Have a good weekend?"

"Not too eventful, just the usual harem of beautiful women in my bedroom."

David pretended to laugh. He felt much too serious to joke.

"Sal, I received the mass spec results today. It seems that you're doing your job as perfectly as always. Both samples tested out as pure and matched our prior study chemical. Nothing about the test compound appears changed. The neurological problems are hard to explain; I still think they may be a fluke. We're going to require larger numbers of animals in the study—if we can evaluate larger numbers of subjects, a poor outcome in just a few will be much less significant."

Sal had hoped for a different conclusion from the doctor.

"Are we going to continue with the study?"

"I'm meeting with BioVenture on Friday. I think I may end up having to be a lot less demanding in the financial terms I try to arrange in view of our recent developments. I'm going to try to get them to agree to compensate us for our expenses to date and for two years into the future. We can increase our staff and purchase more animals. We'll go for a bigger office and a generous salary for you and a consulting fee for me. Then, if it doesn't work out, we'll at least have something to show for our efforts. If it does work, we'll get our piece of the drug development money and future royalties."

Sal was at a loss for words. He had his own meeting scheduled, and he doubted that Bobby Volpe was going to be as pleasant as the investors from Bio Venture.

"I'll keep plugging away, Dr. Layton. I'm sorry the testing isn't going as smoothly as we hoped. I would understand if you wanted to terminate the study. It's not as if we haven't given it our best shot........" Sal knew he was throwing a 'Hail Mary' pass here – he didn't think it would hurt if he let the doctor know that he supported him in ending the research.

"I'm surprised at you, Sal. I never had you pegged for a quitter. Let's see what the Bio Venture guys say and we'll take it from there."

There was nothing more for Sal to say.

"Okay, David."

"By the way, Sal, how's everything in the lab?"

Sal's mind was already contemplating his upcoming meeting and conversation with the crime boss. He barely heard the question.

Sal considered telling David of the increased sexual activity of the mice in the lab, but was eager to end the conversation and saw no benefit to advising Layton of the observations, which seemed so unimportant now.

"Everything's hunky-dory here David," Sal answered with a touch of sarcasm.

If he detected anything unusual in the biochemist's tone, David didn't acknowledge it in his response.

"Great, then I'll talk to you later in the week. I'll need the most up-to-date data on the lab subjects by Wednesday, or Thursday morning at the latest. We'll also need to have pictures of a few of the mice."

"I'll take care of it. Anything else?"

Layton thought he could appreciate something out of sorts in Sal's tone. The fat man sounded down, or depressed. David attributed it to concern over the study.

"No, Sal. Let me let you go. Have a good night."

"Good night, David." Sal murmured.

CHAPTER 59

Detective Collins returned to work on Monday in significant pain. Despite his most gallant attempts and almost religious use of sunscreen, he had burned incredibly while fishing in the Keys. His face was a bright shade of pink, obscuring his usually prominent freckles.

Captain Pincer greeted him.

"I see you're here bright and early—and I do mean bright. Are you going to be able to work today?"

"Absolutely, Captain. Just don't slap me on the back. I'm okay, as long as I don't move too much and nobody touches me."

"So tell me about your trip out to the doctor's office. Anything pan out?"

"I think I'd have to say negative on that one. Both Dan and I feel that there may be something there, but the nurse we spoke to, one of the victim's best friends, corroborated the doctor's story. Maybe if we had more time……"

Pincer cut Collins off in mid-sentence.

"More time is something we definitely do not have. As of this morning, I'm closing the file on Janetta Fannestack. The case will go to the District Attorney and we'll let it be his headache. Frankly, it's one case I'm happy to shut the door on."

Kevin knew it would be useless to ask Pincer for any more time. Anyway, the captain was probably right. It wasn't as if there weren't enough things to keep him and his partner busy.

"Whatever you say, Captain. So what do you have for us today?"

Captain Pincer had a string of high-end auto thefts eagerly awaiting the detectives' attention. The bad guys never took a day off.

CHAPTER 60

Though she had gone to bed early, Lisa did not feel rested. She rarely remembered her dreams, but this morning she recalled several. In one, Janetta was with her in a bar and had gone off to the restroom. Lisa turned around and saw a man placing a pill in her friend's drink. When she looked up to see who the man was, it was her boss, Dr. Layton. When Janetta returned from the bathroom, Lisa tried to stop her from consuming the fluid, but instead, watched helplessly as her friend drank the tainted liquid. The second dream was less disturbing, but certainly interfered equally with her sleep. Lisa was completely naked and lying in her bed. Nate was with her and began kissing her passionately. Lisa had closed her eyes and embraced her husband. She could feel his arms around her and eagerly awaited the culmination of their love-making. When she opened her eyes in order to gaze at her husband, she was disturbed to find that the face of the man in her bed was that of Dr. David Layton, attached to the body of her husband Nate. She had been aroused when she awoke, and felt peeved at her loss of sleep. She wondered whether all of the talk of dreams of a sexual nature at work had stimulated her own imagination.

Lisa was trying to push herself out of bed. She had already dawdled several minutes and did not want the boys to be late for school through her lethargy. Bounding out of bed, she attacked her morning duties.

After the boys were safely off to school, Lisa returned to her quiet home. Only the low drone of lawn mowers and whine of weed-wackers from the neighbor's gardeners broke the tranquility of the silence in her house. She decided to take advantage of her Tuesday off from work to tackle her chores. There were several loads of laundry to conquer. With determination, she began carrying the soiled clothing and towels from the boy's room and the hamper in the closet she shared with Nate. Next, Lisa went about the task of sorting the dirty clothes into lights and darks, with a third pile for the clothing that needed to go to the dry cleaner. Mostly, the dry cleaning consisted of Nate's dress shirts, though now that Lisa was working she occasionally had some of her own items which required the extra care of professional laundering. Like most of her jobs around the house, she found it mostly mindless and thankless work. None the less, it had to be done.

The stacks grew as Lisa was down to the last few items in her laundry basket. There was a blue pinpoint Oxford near the bottom that Lisa prepared to toss into the dry-cleaning pile, but as it passed her face she caught a whiff of an unfamiliar perfume. Her relaxed mental state went from automatic-pilot laundry sorting to red alert. Examining the shirt more closely, she brought it to beneath her nose and inhaled. The sweet odor of a feminine fragrance filled her nostrils. Her morning tranquility was replaced by fears of infidelity on the part of her husband. Lisa examined the clothing again, hoping to extract some clue as to the owner of the scent.

Lisa checked the breast pocket for a phone number, or card or anything suggestive of another woman. Thoughts of the young attorney who had accompanied Nate to lunch filled her mind. No evidence was to be found. She was about to give up her search and place the offensive shirt in the pile with the rest of Nate's soiled laundry when she spotted a red smudge on the inner left side of the collar. A little voice in her head entered uninvited, with the words, "Lipstick on your collar, told a tale on you," part of an old song from a bygone era. Lisa felt betrayed. Was Nate cheating on her? What was she going to do? Now that Janetta was gone, she had no one to confide in. Her best friend was dead and her husband was spending more and more time away from the family and maybe in another woman's arms. She felt all alone and out of control. Throbbing began in her head and she feared a migraine was coming on. In order to circumvent the migraine and to gain some control of her emotions, Lisa turned on the television hoping to be distracted by others people's problems.

CHAPTER 61

"How's it going, Ed?" Manzari was a few minutes late getting to the lab. His employee was already busy at work.

"Same-old, same-old, boss. The animals all seem at peace with the world today. All of the mice are healthy, though a few of them seem a little 'frisky'."

"What do you mean?"

"More mounting activity than usual. I've entered the data into the logs for cages nine, eleven and twenty-two. Also twenty-six, I think."

"I doubt it's anything, especially not likely to be medication related, but we'll have to keep an eye on it. Anything else?"

"Yeah, it's cleaning cages day, would you care to join in?"

Neouri knew better. Sal did most of the jobs in the lab, but cleaning the cages wasn't one of them.

"Okay, Ed. You get started and I'll join you in a little while."

Neouri laughed to himself.

"Sure, boss."

Sal took a walk past the cages and checked on the animals. He reviewed

Ed's meticulous notes for cages nine, eleven, twenty-two and twenty-six. Animal mountings were described, including the time the activity was first noted and its duration. It was likely that there was some activity that was being missed, as the personnel were not always monitoring the cages. The trend was unmistakable. There appeared to be an increase in sexual arousal among the mice. If it continued, he would have to consider sacrificing one of the mice to determine if there were any anatomical or pathological changes which could be evaluated under the microscope. He decided to draw some blood for analysis of hormone levels to see if anything was abnormal. The tests were costly, but much more practical than an autopsy.

It was still early morning and Sal considered heading out to buy a newspaper and catch a cup of coffee before drawing the blood samples on the mice. A phone call interrupted his thoughts. All three employees in the lab were away from their desks, cleaning cages. Sal picked up the receiver and fielded the call.

"Youth Labs, may I help you?"

"Pinching nickels, 'ey Sallie? I like that, answerin' your own phones. Keep the expenses down."

"Good morning, Mr. Volpe." Sal's heart began to race and he felt a pit in his stomach. He had feared a call from the crime boss. He knew that Volpe was expecting some progress on eliminating Dr. Layton from the partnership. Sal had gotten no closer to success.

"So, Sal. How goes it? Everythin' runnin' smooth at our lab?"

"Yes, sir, Bobby. No problems here."

"And our little difficulty with your partner?"

Sal hesitated. There was no use lying. In a sullen voice, Sal responded, "Mr. Volpe. I haven't been able to get him to back out yet. I'm trying my hardest."

There was an icy cold edge to the words Sal heard next.

"You disappoint me, Sal. I don't like to be disappointed. We have a deal. I'm afraid ya haven't fulfilled your part of the bargain."

"But, Mr. Volpe, I…"

"Sal, don't but Mr. Volpe, me—I'm sure ya tried, but it would appear that you're not up to the job. This is business; serious business. I'll have to take care of things myself. And unlike you, I will be sure to get the job done. But it will cost ya for my extra efforts. I'm goin' to have to cut your pay by twenty percent and you'll owe me a favor as big as the one I'll be doin' for ya."

"If I could have a little more time, Bobby, I think I could take care of it myself."

"Sal, ya stay right where you are and continue doin' just what you're doin'. You're a lab guy. Let me take care of the other business arrangements. Keep ya nose to the grindstone and just make sure everythin' in the lab goes the way it's supposed to. If you screw up there I won't be so understandin'."

Sal was distraught. He liked Dr. Layton and didn't want anything bad to happen to his partner. Things felt like they were spiraling out of control.

"Just one more week, Mr. Volpe. I won't let you down."

"No, no more discussion, Sal. I've made my decision. I'll be in touch with ya in a few days. I'll need the newest lab data. We're preparin' a package to 'shop around' to the pharmaceutical boys. The market is so hot for a drug like yours, we'll probably be able to get a 'bidding war' going. Get me some new pictures too. Okay?"

"Sure Mr. Volpe," Sal responded flatly.

"I'll count on it, Sallie. Talk to ya soon."

Sal's skin felt clammy with nervous perspiration. His pulse was thready and he tasted the bitter acidity of the Burger King sausage-biscuit he had purchased on his way to work, rising partially digested in the back of his throat. Sal rushed to the office restroom and locked the door behind him. He hoped no one outside could hear him as he puked three times into the sink. What had he gotten himself into?

CHAPTER 62

The 'mechanic' had been given his orders. It was a clean assignment that paid well. A search through the hacked Florida DMV database had provided the home address for Dr. David Layton along with the make and model of his car. A grey 2005 Mercedes Sedan with a 'Save the Manatee' personalized license plate embossed 'WRNKLMD'.

Security at the condominium consisted of a silver-haired guard watching TV. The guy paid little attention to the mechanic, who parked his car in a visitor's parking spot in the corner shadows. The visitor made his way around the side of the tall condominium and to the first level parking spaces reserved for tenants. He carried a small satchel of tools. A drive through the parking garage earlier in the day had given him some useful information – there was no surveillance camera system in the parking garage for him to worry about. If an emergency arose, he was prepared. I tap on a small bulge over his left breast reassured him that his Walther pistol was safe in its shoulder holster.

Dr. Layton's address was listed in the DMV directory as number 715 of the Surf Tower condominium. The mechanic gazed around the parking lot, stocked with an abundance of luxury vehicles – the three cars directly in front of him were a Lexus SUV, Porsche 944 and an antique Mercedes 450SL. A Hummer was crowded into one of the spots, next to a Prius. At the end of the aisle, parked between a Lincoln and another Lexus was his quarry, a grey Mercedes with a rear license plate bearing the picture of a manatee.

No one was in sight. It was exactly how the mechanic had planned his ten o'clock in the evening visit to the condo. Early enough for the guard not to notice someone visiting, late enough for pedestrian traffic and other visitors to be at a minimum. He made his way to the Mercedes, and tried to remain in the shadows of the parking area.

A casual observer might have mistaken the mechanic for a doctor. He had a black bag, not very unlike a physician's bag. But its contents were meant to serve a very different purpose. He approached the front of the vehicle and silently slid under the car. He worked quickly and efficiently, in many ways similar to a medical surgeon. The mechanic identified the rubber housing covering the assembly leading to the brakes of the left front wheel. He peeled it back and removed a sharpened pipe-cutter from his bag. The man meticulously cut the tube, creating a breach in the braking system of the Mercedes. The entire procedure had taken less than a minute, and had taken place in nearly complete silence. The mechanic repeated the same procedure on the braking assembly of the front right wheel. He placed his tools back in his bag and departed from the shadows as silently as he had arrived. The guard seemed content to continue watching the end of the National League baseball playoffs. He would never recall any suspicious vehicle or driver entering the parking area during his watch.

CHAPTER 63

Lisa had just finished reading an article in her Newsweek magazine. The bed covers were tucked up to her neck and she was enjoying some late-night peace and tranquility. Nate was puttering around in his study and the eleven o'clock news was playing on the television. Was he avoiding her? Lisa had no idea how to ask her husband about the incriminating evidence she had found on his shirt. Maybe he was bored with her. Maybe it was that young attorney; she was certainly sexier looking than his old dowdy wife.

"Nate, why don't you come to bed?" she called through the house.

"In a few minutes honey, I'm just finishing up here."

Another car bomb had exploded in Iraq, killing eight civilians. The miseries of the world sometimes helped remind her of how fortunate they all were and helped place her relatively minor problems into perspective. However, tonight Lisa was feeling much too sorry for herself to feel any sympathy for anyone else's troubles.

Lisa thought of calling to Nate one more time. Instead, she picked up her magazine and continued to read. The article was mildly interesting.

It presented the craze of Texas Hold-Em poker sweeping the younger generation, especially teenage boys. The argument was whether it was good; and teaching the kids the rules of mathematical probability and odds, or bad; creating a future generation of compulsive gamblers. Lisa's eyes grew heavy with fatigue.

Thirty minutes later, Nate came to bed. Lisa was already asleep with the magazine askew on her chest, where it had fallen when she had nodded off. Nate removed it delicately, so as not to wake his wife. After finishing with his nightly routine of tooth brushing and face washing he too drifted off to sleep.

CHAPTER 64

For a moment, David forgot where he was. After his eyes focused on the distant wall; he recognized the comforting outlines of his bedroom. He had awoken to his alarm, but had been deep inside a dream. The abrupt awakening allowed him to remember visions from his sleep that he might otherwise have forgotten. David recalled being out to dinner on a date with the beautiful Kerri Colle, but she had gone to the bathroom and in her place, his receptionist Becky had returned. In his dream, he had wanted to take Becky back to his apartment. She had joined him at dinner, and began touching his thighs beneath the restaurant table. His desire for her grew and he wanted to leave with her without finishing the meal. Becky stood up, but asked him to wait for her while she took her own turn in the restroom. David waited for her patiently. She returned, but as she came close to the table, her silhouette became that of her strapping fireman fiancé. He seemed furious with the doctor. They glared at each other and David sensed that they might come to blows. That was when his alarm had gone off. It seemed like a good time to get up!

Dr. Layton had a fast, cool shower. Feeling invigorated, he attacked a bowl of oatmeal and a glass of fresh orange juice—at least as fresh as the health food store could provide. Coffee would be at the office. David dressed quickly and left his apartment only twenty minutes after his alarm had first awakened him. He opened the door to his Mercedes, hopped in the seat, and switched on the radio. It was his favorite 'driving to work tunes'. He had always been a Rock and Roller, but had been turned on to country music by an ex-girlfriend. She was long gone, but his taste in music had been forever altered. Gator Country's morning show with Val and Scott was on. They were playing some song from Taylor Swift who always seemed to be whining about some boyfriend or other in her songs. The car started with a gentle roar. David immediately noticed that the brake light remained on. He tapped his brake, and everything seemed normal, but the light remained lit.

"Damn it, I'll have to bring the car to the dealer," he muttered.

David placed the car into reverse and maneuvered his way to the condo gate. His remote control raised the barrier and allowed him to exit without stopping. He flew out onto the main street, leaving the Surf Tower Condominium behind. Traffic was light, mostly consisting of parents taking their kids to school and some working-class stiffs. Dr. Layton came to the light at the corner of Queen Palm Drive and Tamiami Trail, also known as US 41. The road connected Tampa to Miami and had provided for much of the development of the area prior to the creation of the interstate highway system in the sixties and seventies. Tamiami Trail was congested with an awful array of strip malls, banks and gas stations. The only redeeming quality at this time of the morning was that it did have some stretches where he could take the car up to fifty-five, and there were a few miles of four lane road before he reached the office. There were no traffic lights and he could cruise while he listened to the radio, and relax before entering into the center of town, traffic and lower speed limits. As he brought the car up to cruising speed, he switched the radio to another favorite station, Quiver 94.5, which played old rock and caught the end of Springsteen's "Thunder Road". He cranked up the volume and sound blasted from the eight speakers of the Mercedes.

"Carpe diem, Bruce," David mused.

Dr. Layton accelerated, his car's speed rising to meet the tone of the music. At sixty-five miles per hour, David lightened his pressure on the gas and allowed the vehicle to begin to slow. About half a mile away, the first traffic lights beckoned, indicating David's entrance into the heart of town and lower speed limits. The legal speed diminished to forty-five and the doctor pressed lightly on the brake. Nothing happened. He pressed more firmly and felt terror as the pedal sank to the floor. The car continued at fifty-three miles an hour and the traffic around the Mercedes intensified as the drivers on either side of his car slowed as they entered a more congested part of the roadway.

Mercifully, the cars in front of David were speeding up, or at least not slowing down, as they tried to cruise through the light up ahead, which was still green.

"Please, please, stay green," David prayed out loud. Only Bruce Springsteen and God could hear his words.

He was almost at the intersection as the light flashed yellow. His speedometer read forty-seven miles an hour. Dr. Layton inhaled deeply. Only one more vehicle stood between him and the intersection. Cars on either side of him were speeding up, trying to make it through the light before it turned red.

The teenager in the Volkswagen Beetle in front of him decided not to run the yellow light and slammed on the brakes. David watched as if in a trance as the distance between his Mercedes and the pale blue Bug halved, then halved again. There was insufficient time for any evasive maneuvers.

Most accidents are accompanied by a screech of tires. This time there was none. Dr. Layton's car tore through the small Volkswagen. The last thing David remembered was the radio's opening lyrics to the Allman Brother's "Rambling Man." Then there was only darkness.

CHAPTER 65

"Welcome back to the world of the living, Dr. Layton."

David forced the cobwebs from his brain. He realized that the woman who had spoken to him was a nurse; she was dressed in a starched white uniform and had a grin on her face. Her name badge said she was Virginia. Dr. Layton imagined she was about fifty, and about as many pounds overweight as her age. She peered at him over her reading glasses and her voice sounded as if it were coming from far away. David felt disoriented and he hurt all over. His chest felt like it was on fire and he had an awful headache.

"Where am I?"

"You're in the Emergency Room of Pelican General, Dr. Layton. We're glad to have you back with us. You've been out for over an hour. Do you remember the accident?"

Slowly, things came back to David.

"I remember being unable to get my car to slow down—the brakes must've failed. And then I came to an intersection. There was a kid in a blue car in front of me. That's the last thing I remember."

"He came in and has already been discharged Dr. Layton. You were both lucky. The airbags saved you. From what I hear, he did a lot better than his car. I think your insurance company is going to want to have some words with you! And your airbag did a little job on your chest and chin."

David was vaguely aware of a burning sensation on his chin. He raised his arm to touch it and was restricted by the intravenous lines which had been inserted into both forearms at the antecubital fossae on the front side of his arms opposite his elbows. There was a bandage on his chin.

"Dr. Greider will be very happy to hear you're awake. He'll want to do a quick neuro evaluation on you. You've got a bruise on your forehead, and he may want to order an MRI as part of the protocol for your loss of consciousness. I don't think you'll be going home for a bit yet."

Dr. Greider had heard the conversation and was comforted to see his fellow physician awake and more or less alert.

"Good morning, Dr. Layton, I'm Dr. William Greider. I don't think we've met before."

"Pleased to meet you Dr. Greider."

"Call me Bill."

"David." Dr. Layton extended his hand, iv and all, across the bed to Dr. Greider and the colleagues shook hands. David didn't realize that the handshake was also Greider's way of evaluating the plastic surgeon's strength and appropriateness of response; part of an informal neurological evaluation.

"David, you took quite a beating in the accident. Are you hurting any place in particular?"

David took a deep breath, searching for discomfort. His stomach felt normal, but after he had taken half of the breath, the added expansion of his chest became uncomfortable, though not terribly so.

Greider noticed Layton's discomfort.

"We don't think you've broken any ribs. The airbag really helped, though it did give you some abrasions that'll take a few weeks to go away. Because of your prolonged loss of consciousness, I would like to check an MRI just to be sure nothing is amiss before we send you home. I understand you live alone?"

"Yes, I do."

"It would be entirely reasonable to spend at least the daytime hours here for observation so that we can do thorough neuro checks on you for the next twelve hours. Then, if everything is okay; if you can get someone to stay with you, or a visiting nurse to spend the night, we can send you home. Or, since the hospital really isn't too crowded right now, we can just keep you overnight."

"Why don't we see how it goes? I really feel pretty crummy right now. I can't imagine taking care of myself, even though I'm no wuss. When I leaned forward to shake your hand the room spun a little and I ache all over."

"Okay, David. Let me do a quick neurological exam on you now that you're awake. Then we'll get you down to radiology and take care of the MRI."

"I'm all yours." Layton tried to turn his body to better face the doctor and felt discomfort in his back and throbbing in his head. He tried to force a smile on his face for Dr. Greider's benefit.

He endured a quick, but thorough examination. There were no findings suggestive of brain injury or neurological damage. Now that David was awake, the emergency room physician was able to probe Dr. Layton more thoroughly for any discomfort. He had David move each of his joints, evaluating all areas for disability.

"Ouch, man that hurts, Bill."

Greider had been pressing on the center of David's sternum, where a bruise and air bag abrasion were clearly visible. Dr. Layton tried to shift his body away from the pressure.

"I don't see any deviation of the bone, and your cardiogram is normal. It's unlikely that you've suffered any cardiac damage, but I think we should order a set of cardiac enzymes just to be sure you didn't suffer a contusion of your heart. It appears that the worst of your damage was to your chest wall, but since you had that coma, we've got to be careful about your brain too."

"How's my car?"

"I'm afraid you won't be driving it anytime soon. From what I heard from the police report, the entire front end got crunched. The radiator was destroyed and there was antifreeze all over the road. I don't think it was anything that can't be fixed, though. Don't worry about that now— let's just work on getting you out of here."

"Whatever you say, Bill. Has my office been called yet?"

"Actually, yes. We took the liberty of answering your cell phone when it rang. It's about 10:00 now, and when you weren't at work by nine, they called looking for you. I think it was someone by the name of Becky."

"That would be my receptionist."

"You may want to call her and tell her you're okay."

"Can I use my cell phone?"

"Not in here, David. But I can get you a hospital line for you to use."

"Great, let me do that so they don't all worry about me needlessly."

"Dr. Layton, I am going to recommend you stay here overnight. I don't like the way your chest looks and you still seem a bit groggy. I just don't feel comfortable sending you home, even if the MRI ends up being totally normal."

"You won't get any argument from me, Bill. I hate hospitals and I hate being a patient, but a day to recover sounds pretty good right now."

"Done, then. I'll have the unit clerk take care of everything.

CHAPTER 66

The entire office was abuzz with the news of Dr. Layton's accident. Becky was busy at work, canceling the day's remaining appointments. Dr. Layton had called

just a few minutes earlier. Lisa had spoken with him the longest.

"Is he okay?" asked Paula.

"He sounded tired. He said he thinks he'll be okay. His chest is sore and they still need to make sure no bleeding occurred in his brain, but apparently he was very lucky."

"I don't understand what happened. I mean it wasn't raining or anything. Do you know how the accident occurred, Lisa?"

"I only know what Dr. Layton told me. The last thing he really remembers is that he hit the brakes and his car wouldn't slow down. The car was towed away. I'm sure his insurance company will check out the car and try to figure out what happened. He asked me to run some errands for him. The police were smart enough to remove his key ring from the car key. His condo keys are at the hospital with him. He wants me to go to the hospital and pick up his house key and run over to the condo to pick up some toiletries and a change of clothes."

"That's just like Dr. Layton to be worrying about how he looks, even after a serious accident. I guess if he's worrying about his appearance he can't be hurt too badly," joked Paula.

"Have you ever been to his apartment?"

"No, I haven't. I know Barbara's been over there—a few times when he's gone on vacation he's had her check on things and water his plants while he was away. I hear he has quite the view."

"I won't have time to enjoy the vistas, I'm afraid. I'll have to rush to get to the hospital, to his apartment, and back to the hospital before I have to pick up the boys. Do you need me to do anything before I go?"

"No, Lisa. We're all set. It's going to be a quiet day at the office without the doctor here. I just hope he's alright."

"Me, too. I guess you've gotta worry when even an almost new Mercedes has mechanical problems. They just don't make things like they used to. I'm gonna go, Paula. I'll see you on Monday. I'm off the rest of the week."

"We all may be off the rest of the week. Have a nice weekend, Lisa. And drive carefully!"

CHAPTER 67

The Mercedes dealership did not do collision repairs. They referred all their work to Pelican Auto Works. David's car was on a lift, and the undercarriage was being examined by Mario, Pelican's owner.

"Well, the front axle looks alright, but the radiator will have to be replaced. The driver side quarter panel and deck lid will both need replacing, both headlights and the front bumper too. Let's see what the brakes look like, Frankie. There were no skid marks at the scene of the accident, and the police said they thought the doctor may have lost control of the car 'cause his brakes failed."

Frankie was the spitting image of his father. Both men had dark shocks of black hair, though flecks of silver had appeared in the elder mechanics' mane. Frankie stood a bit taller, at about six feet, but both had the athletic builds of men who worked hard and took care of themselves. Mario still played soccer and his son went to the gym three times a week.

Frankie used the pneumatic tool and quickly removed the lug nuts from the passenger side wheels, then repeated the procedure on the driver's side. He grabbed a shop rag and placed it over his hands as he removed the wheels from the car and laid them aside. Mario watched approvingly as Frankie conducted himself neatly in his tasks. The older man took pride in maintaining a clean shop and felt disdain at mechanics that were sloppy in their work. Mario felt like an artist or surgeon in his shop and tried to conduct himself in the manner of a professional. There was little wasted motion or effort when he was working. And any messiness was kept to a minimum.

"Look at this, Pop. There's a nick in this brake line. And it looks pretty fresh—the metal is still shiny on the cut surface."

Half way through the brake line, a cut was clearly visible.

"He probably hit something sharp in the road."

"I don't know, Dad. That would make his brake light go on, and he might notice the car handling funny, but he wouldn't lose control. That would take a loss on both sides. It wouldn't explain the accident."

Frankie made his way over to the driver's side of the car. In almost the identical location on the opposite side of the car a nick was clearly visible in the brake line tubing. The metal glistened.

"Wow! Somebody must not like this doctor very much. I feel like I'm in an episode of CSI or something. The cops will need to know about this, Dad."

"You're probably right, Frankie. I just hope there's a better explanation than somebody wanting to hurt the Doc. I always thought he was a nice guy. Remember when he donated all that money to Frankie Junior's Little League for the new sign in the outfield?"

"That don't mean he doesn't have people who don't like him, Dad. I'm going to look over the car some more and enter the damage log into the computer. The sooner we get it done, the sooner the insurance adjuster can come down and sign off on it. We're obligated to call the police. Hopefully, they won't make us wait too long on doing any repairs. This will be a big job. Probably be able to get $15,000 out of it."

Frankie and Mario took meticulous notes on the damage as they surveyed the car. They had an excellent reputation with the local insurance adjusters as being honest and accurate in their description of the damage to vehicles in their care. Most times, the adjusters would give a quick examination of the car, then review the printout of the estimated costs of their repairs. The process was very straight-forward, and usually resulted in the body shop being paid their charges as soon as the work was completed. The only fly in the ointment might be any investigation of the accident requested by the police. Mario left Frankie to finish the estimate and walked over to his Rolodex to find the phone number of his friend at the police department, Dan Levine.

CHAPTER 68

David Layton appeared as if he had aged five years since the last time Lisa had seen him. He was dressed in rather generic hospital garb. Uncharacteristically, his hair was unruly and his complexion was pale. A bluish bruise was visible on his forehead.

"I'd hate to see the other guy, Dr. Layton."

David forced himself to laugh.

"Me too. Thanks for coming Lisa. I appreciate it."

"So how are you? Are you alright?"

"I ache all over, and still feel a little woozy, but it looks like I'm going to be okay."

"How long are they going to keep you here?"

'Here' was a private room on the neuro floor. Most of the other patients on the unit were recovering from cerebrovascular accidents, commonly known as 'strokes'. David had returned from his MRI just moments before Lisa arrived. The test had been uneventful, with no abnormalities noted, though the final reading would not be available until later in the day.

"I expect I'll be going home tomorrow morning."

David was no longer attached to an iv, though the doctor had left a 'hep lock' in place—a small port which provided simple access to Dr. Layton's veins and blood supply in case of an emergency. He walked over to the nightstand and picked up his house keys.

"Here are my keys. The transponder for access to the condo is still in the Mercedes, so you'll have to give the guard your name to get in. I'll call over there so that he'll be expecting you."

"What would you like me to bring back?"

"Good question. In my bathroom, you'll find my toothpaste and toothbrush. Please bring my hairbrush too. In the walk-in closet are drawers with my folded clothes. If you don't mind, bring me an extra polo shirt and a pair of boxers. And on my nightstand, you'll find a copy of a book I'm in the middle of, The Sisterhood, by Michael Palmer."

"Okay. I'd love to stay and keep you company, Dr. Layton, but if I don't get going soon, I'm afraid I'll hit traffic when I have to go to pick up my kids."

"Don't let me keep you then. Call me if you have any problems."

"I'll be back soon, Dr. Layton. Glad to see you're alright." Lisa left the room and walked briskly back to her car.

The ride to David's condo took less time than Lisa expected. As Dr. Layton had promised, the guard had been advised of her arrival in advance. Lisa parked her car in David's assigned parking spot. She rode the elevator up to the penthouse. The lift was decorated in rich cherry wood, and except for a soft 'whoosh', was silent as it ascended to the uppermost floor.

Lisa experienced a sense of déjà vu as she entered the doctor's apartment. When she had snooped around in David's office, she had done so uninvited. At least now she had the advantage of an invitation and the greater advantage of privacy. She locked the door behind her, and admired the décor of Dr. Layton's apartment.

Although its ambience was more masculine than that of her own home, it was warmly decorated in bright Florida hues with great attention to detail. There were three layers of crown molding on the ceiling, and the walls of the entrance room were faux painted with patterns resembling bamboo placed on the walls in an intricate pattern that complemented the room beautifully. The floor was covered in an exotic dark wood, polished to a bright finish. Lisa forced herself to look past the room decorations. If Dr. Layton had secrets, perhaps she could find some answers here. His home seemed a reasonable place for him to hide anything he would not want stored in the office, perhaps even Janetta's missing records.

She began her search in the bedroom, eager to gather the items David requested so that she could get along with her exploration of the apartment. Lisa walked down a narrow hallway to David's bedroom. A massive four-poster bed stood against the wall in the middle of the room. Lisa walked past the bed, and again experienced the sensation of being an intruder. She walked into his bathroom and quickly gathered the articles he had requested. Next, Lisa selected a couple of pairs of boxer shorts and a J. Crew polo shirt and placed all of the items in a small carry-on bag she had found in David's closet. Her eyes searched his room for an area appropriate for the storage of files. None were in view. Lisa checked his nightstand and peaked into all of the drawers in the bedroom. She found nothing of interest. There were no files to be found. Lisa retraced her steps and walked back down the hallway.

Dr. Layton's study was the centerpiece of his apartment. This was his room. Several old maps hung on the wall, including an ancient fragment identified by a plaque below its frame as "Roman Empire". It was yellowed and smudged with age, and appeared very ancient. Several pictures covered the walls, a few with celebrities Lisa recognized. Lisa walked over to his desk.

She opened the uppermost drawer. Her heart began to beat faster as the yellow tops of several files, pressed tightly together, caught her attention. She removed a few. The first was labeled Bank of Florida, and the second Chase Visa. Each folder contained copies of monthly statements. She began to think that her search would be a waste of time. Lisa's heart returned to its slower rate as she placed the files back in the drawer. Lisa closed one section as she simultaneously opened the next drawer.

This time she knew that her detective work had paid off. Lisa immediately recognized the folders she had seen previously at Dr. Layton's office. Lisa removed a large handful of charts and placed them on the desk. Her hands were trembling as she read the name Janetta Fannestack on one of the charts.

Lisa went back in to the drawer and removed more files. They were still in alphabetical order. These were not the standard folders she was used to seeing in the office. Demographics on each patient were absent, but each file contained annotations regarding dosages of Botox administered. No other treatment data were contained in these records. Many of the charts contained before and after photos. Janetta's chart was like the others, with a sheet of paper containing information regarding the dosage of drug administered, lot number and side-effects noted. Lisa placed Janetta's chart back with the remainder of the pile, and rapidly read through the names on the files, advancing past the letter 'F' all the way to 'M'. Lisa felt a sense of foreboding as she read the name 'Martin, Lisa' taped to the top of the file now resting on her hand. She removed the folder and examined the entries on the form. Lisa recognized the precise, neat penmanship of Dr. Layton and reviewed her file as if in a daze. On the top of the page, in heavy black ink, she stared at the entry, 'Subject # 71.' Lisa quickly skimmed the remaining charts, each containing a separate subject number and data for Botox treatment administered over the past few months. Was Dr. Layton somehow testing Botox in his office? Since the drug was already approved, what exactly was he doing? In any case, she was out of time – she had to get back in time to pick up the boys. She carefully returned the charts to the drawer and closed it.

The last place she wanted to go at that moment was back to the hospital and have to confront Dr. Layton. Lisa took a deep breath, closed her eyes, and thought of her friend Janetta. In her friend's memory, she would do whatever was necessary to figure out exactly what David was doing. Lisa rushed from the apartment, and her hand was shaking as she tried to insert her key and lock the door behind her.

CHAPTER 69

"Hey, Levine, there's a call for you."

"Thanks, Pat." The desk sergeant relayed the incoming call to the detective's desk.

"Detective Dan Levine."

"Hi Dan, it's Mario Nocera, at Pelican Auto Works."

"Hey. Hi, Mario. Good to hear from you again. I never got to thank you enough for the job you and Frankie got done on repairing my nephew's busted up Camaro. He also really appreciated the break you gave him on the body work. It looks better than new. So what can I do for you?"

"You know how I like to help you guys out whenever I think something don't look Kosher?."

"Sure do and we appreciate it. Do you have another case of someone trying to cheat their insurance company?"

"No, nothin' like that. This time, I think it's worse. This late model Mercedes was cracked up pretty good. End's up lookin' like it's cause the brakes failed. No big deal, until we check the lines and it looks like they've both been intentionally cut."

"No kidding! Was anybody hurt?"

"Mostly just the cars. A doctor was driving the car Frankie and I are working on. I think he's in the hospital, but from what they tell me, he's okay – a Doctor Layton."

Dan couldn't believe what he'd just heard. It seemed that as much as he and his partner wanted to part ways with David Layton, his name kept popping back up.

"So you're pretty sure about this? The only way this could have happened is if someone intentionally damaged the brakes?"

"That's about it, Detective. I've never seen both brake lines have problems like this at the same time. Both have fresh cuts that look too sharp to be from road debris. No, somebody was definitely trying to get put a serious hurt on this doctor."

"Well, thanks for the heads up, Mario. I'm going to find my partner and come down to the garage and photograph the car ourselves. Don't let Frankie or anyone else do any work on the vehicle until we can come down and check over everything first. Were there any other signs of foul play?"

"None that I found, Detective. But we haven't finishing looking over the entire vehicle yet. When do you think you'll be here?"

"An hour tops, Mario."

"Perfect, I'll still be here. You still play soccer, Dan?"

"Yeah, I'm still with the same guys." Dan played soccer on an adult men's team which competed in the same league as Mario's team. Whereas Mario's team usually won, Dan's was the exact opposite and usually lost. Dan played defense, and had been on the opposition many times facing Mario's quick footwork.

"Well you're not too bad for an old chubby white boy!"

"Hey, watch it, Mario. I may have to check to see if you're really young enough to play in our league anymore." Mario was older than some of the men, and now it was Dan who was teasing.

"Very funny, very funny. It's a shame your feet aren't as fast as your tongue!"

Both men laughed into their phones.

"Hey, Mario, let me go so I can round up my partner and head over to you."

"Sure, Dan, Ciao."

Dan hung up the phone and craned his neck, searching for the red-headed silhouette of his tall partner. He spotted Kevin by the coffee machine and made his way over to him. It looked like he and his partner would be making at least one more call on David Layton, though this time it would be at the Pelican Cove Hospital.

CHAPTER 70

Wednesday afternoon, and Sal hadn't heard from Dr. Layton. He was surprised. The meeting with BioVenture was only two days away, and as requested, Manzari had organized the animal data and photos for David's presentation. Sal assumed that Dr. Layton would want to review the material in advance, which only gave him one day, tomorrow, to do so. Sal figured it was time to call his partner.

"Good afternoon, Dr. Layton's office. Can I help you?"

Sal had called often enough to recognize Becky's voice.

"Hi Becky, it's Sal Manzari. Is Dr. Layton available?"

"Gosh, Mr. Manzari, I guess you haven't heard. He was in a car accident this morning. Right now he's in the hospital for observation. Thank God he seems to be alright."

"What happened?"

"From what they tell me, he had some problem with his brakes. He collided with another car at an intersection. The cars took most of the damage, but Dr. Layton did lose consciousness."

A gray cloud of apprehension entered Sal's thoughts. Maybe this wasn't the accident it appeared to be. He knew David was a good driver and took good care of his expensive new car. It would be most unlikely that the brakes on the doctor's new vehicle would fail. Sal kept his concerns to himself.

"Is he at Pelican General?"

"Yes, Lisa, one of the nurses from our office just went over to his apartment to bring him some overnight things. He's going to be on the neuro observation ward and go home in the morning if everything's alright."

"Thanks, Becky. I'll call over there right now."

"Say 'hi' to Dr. Layton for me when you talk to him."

"Sure thing. Have an uneventful rest of your day-and drive carefully!"

"You can count on it. Take care, Mr. Manzari."

"You too, Becky."

"This is the automated routing system for Pelican General Hospital. If this is an emergency, dial 911. If you know your party's extension, you may dial it at any time. For the emergency department, please press 'one'. For critical care, please press 'two'. For ambulatory surgery, press 'three'. For billing and account enquiries, press 'four'. For admissions, please press 'five'."

Sal wondered how many numbers they had in the stupid system. He hated these automated call programs and decided to press 'zero' and see what happened.

"Operator, can I help you?"

"Neurological observation unit please." Sal requested.

"Is there a room number you would like to be connected to?"

"I don't know the room number, but the patient's name is Dr. David Layton."

"I'll connect you, please hold."

The phone was momentarily silent, then a familiar voice came on the line.

"David Layton."

"Hi, David, it's Sal."

"Sal, I guess you know I had some trouble with my car!"

"That's what I hear. Becky told me you're okay more or less."

"Yeah, I'll live. I'm still a little groggy, and I ache all over, but I think I'll be going home in the morning. I had an MRI but I don't know the results yet. I guess if they were bad, they'd have told me by now."

"I know you've had other things keeping you busy David, but is the meeting still on for Friday with BioVenture?"

"SHIT, it slipped my mind Sal. Tomorrow's Thursday and I haven't gotten to review and organize the data, plus it looks like I'm going to have a shiner by tomorrow. My chin looks like somebody put sandpaper to it. The air bag blew up into my face. I think it might be best if I try to postpone the meeting for a week."

"That sounds good to me, David. Is there anything you need me to do?"

"No, not really, Sal. Is everything okay at the lab?"

"No problems there, Dr. Layton. I have the updated files and photos for you. Do you want me to bring them over to you?"

"No, Sal. I'd rather wait till I'm discharged and feeling better. Maybe we can get together this weekend for breakfast or brunch and go over the material then."

"Sounds like a plan. Call me when you're home tomorrow and we'll set up a time. What are you doing for wheels?"

"I've already talked to Mercedes. They're going to have a driver pick me up from the hospital and take me home. They said they'll have a car waiting for me at my condominium while mine is being repaired. I think they're a little concerned that the accident may have been caused by mechanical failure that they should have detected when they serviced the car."

Sal saw no reason to argue with Dr. Layton, though he suspected that poor service had nothing to do with the problem with the Mercedes.

"I guess everybody is always worried about being sued these days. Well, if you need a ride or anything, just give me a call. Otherwise, I'll wait to hear from you tomorrow."

"Thanks for calling Sal."

"Glad you're okay, David. Try to get some rest."

David hung up. Sal stared at the phone for several moments. Apprehension and fear cast a shadow on his already somber mood. He rose from his chair and headed over to the lab table where the remains of his Subway sandwich were being examined attentively, from a distance, by several of the caged lab mice. Maybe some food would calm his gloomy thoughts..........

CHAPTER 71

By the time Lisa got back on the road, the traffic had increased. The clock on the car dashboard read 2:36. She doubted she would have the time to drop off Dr. Layton's things at the hospital and drive back to the school to pick up the boys by their 3:15 dismissal time. The school had a strict policy and she had been warned in the past about allowing her boys to wait outside the school past the 3:45 deadline for student pick-ups.

Lisa kept her eyes on the traffic massing around her car as she reached over to her purse and removed her cell phone. She pressed the speed dial number for Nate.

After three rings, she heard his voice transmitted through the phone. Lisa cut in, "Hi, Nate…….."

She felt foolish as Nate's voice on the other end continued despite her attempt at conversation. "Hi, this is Nate Martin. I'm sorry I can't come to the phone right now. Please leave a message at the sound of ………."

Lisa hung up. She pressed the next number on her speed dial, Nate's office number.

"Walker and Pakeman, can I help you?"

"Nate Martin, please."

"Whom can I say is calling?"

"It's his wife, Lisa Martin."

"Hello, Mrs. Martin. I'll try his office. Hold please."

Lisa waited. Moments later, the receptionist came back on the line.

"I'm afraid he signed out at noon, but still hasn't returned. Would you like to leave a message on his voice mail?"

Lisa wondered if his prolonged lunch break had anything to do with his attractive female coworker. She felt herself becoming irritated. In any case, he wouldn't be able to help her pick up the boys.

"No, I'll reach him later. Thanks."

"You're very welcome Mrs. Martin."

Lisa decided to pick up the boys first, then head back to the hospital. Her revised plans gave her a little time to kill before school let out. Lisa's mind wandered back to Nate. She wondered if at that moment he was keeping company with another woman, and on a hunch, drove back through town, making only a slight detour from her route to the school. Lisa peered like a hawk, craning her neck back and forth as she drove down the narrow posh street of Pelican Cove's tourist district. The area on Second Avenue was especially full of small restaurants and bistros. These were among the most popular places for power lunches. She passed Chez Golton, the establishment where she had found Nate with Sandy Parker. Her husband's car was nowhere to be seen, and at this in between time of the day, most of the tables at the establishments were vacant. Only Starbucks seemed to be doing any business. Lisa parked her car a few spaces from the coffee shop and ordered a large vanilla hazelnut frappuccino. She drowned her anger, frustration and loneliness in the sweetness of empty calories. Deep down inside, she was happy she hadn't found her husband enjoying a long philanderous lunch and drinks with another woman. Lisa finished off the whipped topping, and walked briskly out of the Starbucks. The strong aroma of freshly brewed coffee accompanied her out into the humid and sticky afternoon Florida air.

The Starbucks was part of a small complex of six stores sharing a common roof. Two doors down was one of the last remaining 'Mom and Pop' type stores in downtown Pelican Cove. It was a somewhat tacky general store that catered to tourists. A couple of years ago, when Beanie Babies were the rage, it had made a bundle selling the small stuffed animals. Now, its shelves were stocked with boxes of copies of designer sunglasses, beach towels and T-shirts with witty sayings on them, and lots of creams and lotions for tanning, preventing tanning, and treating sunburn. It was only a matter of time until the high costs of rent, employees and insurance would force the store to close, ushering in another chain coffee shop or yogurt palace. In a corner, near the checkout counter at the front of the store, stood a small rotating carousel containing an assortment of blank keys, meant to be converted to functioning copies when placed in a machine operated by one of the employees. Lisa had an idea.

She removed the keychain Dr. Layton had given her from her purse and detached the door key to his condo from the ring. She handed the key to the older gentleman tending the cash register. The man was forgettable in every way, except for a wildly thick white handlebar mustache which extended outward from his upper lip in two exotic curls. He smiled at his attractive customer, revealing perfect teeth that seemed slightly too large for his mouth. Lisa imagined that they must be false.

"Good afternoon young lady. How many copies would you like?"

Suddenly, Lisa was quite self-conscious. She felt herself blush. She had no right copying Dr. Layton's key. Then she thought of Janetta, her death and the suspicious charts hidden in her boss's desk and forged the courage to continue.

"Just one would be fine, young man. That's a great mustache you have."

The cashier broke into a broad smile, lifting the ends of his wild mustache higher over his cheeks.

"Well, that's the nicest thing anyone has said to me all day." He glanced quickly at her left hand and the twinkling diamond ring on her finger.

"Your husband is a lucky man to have such a beautiful lady as a wife."

The compliment made her smile, but the effect lasted only the briefest of moments, as mention of her spouse reminded her of what had brought her downtown in the first place and her concerns regarding Nate's fidelity.

"That's very nice of you to say." Her final words were partially drowned out by the metallic grinding sound of the machine etching the proper grooves onto the newly minted key.

"Will that be all?"

"Yes…thanks…… Cliff." Lisa read the name off the older man's name tag.

He smiled broadly once again.

"Well, you're so pleasant, I'm tempted to give you this little key for free, but I'm afraid if I don't my boss will fire me and I'll be forced to become a 'greeter' at the Wal Mart. It'll be $2.12. Do you need a bag?"

"No, I can just put it in my purse." She had an urge to get the key out of sight as quickly as possible, wondering if she had the nerve to carry though with her plan. Lisa handed over the cash and placed the key in her bag.

"Have a nice day now, and please come again."

"I will." Lisa gave the clerk a parting smile and walked out the door.

A few steps later, she was in her car. Lisa drove away and arrived at Pelican Elementary in plenty of time to pick up both boys from their school.

CHAPTER 72

Nate felt his cell phone vibrate against his waist. He checked the message area and saw that it was a 'missed call' from his wife. He ignored it. At the moment of it's vibration he was enjoying a mesmerizing, pleasant conversation about the quality of the sushi being served. Nate was sitting at a small table in the corner of Sashimi Mi, arguably the best sushi restaurant in Pelican Cove. There were only three in the town, but the food at Sashimi Mi was superb. His judgment regarding the quality of the food may have been elevated somewhat by the fact that he was finishing his third martini. His spirits were buoyed by the titillating conversation, and his companion, Sandy Parker.

Nate knew he shouldn't be sharing an extended lunch with his associate. It was only a matter of time before people would start talking about seeing him out past normal lunch hours with a woman other than his wife. But he couldn't deny the pleasure Sandy's company brought him. Unlike Lisa's frequent dissatisfaction and complaining, his law associate's demeanor was always pleasant. Of course, it didn't hurt that she had a body to die for and seemed to enjoy his company as much as he did hers.

Nate looked up into Sandy's dark brown, doe-like eyes. Her complexion was flawless, framed by long silky-brown hair and a trim, statuesque figure. Sandy stood about five-seven, and had beautiful full breasts. Nate expected that they had been enhanced by implants, but appreciated the results none the less. It was all he could do to keep from glancing down at them from time to time, and he was sure that any failure on his part to maintain eye contact was noticed by Sandy. He had read somewhere once that women always know when a guy is staring at their chest, even when he thinks he's fooling them.

"We probably should be getting back to work, Sandy."

"How are we going to explain being away for half the afternoon?"

"Car trouble usually works." Nate responded.

"It does when you don't smell of alcohol! I'm afraid we've both had too much to drink. I only live about a mile from here. Want to grab a coffee back at my place and freshen up a little before heading back to the office?"

Nate couldn't believe what he was hearing. It had been quite a while since a woman had tried to seduce him, but it did appear that Ms. Parker had him in her sights. Rapid beating of his heart betrayed any attempt on his part to remain calm and collected. He knew that coffee wasn't the only thing that would be waiting back at her apartment.

Yet he hesitated. The phone call from Lisa had initiated a reminder signal from his cell phone. It vibrated briefly on a regular basis, alerting him to the missed call. It reminded him of his vows and responsibilities. Nate inhaled deeply, sighed to himself and knew that he would probably regret what he was about to do next.

"Sandy, I think what we better do is go back to the office. I'll take you back and drop you off. I'm going to run an errand and by the time I return, no one will know we were out together. I don't want to stir up any gossip at the office. But I had a great time at lunch with you."

Nate looked back into Sandy's eyes and was amazed that he was going to let the opportunity pass. Sandy smiled at Nate, then caught him completely off guard as he felt her stocking toes catch under his pants leg and inch their way up his shin bone. The tightness of his pant leg caught against her foot, which she withdrew. She then began to run her foot onto the outside of his leg. With nothing standing in her way, her toes made their way toward his knee, advancing up to his thigh. Nate blanched, then flushed and felt his throat grow dry. He swallowed self-consciously, and bumped against his chair as he moved away from her probing foot.

Nate managed an awkward smile back at Sandy.

"I think that's more dessert than I can handle right now Ms. Parker."

"We'll see, Mr. Martin. We'll see."

CHAPTER 73

David watched as Lisa exited from his hospital room, boys in tow. She seemed to be able to do it all. He appreciated his clean clothing and toiletries and wished that she could have stayed to visit, but she said she had to get home. Lisa had seemed unusually tense. David hoped that she was not still uncomfortable around him because of any past awkwardness. He knew that his advances toward his employee had been inappropriate. Despite his remorse, Dr. Layton couldn't deny his attraction toward Lisa Martin. In any case, now that she was gone, he turned his attention to his next task. David picked up his cell phone and speed-dialed the phone number for Neville Cooper of Bio Venture. Cooper picked up on the first ring.

"David, how are you?"

It was still unnerving for Dr. Layton that when you called someone you didn't have to say hello in order for them to recognize your voice and know who was calling. Now, the caller ID tipped them off.

"Actually, I could be better Neville. That's why I'm calling. I was in a little accident with my car. I'm in Pelican General right now recovering.

I should be getting out tomorrow, but I'm a little banged up and was wondering whether we could postpone our Friday meeting until next week."

"Are you alright, David?"

"I seem to be. I've got an assortment of aches and pains, but it looks like the only lasting damage will be to my car."

"Well as long as you're okay. Listen, the investors are going to be a bit disappointed, but under the circumstances, they'll understand. If I can get them together, do you think we can do it for Tuesday next week?"

David considered.

"I think that should be fine. I have patients scheduled during the day, and the time I'm missing because of the accident is going to force me to work longer hours next week. I'd prefer not to have to interrupt the day too much on Tuesday. Do you think we could meet in the late afternoon or early evening?"

"How about we meet at my office at 5 p.m. on Tuesday? I'll have it catered by Emilio. Have you ever had his food?"

Emilio was becoming legendary in Pelican Cove. The affluent residents of the town supported a vast array of charities, each of which had its own yearly fund raising function. Emilio was known as the best of the best. His catered affairs were always fully attended and his services usually had to be reserved months in advance.

"I'm impressed. How will you be able to book Emilio on such short notice?"

"Well, it's not easy, David. Except he hopes to be one of the investors in your drug. Consider it one of the perks of our partnership."

"After eating here in the hospital, a Wendy's hamburger sounds gourmet to me. Tuesday sounds great, and sorry for any inconvenience I've caused."

"Nonsense, David. I'm relieved to know you're okay. What caused the accident anyway?"

"The brakes on my car failed. I was lucky I wasn't killed."

"On that new Mercedes you drive? How odd. I've never heard of such a thing. Maybe I should have mine checked. Well, we'll look forward to seeing you on Tuesday then. If you run into any more problems, please give me a call. I know the group is really looking forward to your presentation. They've literally got money burning a hole in their pockets. We need to get these guys signed on and committed before they have a chance to look to another place for their money."

"I hear you, Neville. Five p.m. at your offices then. See you Tuesday."

CHAPTER 74

"Are you sure you're not just a little bit obsessed with this doctor, Kevin? First you were considering a conspiracy involving the deaths of those women, now you think someone is out to off the guy."

"Chief, something's not right with the guy. Let Dan and I pay him a visit at the hospital. He may not even know that his brakes were tampered with. If someone is trying to harm him he certainly should know, and we may need to protect him. Remember our motto, "To protect and serve.""

Chief Pincer sighed. Detective Collins was one of the most capable officers in the precinct. It was tiresome having to admit that there was something as vague as intuition and 'feelings' that could still play a role in police work. Whatever it was, Kevin Collins was a better detective because of it.

"Fine, you and Dan go over there. You'll have to get a forensics unit to the garage to check on the doctor's vehicle, though I have no doubt that what Mario told you is accurate. He knows his stuff. Make the visit as brief as you can. I don't want to get the gossip mill going."

"You got it Captain. We'll be back in a couple of hours."

Lisa and the boys had been gone less than thirty minutes when Dr. Layton's unexpected guests arrived. They were dressed in their undercover civilian garb. Even out of uniform, Collins had the demeanor of a police detective; his ever-inquisitive eyes scanned the room and settled on the doctor.

"Hello, Dr. Layton. Sorry about your little accident."

"Good afternoon Detective Collins, Detective Levine. I'm afraid it was a little more than a 'little' accident, but all in all, I can't complain. I'm still here! What brings you two to the hospital? Still investigating the Fannestack case, or is there something new regarding my nurse Shirley?"

"Neither of those, Dr. Layton. We received a call from the mechanic working on your Mercedes. It doesn't happen often, but whenever they find something suspicious involving a motor vehicle accident we get a call. It appears that someone may have tampered with the brake lines to your car. Your accident may not have been an 'accident' at all."

David was shocked. The thought of someone trying to intentionally hurt him had never crossed his mind. He just didn't know what to say.

"How do they know the car was tampered with?"

"Both brake lines showed evidence of having been cut recently. The metal of each of the lines was shiny in the areas where they had been partially cut. If it had happened over a longer period of time we could expect the area of weakness to be corroded and covered with debris. And both lines showed the same evidence, making the possibility of product failure or wear and tear extremely unlikely. Since it was so blatant, we suspect that the person doing the work is an amateur or maybe was trying to make a point or wanted you out of the way for awhile. Have you received any threats from anyone lately?"

David considered the detective's question. Although he tried to avoid crossing paths with anyone, in his profession, as with any business, disagreements were unavoidable. There were several patients who were unhappy with either their surgical outcomes or their bills. Perhaps one the women he had operated on was unhappy, or maybe one of their spouses or boyfriends had an axe to grind. He had also been involved with many girlfriends over the years. Several had also been enmeshed in relationships at the time he had dated them. David searched his memory for any one that stood out as having the potential for an angry stalker.

"I haven't received any threats, though I imagine everyone could probably think of someone who doesn't like them for some reason. What do I do now?"

Dan spoke.

"Money's tight, so I don't think our Captain will allow the department to provide 24-7 protection, but we can increase the car surveillance traffic of our cruisers around your residence. You may want to consider having someone provide security for you, maybe even a driver to take you to and from work for awhile. Under the slim chance that you could receive a call from the perpetrator, we can wire your phone so that any calls are recorded and can be traced back at the department. Where do you live?"

"In the Surf Tower condo, on the beach."

"You might want to tell the security at the gate to be extra vigilant in case of any intruders, since that's probably how access to your car was obtained. Do many people have access to your unit?"

"No, the only people with keys are myself and my cleaning person, and she's been with me since just about when I first arrived in Pelican Cove seven years ago. I've had handymen do repairs from time to time, and I've given them keys, but nothing recently."

"You may want to consider changing your locks. We don't want to alarm you, but obviously your accident could have had a much more serious outcome than it did."

"I appreciate the heads up, officers and your concern. I'm still shocked by it all. The idea that there is someone trying to harm me is pretty scary."

"As long as we're here, have you found any more information in your office regarding Janetta Fannestack or Roberta Cook, or your nurse Shirley?"

David froze. The change in subject was sudden. He was ill-prepared to face additional questioning regarding the dead women. Why did the red-headed detective keep probing? Did he suspect something? His own accident had pushed such thoughts from his mind. The hesitation in his response was not lost on Detective Collins.

"No, we didn't find any more information. To tell you the truth, I thought that you boys had closed that case. I don't think I can be of much help there. Right now, I'm so preoccupied with the tampering with my car, and possible attempt on my life, that I can barely think straight."

"That's quite understandable. Well when you're back at work, let us know if you find anything. Did you want us to put a trace on your phones?"

David considered. A tap on the phones might help him find out who had tried to harm him. But he didn't want anyone to hear his private conversations with Sal Manzari or anyone else involved in his drug research. He could use his cell phone, but that wouldn't eliminate the possibility of receiving unexpected incoming calls at home. He didn't want the police department to have access to his conversations.

"For now, I think I'll ask the security staff at the condo to be extra vigilant. I'd appreciate any help your department can provide with added surveillance. I'm going to upgrade the alarm on my Mercedes to one that goes off when anyone touches the car—at least I will as soon as I get the car back from the body shop. Maybe I'll even get a deadbolt installed on the inside of my condo unit."

Neither detective acknowledged their suspicions regarding Dr. Layton's refusal for phone surveillance.

"Well, I think we're done for now," responded Detective Levine. We'll see what the department can do and we'll let you know if anything else turns up with your car. We'll also increase our patrol car drive-bys at your office. If anything comes to mind, if you think of anyone that might want to harm you, just give us a call." Levine handed David his card.

"Anything else officers. I think I'm about ready for a nap."

"No, I think that's it," responded Collins. "Will you be discharged soon?"

"I'm probably going home tomorrow."

"Well, have a good evening. I hope we didn't scare you too much with our news."

"I can't say I'm pleased, but what can you do. I've never been one to be afraid of things, and I don't plan to start now." David hoped that by saying the words, he would convince himself that they were true. In reality, he was quite shaken by the accident, and shocked to have to consider that someone out there might have tried to harm him.

The two detectives were alone in the hospital elevator.

"So what do you think about his refusal for the phone tap."

"It got my attention, Kev. I just don't know what he's hiding. We both know that the chance of a perpetrator actually calling him are about zero. But your idea of using the offer to see if he might be hiding something was a good one. I think most people would do anything they could after an attempt on their life to try to catch someone. The fact that he turned us down certainly implies that he's got something to hide."

"Now, all we've got to do is convince the Captain to allow us to follow up on it. I don't think it's going to be too easy. He was pretty clear that he didn't want us to spend much more time investigating Dr. Layton."

"With your Irish charm, it'll be a piece of cake, Kev."

Collins smiled. He hoped his partner was right.

CHAPTER 75

S al made his early morning rounds of the cages. Ed was out behind the building taking a cigarette break. The other lab techs were off for the day. All of the rodents seemed healthy. But two of the mice were squeaking loudly and involved in mounting activity. There were two mice in the position in cage seven and two more in cage thirteen that had been similarly involved, separating only when Sal came over to add water to their cage. Manzari documented the behavior in the notes attached to the clipboard for each of the respective cages. A knock on the locked front door interrupted his thoughts..

"What's a matter, Sallie, ya doin' somethin' you shouldn't be doing with your friend Ed? What's with the locked door? I know he's a pansy, but I never figured you for one." It was Sam/Knuckles. This time he came alone.

"Sometimes we lock the door early in the day. There are some homeless people that live in the woods around here and we don't want them wandering into the lab. Where's your buddy, Vic?"

"He hadda take his mudda to the doctor. She ain't doin' too good.

Somethin' with her ticker."

The thought of the hulking criminal having a mother that he cared about was somehow jarring—incongruent with his means of employment, but Sal guessed that even hoods have caring mothers.

"What can I do for you Knuckles?"

"Bobby wants to talk to ya. He wants to see ya right now. It don't look like you're in the middle of anything' too critical. Let's go."

Sal knew better than to argue.

"One minute, let me go find Ed and tell him I'm leaving."

Knuckles smiled.

"Give 'im a little kiss for me too."

Sal ignored the rude comments. He found Ed at the service entrance to the lab, next to a dumpster. Ed's cigarette was nearly finished.

"I've got to run an errand. I'll be back in a little while, Ed."

"No problem, boss. Anything special I need to do while you're gone?"

"No, everything's fine. If you get around to it, make sure all the files are copied. I'm probably going to meet with Dr. Layton this weekend and he wants all the most recent data. I don't think we need to do any more injections until next week, so today should be a short day for you. If I'm not back by noon, just close up the lab when you're done. You can take Friday off. Rick will be in tomorrow and on the weekend to check on everything. I'll probably be by on Saturday or Sunday before I meet with Dr. Layton to pick up the data and photos. Any big plans?"

"Not this weekend. I think I'm going to go to the beach and catch some rays. I've got a Grisham novel I'm in the middle of that I want to finish. I may go out for dinner Saturday night. You doing anything special?"

"You know me. Nothing big on the agenda. I'm registered in a fifty dollar buy-in Texas Hold Em tournament on Saturday evening. If I win that, I may not have to come to work on Monday. The first prize is

$25,000."

"Good luck, Sal. But I imagine I'll see you on Monday."

"Afraid so, Ed. Have a good weekend."

Bobby Volpe was seated at his desk with a copy of the Pelican Cove News in front of him. He was reading the sports pages, and a smile appeared on his face.

"Gotta love those upsets. We made some money last night. So, how are ya, Sallie, been playin' any poker?"

"Not too much, Mr. Volpe. Not too much."

"That's good. Stay outta trouble. Talkin' about trouble, did ya see what happened to Dr. Layton?"

Sal swallowed. His throat suddenly felt as dry as the Mojave.

"Yes, bad car accident." Since it hadn't been in the paper, Sal assumed that Bobby had heard about it from his paid informants on the Pelican Cove police force.

"Frankly, Sal, I'm surprised it wasn't worse. He got away lucky. But accidents happen, if ya know what I mean. Is he goin' to be able to go back to work?"

"Yes, I think he's planning on going back tomorrow. He really wasn't hurt too badly." Sal answered.

Volpe frowned.

"Well, I guess that might be good for him. You'd think after a little accident he might become too preoccupied to run both his practice and his lab. So what's up with the research?"

Sal was dreading what he had to say next.

"Dr. Layton is still planning on meeting with a group of investors this week. I don't know what to do, Mr. Volpe."

Bobby sighed. He realized that sending 'the mechanic' had been a mistake. Knuckles probably would have been a better choice. His head henchman wasn't too bright, but he was effective.

"Sal, does Dr. Layton have any nasty habits?"

Manzari thought he knew where this was going. He spoke before thinking—

"Did you damage the brakes on Dr. Layton's car?" Immediately, Sal regretted asking the question. He didn't know what had come over him. Volpe's face became contorted and turned livid. The mobster stood up.

"Sal, I'm gonna say this once, and only once. Ya knew who and what I was when ya first came to me for help. Don't ever ask me nothin' about what I do. If ya hadn't screwed up, this would have been a nice, clean deal. Now, I'm stuck cleanin' up your fuckin' mess. I've been lenient with ya because ya have something' I want. But don't overstep. Capiche?"

Sal's heart was racing a mile a minute. His head throbbed and large circles of sweat had broken out underneath both armpits.

"Yes, Mr. Volpe," Sal responded subserviently.

"Now I asked ya, does your partner have any vices?"

"He's a little vain, and he likes the women."

"That's better, Sal. Does he have a wife or steady girlfriend?"

"No, he lives alone, never been married, and dates lots of women."

"My kind of guy. Ya should learn from him. Does he gamble?"

"No, he's pretty above board, doesn't drink much, do drugs or gamble. Just women."

"Okay, Sal. At least I've got something' to work with. We need to make sure that he doesn't meet with any investors and sign any papers. If he does, it will get much more complicated for us. Ya need to make sure that no matter what, that meetin' never happens. Do ya understand?"

"Yes, Mr. Volpe."

"Great. We're gonna to have a meetin' of our own. Do you think the data is ready to present? I have investors ready to give us big money to get involved with this thing."

"Yes and no. I tampered with the Botox chemical a little, to try to discourage the doctor from continuing with the research. It didn't work; the bad results with the new drug weren't enough to discourage him. A few women became sick." Sal decided not to mention how sick they had truly become.

"Wow, this doctor is more screwed up than I imagined. So he just ignored the fact that the medication could harm them?"

"Yes, he denied that the drug was to blame. You know, we did have a lot of success with the injections until I altered it. I just think he couldn't believe that the drug was causing the problems. And I couldn't very well tell him that I had changed the chemical. Also, the lab animals have been acting weird lately. They seem to be hypersexual."

"Hyper what?"

"Hypersexual. They're mounting each other and doing things that they usually don't do. Males are mounting other males, and females are going after the females."

"Sounds like this might be one popular drug if ya ask me, Sallie. Gets rid of wrinkles and makes ya horny. Was the original compound ya guys manufactured safe?"

"I think so, I checked over the lab data and it seems that it might also be inducing some increase in sex drive in the mice."

"And this is a bad thing? I think that might be better than getting rid of wrinkles."

"It's bad if it causes problems in the brain. I haven't sacrificed any of the animals yet to see if they have brain changes accompanying their altered activity. The animals that died had all received the modified drug. The ones that are living, and have increased sexual activity are a mixture of groups; those that received the original drug and those that received the altered Botox."

"So if I understand this correctly, the Botox ya were usin' originally seemed to work well, but it may make its users horny. And the chemical ya messed around with is dangerous."

"As much as I can tell. I don't know if Dr. Layton always tells me everything that goes on in his office. He keeps his own charts on his patients. He used to keep them in his office, but he told me that now he keeps them at home."

"I may wanna have a look at those records. Do you think ya can get at them?"

"Maybe, but Dr. Layton is pretty possessive of his office charts. I would need some kind of pretext for needing to see them. Frankly, since I run the lab and treat only the animals, I can't think of any reason why I'd need to have access to them."

Bobby seemed to be considering his options. Finally he said,

"Don't worry, Sallie. I'll take care of it. Ya just make sure that Dr. Layton speaks to as few people as possible about his drug, and keep him from makin' any meetin' with any investors next week."

"Hey Knuckles; come over here and drive Sal back to his lab."

The henchman didn't mind taking orders from his boss, but he resented doing so in front of a soft slob like Sal. He was smart enough to hide his dissatisfaction behind a stoic expression of obedience.

"Certainly, Mr. Volpe I've got the Caddie parked out back."

Sal had visions of getting into the Cadillac and having a gun held to his head. He would be shot in the temple, and rolled out of the car on some country back road, or loaded into a fifty gallon drum with cement and lowered to the bottom of the Gulf. He knew it was possible, but just as certainly, he knew he was being ridiculous. As cold and vicious as the mob boss might be, Volpe was a businessman first. Sal had something the mobster wanted that meant Sal had some control. He would have to be certain to keep it that way if he wanted to live. Manzari felt remorse in the knowledge that he had placed Dr. Layton's life in danger through their tainted partnership. At this point, extricating himself from either business involvement seemed impossible, and as much as he was concerned for David's life, he also feared for his own. He forced himself to focus on the matter at hand.

"Sal I'm counting on ya to not let me down. I don't know if you realize how big a deal this drug can be. Even my wife is hooked on the stuff. She gets shots for her wrinkles all the time. It's crazy, but a dollar is a dollar. This is your chance to get out of hock and my chance for a solid legit business."

"Yes, Mr. Volpe." Sal felt like he was going to throw up. He had a flash of some stupid television commercial where this guy does something really, really embarrassing, and the voice on the commercial says, "Want to get away?" Sal just wanted to get away; forget about his gambling debts, forget about the mice and forget about the study and the adulterated Botox. He took a deep breath – it was too late for any of that.

CHAPTER 76

D avid had never spent a night in the hospital before. At least not
as a patient. He had endured his residency, when most nights he
barely got an hour's worth of sleep. His night under neurological
surveillance was not much better. It brought back memories of his time
in training. Every hour or so, someone came by his bed and checked to
make sure he was breathing normally. At one point, when it was about
three in the morning and he had actually awoken before the nurse came
to check his vitals, he considered pretending to be having a seizure, just
to shake her up. He realized that he was being petulant and tolerated the
inconveniences, understanding that it was only temporary and that he
would be going home in the morning.

David greeted the first rays of sunshine at a little after six. He figured
he couldn't be doing too badly, as he has made it through the night with
flying colors and his appetite had returned. He was starving. The nurses
on the night shift certainly weren't anything to look at. His evening
nurse, Leslie, finished her shift at eleven. She was about five foot two and
had to weigh over two hundred pounds. She had stubble from dark hairs

on her chin and a bad case of acne. Probably some type of hormone problem Layton guessed. Leslie was replaced by the eleven to seven nurse, Denyse Weatherspoon, every bit as skinny as Leslie had been fat. Denyse was young, about twenty-five or so, and had a plain, flat face like the women in that picture of a guy with a pitchfork standing in front of a barn or something. David thought it might have been titled American Gothic.

His day was saved when the shifts changed at seven AM. His new nurse was Ashley, a pert blond. None of the nurse's name tags stated their last names. Several years ago, a disgruntled patient had learned a nurse's name from her name tag and after his discharge had stalked her home. Since then, last names were kept private. David imagined that anyone who was crazy enough could find anyone if they really wanted to. Ashley was also young, with a clear, creamy complexion. She had a huge smile, and expressive brown eyes that twinkled. Both his breakfast and his new nurse arrived at the same time, and David couldn't decide which to give more attention to first.

"How are you, Dr. Layton? I'm Ashley, and I'll be your nurse this morning. I understand from Denyse that you're probably going home early today."

"Yes, I'm planning on it, Ashley. I'm sorry that I probably won't be here long enough to get to know you." David glanced at Ashley's left hand. No wedding ring. It was a reflex for him and one not missed by the nurse.

She smiled. Ashley was accustomed to the flirtatious behavior of patients. Dr. Layton was certainly a handsome man, though somewhat old for her tastes. She decided to play along with his machinations.

"Same here, Dr. Layton. Maybe some other place and some other time. Pelican Cove is a small town. We'll probably meet again. Dr. Cleary has asked that Dr. O'Connell see you before you can be discharged.

Technically, you're actually on Dr. O'Connell's service while in the Neuro unit. He's in charge of all 'unassigned' patients, which includes you. He'll be making rounds here soon."

Dr. Layton smelled the aroma of fresh coffee and the more subtle 'fragrance' of steamed eggs. At the same time, he was pleasantly distracted by the beautiful curves of Ashley's taut young body. He was tired, and barely heard what she was saying about the doctors, though he did listen closely enough to understand that his doctor would be making rounds shortly.

"I'm famished, Ashley. Care to join me for breakfast?"

"I wish I could, Dr. Layton. I'm afraid they don't pay me for that. You enjoy your meal. When I see Dr. O'Connell, I'll tell him you're doing well, and he'll probably see you first so that you can go home."

David smiled.

"Thanks, Ashley." He winked at the nurse. "Maybe I'll be lucky and he'll keep me another day."

Ashley didn't know what to say, but decided that the flirting had gone far enough. She smiled at the doctor, though this time with a little less enthusiasm.

"I'll let you eat. Nice meeting you, Dr. Layton."

"Call me, David."

"Sure, okay. I'll be back when Dr. O'Connell arrives."

Ashley's somewhat cool reception to his flirting disappointed David. He wondered if he was losing his sex appeal. "Oh well, maybe I'll do better on a full stomach!" he said to himself. He attacked his scrambled eggs, toast and coffee with reckless abandon.

David was just finishing up his coffee when Ashley returned. Preceding her into the room was a thin and fit appearing, fifty to fifty-five year old gray-haired man in a white coat. The embroidered name on his white jacket read Dr. Tom O'Connell. For some reason, Dr. Layton thought he looked more the part of a priest than a doctor. Although he wore a faint smile, he appeared serious.

"Good morning! I'm Dr. Tom O'Connell."

"David Layton, or at least what's left of me." David extended his hand and greeted Dr. O'Connell, whose hand reached across the surgeon's meal tray in a firm hand shake.

"So when are you going to spring me out of here, Tom?"

The smile left O'Connell's face.

"I think you can leave whenever you're ready. Your neuro checks through the night were fine. There's no evidence of any injury that we need to keep you here for. I did want to discuss your MRI with you though."

Even after years away from the uncomfortable task of having to present patients with bad news, David recognized the tone of voice and subtle change in Tom's tone and words. It was the serious approach that often preceded the pronouncement of bad news.

"I thought the MRI was normal, Dr. O'Connell."

"To the casual observer, it was. The staff who had performed the test and the ER doctor who had reviewed it were within reason to consider it normal. But I got the final reading from the radiologist early this morning before I came here. You have some subtle changes that concern me."

David became apprehensive. "Such as?"

"You seem to have some shrinkage of the hippocampus. It's mild, but definitely on the low side of normal. Similar findings can predate the onset of Alzheimer's disease by one or even two decades. Have you had any trouble with your memory?"

"I've noticed some memory lapses, but have written them off as age-related stuff. Nothing really serious, though I have noticed it more the last few months. It's concerned me more lately, because I recently found out that my father has been diagnosed with Alzheimer's."

"It can run in families, David. The other finding was more unusual. There seemed to be some hypertrophy in the area of the fornix. Again, a subtle finding, but a most unusual one. It may have no significance at all. Normally, we think of it as a relatively unimportant portion of the brainstem."

Dr. Layton felt that it was likely to be anything but unimportant. For a brief moment he considered mentioning that he knew of other recent cases involving hypertrophy of the region, but held his tongue. David remembered his vivid dreams of a sexual nature and recalled that the fornix could affect sexual drives. He pushed these thoughts from his mind.

"Do you think I have Alzheimer's?"

"It's probably too early to say. I do suggest you monitor your mental functions and memory. Also, sequential MRI's may be beneficial to check any changes in both areas. There are some investigations going on with what are called 'functional' MRIs whereby we can evaluate activity in different parts of the brain in a more objective way. The tests are experimental, but you may be able to enter a study and have the tests done in Tampa. If you wish I can contact my colleagues there for you."

"This is all kind of shocking to me, Tom, but please check with them if you don't mind. Right now, I'm awfully tired and would just like to get home and catch some rest. Is it okay if I leave the hospital?"

"By all means. I'll give you a call tomorrow or early next week regarding the functional MRI. I do recommend that at the least we repeat your MRI here in three months."

"That sounds easy enough. I'm ready to leave whenever you give me the word, Dr. O'Connell."

"No problem, let me just finish the discharge paperwork. It shouldn't take long, Do you have a ride home?"

"The Mercedes people are going to take care of it for me. All I have to do is call."

"I knew I should have been a plastic surgeon," O'Connell teased. "Me, I drive a Chrysler."

David smiled. His mind was in a tumult, unable to absorb the frightening news of the morning.

CHAPTER 77

U pon awakening Lisa's thoughts were on Dr. Layton's practice. It was hard for her to believe that he would do anything to intentionally harm any of his patients-not to mention his own nurse. Certainly, if he knew anything that pertained to Shirley's death he would have revealed it to the detectives. Then again, he had withheld information from the detectives regarding Roberta Cook and Janetta. Was he protecting patient-doctor privilege? Lisa was certain that such considerations were not valid when someone had died. The fact that the doctor had withdrawn the records to his home office seemed a testimony to his guilt; Dr. Layton was certainly hiding something.

Her brief look at the records had been inadequate. Lisa considered going to the detectives with her information, but when it came right down to it, she enjoyed her job and liked the doctor. He seemed to be a decent man and had treated her with respect. She wanted to provide him with every benefit of the doubt before considering him guilty of any disservice to his patients. Going to the detectives would be the wrong thing to do at this point. In addition, she would have to admit to snooping around David's home, which in itself was wrong. And then she had a copy of the door key.

Nate had purchased a new Canon digital camera. The little silver box was barely larger than a pack of cigarettes, but took amazingly clear pictures. Lisa had used it to take photos of the boys' artwork when their creativity had been on display at the mall. She had been able to enlarge the pictures and had placed them in simple frames and mailed them to family up North, all of whom had enjoyed the quality of the reproductions.

Lisa wondered if she could use the camera to help in her investigation of Dr. Layton. It wouldn't be exactly high tech, but she could slip into his apartment when he was away and copy the records by taking a picture of the two or three pages in each chart. It would probably take no more than an hour or two to copy all of the records. That way she could 'read' the photos at her leisure and review the notes on each of the patients, including those of her friend Janetta. If things looked even more suspicious, she could then think of some way to tip off the detectives.

Lisa tested the camera on her copy of "Bon Appetit" magazine. She focused the camera on an ad for Rachael Ray's holiday recipes for Thanksgiving. After the picture was taken, she pressed the 'review pictures' button on the camera and was rewarded with a crystal clear picture of the TV chef's perky smile and the text of an advertisement for using Nabisco crackers and Triscuit in recipes. The quality of the pictures was certainly more than adequate for the task she was considering.

The thought of returning to Dr. Layton's apartment for the sole purpose of copying records terrified Lisa. She wished she could just rush over there and do it now, before she had time to reconsider, but knew that her boss would probably be discharged from the hospital and be returning home at any moment. She would just have to suffer through the next few days until she could put her plan into action.

Patience had never been one of her strong suits. Even as a young girl, she would pressure her parents into giving her birthday presents days ahead of the occasion and Christmas was a similar ordeal. Perhaps if she had not had such success with her persistence, she might have learned to be more patient as an adult. Unfortunately, it was a lesson she had never learned.

Lisa decided to go to the gym and do some aerobics; it always cleared her head. There was a ten o'clock workout on Thursdays at the YMCA with a great class leader. The time taken up by her new nursing job had forced her to significantly cut back on her athletic conditioning, but she refused to let her body grow soft. Lisa had found time for jogging once or twice a week, but enjoyed the workouts at the 'Y' much more. She slipped out of her jeans and T shirt and into a pair of stretch workout pants, a sports bra and stretch top. Lisa admired her silhouette in the wall mirror. She sucked in her stomach, in an attempt to eliminate the midriff bulge that had grown over the last few years. She looked great- until she had to breathe. When she let out her breath, the small bulge returned.

"What the hell, I could look worse!" Lisa exclaimed in the empty room. Lisa quickly laced up her workout Nike's and she was out the door in a flash.

CHAPTER 78

Sal was desperate. Disappointing Mr. Volpe would have dire consequences; however his leverage in controlling Dr. Layton's behavior was very limited. Volpe was insisting that Sal persuade David to cancel the upcoming meeting with the BioVenture group-but how?

It was Friday morning and Sal was alone in the lab. He expected the doctor to call later in the day to arrange their weekend meeting. David needed the updated lab data and photos for his re-scheduled investors meeting. Sal had an idea. It was his only chance. He walked over to one of the storage cabinets in the laboratory. Inside he found a bottle of xylene, a solvent used in the lab. It was the most flammable chemical they used. Sal gave the pint-size can a shake, making certain that there was sufficient fluid for his purposes.

Next, he rounded up all of the papers from the clip boards and from the cages. There were over one hundred pages of information which he placed face down by the copier. He pressed the auto-copy button and watched the machine systematically copy the sheets. Sal placed the copies in a folder and returned them to the briefcase in his office.

There were two fire extinguishers in the facility; one by the entrance and one by the back door. Sal removed them both, and carried them over to the area of the cages. Next, he poured the xylene from the can, the fluid pooled on the floor near the cages. He ran a trail over one of the laboratory tables continuing it to the copier. He placed the originals of the laboratory data sheets on the copier. The chemist grabbed a match from the small box on Ed's desk. "Here goes," he thought to himself.

Sal struck the match and tossed it onto the trail of xylene at his feet. The result was an almost instantaneous flash of flame spreading in both directions from his match. One trail of fire stretched backward, toward the cages. The other rapidly spread upwards and engulfed the copier burning data sheets into ash.

Reacting quickly, he used one fire extinguisher to put out the flames spreading toward the cages and the fire died in seconds. At the same time, the fire he had started at the copying machine had grown.

The table the copier rested on was made of particle board and wood fiber and quick to burn. In addition, the plastic of the copier had caught fire and was dripping molten droplets of plastic and rubber onto the floor. Sal rushed over to put out the flames. Small pieces of charred paper were floating in the air like the ash of the Mount St. Helens eruption. The air had become smoky and was thick with the acrid smell of burnt wiring and plastic. Sal aimed the second fire extinguisher at the base of the machine and was relieved to see the fire immediately diminish in intensity.

Then all hell broke loose. The overhead sprinkler system was triggered by the heat of the fire. Sal became drenched with water and deafened by the noise of the smoke alarms which were now blaring throughout the lab. With the help of the sprinklers, he was able to eliminate the fire at the copying machine and by opening all the doors to the lab Sal was mercifully able to stop the alarms. He then found the sprinkler system shut-off valve and the spray of water stopped. Manzari surveyed the damage.

The copier was destroyed, as was the table it had rested on. The only remains of the lab data was a burned sodden pile of blackened paper. Some of the floor tiles at the base of the copier were charred. Other than that, the damage was minimal. Sal had successfully executed the first part of his plan.

From somewhere in the distance, Sal could hear the sound of the alarm signal for the volunteer fire department.

"Shit, shit, shit." Sal exclaimed loudly. "I'm such an asshole."

He had forgotten that the sprinkler system was automatically wired into the fire department response system. They were already on their way and Sal prepared himself for their arrival.

Pelican Cove had an all volunteer fire department and the wealth of the community provided for the latest in modern equipment. The station dispatcher was able to identify the source of the alarm from the coded sprinkler GPS identification signal. In moments, a new gleaming red fire truck arrived at the scene. From the time of the triggered alarm to their arrival at the smoky lab, only six minutes had elapsed.

There were four men on the truck. The vehicle filled the small parking area in front of the building. All four firemen jumped off the vehicle and came through the front door. The first one to enter was also the largest, a bear of a man in a black, fire-resistant suit.

Brian Venible slowly moved his eyes across the open space of the lab. He focused on the smoldering burnt out hulk of the copying machine.

"Hey, I'm Brian. We got a signal that your sprinklers were triggered. Now I can see why. What happened?"

Sal looked at the firefighter. His uniform made him look large, but Sal wagered that even out of the fireman's suit the man stood over six foot-three and two hundred and fifty pounds.

"I'm Sal Manzari, the bio-chemist here. I was moving some xylene away from the hood and spilled it onto the copier. It ignited somehow and did a job on the copier, but I was able to put it out with the extinguishers. The damage was pretty much limited to the copying machine and some papers. I'm sorry to have made you guys come out here for nothing."

"Don't sweat it, we live for this." Venible smiled.

Sal forced a smile onto his own face.

"It looks like you could use some dry clothes!"

"Yeah, I'm going to mop up this water, then I'll change. You guys can go home. I'm fine."

"Will you need a report for your insurance company?"

Sal thought quickly.

"No, we have a deductible higher than the value of the copier and flooring. I don't think we'll be filing an insurance claim." Sal knew that an insurance claim might initiate a police report and Sal wanted to keep this mishap as private as possible.

"Okay then, we'll get out of your hair. Be careful with those flammables- you should really only use them under a hood."

"I know, I know. I've learned my lesson."

"Hope the rest of your day is better than the start, Mr. Manzari. Bye."

The firemen left the building. Sal was all alone and felt that the morning had actually gone quite well. Now all he had to do was call Dr. Layton and give him the news.

CHAPTER 78

D r. Layton had cleared all surgeries from the schedule for his first day back at work so his Friday schedule was light.

Paula and Lisa were working the examination rooms with Dr. Layton.

"Would you like some make-up to cover your bruise Dr. Layton?" Paula was staring at the dry scab on David's chin.

"Don't make me more self conscious, Paula. I've already got some cover-up on it. Does it look bad?"

"No, I'm just busting your chops. Do you feel alright?"

"Actually, I do. I got quite a bit of rest at home yesterday, and most of the soreness from the accident has faded away. I'm still a little tired, that's all."

"Are you ready to start? Should I begin putting patients in the rooms?" David smiled.

"I need one thing first."

Paula grinned back.

"That's the old Dr. Layton. I'll fix your coffee right away. Lisa, can you get a couple of patients ready?"

"Sure, but set aside a cup of coffee for me too. I left in a hurry this morning and didn't get my caffeine fix yet."

"Two coffees coming right up." Paula marched off to the kitchen.

Lisa walked in the opposite direction, to the front desk. The charts of three patients were resting on the counter, indicating that the day had begun. David walked back to his office and had a seat. He felt spacey, having had two days off from work in the middle of the week. It seemed like it really should be Monday. He had lied to Paula when he stated that he felt good. He still ached quite a bit and now was burdened further by the knowledge that his MRI was abnormal.

David unlocked his files and pulled open the lowermost drawer. He was surprised to find it empty. Then he remembered he had moved the records to his home. David wondered if the momentary memory lapse was a manifestation of his possible Alzheimer's disease. Would this be the way it would be for now on – every time he forgot something he'd be wondering whether he was one step closer to Alzheimer's?

Paula entered carrying Dr. Layton's coffee. There was also a jelly donut on a napkin.

"You're spoiling me, Paula."

"You need some pampering every now and then, Dr. Layton. Now eat up, and let's get started. It's Friday. We all want to get out on time."

"Aye, aye, captain. David made a mock salute at Paula, who seemed to be taking on many of the responsibilities and tasks that Shirley had managed prior to the senior nurse's death. The fleeting thoughts of Shirley saddened Dr. Layton, though not as much as it might have a couple of weeks earlier; time was healing his wounds.

The first patient was Sharon Faylon, a forty-eight year old who was new to the practice. Lisa brought her back into one of the exam rooms.

"Good morning, Mrs. Faylon, I'm Dr. Layton's nurse, Lisa. How can we help you?" Dr. Layton.

"I'm new to Pelican Cove. I used to live in Miami, and received Botox there, but it's just too long a drive. I had Dr. Sebastian Cohen. Have you heard of him?"

"No, I'm sorry, I haven't. Did you want additional Botox treatments?"

"Is it that obvious that I need it? I'm just kidding Lisa, yes. I haven't had a treatment in six months and I'm starting to droop again." For emphasis, the women pushed up the corners of her eyes and face with the palms of her hands.

Lisa had a moment of déjà vu, and remembered when she had conducted a similar performance in front of Nate. She wondered if she had looked as ridiculous as Mrs. Faylon did making that gesture. Lisa tried to be diplomatic.

"I think you look great. As a matter of fact, I didn't realize that you're forty-eight. You look like someone in their thirties." Lisa thought a little white lie never hurt anyone.

"You're just flattering me, but thanks anyway. I heard that Dr. Layton is the best. Do you think he'll be able to treat me today?"

"Maybe. With new patients, he usually wants a consultation first, but since you're experienced at receiving Botox, he may be able to provide the injections on your first visit. He'll be here in just a minute. I'll tell him you would like treatment today if possible."

"Thank you, Lisa."

Lisa walked toward Dr. Layton's office. He had finished his coffee and was on his way out the door. They almost bumped into each other in the hallway. The narrowness of the hallway and their near collision brought their bodies close to each other. For a moment, Lisa felt her heart speed up and the attraction of weeks past reassert itself. This time, it dissipated quickly although she still stumbled for words.

"You have a new patient, Mrs. Sharon Faylon, in room one. She's had Botox before, and wants to start treatment here. She lived in Miami and was receiving the medication there."

"What's she like? Is she nice?"

Lisa smiled.

"A little nutty, but no more than a lot of our patients."

David had to smile too. Many of his patients were a little eccentric and Lisa was starting to appreciate their somewhat narcissistic and at times demanding nature.

"Lisa, go into the refrigerator. We've got some new vials of Botox. They're in a gray sealed box. Please get me a new vial and meet me in room one," directed the Dr.

Lisa wondered if the grey boxes were special. If there was any risk of hurting a patient she knew she should prevent David from completing the treatment. She didn't know what to do. She walked slowly away and her only response to Dr. Layton was a terse, 'okay', muttered in a low monotone.

The refrigerator contained several small vials of Botox. Lisa noticed that the opened vials contained the standard labels from the manufacturer, but also bore additional numbers written on them by hand. The first one she was holding had #29 and a B written in magic marker on the white paper of the label. There were several more opened bottles in the refrigerator, all with a different number, though several shared the same letter. Lisa noticed that the small rubber stopper on top of each bottle contained multiple puncture marks, indicating past usage of the vials. She found the box that Dr. Layton had asked her to open. It contained six small grey boxes, sealed in thin plastic from the manufacturer. Each was labeled Botox. Lisa removed the outside wrapping, and removed one of the boxes. She opened the cardboard flaps of the small box and removed the vial of Botox. It was almost identical to the already opened specimens she had been examining. There was one difference. The new vial had a metal seal around the top, indicating that the drug had never been used. The top of each vial contained a small, thin, circular metal disc which was meant to be removed by the doctor or nurse prior to inserting a syringe in order to extract the medication. Once the disc was removed, it would leave behind a thin rim of metal, which kept the rubber stopper sealed on top of the vial and protected the contents within from contamination.

The small bottles were not meant to be reused, and were disposed of when empty. The metal rim was missing on almost all of the partially used vials in the refrigerator. Lacking any other explanation, it appeared that Dr. Layton was reusing his Botox vials. Lisa felt reassured that she was at least delivering an unopened, apparently unadulterated vial to the new patient. Armed with the medication, she returned to the examination room.

Dr. Layton accompanied Lisa into the exam room. If she hadn't known better, Lisa wouldn't have been able to guess that he had been in a serious auto accident just two days earlier. He walked into the room as if he had not a care in the world, and moved with the smoothness and athleticism of a young man. His face seemed carefree, and as he opened the door, a smile appeared on his handsome face.

"Good morning, I'm Dr. Layton." He reached out and gently took Mrs. Faylon's hand in a respectful greeting.

"Glad to meet you at last, Dr. Layton. I've heard so much about you." David smiled.

"All good, I hope."

"Of course. They say you're the best in Pelican Cove."

There were two ways of taking the compliment, and David knew that Mrs.Faylon probably meant the comment on both levels. On the first, she did think he was the best in Pelican Cove, but on the second level, she probably consciously, or subconsciously, felt that all of the doctors in Pelican Cove were inferior to her doctor from the great city of Miami.

He understood the bias toward thinking that the better physicians practiced in the bigger cities, and took little umbrage at her comment.

"Well thank you. I understand that you've had Botox before and wanted some additional treatment.

"Yes. My eyes and the corners around my mouth could use some. I would really appreciate it if I could do it today. The National Cancer Society fund raiser is this weekend and I want to look my best. I'm on the Board."

"Certainly, that should be no problem at all. Now let me have a look." David adjusted the overhead lighting and examined her skin.

"No problem, Mrs. Faylon. I can treat you today if you'd like."

"That would be fantastic, Dr. Layton. I'm ready and really appreciate not having to come back for another visit."

"Great, Lisa will need to get your informed consent and then we'll be all ready."

Once the paperwork was completed, David picked up the Botox vial and flicked off the metal seal. Although it had never been exposed to the air and was sterile, by reflex he cleaned the top of the vial with an alcohol swab before puncturing it with a sterile needle. He injected some air into the vial to provide back-pressure in order to allow the syringe to fill with the medication. When a sufficient amount was withdrawn, he removed the needle and capped it.

"This is going to hurt just a little," David warned.

"I know, doctor. I'm ready." She closed her eyes and appeared to be gritting her teeth.

"Try to relax, it'll hurt less. Lisa, hold her hand. Please."

Lisa knew that holding Sharon's hand would decrease the pain by distracting her. She grasped Mrs. Faylon's right hand while David injected the left side of Sharon's face. Then they switched sides and repeated the procedure for the wrinkles on the other side.

"You did great, Sharon. How was it?"

"I have to say, you hurt less than Dr. Cohen. I should have come here sooner."

David smiled. Another thing he had learned was that although his patients might praise him mightily one day, they could just as easily turn on him the next. He had no doubt that the next time Mrs. Faylon returned to Miami she might tell Dr. Cohen how much she missed him and how much gentler he was than the doctor in Pelican Cove. Or maybe not – perhaps she truly meant it.

"Lisa, ice the injection sites for her please. Is there anything else I can do for you Mrs. Faylon?"

"No, you've been great, Dr. Layton. I'm going to brag about you to everybody. I'll probably never be able to get an appointment with you again; you're going to be so busy."

"Nonsense. I'll always have time for someone as nice as you. It was a pleasure meeting you."

Lisa understood why all of Dr. Layton's patients loved him so much. His bedside manner was the best, he was easy to look at, and he was skillful. Mrs. Faylon flashed a big smile.

"Thank you so much Dr. Layton."

They shook hands and David left the room.

The very next patient was also new to the practice. She had called just yesterday, and was able to get an appointment vacated by David's surgical schedule cancellations. He had been forced to cancel two major liposuction cases as the work required physical exertion which his hospital physician had advised against until the following week.

Many beautiful patients passed through Dr. Layton's doors, but even in a practice based on cosmetic procedures, where beauty was prized, this patient stood out head and shoulders above the rest. Becky was the first to greet her and hand the young woman the initial paperwork necessary to open a file.

Cherie Steele stood about five foot six inches and carried herself with confidence and dignity. Her hair was an auburn-blond color with a beautiful sheen and golden highlights. She had lightly tanned skin, with no wrinkles and a flawless smile. Slightly broad shoulders joined a graceful neck. She was wearing a tight fitting short-sleeved blouse which complemented her athletic figure and ample cleavage. The size of her chest suggested augmentation surgery, though perhaps on a person this perfect, the breasts were just one more gift from God. Her toned thighs were youthfully accented by a pair of tan slacks that completed the package perfectly.

Becky knew that the young woman was at the office for a cosmetic consultation, though beyond that, the nature of the visit wasn't noted in the appointment book. When the mystery woman returned the paperwork, Becky learned two additional pieces of information; the new patient was thirty years old, and was seeing Dr. Layton for a consultation regarding augmentation mammoplasty-she wanted bigger boobs.

CHAPTER 80

Detectives Collins and Levine were about to call it a week. Both detectives had the weekend off and decided to run one errand before checking out. They pulled into the visitors parking spot at the gatehouse of the Surf Tower condominium.

Dan groaned as he pulled his body up from his seat and got out of the car.

"Man, Kev, I'm getting too old for this. I'm tired!"

Kevin smiled.

"Dan, I think you'll still be doing this when you're seventy!"

Levine's entire family had been in law enforcement, including a brother who was on the force in Chicago. It was no secret that Dan enjoyed his job.

"God forbid. One of these days I'm gonna hit those lotto numbers."

They walked over to the frosty-haired gate attendant. He was watching TV and the door to the guardhouse cubicle was closed. A wall-unit air conditioner was blasting. The odds were more likely that the Cubs would win a pennant than an isolated intruder being heard or seen by this man.

Kevin knocked on the sliding glass window of the guardhouse. The man inside turned his attention from the TV to the interruption. He smiled at the officer.

"Hey, where's your car?"

"I parked it! You were busy watching TV and we decided not to interrupt you," Collins quipped.

The attendant didn't know if the visitor was joking or not. Kevin decided that he best not confuse the old guy. He flashed his badge.

"I'm Detective Collins and this is Detective Levine. We have reason to believe that an intruder visited your parking area and tampered with Dr. Layton's vehicle. I don't know if you knew this, but the doctor was in a serious auto accident this week."

"My name is Jake, Jake Callahan. No, actually I hadn't heard about it. Dr. Layton has a pass, so he doesn't have to stop to be let in. He just enters on the resident's side of the gate. I did notice that he was driving a new car today, but that's no big deal for him. He gets a new car every year or two."

"Well, the accident could have been very serious. His brakes failed. We're here to let you know that we'll be having marked and unmarked cars patrolling the area on a more frequent basis in case someone decides to come back. We'd like you to keep your eyes peeled for anything or anyone suspicious. It might help if you kept the TV a little lower than usual and maybe open the glass slider a little so you might hear someone more easily."

The attendant seemed slighted at the suggestion that he might not be up to the job. "I'm sorry; I really love my position here. It keeps me from getting under the wife's hair and gives me enough money to golf on the weekends. Unfortunately, my hearing ain't so good. These hearing aids help, but if I don't crank up the TV I can hardly hear it. I'll try my best though. I'll look around every now and then and keep the slider open.

I'll even turn the air down a little so it won't run so loud."

Kevin really didn't mean to make the guard feel badly, and doubted that any added surveillance from the old man would catch a professional who was trying not to be seen. But none the less, it couldn't hurt.

"That sounds great, tell the other guards too. But otherwise, keep what I told you to yourself. You wouldn't want to frighten all the rest of the residents. The investigation is still ongoing and our chief might not even like it that we told you-consider yourself our deputy."

Kevin would have thought the man had just won the lottery. His face lit up and he grinned back at the officer. It was clear that he liked to feel important, and was proud to be of use to the officers.

"I'm honored. Truth is, I always wanted to be a police officer, but I had a bad back and it kept me out of the police academy. Ended up working in Detroit instead, back when we were making all our own cars. Still get a good pension out of it. Never thought I'd be deputized at seventy-six though," he chuckled.

"Well don't do anything crazy. Just call us if you see anything out of the ordinary. There may even be a reward if anything you provide leads to an arrest."

"Detective, I would be happy to do it for free, to help out Dr. Layton. He's always been nice to me, especially at Christmas. I believe in doing the right thing I'll keep my eyes open. Is there anything else I can do for you men?"

"No, that's about it. Here, take our cards, Jake." Both Dan and Kevin handed the guard their police ID business cards.

"Thanks for your assistance."

"No problem. Good luck with your investigation officers."

The detectives returned to their unmarked Mercury Marquis and drove away.

CHAPTER 81

"Is the next patient ready, Lisa?"

"Yes, Paula brought her back." Then in a lower voice, Lisa added, "She looks like a model."

David smiled at his nurse. "You look like a model, Lisa."

She blushed.

"I'm sorry, Lisa. I didn't mean to embarrass you. But you do look great," he said as he entered the patient's room.

Cherie Steele was seated with her slim legs crossed and her ample cleavage clearly visible. David found himself staring at his newest patient. She was the most attractive woman he could recall having seen in a long time. It was difficult for him to see how he could possibly help her with her appearance. He glanced down at her chart, and noted that she lived in the adjacent town of Manatee Bay, was single and had no significant prior medical history other than her plastic surgery.

"Hello, I'm Dr. Layton."

"Hi, Cherie Steele, call me Cherie." She extended her hand.

"My pleasure. What can I do for you Cherie?"

"I feel a little uncomfortable asking you this, but I guess I might as well just spit it out. I take care of myself and all, and I'm in pretty good shape."

"I'll say," thought David to himself.

"I had some plastic surgery two years ago and had my breasts enlarged. At the time, the surgeon talked me out of going as big as I had wanted. Now, I'm disappointed. I'd like to go a little bigger and I hear you're the man to see."

"What kind of work do you do Cherie?"

"If you're asking if I'm a dancer or anything, I'm not. Right now I'm not working, though I'm sure more breast enhancement surgery won't hurt me any in finding a job."

David felt that no improvement was necessary.

"Do you mind if I examine your prior surgery?"

For some reason, Layton felt uncomfortable around the new patient. He had been a plastic surgeon for enough years to sense when something was wrong. He didn't know what it was, but he was on his guard. Never the less, he did need to see her surgery and breasts if he was to try to satisfy her wishes.

"Of course not. I had the surgery done through my armpit area. The doctor who did it did a great job, but he's in California, so now I'm here. Do you want me to disrobe?"

"No, for this, I can just have you remove your top. But I need to have you up on the exam table please."

Cherie rose from the chair and simultaneously pulled her top off. She wore no bra and seemed to have a flawless body. As she moved toward the table, she brought her body close to Dr. Layton who couldn't help but appreciate her appearance. Lisa thought she saw him blush slightly. Ms. Steele had firm breasts which appeared natural, if not somewhat large for her trim, shapely form.

"I'd like to examine the scars from your prior surgery, Cherie."

"Sure, Dr. Layton." Cherie raised her left arm above her head, and David examined the small, well-healed scar within her left axillary area. Next, he checked it's mate on the right side.

"Do you think you can help me, Dr. Layton?"

"I try to satisfy the needs of my patients, Ms. Steele. Honestly, I think you look perfect the way you are. Are you sure you want to do this?"

David knew from experience that life changes, such as a divorce or stressful life event often triggered a patient's desire for cosmetic surgery.

"Has something changed in your life or is someone else asking you to have this surgery?" he continued to question.

"No, Dr. Layton, I want this for me." Cherie assured him.

"Okay, what I'd like to do is take some pictures and get them in the computer. Then with our computer software I'll be able to show you what you'll look like after the surgery. It will help us pick the breast augmentation that best satisfies your needs."

"That makes sense to me."

David was hoping that after seeing the pictures she would realize that she might be better off without additional surgery.

"Lisa, have Paula get the camera since she's done this before. Just ask her to take the pictures for me and get them into the computer. When she's finished, bring Ms. Steele into my office and I'll review the computer shots with her."

"I'll see you back in a few minutes, Cherie," Dr. Layton said over his shoulder.

David returned to the solitude of his office. As much as he wanted the business, something told him to steer clear of this patient. His warning system had been triggered; something here didn't seem right.

Layton had enough time to review some of the messages which had gathered on his desk during the two days he had been out of the office. He was still involved in poring through the pile of calls and notes when Cherie returned, accompanied by Lisa.

"Have a seat, Ms. Steele. Lisa, you don't have to stay for this. I'll call you when we're finished."

"Do you want me to close the door?" Lisa asked.

"No you can leave it open. Have Becky get a breast surgery patient folder out for Cherie. She can take it home and read it before committing to any surgery."

"I'll get right on it, Dr. Layton." Lisa left Dr. Layton alone with the new patient.

David got up from his chair and turned his laptop at an angle so that Ms. Steele could see her proposed augmentation photos. "Let me move your chair so that you can see better."

Cherie rose and David moved her seat close to his own. For a brief moment, their shoulders touched. They were close enough for the surgeon to be able to smell his patient's perfume – a slightly sweet scented mixture of almonds and perhaps vanilla.

David pressed a computer key and the program appeared on his laptop monitor. The screen was split in half. The left side showed 'before' pictures, while the right side contained three 'after' images, with augmentation of twenty percent, thirty-five percent and fifty percent. Further increases were possible, though David knew that such a change, especially in Cherie's case, would appear grotesque.

"These are your pictures as you appear now, and on the right you can see your post-op expected results. Do you have any questions?"

"No, I don't want to look weird or anything. I think the middle one with the thirty-five percent increase would be great."

"I'd like you to read the materials in the package that my receptionist Becky will give you on your way out. If you have any questions, just call.

To be honest with you, as much as I'd like to satisfy your needs, again, I think you look great just the way you are.

"I appreciate your integrity Dr. Layton. I'll think about it. Maybe you're right, There is one other thing."

David waited as she paused.

"If you're not able to do my surgery would you be available for dating?"

David was speechless as well as flattered. Cherie was such a beauty. But something in her behavior felt wrong. It helped him formulate a response.

"I'm very flattered, Ms. Steele, but I make it policy not to date my patients."

"What if I didn't have my surgery or had it elsewhere, could we go out then?"

Layton was surprised at her persistence. She was 'off' somehow.

"I'm sorry, Cherie. I can't. I'm rather spoken for."

For a moment, David thought he could perceive a flash of anger in the woman's eyes. A furrow appeared between her eyebrows.

"Okay forget I asked." Cherie rose abruptly. "I'll get the folder on the way out and think about it."

"I guess that'll do it then. I hope I haven't hurt your feelings or anything."

"Don't flatter yourself too much, Dr. Layton. I'll be alright." The young woman now seemed clearly angered and David was eager for her to leave.

His wish was promptly fulfilled. Within moments, Cherie had paid cash for her consultation and departed from the office.

CHAPTER 82

S al decided that it was about time to call Dr. Layton. It was a little past noon; hopefully he would catch David on his lunch break. He tried him on his cell phone. David picked up on the second ring. Sal's number showed on the digital display of the phone.

"Hi Sal, what's up?"

"I'm afraid I have some bad news, David. There's been a little accident at the lab. Some Xylene caught fire near the copying machine. I was in the middle of copying the lab records from the last few weeks and everything went up in flames."

"Oh my God! Are the animals alright?"

"Yes, they all seem fine. I was able to put out the fire with the extinguishers. By the time the fire department arrived it was all out. There's some damage to the floor, the copier is a total loss, and the place stinks to high heaven from burning plastic. The worst part though is that the information from the animals is lost."

"Not completely, Sal. I've already got copies of a lot of our data. I imagine it will be enough to go ahead with my presentation to the

BioVenture group on Tuesday. At this point, I just want to get the damn thing over with. I'm beat. I've got the pictures you've already given me and if things go well, I may hint at the preliminary human data, at least acknowledging usage of the drug in our nurses and myself. That alone may convince them to come aboard and fund us. I think we'll be alright."

The plastic surgeon was like a dog with a bone - he just wouldn't let go. It appeared that no matter what Sal did, he couldn't get Dr. Layton to give up on the Botox study. Manzari was getting concerned – if he couldn't dissuade David from continuing with the study he was sure that Bobby Volpe would find a way to do so.

"David, are you sure it's not your recent accident talking. We're not in that much of a hurry. Maybe we can put the meeting off for another week or two. We can try to piece together the missing data and have the most recent findings to present along with up-to-date pictures. In the end, we may be able to get more out of the investors with a stronger presentation."

"I've made up my mind, Sal. I'm not going to put these guys off again. The first missed meeting was understandable, but I don't want to try their patience any further. The venture capital market is very competitive right now – there's not as much money as there used to be. Trust me. It'll be fine and we'll get exactly what we want."

Sal paused. "Alright David, I hope you're right."

"I know I am, Sal. Don't be such a worrier. Will you be able to clean up the damage from the fire yourself?"

"Yeah, no problem." Tidying up after the fire wasn't what concerned Sal at all. Manzari felt as if the walls were closing in on him – he had placed Dr. Layton's life in danger and was running out of ways to keep him out of harm's way.

"Well, if you need any help, give me a call. I guess we'll have to get in touch with the copier company. It was being leased, but I purchased a service contract and we'll get it replaced. Don't worry about the meeting it will all go as we planned."

"Terrific David. Just let me know...."

"Count on it partner. They won't know what hit them."

Sal closed his eyes and said a silent prayer for his doctor friend.

"Knock 'em dead."

CHAPTER 83

Bobby Volpe rode in the passenger seat of the spacious Cadillac. Knuckles, in a dark black suit, occupied the driver's seat. They drove at a leisurely pace through the midday traffic, heading toward the edge of town.

"Hey, Knuckles, slip somethin' nice in the CD will ya. Get rid of that rock and roll."

The music that had been offending Bobby's ears was a new Christina Aguilera hit. Within seconds, the speakers emitted the soothing sounds of Frank Sinatra, crooning about how Chicago was 'his kind of town'. The car drove past a Greyhound station and a Seven-Eleven. Several Hispanic day laborers jumped off the back of a pick-up truck, ready to call it quits for the day. Two of them were already getting onto their bicycles, which had been chained to a small fence. From the Seven-Eleven, they would drive three or four miles to their trailers on the edge of town, or if they were less lucky and had nowhere to live, into the pine woods surrounding the affluent community. There, they would try to avoid the occasional police officer performing his duty at keeping the homeless away from those with fenced-in estates.

Bobby marveled at the hard work the day laborers endured in their efforts to make a better life for themselves. Then again, it wasn't much different for his father Giuseppe when he had first come to America in the 1920's. Volpe's father had been a minor soldier in the Amalfi crime family. His labors provided steady income for the family and a college education for Bobby's younger brother and sister. Bobby had neither the grades nor the desire for higher education, and followed his father's footsteps into the family business. His father's reward for working hard had included a seven year rap for extortion. While the senior Volpe was in prison, Bobby and his mother were well cared for, with regular supplemental income provided by the Almalfi family. His father had come to an unfortunate end, when a fight in the prison yard had ended with a shank to the chest. He died on the way to the hospital.

Bobby was only seventeen, and his entry into the crime family began only a few weeks later. He was a fast learner and his ascent through the ranks had been rapid. His rise in their hierarchy was aided by an ability to carry out his orders completely and discreetly. In his younger years, he had the earned the reputation of a cold-hearted assassin. Now, he was known as a shrewd businessman. He ruled his mob family with firmness and an iron fist.

After driving two more blocks, they passed a Lickin' Chicken restaurant and an adult book store. The storefront at the corner was their destination—the VIP Velvet Lounge. It was marked by a neon sign, spelling out the name of the lounge, followed by the neon silhouette of a reclining nude woman holding a champagne glass. Even at a little before five in the afternoon all of the parking spaces in front of the business were taken, and there were several cars in the back, including one large eighteen wheeler. The establishment benefited from its location close to the entrance and exit ramps of the adjacent interstate highway

75. The club was another of Volpe's investments, managed by one of his captains, Carmelo Niantic, also known as "Mello". The entrance to the lounge was marked by a non-descript black door, with the hours of operation and a 'no minors permitted' sign.

Knuckles parked the car and the men entered the dimly lit lounge. Most of the patrons were seated at the semicircular bar, holding their drinks and ogling the two dancers who were nude from the waist up, and dressed only in thongs from the waist down. The sole purpose of the thin garments was to hold the bills of various denominations placed there by the admiring men. It also allowed the lounge to pretend to be in accordance with the local laws prohibiting full nude dancing in the county. A few of the men were seated at private tables, purchasing overpriced drinks for themselves and the dancers and negotiating other 'services' with the ladies – services provided in private rooms located at the back of the lounge.

The bartender was opening a case of Budweisers and placing the bottles in the cooler at the end of the bar.

"Hey Al, is Mello around?"

"No, Mr. Volpe, I haven't seen him yet today."

"How about Cherie, is she here?"

"Yeah, I saw her pull up a little bit ago. She's probably in the back getting ready to come out. She starts at five."

"Thanks, Al. I'll find her."

Volpe walked toward the back of the lounge, past the bathrooms and down a narrow corridor. There were three doors marking the entrance to small rooms. The door to one of the rooms was closed and the unmistakable sound of a man groaning was easily audible.

"Sounds like somebody is gettin' his money's worth," Bobby declared to Knuckles.

"Sure does, Mr. Volpe. Nodda bad way to spend a Friday afternoon in

342

my book."

They continued walking and reached a small staff dressing area. It contained a mirror, some chairs, lockers and a closet with hangers and various outfits used by some of the dancers. Two of the chairs were occupied by extremely attractive women. The shorter of the two appeared to be Hispanic, with dark brown hair and a slender body. Her breasts were rather small, covered only by two half-dollar sized 'pasties' in the shape of American flags. She wore a pair of very small, very tight shorts, also in a patriotic red, white and blue motif. The second woman was blond, taller and also extremely attractive. She was still dressed in her street clothes, a tight short-sleeved blouse and red slacks.

When the men entered the room, both women looked up.

"Hello ladies. You two look like you're ready to make lots of money tonight."

The blond nervously bit her lower lip.

"Hi, Mr. Volpe."

The patriotic dancer smiled nervously at her boss.

"Hi."

Bobby looked at the second dancer; he couldn't remember her name.

"Sweetheart, could you go up front and leave us alone with Cherie for a few minutes?"

"Sure, Mr. Volpe. She picked up her small purse and grabbed her cigarettes and lighter from the area in front of the mirror. In a flash, she was headed down the corridor and back to the bar. As she walked away, the sound of her red, white and blue sequined platform shoes echoed down the hallway, becoming softer as she disappeared from the back of the lounge.

"So Cherie, how'd your appointment with the doctor go?"

Cherie inhaled deeply before answering. She bit her lower lip again.

"I tried my hardest, Mr. Volpe. I did everything you told me. Maybe he's gay or something, but I couldn't get him to go out with me. He told me he doesn't date patients. When I told him I could go out with him and end our doctor-patient thing, he just said he already has a girlfriend. I felt like a jerk. I even took my top off in the room. Nothing worked."

A dark cloud appeared to pass across Volpe's eyes. He looked very angry and his brow became furrowed. Layton was proving to be a bigger problem than he had anticipated. Using Cherie to get into the physician's apartment—to access his office and lab records—had been his last subtle plan. He quickly shifted gears.

"Knuckles, ya look like ya could use a drink. I'm going to stay back here for awhile. I'll be out in a bit. Wait for me at the bar and when I come out we can think about catchin' some dinner."

"Sure, Mr. Volpe." Knuckles looked approvingly at Cherie's beautiful body as he made his exit from the room.

"Cherie, let's finish our discussion in private."

Bobby got up and walked over to Cherie. He kissed her softly on the side of the cheek. Hand in hand, they walked to the first of the open doors in the dark, dingy corridor. Bobby closed the door behind them. Knuckles was half way down the corridor as he heard the sound of tossed shoes hitting the floor and the creak of a bed sighing under the weight of two bodies. A smile creased the corners of his mouth – at least the boss might be happy when he arrived for dinner.

CHAPTER 84

L isa felt relieved to be finished with work for the week. "TGIF," she said to herself. Lisa was guiding her car out of the parking spot at Dr. Layton's office. She had over two hours before she had to pick the boys up from school. She was tired and in no mood to do food shopping that needed doing and really wasn't in the mood to have to prepare a big dinner. Nate had advised her that he would be home by six. Lisa made an 'executive' decision—it would be Pizza Hut for dinner. She would make it more nutritious by adding a salad and entice the boys with some cinnamon crust breadsticks. With the dinner plans out of the way, Lisa tackled her more vexing decisions.

What was she going to do about the events surrounding Janetta's death, the pilfered records at David's home, and her suspicions regarding his Botox treatments? She could still just go to the police, but besides her concerns for Dr. Layton, preferred not to do so. When she was in college, her roommate had been incorrectly identified as a drug dealer and was removed from one of her classes and taken to the police station for questioning. Circumstantial evidence and eyewitness accounts had forced her friend to have to hire an attorney. There was enough of a case to merit an investigation. Her roommate, Kay, totally fell apart. She couldn't concentrate on her work and failed two of her four classes for the semester. Kay's own parents were uncertain as to their daughter's innocence. Six weeks later, new evidence from the true dealer led to the arrest of the real criminal, who bore an amazing likeness to Kay. Lisa's roommate never got over it. They lost touch after college, but Lisa never forgot the experience. No, before taking the chance of harming Dr. Layton's reputation, she would be certain an investigation was justified.

Lisa opened her purse and found the key she had copied the prior day. Did she have the nerve to return to Dr. Layton's condo and search through the files in his apartment? Lisa had driven half a mile on auto-pilot. She passed a beauty supply shop and had an idea. The sign out front read, "Rhonda's Beauty Supply", and below this, another sign pronounced, "Wholesale and Retail, Wigs and Hair Cosmetics". Mrs. Martin parked her car in front of the shop. She pushed open the door and a small bell tinkled, signaling her entry. A large dark-skinned woman appeared, entering through a curtain from an adjoining room at the rear of the small shop.

"Can I help you?"

The woman must have weighed about two hundred pounds and stood about five-three. She had beautiful chocolate skin and a round, smiling face. She wore bright red lipstick and was wearing a yellow cotton blouse that proclaimed her name, in elaborate script, as Rhonda. She had beautiful long black hair, flipped at her mid neck, in a style that had been popular in the early 1960's. She looked like a singer from one of those Motown girl rock and roll groups from a few decades earlier.

"I'd like a wig. Nothing too expensive, or anything, just something to surprise my husband."

Rhonda's smile grew bigger.

"You've come to the right place. Do you have a special color and length in mind?"

"Black and long— kind of like your hair." Lisa looked around the shop, and spotted several wigs on Styrofoam molds. None exactly looked like what she wanted.

Rhonda laughed.

"I don't have one of those out on display, but I have some in the back."

Then she shocked Lisa. Rhonda pulled backwards gently on the front of her forehead and pulled her hair from her head. The wig separated itself from the obese woman's natural hair, which was rather stubby, much sparser than normal and silver speckled.

"When I got chemo for breast cancer two years ago my hair came in weird. It's been gray ever since and doesn't get too long. I already had the beauty shop, but thought that it would be a good time to add wigs. It was kind of like a message from above. I hope I didn't embarrass you. I just wanted to show you the quality of our wigs."

Lisa smiled back.

"I appreciate all you must have gone through. It must have been very hard to lose your hair and all. Your wig is beautiful and very natural appearing. Do you have one like it at a reasonable price?"

"This one is actually several hundred dollars, but I have a synthetic and human blend that looks almost as good and costs only fifty dollars."

"That's my price range. Can you show it to me please?"

"No problem."

Rhonda returned with a long black wig, slightly longer than her own artificial tresses. Otherwise it appeared almost identical. She carried it draped across both of her outstretched forearms, and it vaguely reminded Lisa of a skinned animal.

"Go ahead, try it on." Rhonda gently handed the wig over to Lisa.

Lisa slipped it on. The fit was imperfect; it required pinning up of her natural locks to rest properly, but the transformation was truly amazing. Simply changing to dark, long hair altered Lisa's appearance significantly. Mrs. Martin admired herself in a mirror placed on the counter for just that purpose.

"That's exactly what I wanted. Thanks, I'll take it." She handed the wig back to Rhonda.

"I'll throw in the head mold at no charge. Are you sure you don't want to wear it out?"

"No, I have to pick up my kids, and I think they'll be too surprised if they see me with the wig on."

"Okay, will that be charge or cash?"

Lisa handed over three twenty dollar bills. The new big faces and multi-colored hues of the recently minted new currency made her feel like she was paying with play money.

Rhonda handed back the change along with a rectangular box made to fit the wig and mold.

"If you ever have any problems with it, just give me a call." The store owner handed Lisa a business card. "For taking care of it, just wash it gently with soap and water and style it on the low setting of your hair dryer. And keep it away from very high temperatures—that can be rough on synthetic hair."

"Thank you very much." Lisa said.

"Thank you. I hope your husband likes the wig."

For better or worse, Lisa knew that she had crossed the threshold, and was now committed to her plan.

CHAPTER 85

Saturday morning in October. It was a bright sunny day, with the high expected to get into the eighties. Sal had no real plans and awoke to fresh concerns regarding the lab. He was trapped. There was really no way out of his obligation to Bobby Volpe, excepting his death. It was a 'deal with the devil.' He could live with the sale of his soul if it only affected him, but he had real fears for Dr. Layton. Then again, he had tried all he could do to save David and it was the Dr.s own greedy tenacity that kept him in harms way. As a means of some kind of mental escape, he went over to his computer and clicked on Google, then entered InternationalPoker.com. This was a new site that let him play Texas Hold 'Em for free. The prizes were nominal, always less than one hundred dollars, because they were paid for by the advertisers. At this point, a free site sounded good to Sal-he was just about broke.

Sal clicked on the web portal and began to play. It was a little different playing for small stakes and not having any real money on the line. Everyone played less predictably and it was much more difficult to gauge opponent's cards. Sal lost himself in the game and methodically moved up in the ranks, clearing one table of opposing players after another. The tournament had started with two hundred and forty competitors, and was now down to thirty-one. The top ten spots won money, and Sal was feeling pretty good about his chances of coming away a winner. Now, he wished he had been at one of the 'real' cash sites, where he could have been winning some serious green.

The phone rang and Manzari answered it while continuing to play.

"Hey Sal. Hope I'm not botherin' ya on this glorious day. I'd like to meet with ya today. How about noontime at Manatee Park?"

Sal recognized the voice of Bobby Volpe, who assumed correctly that Sal recognized his voice from prior conversations. The caller ID of the phone indicated a blocked call from an unknown number; Volpe didn't like people identifying who he was when he called. Sal sighed. A meeting with the gangster was not what he had in mind for the beautiful afternoon, but he knew that there was only one acceptable answer to Bobby's request.

"Sure, Bobby. Anything special I need to know? What's up?"

"You know, Sallie, I don't like to talk much on the phone. I'll see ya at the entrance of the park under the big oak tree at noon. I'll even spring for lunch."

"Okay, I'll see you then." Sal spoke.

Sal went back to his game of poker. The field was now down to twenty-two players. Manzari had accumulated a big stack of chips, and was in sixth place. First place was a prize of one hundred bucks and an entry into a future tournament where the winner would receive a $10,000 all expenses paid admission to a World Series of Poker event in Las Vegas. Sal wondered if he had the skill to play with the heavy hitters in Vegas. He got his first two cards, a seven and eight of spades. Sal decided it was worth playing them and paid to stay in the pot. The three cards of the flop came and were a six of hearts, nine of spades and queen of spades.

Manzari was excited. He was one card away from a flush, and had two cards, either a five or nine, that would give him a straight. With so many ways to win, betting became important. He wanted as many opponents as possible to stay in the game if he 'hit' the cards he needed, but didn't want to pay a lot of his money to receive the next card, in case his hand wasn't a winner. Without the straight or flush, his cards were weak.

One of the other players raised, and another re-raised. It wasn't what Manzari had hoped for, but he couldn't force himself to quit. "Anyway," he said to himself, "It's not like it's real money." He stayed in the game. The next card revealed was a ten of diamonds. Sal had made his straight. Time to rake in some money. The betting made its way around the table and before it reached Manzari, the same two players who had been betting all along bet again. Sal decided to try to fool the other players into not thinking that he had a good hand and didn't raise them further. The pot was getting large. If he won, his chip total might place him into first place and he might be able to simultaneously eliminate several challengers from the table.

The last card, the river, appeared on the computer screen. It was the king of spades. Even though the stakes were low, Sal was excited. He now had a flush. Only a higher flush could beat him. The betting began. One player ahead of him bet half their pile of chips. The player next in line to bet folded their cards and went out. When it came to Sal's turn in the action, he raised his entire pile of chips. He was 'all in'. Only one other player at the table, the one who had bet originally, stayed in the game. His competitor had enough chips to meet the raise. The pot was huge.

The computer turned over the cards of both players, and Sal watched as the computer awarded the entire stack of chips to his opponent. "Damn" Sal shouted at the computer. His competition had a jack and two of spades, and won with a higher flush. Manzari was out of chips and eliminated from the tournament.

Sal wondered if his luck would ever change. He walked away from the computer screen and made himself some breakfast. The distraction of the game was gone, and now his stomach was in knots at the thought of his meeting with Volpe. A few minutes before noon, Sal was positioned under an ancient huge oak tree at the entrance to Manatee Park, one of the many small green spaces in Pelican Cove. The park had three baseball fields, a couple of basketball courts, and two tennis courts. There was a small lake with paddle boats and a concession area with hot dogs and hamburgers. Sal didn't have to wait long. He saw Bobby approaching from the parking lot, dressed stylishly in a black short sleeve knit shirt and black slacks. He was accompanied by a driver Sal hadn't met before, a well-groomed man of average height wearing a pin-striped black suit. The chauffeur was remarkable for his puffy hairdo, jet black and combed back over his head. He looked like a mafia version of Donald Trump.

"Hey Sallie, glad to see you're on time. This is Lanzo, my driver."

Lanzo picked his head up in greeting, and extended his hand to Sal. Sal's smaller paw was swallowed in a handshake.

"Let me get us something to eat. Lanzo, get us a couple of hot dogs. Sal, they've got the best hot dogs in all of Pelican Cove here. Hebrew Nationals. Say what ya will about the Jews, but they make the best hot dogs."

Sal doubted that it was the Jews that made the hot dogs, but kept his mouth shut.

"What do you want on yours, Sal?"

"Mustard and sauerkraut would be great and a Diet Coke."

"Glad to see you're watchin' your calories. Wouldn't want my partner to croak. Get me a Diet Coke too, Lanzo, and a hot dog with a little mustard."

"Sure thing boss. You want me to bring them over here, or are you gonna eat at the tables by the concession place?"

"We'll be over there in a couple of minutes, Lanzo. Just wait over there for us."

Lanzo walked away and Volpe gave Sal his full attention.

"So how's things, Sal?"

"I'm afraid they could be a little better, Bobby. I tried to slow Dr. Layton down, like you asked. I made a little fire in the lab. I made a copy of the data for you, then burned the originals. And even though I told the doc that all the records were ruined he still plans on meeting with some investors on Tuesday. I just don't know how to stop him."

"I'm afraid we're runnin' outta easy alternatives, Sal. How are things in the lab?"

"Fine. And I've got the data saved for you, for whenever you need it."

"I'm going to be ready to move ahead with incorporatin' and gettin' all the legal stuff completed next week. The only thing we gotta take care of is Dr. Layton. I'm afraid we havta have a more permanent solution."

Sal didn't like the way that had sounded but he knew to hold his tongue.

"Come on, let's go get our hot dogs."

Any appetite that Sal had was gone. The smell of the hot dogs and sauerkraut nauseated him.

"I will need all the records and the most recent before and after pics from the lab, Sal. Most of it is mumbo jumbo to me, but I'm gonna have you meet with my attorney. He's a real sharp guy and will put us in touch with who we need to get this thing goin'."

"Sure Bobby."

Sal found himself answering methodically as if in a trance. He knew he couldn't continue their partnership. Sal would have to do something to get out of their deal and keep Layton out of harms way-he owed him that didn't he? Sal hoped he had the nerve to make his final plan work.

CHAPTER 86

D avid had trouble sleeping. He thought he might have been dreaming, but couldn't recall what had awakened him. He remained in bed, hoping to fall back to sleep. Instead, he just continued tossing and turning and thinking about his abnormal MRI. The bedside clock indicated that it was only five in the morning. David decided to get out of bed and have a leisurely breakfast before work. It was useless to try to go back to sleep, he was just too wired.

After pouring some orange juice into a small glass, David opened a box of Special K cereal and added some slices of fresh banana. He was about to sit down to his breakfast when he stopped realizing that he had just placed the cereal box back in the refrigerator, and the milk was in the cupboard where the cereal belonged. Dr. Layton shook his head and wondered if it was just too early to be awake or if he was losing his mind. After re-placing the food items back where they belonged he ate his breakfast.

David pondered his agenda for the day. Nothing unusual, though he did have several surgeries scheduled. It was to be his first day back performing surgery since the accident. His wounds had improved significantly, and he felt eager to get back into the normal routine of his work. He tried to put the accident out of his mind and succeeding. Unfortunately, he could not similarly ignore concerns regarding his Botox study. David wasn't sure if he was adequately prepared to meet with the venture capital funding group the next day despite what he said to Sal. The events of the past few weeks had him questioning whether FDA approval for the drug would be achievable. He again pushed these negative thoughts aside. If he played his cards right, the investors might purchase rights to the drug outright with enough of a one-time payment to satisfy both he and Sal Manzari.

The surgeon walked to his study and gathered the folders he would use in his meeting with the BioVenture group Tuesday. The pictures of the mice before and after treatment were impressive. His data, indicating up to eight months without recurrence of wrinkles, accompanied by standard Botox data indicating efficacy of three to six months should be sufficiently convincing to satisfy the investors. If all that wasn't enough, David had some dated photos of himself before and after the Botox, as further support of the long-term usefulness of the drug. Passing the responsibility of obtaining FDA approval over to another group of investors and researchers now seemed like an excellent idea. Whether the drug panned out or not, he hoped to receive a windfall that would secure his retirement. David showered, dressed, and got ready for work. He actually felt more rested than he expected and as usual looked forward to a busy, routine day.

The police cruiser drove past the Surf Tower condominium. The officers inside had been advised that one of the residents, a doctor, was a potential target. Watching for suspicious activity was a low-yield part of the business. The bad guys might strike at any time, and usually did so in the middle of the night, when surveillance was most difficult. Short of a full-time stakeout, drive-bys were mostly to satisfy the neighbors that the police were 'on the job.'

The two officers in the car enjoyed the view of the Gulf of Mexico, visible behind the condo tower. An older man was visible in the security office at the gate. Everything seemed quiet and the patrol car continued on its way.

CHAPTER 87

Anthony Amari lived in Tampa and was part of the Ferraro crime family. From time to time, his special skills were requested by operators outside his area, and with permission from his capo, he might travel elsewhere. It always came down to the money. For enough of it, he would go anywhere his boss allowed.

On Sunday, Amari was leaving church with his family when his cell phone rang. A private meeting later that day had provided all the information he would need. The mark was a doctor in the ritzy town of Pelican Cove. It really didn't matter to Amari who the target was, but it was always nice if it was someone who wouldn't put up too much of a fight. He figured a rich, wimpy doctor wouldn't be too tough. He had to drive to Pelican Cove that afternoon, meet up with the local cheese, Bobby Volpe, and get his detailed orders there. The money was good. He was going to get paid $50,000 for the hit and another $50,000 if it got in the papers as a suicide and didn't stir up trouble for the local crime family. That made the job harder, though Amari thought that with any luck, and his always meticulous planning, he would be able to pull it off.

Anthony stayed overnight at the Budget Six Motel in Pelican Cove, paying for his stay in cash. He dressed casually and kept to himself. In the morning, he had a small breakfast and got ready for work. First, he stopped at a Goodwill store on the edge of town. Amari drifted through the racks of clothing until he found what he wanted. An old, but serviceable shirt embossed with the name, Supreme Electric, and in similar script beneath that, the name 'Dave'. It would be a useful cover if anyone in the building spotted him and wondered what he was doing in the condo. Usually, Anthony would be able to come and go unnoticed. Years of practice had taught him how best to fit in. He never drew any attention to himself and was careful to look as 'average' as he could. The work shirt would help.

Amari reviewed his other supplies. A bottle of Oxycontin, a garrot, gloves, his lock picking equipment and a few other tools. All fit neatly into a case which would match with his cover as an electrician. And at his hip, hidden from view, a 9mm Walther with an attached silencer. It was only for emergency use and Anthony had every intention of keeping it holstered and collecting the extra $50,000 for keeping the job below the police radar.

It was still early. Anthony decided to make a little dry run and check out the neighborhood of the condominium. Amari was impressed by the wide boulevards, lush vegetation and landscaping, even in the medians of the Pelican Cove streets. Everything in the town spoke of money. When he approached the area of the condo he studied the parking arrangements. He knew from experience he could not go through the front gate. That as meek as the guard might be, he was unlikely to allow him in without someone in the condo confirming the call for electrical repairs or service. There was adequate parking across the street, where there were some smaller condos. These units were not of the high-rise variety and were not as ritzy. They had no guardhouse and had spots in front labeled 'visitor'. Anthony would park in one of these, just up the street from the Surf condo building, cross the street and quietly make his way into the condo. Once inside, he might be seen by tenants, but his presence was unlikely to raise any questions. If he did his job well, there might not be any significant police investigation. He and his boss would be $100,000 richer by morning.

With that out of the way, Amari decided he might as well relax. He drove down to the public beach and purchased a cherry Italian ice from a street vendor looking every bit the relaxing tourist as he walked along the shore.

CHAPTER 88

Lisa awoke with the first rays of sun penetrating through her window. Before getting out of bed, she had to guess what time it was. Lisa hadn't played her game in several days, and wanted a good guess here to portend an auspicious day. 6:18, yes, 6:18 felt right. She looked up at the digital display on her bedside clock and congratulated herself on a 'hole in one'. The clock time was 6:18. Lisa hoped the rest of the day would go nearly as well.

Nate was still asleep, as were the boys. Lisa turned off her alarm, which wasn't set to go off for several minutes, so that it wouldn't chime and awaken Nate. Grabbing a backpack from her closet Lisa placed the Canon digital camera in the bag and added a pair of jeans and a comfortable T shirt. Next, Lisa walked out to her car where she had left the wig in her trunk. Lisa removed it from the head mold and placed it in her backpack alongside the camera and change of clothes. That would be all she would need. The camera had enough storage space for over four hundred pictures. After reviewing the files, she could forward the material to the police, or confront David with the information. She would decide what to do later. For now, it was all she could handle to try to steady her nerves and face the day. Lisa locked the bag in the trunk and went back inside the house. When she returned to her bedroom, Nate was still fast asleep. Lisa walked over to his side of the bed and lightly touched his shoulder to awaken him. Nate rolled over onto his back and gave his wife a sleepy smile.

"What are you doing out of bed, honey? Come on back here and let me wake you up properly."

She smiled at his invitation.

"Not now, Nate. I've got to get the boys ready for school. How about we settle for a nightcap when you get home?"

"How about one now and one later, like in the old days?"

Lisa knew Nate was teasing—he was already lifting the covers from around his trunk and getting out of bed.

"How about we just try for two later? Do you know if you'll be working late?"

"You know how Monday's can be. I'll try my hardest to be home for dinner at six. I'll call you if I'm running late. I should know by about three. I can call you before you pick up the boys."

"Sounds like a plan. And remember, we have a date at eight so don't be late!"

Nate smiled at Lisa's play on words. He was now standing at the side of the bed in his boxers and leaned over and gave his wife a warm kiss. She reciprocated by wrapping her arms around him. They held each other for a moment. Lisa sensed that Nate was not satisfied with just a kiss.

"Looks like part of you doesn't want to take no for an answer."

"Is the answer still no? " Nate asked.

"Only for now, Nate. Promise me you'll be on time."

Nate scowled.

"I'll make it my highest priority honey. I guess I better get going too. The sooner I get to work, the sooner I can get home."

🕮

Lisa got the boys to school and made it to work just as Becky was arriving. Dr. Layton was already in the office and, uncharacteristically, had gotten the coffee started.

"The doctor got an early start today, Lisa."

"I guess so. That coffee does smell good. I think I'll have a cup. How about you, Becky?"

"No thanks, I'm trying to cut back. Looks like we've got a busy day of surgery."

"I know, but Dr. Layton's only had us schedule patients until three-thirty so it shouldn't be too rough. It'll be nice to be doing surgeries again. The day seems to go faster when we're operating."

"I know what you mean. I'm going to get the computer started and get ready for work. Why don't you go see if Dr. Layton wants some coffee?"

"Sure." Lisa walked down to the doctor's office and knocked on the door.

David beckoned her to come in. The doctor had papers spread across his desk in addition to folders with pictures of mice taped inside. He quickly brought the papers together into a neat pile and placed them back into a larger folder.

"Good morning, Lisa, did you have a nice weekend?"

"A quiet one, we went to the beach on Saturday for awhile and hung around the house yesterday. How about you?"

"Same here. Are there any patients here yet?"

"No, no one is scheduled till 8:30. We've got about twenty minutes. Did you have any coffee yet?"

"No, I started it, then forgot all about it."

"Want me to get you a cup?"

David looked up at Lisa. Lisa felt her heart speed up and melted as she looked into his sparkling eyes. He smiled at her and she forced herself to look away. What was it with the doctor that always seemed to unnerve her?

"Sure, Lisa. A little cream and a little sugar please."

"Coming right up."

The day was uneventful. David seemed a little more tired than usual, but finished off his morning surgeries without a glitch. As the time for her departure came closer, Lisa began to feel herself becoming nervous. Her mind wandered as she considered the secret endeavor she had planned. Lisa worried about being seen in the building or being cornered by a neighbor. All kinds of things could go wrong but memories of Janetta firmed her resolve. After lunch, she assisted David in a time-consuming liposuction on a twice-divorced obese sixty-year-old about to go back into the market in pursuit of her third husband. Lisa found liposuction cases boring, and in her current state found it especially difficult to remain focused during the surgery. When the case was finally over she was happy to clean up the room and get ready to leave. It was almost two o'clock.

She said her goodbyes and drove away.

At a small strip mall five minutes from David's office she stopped the car and parked under a tree, away from the other parked vehicles. Lisa opened the trunk and pulled out the backpack. She clipped up her hair and pulled her new black wig over her own locks. Once back inside her car, she admired her appearance in the rear view mirror. It was amazing how different she looked. Maybe she would surprise Nate tonight when he came home. She quickly slipped out of her work uniform, ducking down in the back seat of her Volvo as she slipped into her blue jeans and T shirt.

Lisa drove the rest of the way to the condo. She had decided to leave her car at the beach access parking lot one block away from David's apartment. She could easily enter the condo from the beach and was unlikely to be questioned. Lisa patted her pants pocket just to be sure she still had the copy of David's apartment key. It was still there.

The beach parking lot was almost completely empty. Lisa placed the camera in her purse and parked the car. She made her way to the condo, walking along the beach. When she got to the Surf building, she was greeted by a sign warning that the building was a private residence and that trespassing was not permitted. Lisa tried to fight her fear and entered the property of the Surf Tower Condominium.

The place was empty. Many of the residents were still not back form their summer places up North. Just as many of the year-round residents were either still out golfing or working. Lisa entered the first floor lobby and rode up the elevator without seeing or being seen by a single occupant of the building. She was pleased at her good fortune.

Lisa arrived at the 15th floor penthouse and used her key to enter Dr. Layton's apartment. She had an initial fear that he might have changed the locks on his apartment, as he had mentioned doing, but he must not have gotten around to it yet. She had another fear, wondering what she would do if anyone was there to greet her when she opened the door, but both concerns proved to be needless, as no one was in David's apartment. She had the place to herself. Lisa locked the door behind her. Now that she was no stranger to his home, she knew exactly where to go. Lisa headed straight to David's study and opened his desk drawer. The files were where they had been the last time she had been there. Lisa removed the entire collection and prepared to photograph them. She spread out the first file and took a picture of the contact information page. When she checked the quality of the photo, she was disappointed to find it appeared somewhat dark. Lisa turned on a desk lamp situated on David's desk, and also switched on a lamp on the floor next to his desk. She took the picture a second time and reviewed it in her viewfinder. She was pleased with the result.

It was now almost 2:30. Lisa had less than an hour to finish taking her pictures before she would have to pick up the boys from school. She set herself to work, snapping one picture after another. After only twenty minutes she had finished more than half of the charts. Since she was running ahead of schedule, Lisa allowed herself the luxury of going to the bathroom.

Like everything else in David's apartment, the restrooms were fancy. He had a large Jacuzzi tub off to one side of the huge bathroom. The countertops were a beautiful blend of green and grey granite, with intricately carved borders. Although the bathroom was almost as large as her master bedroom, it had warm lighting and subtle faux painting, creating an intimate sense to the room. After washing her hands, Lisa grabbed a towel, and was pleasantly surprised to find the towel rack heated. She promised herself a luxurious bathroom like Dr. Layton's as soon as Nate made partner at the law firm.

Lisa was almost back to the study when she thought she heard a tap on the condo door. She froze and felt blood rush to her temples. She heard the sound again. Someone was at the door.

Lisa ran to the study and grabbed the charts. She lifted them back into the desk drawers and tried to return them back to their proper places. Lisa knew they were not as neatly placed as they had been, but she managed to get them all back into place. She moved the lamp back, grabbed her camera and shut the lights.

The sounds at the door continued. Lisa ran down the hallway and into David's bedroom. She heard the door to the apartment open and the echo of footfalls as David entered his home after a hard day at work. What was he doing home so early? Lisa got on the floor and squeezed her body under his bed. She peered out from under the dust ruffle surrounding the frame of his king-sized bed. She was trapped.

CHAPTER 89

Amari knew that Dr. Layton might not get home until after six; waiting was tiring him.

The doc probably has some nice digs, "I might as well wait for him at his place," he thought to himself. Amari was eager to get the job done and get back to Tampa. The assassin felt his stomach grumble and realized he hadn't eaten since breakfast. The picture of a girl in pigtails on a Wendy's sign beckoned from the distance and Anthony pulled into the drive-thru. His bacon cheeseburger disappeared in a few bites, but the Frosty was another story. After a few attempts at sucking the concoction through the straw, Amari gave up and used the spoon. He was eating and driving at the same time, navigating the spoon from the cup to his mouth while attempting a left turn.

"Shit," he cursed. A mound of chocolaty mush fell from his spoon onto his blue custom-tailored silk Adolofo shirt. The veins at his temples bulged in anger as he threw the Frosty out the window. A silver-haired elderly man in the Taurus in the next lane yelled something at him about not littering. Anthony was about to give the old coot the finger and yell back, when instead he closed his eyes and tried to control his anger. "Stay cool," he thought and Amari reminded himself that the hundred thousand dollar prize was almost his. Just a few hours of work. He certainly didn't want to draw attention to himself now.

It was almost two-thirty when Amari pulled into a quiet cul-de-sac and changed his soiled shirt for the white Supreme Electric uniform and substituted his black trousers for a pair of blue Dickies work pants. When he pulled into the parking area across the street from the Surf Tower Condominiums he was a presentable blue collar worker that no one would confuse with a professional killer. Anthony removed his equipment bag from the car and walked at an angle across the street toward the Surf Condo and entered the alley between the parking area of the Surf and the adjacent Javelina Condo. The two were separated only by a thicket of beach plums. After quickly looking around, Amari felt certain that no one could see him as he entered the parking lot on the Javelina side of the beach plums and exited on the Surf Condo side, out of sight of the gatehouse guards.

Anthony walked rapidly to where he could see the main entrance to the condo. Although many condominiums did have a security guard of some sort in their lobbies, the Surf, and most of the condos in Pelican Cove did not. Amari laughed to himself. No guards were necessary since no one ever committed much crime in the retirement community of Pelican Cove.

So far, so good. Anthony arrived at the elevator and pressed the call button. The elevator was on the seventh floor and on the way down. At that point, Amari ran out of luck. One of the tenants of the building walked in the front door and signaled with his index finger that he needed Anthony to hold the elevator for him. The assassin had no choice. As the doors opened, he held them open with his foot. A gasping, short, white-haired man with a goatee joined him on the elevator. The man must have been about seventy-five and was wheezing from the exertion of catching the elevator. He looked one wheeze away from a heart attack.

"Thanks, buddy," he said between two deep wheezy breaths. "Could you press six for me please? Well, that's my exercise for the day." He noticed the script on Amari's shirt and the equipment bag in the visitor's hand.

"Hey, if you've got a minute, I have a fan I bought and I've been having trouble getting anyone to come down to install it. It shouldn't take too long; I can pay you some extra cash if you'll put it in for me."

"Sorry, sir, my company doesn't allow any me to freelance. I'm here on a call." Amari hoped this wouldn't go any further. He really hadn't planned on having to speak with anyone and hadn't worked out a good cover story.

"Can you give me your business card then and I'll call your company myself."

"I'm new and I don't have any cards, but we're in the phone book."

That seemed to appease the man. In any case, the elevator had arrived at the sixth floor.

"Okay, I'll do that. Don't work too hard."

He was relieved when the elevator door closed, terminating their conversation.

There was only one apartment on the penthouse floor. Dr. Layton had it all to himself. Anthony walked up to the door. Truth be told, he loved his job. And one of the parts he enjoyed most was picking locks. He loved the challenge, though usually a residence like this was child's play. Looking down the hallway he slipped on a pair of thin rubber gloves. Next, he expertly inserted his metal 'feelers' into the solitary lock. The first had no effect, and he inserted two others. Amari closed his eyes and tried to picture the surface of the lock as his thin metal probes pushed their way into the space normally occupied by a key. Simultaneously, he applied gentle pressure on the door handle, waiting for any movement. A click alerted him to his success. The door opened. He was in the apartment. Anthony locked the door behind him.

Amari whistled softly to himself. Wandering from room to room he noticed the views were exceptional. He regretted having tossed his Frosty out the window because he was still thirsty. Deciding to raid the icebox he found a small green bottle of Perrier that hit the spot. Anthony looked at the clock. It wasn't even three o'clock yet. Depending on how late Dr. Layton worked, he still could have several hours of waiting ahead of him. He picked up his bag and continued his exploration of the spacious apartment.

The bedroom had a thick king size bed with a heavy wooden frame. Opposite the bed, a large flat screen Sony covered half the wall. Amari found the remote and clicked on the TV. He lowered the volume. It was some cooking show-Rachael Ray showing the best way to prepare Shrimp Scampi. As she emphasized the need to use fresh garlic, Anthony thought she was a hell-uv-a lot easier to look at than that old hag Julia Child or that Emeril guy. Amari sat on the edge of the bed and wondered whether Rachael Ray's boobs were the real thing. He made sure to leave his thin gloves on—no way was he going to leave any evidence, slip up and get caught. The intruder channel-surfed, but he found himself edgy and couldn't relax. He shut off the TV and wished the doctor would just get along with it and come home.

Lisa had worked with Dr. Layton long enough to recognize the sound of his footfalls. The man in the apartment was not her boss. She had seen the stranger's black shoes through the space under the dust ruffle and knew that they did not belong to David. The intruder's ankles were thicker and he smelled of some strong cologne that was unfamiliar to her. These things she realized as she lay trapped under the bed.

Minutes ticked by. Lisa was becoming cramped in her tight space beneath the bed and her mind was reeling. The man lying above her wasn't moving. Maybe he had fallen asleep? She dared not venture out. Lisa closed her eyes and tried to think of what to do. She had to pick her boys up from school. She hadn't finished copying the records. Who did she think she was breaking into her boss's place? Who was the man who had access to David's apartment?

Lisa was about to try to shift her position slightly in order to bring some feeling back to her fingers, which had become numb. Then disaster erupted. The silence of the room was broken by Elton John's Rocketman ringtones launched from her cell phone as it came to life. Too late, Lisa remembered Nate's promise to call her. She reached down to her side to shut off the phone, but in the crowded space all she managed to do was switch the little Motorola instrument into the speakerphone mode. The ring tone continued and Lisa felt the weight of the man above her bounce off the bed and felt the floor shake as he jumped from the bed. Two dark eyes stared at her from under the fringe of the bed coverings while the business end of a black revolver pointed at her face.

"What do we have here? I didn't know the doctor kept any woman friends in his apartment. Come out from under the bed, and shut off that phone right now."

Lisa was speechless. She tried to turn off her cell phone, but couldn't find the correct button. Her fingers were numb with 'pins and needles'. Instead, she pulled her body out from its hiding place. Her head and shoulders became exposed, and she felt strong arms grasp underneath her armpits and pull her away from the bed. The man grabbed the phone from her hip and shut off the power switch. Neither of them heard Nate's voice as he searched for a response to his 'hello.' The room was again silent.

The man was standing at the foot of the bed.

"Get up off the floor and come up here where I can see you."

Lisa picked herself up and sat down on the corner of the bed.

"Who are you?" she asked.

"I'm an electrician. Can't you tell from the uniform? Who are you?"

Lisa felt very vulnerable. She wondered why repairman was would need to carry a weapon. The presence of the gun made honesty seem like the best course of action.

"I'm Lisa, one of the doctor's nurses. I came here to get something for him."

Amari looked at the attractive dark-haired woman sitting in front of him. She was definitely a looker. The doctor had good taste.

"Well I guess that would explain why you were hiding under the bed when I came in. Want to try the truth?"

Lisa tried to calm herself. She thought it best not to tell the armed man the entire story of Janetta, the hidden files and suspicions regarding Dr. Layton's Botox treatments. She thought of something simpler.

"I wanted to surprise David when he came home from work. I didn't want him to know I was here, and when you came in, I knew you weren't him and I was afraid to come out."

"That's more like it. The truth will set you free. Now we have a little problem, Lisa. You see, I wanted to surprise the doctor too. It's going to be a hell-uv-a a lot harder to surprise him with you here, but then I can't very well let you leave; you might ruin my little surprise. No, it looks like we're going to have to keep each other company for awhile."

"I thought you said you're an electrician."

"Let's just say I came here to fix something."

As he finished the sentence, Lisa noticed that the stranger had gotten a look in his eye and was staring at her in a way that made her uncomfortable.

"I have two small boys waiting for me to pick them up from school."

"Well, I would call that very poor planning. You must not have really anticipated picking them up if you were going to stay here and wait for the doctor." The assassin smiled at Lisa with a crooked grin.

"Were the two of you going to have a little nooky on the side?" He glanced at Lisa's wedding ring. "You're married, and Dr. Layton isn't. This looks like a little walk on the wild side to me. Not that I can blame the guy, you're a beautiful woman."

The man's comment made her feel dirty.

"Please let me leave." Lisa stammered.

"I already told you. I can't."

Amari was trying to think of what to do with the woman. He knew he could eliminate both the nurse and the doctor, but that would mean that he would have to kiss away the extra $50,000; it would be much harder to make it look like a suicide if both the woman and Dr. Layton were 'offed.'

"I'm not really that bad a guy. Here's the deal. I'll give you a couple of sleeping pills and let you go back under the bed to sleep. When the doctor gets home, I'll just tell him what I came here for and be on my way. Then, when you wake up, Dr. Layton will probably already be asleep and you can surprise him."

"And what if I say no?"

"There is only one answer here, and it's not no."

Lisa feared for her life. She thought of her boys. If she had thought things through she might not have done what she did next.

She screamed "HELP" at the top of her lungs. The yell sounded muffled in the penthouse compound. The sound of Amari's open hand slapping Lisa's cheek was much louder.

The force of his blow sent Lisa reeling and she ended up lying on her side on the bed. In a flash, Amari was on top of her. He straddled Lisa and looked down at her face. A hand-shaped welt was already appearing across her left cheek where he had struck her.

For a moment, Anthony almost forgot why he was in the apartment and considered continuing his assault on the beautiful woman. She had asked for it, and obviously she wasn't a saint; a married woman sneaking into her boss's apartment. Then he remembered his reason for coming to Pelican Cove and the cash awaiting him upon completion of the job. He closed his eyes for a second and took a deep breath.

Amari grabbed a handful of Lisa's hair and pulled her head back towards his right leg which was anchored across Lisa's hips. To his surprise, he found himself with a handful of black hair. Lisa's wig landed in Anthony's lap. A look of surprise appeared on his face.

"Your own hair is even prettier than the wig. I guess you were really trying to be undercover with your boss. Look I don't want to hurt you, but you can't scream or disobey me again."

Amari raised his gun and pointed the shiny black silencer attached to the weapon at Lisa.

"If you behave, in a few hours you'll be back home with your kids and husband. If you don't, your kids may have only one parent in the morning. It's as simple as that. Trust me, I really don't want to kill you, but I will if I have to. Capiche?"

Lisa felt an urge to cry, but fought back her tears. She nodded and whispered a subdued,

"Yes."

"Look, I'm not going to give you too much medication or anything. Just enough to get you out of my hair for a couple of hours."

Amari lifted his body off Lisa and stepped off the bed. He removed a vial of pills from his workman's bag, and removed two tablets from the bottle.

Each pill contained 160mg of Oxycontin, the highest strength of the medication that was available. The manufacturer's recommended starting dose was 10mg – higher doses were only meant for those used to taking the drug for chronic pain. The assassin knew this. He also knew that breaking the pills into smaller pieces would intensify their strength.

"I'll even crush the tablets for you and get you something to down them with." Amari found a drinking cup in the adjoining bathroom and filled it with water.

He returned to Lisa, who was now sitting up in the bed. The clear imprint of four red fingers could be seen across her cheek. Her eyes had the flat appearance of someone in shock.

Lisa was paralyzed with fear. Her main concern now was survival. The outstretched hood's hand reached across the bed, offering Lisa the crushed pills and water. She remembered Janetta and the Roofies that her friend had unknowingly taken. The thought of her misadventure coming to a similar end terrorized her. Lisa said a silent prayer to Jesus and Saint Margaret, the patron saint of nurses. Visions of the faces of her children preoccupied her thoughts as she accepted the broken pills and cup of water and downed both in one frightening gulp.

CHAPTER 90

"Mr. Martin, this is Caren Weinberg at Pelican Elementary. We have Josh and Shawn here. No one's come to pick them up from school, and it's almost four o'clock."

"Did you try my wife?"

"Yes, but she isn't answering her phone."

Almost an hour earlier, when Nate had tried to reach Lisa, the phone had rung several times. He thought that she had answered the phone, but was surprised by what he thought might have been a man's voice in the background just before the connection was terminated. When he had tried to call her back he got her voicemail, which meant that either she was on the line or had the phone switched off. He was immediately concerned. If she had been unable to pick up the boys she would certainly have called him for help.

"I'll be right over to pick them up. I'm not sure what happened to my wife; it's very unlike her. Sorry for the inconvenience."

"No problem, Mr. Martin. The boys will be in the administration office."

Nate broke the connection and speed-dialed his wife's number.

"Hi. This is Lisa. I can't come to the phone right now. Please leave a message at the tone and I'll be sure to call you back."

Nate quickly tried their home number. No answer. Next, Nate tried her work number.

"Dr. Layton's office, Becky speaking. How can we help you?"

"Hi Becky. This is Nate, Lisa's husband. I'm trying to find her and she's not answering her cell phone. She's not at work by any chance is she?"

"No, she left a little before two o'clock. Is everything okay?"

"I'm sure it is, Becky. I'll find her."

"Well, good luck, Mr. Martin, ss there anything else I can do for you?"

"No, sorry to bother you."

Nate had no idea where his wife was. First things first, Nate packed up his briefcase and quit work early to go pick up the boys.

CHAPTER 91

"That's better, Lisa. Now just relax. Just two things—no more screaming out for help and don't use the phone. I'm out of patience. If you behave, I'll chat with Dr. Layton and be on my way. Just don't cross me."

As he said these words, Amari stared into Lisa's eyes. His dark pupils were hard, cold, and emotionless. She tried to figure out some plan of escape, some way to get away from this frightening thug. But his gun, and her fear of provoking him into an action which might end her life, kept her in complete submission.

"Don't worry, I wah't." She had meant to say won't, but heard herself slurring the word. Lisa thought her voice sounded slightly distant as she spoke, as if the words came from behind her. She felt drowsy, realizing that it was probably the medication taking effect.

"You look tired Lisa. You know what?, it really won't do much good if I leave you here on the bed. It'll ruin my surprise for the doctor. Would you mind if I had you get back under the bed just so that Dr. Layton doesn't see you when he comes in? It'll make it easier for you to surprise the doctor too."

Lisa considered his offer. At this point she was getting very sleepy. The idea of going under the bed for a nap didn't sound so bad. It would get her away from the hood and into the relatively protected environment underneath the bed.

"Okay, as long as you don't forget me undah theh." Her last words were slurred and her tongue felt thick. She was having trouble keeping her eyes open.

Amari supported her body as she leaned heavily coming off the bed. His right arm slipped across her back and around to the front of her chest. For a moment, his hand fell across her right breast, with only the thin material of her Victoria's Secret bra between his fingers and her flesh. It thrilled the assassin, and he considered how easy it would be for him to have some fun with the nurse before getting back to work. He thought about it for a moment, then fought back the desire to undress her and continued guiding her down to the floor.

Amari supported her body. She was now lying next to the bed, on the carpet.

"Dank you, I'm berry tared. Ahm just dowing to go to sleep awhile." Lisa closed her eyes.

Amari looked at the woman with little remorse in his eyes. He stood up and went to the head of the bed and picked up a pillow. Without hesitation, and in a fluid motion, he placed the pillow over Lisa's face. He exerted strong, even force as he pressed down on the stuffed cushion, blocking the entry of air into her lungs.

Lisa partially awoke from her drowsy state. She wanted more air. She wanted to breathe! Her chest felt feeble and grasping air was terribly difficult. Everything around her was dark and she felt the weight of Amari's force on her face. She tried to kick free from his hold but could barely move.

Lisa wondered if she would ever see her boys again. Her body would no longer follow her commands. She stopping kicking and felt her breathing diminish. Everything became dark. She no longer felt any weight over her face. Lisa felt tears welling in the corners of her eyes as she took her last weak gasps of air.

The woman had stopped breathing. Almost simultaneously, Amari heard a key in the door to the apartment. He quickly shoved Lisa's inert body from its position on the floor to a more hidden repose beneath the bed.

The hired killer held his gun in his right hand and pressed his body back against the wall of the hallway. He was invisible from anyone who might enter the apartment. He would see them before they could see him and he would have the advantage of the firearm. Amari wanted to be sure that the door would be closed behind whoever entered before he let his presence be known.

The door opened and a well dressed, good-looking man entered the apartment. He was alone. Amari recognized his features as those matching the picture he had been given by Mr. Volpe. It was Dr. Layton. The doctor entered the apartment and shut the door behind him. Amari relaxed, he was in the 'zone', ready to strike.

Anthony allowed the man to settle in. Layton walked from the foyer into the kitchen and placed his briefcase down. The doctor then began to rifle through the day's mail, which he had brought up the elevator with him from the mailboxes in the lobby. His back was partially turned to the assassin when Amari struck.

The intruder passed through the foyer and into the kitchen area with the stealth of a stalking leopard. His silenced Walther gleamed in the light and was pointed at David's chest.

"Good afternoon, Dr. Layton. Nice apartment."

David was startled into attention. The man with the gun looked like a plumber or electrician. He had a work shirt with some script on it that read Supreme Electric.

"Who the hell are you and what are you doing in my apartment?"

"Who I am really doesn't concern you. Your only concern Dr. Layton should be how to get me to leave your apartment without you meeting your maker. I've been hired to come here and get some files. If you don't waste my time, and if you give me what I want, I'll let you live. If you don't, I'll have to kill you. It's as simple as that."

David was used to being in control and was not used to being threatened. From what he had read and seen on TV, he knew that the best thing to do was to cooperate. He had been caught by surprise and had no means of defense.

"What files do you want?"

Amari smiled.

"Thatta boy, Doc. Just cooperate and we'll get along fine. You have some files about a drug you've been testing. Someone I know needs them. He gets the files, you get to live. That's the deal."

David's jaw dropped. Who could know about his files? Sal knew about the files, the police might suspect-certainly this guy had nothing to do with the police. Or could he? There were crooked policemen. Maybe they hired someone to get the information they wanted. Then it struck him. It was someone connected with the venture capitalists; they were trying to cut him out of the deal and figured it was cheaper to steal the information than to buy it. Did they have something to do with the tampering of the brakes on his car? But it just didn't make any sense; surely they knew he would report them. Would they really kill him rather than deal with him above-board?

"Who sent you?"

Amari walked over to Dr. Layton, gun raised, and pointed the muzzle at the doctor's head.

"Listen, I'm not here to chat. I can kill you, and look through your apartment, or you can get me the files and I'll let you live. Simple. You're a smart guy. You wanna live, give me what I want. NOW!!!"

David's heart was racing. He didn't expect any visitors, so no one was going to come to his aid. He was alone. David considered trying to overpower the man, but had little doubt that the thug would use his gun as promised. He had no choice.

"The files you want are in my study."

"Walk. You get them and I'll be on my way."

David led the man out of the kitchen and into his study. Amari followed close behind, with the gun aimed at David's back.

Dr. Layton removed the files and placed them in a pile on his desk. "Here they are."

Amari walked over to the desk and flipped open the front of the first folder. They appeared to be what he had been asked to find.

"Is this all of them?"

"It's all I have. I guess it's what you want." David suppressed the desire to ask him once again who had sent him.

"One more thing. I can't have you come after me or call the police or anything. All I want is a head start to get out of here. I brought some sleeping medication with me. You take it, have a nice little nap, and wake up in the morning to a bright new day. Don't call the police and you never see me again. Deal?"

"How do I know you're not going to poison me or kill me when I'm knocked out?"

"Look doc, if I wanted to kill you, I would have done it already. And in case you didn't notice, you don't have much leverage here. We're all alone, and I've got the gun. Save us both any trouble and just take the pills and catch up on your sleep. Then 'poof', I'll be gone."

David tried to relax. He wanted to believe the intruder. But he had never been one to quit; to give in. What could he do to take control of the situation, to turn the tables on the man without being shot for his efforts? He couldn't think of anything.

Reluctantly he agreed.

"Okay, I'll do what you want."

"Let's go to your bedroom, you can take your nap in there."

The pair retraced their steps, passing through the kitchen and into the bedroom. Amari kept his gun trained on David.

The assassin took two Oxycontin 160 tablets from his pocket.

"See doc, only two pills, you'll catch up on your zee's and wake up rested." He broke them into pieces. Amari kept the gun pointed at the doctor as he filled the water glass for the second time that afternoon.

"Here you go, down the hatch, Doc."

David was somewhat relieved to see that at least it was only two pills, but concerned that the man had broken them into pieces. Dr. Layton had learned long ago, when he was taking pharmacology in medical school, that breaking up or crushing pills could significantly alter their absorption and strength. Maybe he could pretend to swallow the pills and hide them under his tongue.

Amari handed the pills to the doctor along with the glass of water. The hollow end of the silencer was now pointed at David's head. He swallowed the pills.

CHAPTER 92

"Dad, where's Mom?" asked Shawn.

"Yeah where's Mom?" repeated Josh.

The boys were seated in the back seat of his car as they pulled into the driveway of their home. Lisa's car was nowhere in sight. The house was dark. It was getting late and the sun was low. The air was becoming cooler with summer gone and the lower humidity of early fall. Nate tried to hide his concern.

"Mom had some errands to run. She just forgot to tell me, that's why I was late getting you boys from school. When she gets home, we'll get some Pizza Hut."

"Can't we go out to eat? How about McDonald's?" asked Shawn.

Nate laughed. It was nervous laughter, but Nate was pleased to hear it- even if he didn't really feel that way.

"We'll see, Shawn. Let's wait for Mom to get back first." The boys and Nate walked into the quiet house. "Go watch some TV and I'll let you know when Mom gets home."

"Okay Dad," the boys replied in unison as they ran through the home to their playroom. Seconds later, the sound of the television filled the house with life.

Nate walked over to their computer, which occupied an alcove just off of the kitchen. He logged on and waited for the computer to do whatever it did before it presented his Google page and its ubiquitous search engine.

Nate typed in the site for Compustar GPS tracking. As a member of Compustar, he could track the location of either of his cars at any time. Nate entered his member number and password. Next, he clicked on the 'track vehicle' box on his screen, along with the ID for Lisa's Volvo.

Within seconds, the physical location of her car appeared. It was situated at the cross section of Pelican Gulf Blvd and Shore Drive, near the beach. A graphic showed the location of her car on small map, accurate to within one hundred feet.

Nate recognized the location as very close to where Lisa's boss, Dr. Layton, lived. The entire area was residential, and Nate could think of no reason why Lisa needed to be there, other than to visit with the doctor. Layton had been in an accident recently, perhaps she was helping him out. But that wouldn't explain her failure to pick up the boys. Could she be having an affair with the doctor? He decided to try her cell phone again. Nate dialed Lisa's number for the tenth time that afternoon and received the same lack of response.

Mr. Martin had been somewhat remiss in making friends in their small neighborhood. Many of their neighbors were older and only spent part of the year in Pelican Cove. The man next door was nice enough and actually spent all year in town. The guy loved the outdoors and either fished or golfed daily. Nate looked out his kitchen window and through his side yard into Mr. Buckley's home. The lights were on and Nate could see the soft glow of a TV in the family room. He would have to ask a favor.

Nate didn't want the boys to be disturbed. He quietly slipped out the front door and walked over to Buckley's home. Gerald Buckley heard the doorbell and was at the door in a flash. Nate knew he must be close to eighty years old and had already outlived his wife by ten years. He had a thick head of hair, a very dark tan and wrinkles traversed his face in every direction. Buckley smiled at the infrequent appearance of his neighbor at the door.

"Hi stranger, how have you been, Nate?"

"Busy working as usual." Nate felt the need to make small talk, so as not to appear to be visiting only in order to obtain a favor from the man, when in actuality; it was the only reason for the visit. Nate cut to the chase.

"Listen, Jerry, I'd love to talk, but really, what I need is a favor. My wife hasn't come home tonight and I'm worried. It's just not like her and it's never happened before. I think I know where she is and want to go look for her, but I really would rather not disturb the boys. Do you think you could go over to my house and keep an eye on them just for a little while until I get back?"

Buckley could tell that Mr. Martin was distressed and decided not to venture into the cause of the absence of the man's wife. He would never consider turning down a request for help from a neighbor.

"Of course, Nate, and I'd love to see the boys. They're my favorite 'almost grandchildren'. And they're the best kind of kids, I get to borrow them and then return them."

"They haven't eaten yet, Jerry. I'll call Pizza Hut and have them deliver. I should be back in less than an hour."

"You just do what you have to do, Nate. We'll be fine."

"Thanks Jerry. Can you come right over?"

"That's the nice thing about being my age and retired. I can do almost anything I want to do whenever I want to do it. Well, maybe not anything, and not for as long as I used to either." He laughed at his own humor.

Nate felt the pressure of time and wanted to rush over to the location of Lisa's car, but was able to manage a forced smile and a short laugh.

"Great, I'm going to go back and let the boys know I'm leaving and that you'll be with them. And I'll put the call in to Pizza Hut. I'm going to tell the boys that Lisa is having car trouble, so if they ask, you can tell them the same so that they don't worry or anything."

"Sounds good to me, Nate. You get going. I'll just grab a book and the crossword puzzle I was working on and come right over."

Nate found Lisa's car parked across the street from the Surf Tower condo. She was nowhere in sight. Nate knew that Dr. Layton owned the penthouse suite of the posh building. He decided to drive over to the Surf and see if the guard there knew anything about his wife's whereabouts. Nate pulled into the guest side of the guardhouse. He was greeted by a rotund Hispanic middle-aged man whose name badge identified him as Carlos.

"Visiting?" the guard asked.

"Well, no and yes. My wife works for one of your tenants and I'm trying to find her. Her car is parked across the street and I was wondering if she might be in the building visiting her boss. She works for Dr. Layton."

Carlos imagined that the man's wife might indeed be 'visiting' with one of the tenants of the building. It wouldn't be the first affair he had witnessed in the three years he had worked for the Surf Tower. But the mention of Dr. Layton's name had special meaning. The six members of the workforce who tended the gate had all been advised to watch out for anything unusual involving the doctor; apparently there was concern that someone might be trying to harm the man. Although this certainly didn't sound like something threatening, it was out of the ordinary.

"Can I see your driver's license please?"

"Sure." Nate handed him the card.

The picture on the driver's license matched the man in front of him, and the addresses indicated a local residence. Carlos was reassured.

Carlos looked out the back window of his guardhouse. He picked up a small pair of binoculars which the cadre of guards kept on hand but rarely used. The guard identified David's parking spot in the garage and located the loaner Mercedes that the doctor had been driving since the accident.

"I see Dr. Layton's car. Let me call up to his apartment. It'll only take a second."

Carlos rang the unit.

"Hello, if you're hearing this, I'm not at home right now. Please leave your message at the beep and I'll call you when I return."

"No one answers, Mr. Martin. I'm not supposed to tell you this, but I've been advised to report any suspicious activity involving Dr. Layton to the police. I don't know if this is particularly suspicious, but it might help you figure out where your wife is if I call them. Would you mind?"

Nate didn't imagine he would be admitted to the doctor's apartment or even allowed to enter the Surf Condo as a guest without an invitation and pass from the guard. Without the intervention of the police, it appeared that the guard was not about to let him into the building.

"No, I don't see any harm in calling them, though I really would prefer not to wait too long for them to come."

"I'll call them and see what they have to say."

Carlos went back inside the guardhouse and dialed the number for the Pelican Cove police station.

"Pelican Cove police, Maddy Thornberry speaking. How can I help you?"

Carlos described the nature of his call to the operator.

Pelican Cove had little crime, but a well trained force.

"I've been advised to direct any calls pertaining to Dr. Layton to Detectives Collins and Levine. They're both here; I think they're getting ready to go home. Please hold for a moment while I see if I can reach them."

"Sure, thanks."

Nate waited patiently as the guard remained on hold. He was becoming increasingly anxious. Where was his wife?

After several minutes on hold, a voice came on.

"This is Detective Dan Levine, I understand you have a question regarding Dr.Layton?"

"Well sort of. I'm Carlos Rivera, and I work at the gatehouse at the Surf Tower, down on the beach. We were told to call the PD if anything suspicious involving Dr. Layton came up. I don't know if this falls under that category, but there's an attorney here, Mr. Martin, who says his wife works for Dr. Layton. Her car is parked across the street, but he's been looking for her this afternoon and can't find her. She's not answering her phone. Dr. Layton is already gone from his office for the day, and the car he's been driving is parked in his spot, but he's not answering his phone either."

"He's probably out with someone else who's driving their own car or something, but we'll check it just to be on the safe side. I'll be down there with my partner in a few minutes. Please don't let Mr. Martin leave."

"No problem, he was hoping you'd come quickly."

"We're leaving right away. Thanks for the heads up."

CHAPTER 93

The pills tasted somewhat bitter. David tried to hold some of the fragments under his tongue as he swallowed the water, but the majority went down his gullet unimpeded.

"What are you going to do with the records?" David asked.

"Me, nothing. But someone hired me and I don't give a rat's ass what they do with them as long as I get paid so I don't ask questions - neither should you. Want some more water, Doc?"

The small pieces of pill were trapped under his tongue. David saw no real way to get them out of his mouth without being seen.

"Sure."

Amari turned his back to David for a moment while he filled the water glass. The doctor was able to move the medication from under his tongue to the corner of his mouth which he then swiped with the front of his shoulder. Several small pieces of pill fell to the floor. He took the water from Amari.

"So what's it like working on beautiful women all day, Doc? Ever get tired of it?"

"It's a living. Hey, you've got what you came for. Why don't you just take the records and go? I won't call the police or anything."

"Not yet, Dr. Layton. I've got to make sure you can't come after me. Those pills should work soon and then I'll be out of your hair."

Something about the way Amari made his last statement triggered a warning in David's mind.; he wasn't being told the entire truth. The pills were also beginning to take effect. David was feeling little spacey, and light-headed. He knew the pills were a sedative and not a poison but he wasn't sure what this man would do after he was incapacitated.

"Just lay down if you want, Doc. You probably could use some rest after a hard day at work."

An involuntary yawn departed from David's mouth. He felt lethargic and his body felt heavy. The pills were also affecting his ability to put up a fight. All he wanted to do was sleep.

"Some shut-eye sounds good. Hey, I'm not a real fan of the police. You don't have to worry about me calling them. Just don't hurt me and I'll forget you were ever here."

"Sounds good to me, Doc. I'll leave in a minute."

Amari got up and put the TV on. It was the five o'clock news from Fox. The female broadcaster had big blond hair and a low cut blouse revealing the top of her cleavage. Apparently she wasn't hired for her elocution, as she stumbled over one of the headlines in the day's news, relating to unlicensed migrant workers who were working in the construction industry in Pelican Cove.

Amari turned up the volume a little. He turned around and glanced back at David, who was now lying stretched out on the bed.

"Comfortable, Doc?"

"Berry." David heard the word come out slurred and knew that he was at the mercy of the intruder. He was about to fall asleep.

Amari walked over to David and smiled.

"I promised you I'd be leaving as soon as you were asleep, and I will. I just don't know how much waking up I want you to do.

For the second time that afternoon, Anthony picked up a pillow from the bed and in a rapid movement, grabbed each end in his outstretched arms and brought the pillow down over Dr. Layton's face and pressing his body over the pillow.

David struggled to remove his head from beneath the suffocating cushion and release his breath from the crushing weight of the assassin. Every time he tried to take a breath all he could feel was a too small amount of air and the pressure of the Egyptian cotton pillow around his mouth and nose.

Lisa was under the bed, dreaming that she was in a long tunnel, lying on her stomach with beams of light shining over her and ending in a small circle at the end of a cavern. Her head was throbbing but her body felt light as if the beams of light were carrying her toward the end of the tunnel. Now there were other voices and sounds. Something from above was pressing on her back. Reluctantly and slowly she opened her eyes. It was so dark she could barely see but could feel her head throbbing and her neck cramping. Lisa could just make out the silhouette of something in front of her and realized it was a dust ruffle and that she was under a bed.

She was still in Dr. Layton's apartment-alive. A pool of foul-smelling fluid rested against her cheek. Lisa touched it and felt little hard flecks. She brought one to her face and recognized it as part of the pill she had swallowed earlier. Apparently she had vomited after the goon had tried to suffocate her, preventing much of the medication from being absorbed by her body.

As she became more alert she also became aware of a commotion occurring above her; it was what had aroused her from her stupor. The bed heaved, but she didn't dare come out. Lisa reached her arm down her side and felt the reassuring form of her cell phone. She remembered the intruder switching it off and assumed he left is with her as part of his plan. From memory she knew where the 'on' button was and pressed downward. Lisa closed her eyes and said a prayer. Then she reached back down to the phone and searched for the buttons of the number she desired. Lisa played the part of a blind person searching for Braille as her fingers attempted to find the key pad numbers she needed. Mrs. Martin pressed the sequence that she hoped was 9-1-1.

The emergency services dispatch phone rang once and a voice answered.

"Nine-One-One, what is the nature of your emergency?"

The heaving and movements of the bed above her had ceased. The voice repeated itself.

"Nine-One-One, Hello?"

Lisa felt the bed rise away from her body. Amari's feet hit the ground next to the bed. He ripped the dust ruffle upwards and once again grabbed Lisa's hair and dragged her from under the bed.

"Help, I'm trapped in……"

Amari grabbed the phone from Lisa's hip and heaved it against the wall, terminating the call for help.

Lisa was on her back on the floor, staring at the livid face of the assassin.

"What the fuck are you doing? You should have stayed asleep!"

Amari regained his composure. The redness receded from his face. He looked at Lisa.

"We've had a visitor. I think you know him. He's sleeping like a baby now. Why don't you join him in bed? You two would make such a nice couple together."

Anthony lifted Lisa to her feet. She was very groggy and her legs felt like rubber. Amari had his gun pointed at her face. Lisa looked down at the motionless form of David lying on his bed. His shirt and hair were disheveled. His eyes were closed and Lisa didn't know if he was alive.

"What have you done to Dr. Layton?"

"Nothing, little lady. He's just sleeping, just like you should be. I was about ready to leave; at least I was until you woke up. It's past time for me to go, and now you're wasting my time. I've got enough sleeping pills left to keep you out of my hair and get on my way. I suggest you take them."

"Why, so you can try to suffocate me again? You might as well shoot me."

Amari was beginning to see the logic in her statement. Screw the extra $50,000. The main thing was to get the job done and get going. Maybe he could stick the gun in her hand and make it look like a double suicide. Make her shoot the doc, then he could put the gun back in her hand and have her turn it on herself. That might work, but it would be splashed all over the papers. Amari decided to give his charm one more try.

"I wasn't trying to suffocate you; I just lost control when I saw you laying there and wanted to be a little romantic with you. I was trying to make you comfortable and get a pillow under your head. You got all upset and started trying to push me off of you. Then you just nodded off. I treated you right; I kept my hands off of you and stuck you under the bed so we could surprise the doctor when he came home."

Could he be telling the truth? Lisa was still so groggy from the medication that she just wasn't sure. The medication made it difficult for her to remember what had happened.

There was still the matter of the gun and something certainly seemed wrong with David. Lisa hoped that her 911 call might have automatically triggered the Pelican Cove police GPS tracking unit. It was a long shot, but maybe she could stall this guy long enough for the police to come and find her and David.

"I'd much rather have been surprised by you. Dr. Layton is a handsome guy and all, but he's a little soft, if you know what I mean."

Amari looked at the green-eyed beauty in front of him. Maybe he could have a little fun with her before he left. He'd have to be careful though, he certainly didn't want to leave any evidence for the police. It was a shame she'd have to be disposed of.

"Nothing soft here, Lisa. I hope you're not too drowsy for a little fun before I go. Maybe I can hang out here a little longer. Let's leave Dr. Layton alone in here for awhile. He's resting comfortably enough. Does the doc have any booze in this place?"

"I think he has a small liquor cabinet in the cupboard next to the kitchen."

"Let's have a quick drink, then I'll be on my way. And remember Lisa, no funny business. I'm really easy to get along with, as long as you do what I ask."

CHAPTER 94

The assassin was surprised that Lisa had been able to recover from his attempts at suffocating her. Then again, he had been forced to stop prematurely due to David's early arrival home. Amari would be more careful the second time. Some alcohol would augment the strength of his remaining Oxycontin - and a little fun with the nurse wouldn't hurt anything. The sun was setting and it would be easier for him to make his escape from the apartment after dusk and the area surrounding the condo would be darkened and in shadow.

Lisa suspected that Amari had tried to kill her. Dr. Layton might already be dead. The intruder had made no attempt to hide his face, and Lisa had seen enough TV movies and read enough books to know that the killer was not likely to leave her alive to identify him. Her best chance was to buy some time and hope that someone had intercepted her 911 call. Though the thought repulsed her she decided she would give him her body if that was what it took to stall for time.

It had been many years since Lisa had tried to flirt with anyone. She flipped her hair from her face coquettishly and looked back at Amari as she walked down the hallway. He followed closely behind her. She couldn't tell if he had even noticed the gesture. She moistened her lips with the tip of her tongue and tried to swing her hips as she walked. Lisa wished she had learned to defend herself—like Lucy Liu or one of Charley's Angels and envisioned herself kicking the gun out of the gangster's hand. She continued down the apartment hallway. The overhead lighting reflected off the weapon in Anthony's hand, though it was no longer pointed at her and now rested at his side. Lisa entered the kitchen and was able to see the sun setting on the Gulf of Mexico. She wondered whether this sunset would be her last.

Amari came to her side. He held the gun in his right hand and pulled Lisa toward him with his left. She felt the barrel of the gun against the small of her back as he pulled her body against his with his muscular left forearm and hand. His strong cologne repulsed her as well as what she expected might happen next. Lisa's heart pounded in her chest. Clamping her eyes closed, Lisa waited for his dreaded attack on her body. Instead, the room erupted with a cacophony of sound.

The front door imploded and two armed men entered Dr. Layton's apartment. Amari grabbed Lisa by the arm and dragged her back into the hallway corridor, placing her in front of him as a human shield. Lisa heard four words that she hoped would lead to her salvation.

"Don't move, we're the police."

Amari had his left forearm bent firmly across the front of Lisa's neck. She could hardly breathe. He was dragging her down the hallway and her feet barely touched the ground his gun pointed directly at her temple. Lisa recognized the men who had entered the apartment; detectives Collins and Levine. Both officers had their firearms raised; at a standoff with the armed intruder. Levine was speaking into the radio attached to his arm, calling for backup.

Lisa had already seen what Amari was capable of. Instinct instructed her to do the stupidest thing possible. Lisa raised her leg and slammed the heel of her shoe down onto Amari's foot. He released his hold on her neck just enough for her to turn around and kick him in the groin with her other leg.

Unfortunately she missed, and her kick only grazed the criminal along the inside of his thigh. His response was reflexive, and no more intelligent than Lisa's. In anger and pain he fired his gun at the woman. Lisa fell backwards in a heap. Smoke filled the room as both detectives emptied their firearms into the intruder even after he had collapsed to the floor.

Levine rushed over to Lisa. She had landed face down and there was blood on the right side of her neck and jaw. Lisa opened her eyes and gazed at the detective. Blood was exuding from bullet wounds to the side of her neck and top of her shoulder and was pumping from a vessel at the base of her neck. Detective Levine applied pressure to the wound while Collins called the dispatcher who called for an ambulance. The blood continued to pump through the pressure and was pooling under Lisa's supine body.

The sun's last feeble rays disappeared from the wall of the apartment. Their orange hue was the last thing Lisa remembered as she closed her eyes and lost consciousness.

CHAPTER 95

"Now remember boys, the hospital is like church – quiet voices and no messing around."

"We know, Dad. We're not stupid," It was Josh.

"You'll always be stupider than me, squirt," teased his older brother Shawn.

The boys were dressed in matching blue khaki pants and white polo shirts.

Their mom was in a bed on the surgical unit. A tall thin man in a green scrubs greeted the family outside of her room.

"Hi, Mr. Martin, hello boys. Your mom's surgery went very well. She needed some blood and I was worried about her when she first came in, but she's stable now. Mr. Martin, there was a superficial laceration of her external jugular vein that was fairly easy to repair. I stitched up her shoulder wound. I'm afraid she's probably going to have quite a bit of soreness when she wakes up from the bullet tearing up her muscle, but I doubt she'll have any long term problems from it."

"Can we visit with her now?" asked Nate.

"Certainly. She didn't require too much anesthesia for the surgery and she may even be awake now. Let's see."

The group entered Lisa's room.

"She looks pale, Dad."

"She's been through quite a lot, Shawn. But she's going to be fine."

"When will she wake up?" asked Josh. He touched her hand, then withdrew. "Her fingers feel cold."

Lisa stirred. She moved the hand that Josh had just touched. She yawned and her eyes fluttered. Lisa's eyes opened wider as she looked down at the assembled group at her feet.

"Ohhh, boys." Her voice caught in her throat and tears formed at the corners of her eyes. Lisa tried to raise her arms in order to pull her sons closer to her, and cringed.

"What happened?"

"You were a hero, Mom. You should see the papers. They said that because of you, they caught the bad guy and were able to save the doctor."

"Dr. Layton is alive?"

Nate answered.

"They found him in the bedroom. He was barely breathing, but his heart was still beating. They gave him some medication to reverse the effects of the narcotic and were able to get him to breathe on his own. He's still not back to normal – Dr. Layton is in the intensive care unit."

"The guy who was holding me hostage? What happened to him?"

"The detectives took care of him, Lisa. He's dead. They said you acted like a cornered tigress. I don't know how you found the nerve to attack an armed assassin, but you did. The guy had a rap sheet a mile long—he was a cold killer. All the news shows want to talk to you. We've had to fight them off."

"All I want to do is go home with you and the boys."

"When can she be discharged, Doctor?"

"We'll keep her here today, and if there are no problems overnight, she can go home in the morning. After all, hospitals are for sick people, right boys?"

Josh was on Lisa's left, and Shawn was on her right. Lisa and both boys wore big smiles and Nate couldn't remember his family ever being dearer to him than at that moment. He leaned over and gave his wife a tender kiss, then kissed each of the boys on their cheeks.

The doctor quietly left the room and was glad that good fortune had smiled on such a happy family.

THREE MONTHS LATER

Pelican Daily News, January 6, 2009

Trial begins today in the case of Bobby Volpe, the reputed crime boss who is at the center of charges pertaining to his alleged involvement in the "Fautox" murder case. According to papers filed in the docket of the Pelican Cove circuit court, Volpe ordered the execution of Dr. David Layton in order to acquire the patent to an experimental Botox-like medication that the doctor had developed. The doctor is the target of a separate investigation into the illicit use of the drug in his practice. The chemical has many plastic surgical patients of Pelican Cove, recipients of the drug, concerned for their safety. Sworn testimony from the state's witness, biochemist Sal Manzari, indicates that an altered form of the Botox chemical may have exposed many of Pelican Cove's most affluent residents to possible serious side effects of the medication. The doctor is unable to stand trial and is unlikely to recover from an attack at his home which left the intruder dead and one of the doctor's office staff injured. The biochemist is under police protection and has been unavailable for comment. Undisclosed sources suggest that the recent deaths of at least three young women in Pelican Cove may be tied to experimental use of the unauthorized Botox.

EIGHT MONTHS LATER

Rasa Sentosa Resort, Singapore

"Ahhh, Right there, honey. Don't worry about hurting me. I've got enough padding. I hardly feel it."

"Yes sir, Mr. Manzari. You let me know I pressing on you too much though." The raven-haired Asian masseuse leaned harder into Manzari's back as she continued her poolside massage. From time to time, a soft groan emanated from the obese whale of a man as he lay on his rotund stomach.

"You flip over now, time to do your front."

Manzari turned over on his back and placed a small towel over his eyes to block out the bright sunlight. A few minutes later, he removed the shade.

"Darlin', could you get me my drink, please?"

The masseuse handed Manzari a green liqueur in a Martini glass, embellished by a small umbrella.

"If this isn't heaven, I don't know what is," Manzari declared to the young woman.

Alisha smiled at the comment. It was the second time that week she had been fortunate enough to be giving the wealthy American a massage. He was very fat, but very friendly, and had given her a thirty dollar tip the last time. For a thirty dollar tip Alisha was more than happy to give the man his massage.

Manzari's cell phone rang.

"Shit, I thought I shut the thing off." Sal looked at the time on the phone.

"Hey, Alisha, the hour's almost up. How about we finish up now and I'll catch you again maybe tomorrow?" Manzari peeled two twenty dollar bills off a thick roll of green he removed from his pocket and handed them to Alisha.

"Thank you very much, Mr. Manzari. You very nice man."

Sal nodded at the woman and answered his phone.

"Hello, Mr. Manzari, I hope I'm not interrupting anything important."

Sal laughed.

"You can interrupt me any time you want Mr. Ng. So how's the construction going?"

"The lab is ninety percent completed and almost all of your equipment has arrived. Much of it has already been set up. We expect the animals to arrive next week. We hope your accommodations have been satisfactory?"

Sal smiled.

"The Rasa Sentosa is phenomenal. The beach is gorgeous and everyone is so friendly. No complaints here."

"That's good, because it looks like Singapore is going to be your home for a long time. My legal associates tell me that your people in the US are very, very angry with you. If you ever return to the States they'll have you arrested."

"As far as I'm concerned, I paid my dues. I testified and gave them what they wanted. You know, they moved me from Florida to Idaho. No way I could handle any more of that miserable place. They got me a job in a pharmacy filling prescriptions and paid me peanuts—saying I needed to keep a low profile so that my new identity wouldn't raise any suspicions. To top that they were always on my case to try to lose weight so that it would be harder for the bad boys to find me. Fuck that witness protection shit."

Charley Ng was chosen by Emperor Pharmaceuticals as the 'handler' for their promising chemist. Ng felt insulted by the job and had no respect for the slovenly, ill-mannered man he was forced to deal with. Apparently, Ng's superiors didn't see things quite that way. In their opinion, the responsibility of taking care of Sal Manzari was of utmost importance. The preliminary data Manzari had provided regarding his new drug could very well be the foundation of a new blockbuster for the company.

"You never explained to me, Mr. Manzari. How did you get out of your country?"

"It really wasn't that difficult. I wasn't under arrest, even though I wasn't supposed to ever leave the States. I went online and found a guy in Macau who said he could create a forged U.S. passport for a fee. I ordered one under the name of a guy who had just died in my town in Idaho. I was sure that they had my witness protection name and my real name registered in their computers, but the dead guy was a nobody. I was able to get a Visa and plane ticket under his name and 'voila', here I am."

"You certainly seem to have led a charmed life. That mess you were involved with in Florida got news coverage even here in Asia. Any time a drug has serious side effects like that the news agencies just eat it up. There's even talk of a Hollywood movie back in the States. There are lawsuits against that doctor you worked with. If they knew you had money, they'd be after you too." Does anyone from the U.S. know you are here?

"You're probably right, damn lawyers would probably love to get me back there. But no one knows where I am, and thanks to you, and good old Emperor Pharmaceuticals, we'll all be getting rich. This drug will be even bigger than the Botox I was working on. Lots of people get wrinkles, but even more people are into a drug that could affect their sex drive."

"So you're pretty confident that the chemical can be modified so that it increases sex drive without causing side effects? From what I read of the cases in the U.S., the drug caused some serious brain stem swelling. What's going to prevent it from happening?"

"When I was working in the States, we had limited funding and cut corners. The problems produced by the drug I created were the result of wanting too much too soon. Here in Singapore, the pressures for results aren't quite so crazy. I've been promised that we can take as long as we need to create a safe drug based on the portion of the Botox chemical I've identified. A shot that can increase sex drive. Think about it. It's as good as printing money!"

Charley Ng smiled and wondered what made Americans so shallow and vapid. His superiors had advised him that Manzari would be given six more months to produce results. From what Sal's former employee had told Mr. Ng, with the background work behind them, in a few months they should have the work finalized. If Manzari failed it would reflect poorly on Ng. There was no way Charley Ng was going to let this blubberous obnoxious man interfere with his own career plans. The employee, Peter Neori, seemed much more capable than this whale. The assistant had kept copious notes and records throughout the research- including when Sal was risking the lives of innocent people and a not-so-innocent Dr. Layton for his own prosperity.

"Mr. Manzari, my superiors are counting on you using all of your abilities to bring this drug to fruition. Next week we get started. Don't think we don't have pressures here, because we do. We have a board, investors and shareholders who demand results. Some of our bookkeeping methods may be a little less transparent than in the States, but business here is no less cutthroat than in your country. And failure will not be tolerated." Ng was no longer smiling.

Sal felt a pit in his stomach and had a dark moment of déjà vu. He hung his head and finished the remainder of his apple martini—spinning the little umbrella in his drink. From somewhere in his brain, little Dorothy Gale from the Wizard of Oz echoed, "There's no place like home. There's no place like home."

www.ingramcontent.com/pod-product-compliance
Lightning Source LLC
Chambersburg PA
CBHW020321180626
46812CB00001B/4